To Sheila

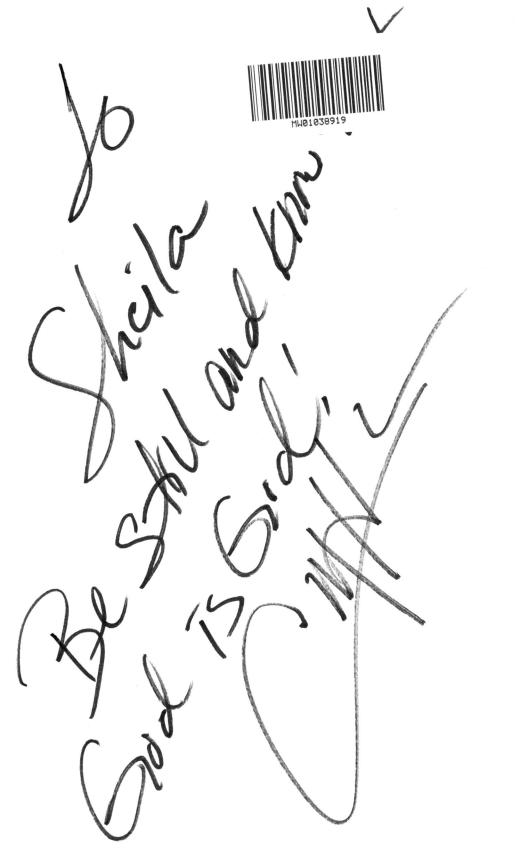

Be still and know

God is God!

The journey to *The Other Side of Through*, concludes with:

The Fight for Life

Cynthia Middlebrooks Harris

T.O.S.O.T. Ministries, LLC
(The Other Side of Through)

Scripture taken from the King James Version of the Bible.

Published by: T.O.S.O.T. The Other Side of Through Ministries, LLC and can be ordered by contacting:

T.O.S.O.T. Ministries, LLC
P.O. Box 565
Waynesville, MO 65583
http://www.tosotministries.org
Email: tosotministries@gmail.com

Available at CreateSpace.com and Amazon.com

Imagery provided by: Cover model David Haynes. Such images are being used for illustrative purposes only.

Edited by Vonnie Scott

ISBN-13: 978-1492733355
ISBN-10: 1492733350

Library of Congress Control Number: 2013922943

T.O.S.O.T. Ministries, LLC rev. date: 2/14/2014

Dedicated to:
Shawndelin Hall
and the Hall family, Dempsey,
Malcolm and Miesha.
My sister in the Lord and dear friend.
By far the biggest fan, encourager,
confidant, assistant, laborer, and
friend to me, the work and T.O.S.O.T.
(The Other Side of Through)
Ministries.

Acknowledgments

I am always and forever thankful to my Lord and Savior, Jesus Christ, and He will always get the Glory first in everything that T.O.S.O.T. Ministries, LLC publishes or produces. We thank Him continuously for the literary gift He has bestowed upon our lives.

I am sincerely grateful to the cover model; Darren Haynes of Shekinnah Tabernacle Ministries in St Robert, Missouri in care of Bishop Willie and Pastor Margaret Curry.

I am thankful to my Pastors, Elder Tim and Miki Collier of (MOEC) Metamorphosis Outreach Empowerment Center of St. Roberts, Missouri. They are super supportive and encouraging. I am grateful for loving and anointed shepherds who keep me covered in prayer. Their wisdom and knowledge are greatly appreciated.

Pastor/Evangelist/Mid-wife & Founder of Still Useable Ministries Susan Marshall continues to bless and back the ministry and the work. I am forever grateful and appreciative of her selfless service and support to the work the Lord has entrusted me with. Susan, thank you so very much.

Special thanks to my editor Vonnie Scott. She is a dear sister in the Lord and now a good friend as well.

Conception, hardship, push and…
…LIFE!

~Chapter One~

She sighed and dropped her head in despair as she read the results of the test, "Positive—ugghhh—why am I so surprised? I knew God wouldn't allow me get away with this. I was fooling myself to think so. Ugghh—Pastor Travis is going to be so disappointed in me. There's no need in putting this off—ugh! I guess I'll call my boyfriend first."

She dialed the number and waited for an answer, "I'm pregnant." She managed to get the words out before she burst into tears.

"Wow—ahhhh—okay. Are you at home?" he nervously asked.

"Yes," she answered barely above a whisper.

"I'm on my way. We'll get through this. It'll be okay. I'm sorry. I pressured you, and you gave in. I'm sorry. I'll be right there," he replied.

"Okay," she said and hung up the phone.

She laid across her bed and cried. This was the one place she thought she would never be. A pregnant teenager. "Why?" she asked herself in despair. "Why did I give in? All the times before—all the other guys. I said no every single time. Why did I say yes? Why did I have sex with him?"

He hung up the phone, breathed heavily and closed his eyes. He said a quick prayer and asked God for his forgiveness. However, he knew what he needed the most from God at that moment was wisdom. He was about to be a teenaged father. He knew although he had performed the deed like a man, he was anything but that in handling the outcome. Nevertheless, ready or not he was about to become a father. He shook his head in disbelief, grabbed his car keys and headed toward town.

*****

"TRREEEEEEE! Oh my God Teddy what—WHAT?" Nevette yelled as she sat on her knees still looking at the television set. The blood all over Tre, and the fact that he was talking and didn't appear hurt, all but told her husband was probably dead.

"Nay Nay—" Teddy said.

"GOD NO PLEASE! PLEASE DON'T DO THIS TO ME. TEDDY PLEASE. PLEASE TELL ME HE'S ALIVE. GOD TEDDY I CAN'T TAKE THIS! PLEASE TELL ME JUSTICE AND TRE ARE BOTH OKAY. TEDDDDDYYYY!" she yelled.

"Tre is fine, but Derrick—I don't know Nay Nay. Nevertheless, Sweet Pea we need to get to the hospital," Teddy replied as he attempted to assist Nevette up off the floor. He knew he couldn't tell her what Lindsay had just relayed to him on the phone earlier concerning Derrick.

"Oh God! Okay, okay, okay," she kept saying again and again as though she were putting forth a strong attempt to figure out what to do next.

"NAY NAY!" Teddy yelled as he grabbed her by the shoulders and shook her. "We have to go now!"

She swallowed hard and batted her eyes repeatedly in an effort to get her emotions under control as she whispered, "All right, yeah—all right."

Teddy grabbed Nay Nay's purse and phone from the counter just in case her mind was blank, and she wouldn't be able to remember any information needed at the hospital.

He managed to get her into the car. As they backed out of the driveway Nevette yelled, "TEDDY STOP! We have to go back into the house."

"Nay Nay—what? You can do this Nay Nay. Come on princess," Teddy replied. He feared he was about to lose her emotionally.

"No Teddy. Please wait, wait! I need to get clothes for Tre," she replied.

"Nay Nay we can take care of that later. Right now, we need to get there," Teddy replied. He put the car back in reverse to continue down the driveway.

"No Teddy! Did you see him on the television? He was covered in his fathers' blood! I have to get those clothes off my baby," Nevette said almost in a panic.

"Okay—you're right. Let's get him some clothes," Teddy replied.

Before he could even put the car back in drive to pull forward, Nevette had jumped out of the car and raced full speed into the house. By the time he pulled up and prepared to exit the car she was on the way back out the front door slamming it behind her. She had a driven and determined look on her face.

Teddy filled her in on everything Lindsay had told him concerning what happened to Derrick as they drove. He omitted anything that concerned whether he was alive or dead and simply said they just needed to get there. He told her that he wasn't sure about that. Which, in essence, was the absolute truth.

*****

Lindsay hung up and sat in the waiting room area. She cradled Tre and rocked back and forth as she began to pray for Derrick, and that everyone would arrive safely. Tre cried and kept repeatedly asking for his father. She neither answered him nor affirmed that she heard his request. She had no idea what to say to him or what to do about the situation. She pondered what she would say to Nevette should Derrick not survive. In the frenzy of the moment, the trauma team assumed she was Derrick's wife, and she had given the go ahead for them to take him into surgery. His vital signs were extremely low, and they had not given a good prognosis on the chances of him even surviving the surgery.

Lindsay started out praying silently because she didn't want to alarm Tre. However, the more she pondered the consequences of her actions the more audible her prayer became:

> *—And God please, keep him. Don't let him— don't allow the enemy to steal him Lord. Please God place Your angels around everyone as they are on their way here today. Clear the roadway God and give them a straight path. I didn't know what else to do God. It had to be done. Someone had to say yes to the surgery and for him to get blood. Oh God please—*

"LINDSAY!" Shaundra screamed as she and Derrick Sr., entered the waiting room area. When Tre saw his grandmother, he jumped from Lindsay's arms and made a mad dash for her.

"The bad man shot my daddy! He's not breathing Grandma. I don't want him to go with Callisha!" Tre cried.

"Oh my God Lindsay!" Shaundra cried as she received Tre. She looked at Lindsay in total disbelief. "What Lindsay? Please—"

"They took him—I had to say yes—I mean they thought I was Nevette—I didn't know what else to do. They needed permission to give Derrick blood—something about a paper Momma G," she replied hysterically.

"All right Lindsay calm down," Derrick Sr., said as he touched both her shoulders forcing her to look at him. "Tell us what's going on."

She took a quick breath and replied, "They needed someone to authorize him to go to surgery and to receive donor blood. They came out and asked. I didn't mean to lie about it, but they needed permission from a family member. I said yes. I pretended to be Nevette. He's in surgery now but the prognosis of him surviving wasn't—" she couldn't finish the sentence.

"Okay," Derrick Sr., said as he nodded his head in disbelief. "Lindsay you did the right thing. He probably would have died had you not been here. It's all right. Everything will be okay. He's in God's hands."

A nurse was sent out by the technician from the operating room to get information about receiving more blood for Derrick from family members if they had arrived. Just as she was about to address Lindsay, Nevette and Teddy burst through the door.

"Mommy!" Tre yelled.

He ran to his mother and jumped into her arms. He began to cry, "Mommy I don't want daddy to go be with Callisha! Please mommy, talk to God and tell Him not to take my daddy!"

Nevette looked him over feverishly and afterwards held him tight. She took a quick second to control herself and said, "Don't worry baby. Daddy is going to be alright, okay. Daddy is going to be just fine."

"Excuse me? You're his mother?" the nurse asked and eyed Lindsay.

"Yes! My husband, how is he? Is he going to be alright?" Nevette asked.

"Ma'am, I cannot answer that question right now. I was told to come and receive any family members that were here and able to give blood. Apparently, you had blood on hold here for emergencies?" the nurse stated.

"Yes we do," Nevette declared. "He and I are both B positive, and we have it here if he needs it."

"Ma'am, we have exhausted your supply here and had to get permission to use donor blood until his parents arrived to give more," she replied, and she again eyed Lindsay.

"Is there something wrong with the blood you've given my husband? What!" Nevette replied now in a panic. "Please how is he?"

"Ma'am, like I said before, I am not sure of your husband's status. I was sent because they are in need of blood from everyone in your family that is B positive," she replied.

Derrick Sr., stepped up and said, "Yes, his mom and I are both B positive as well."

"So am I," Teddy interjected.

"Where do we need to be? Where do we need to go?" Nevette asked.

"You all can come with me," she replied.

Lindsay looked at Nevette and said, "Nevette I'm sorry. There was no one here. I had to—"

"Lindsay. You probably saved his life. It's okay," Nevette said. She looked at Tre and said, "Tre stay here with Aunt Lindsay. She is going to get you changed while we go give blood for daddy."

"No mommy! I want to go with you to see daddy," Tre exclaimed.

"Sweetheart, we're not going to see daddy just yet. You want to help the police find the bad people that shot daddy right? Well, they are going to need your clothes to see if there are any clues on them," she said to Tre as she hugged him again for reassurance.

"Okay mommy," Tre replied.

"The nurses' station will have the proper bags to place his clothes in. They will assist you in storing and preserving them properly," the nurse replied.

Nevette, Teddy and Derrick's parents followed the nurse. Lindsay and Tre headed to the nurses station to get him changed.

"Excuse me, Nurse Howard is it?" Nevette said as they exited. "I work here in the hospital in the physical therapy ward, and I would like my husband in a private room for recovery in ICU after surgery. The cost doesn't matter, plus we have private insurance," Nevette stated as they headed to the blood bank area of the laboratory.

"Yes Ma'am. I will relay your request to the operating room staff," the nurse replied. She was fairly new and Nevette had no recollection of her working at the hospital before now. She looked vaguely familiar but Nevette couldn't quite place where she knew her from.

Teddy and Derricks' parents followed. They took note of Nevette's demeanor and eyed her with concern. They wanted to be on top of any potential breakdown that would threaten to take over her emotionally. She appeared to be running on auto pilot for the moment, and they were somewhat at ease.

*****

"Ughh, why is there so much traffic at this time of the day?" he thought out loud in his frustration. He was in a rush to get to his girlfriend. He left his house without relaying the news to his parents that they would soon be grandparents. He would talk to them later. At that moment, his only concern was to get out of the traffic jam and reach his destination. "This is all my fault. God I can't believe I am about to be a father. Oh God please let there be some mistake in how she took the test."

He knew that no amount of prayer he could speak, would undo his actions over the last few months. It was just like when the ministers spoke to them when they were in Paris, once you open Pandora's Box, there is no going back. You can't control the craving for it.

He was jolted out of his thoughts as the horn from the car behind him honked for him to move over. The traffic was dying down, and his exit was next up on the right.

Her street was only a few blocks from the exit. He pulled into her driveway, parked and walked to the front door. He took a deep breath, rang the bell and waited for her to answer the door.

*****

After they returned from the lab, they sat and played the waiting game. The blood was being processed and prepared for use. Nevette sat with Tre nestled in her arms. She controlled her breathing with the understanding that he would react off of her actions. The controlled rhythm of her heartbeat soothed him, and he relaxed in her arms.

Teddy walked over to her and asked, "Nay Nay do you want anything? Water? Juice?"

"No Teddy I'm fine," she replied. She closed her eyes and kissed Tre on the forehead. She took a few deep breathes to keep her heart rate normal. Her brother coming into her immediate space slightly ignited her emotions.

"Momma—Poppa G—Lindsay, either of you want anything? I'm going to the vending machines down the hall," Teddy asked.

They politely declined, but Lindsay stated that she would walk with him. Nevette's father and other brother Jason were also on the way. Teddy also called his wife Josephine to inform her about Derrick when he was first on the way to get Nevette. He instructed her to stay home and stay put, that he would keep her posted. She'd only just delivered their first baby a few weeks prior. Teddy was somewhat old-fashioned and knew his mother would turn over in her grave if he allowed his wife and new-born baby out of the house before the scheduled six-week exam. Their baby boy was named after his father and grandfather, Theodore Graham III. They nicknamed him G-three. She sent her love and prayers to everyone, of which he relayed.

As they headed to the vending machines Lindsay asked, "So how do you think she really is?"

"I don't know. She appears stable. No at all like she was with Callisha. So far, I'm pretty confident that she is being honest about her state of mind," Teddy replied.

They headed back toward the waiting room. As they rounded the corner, the doctor came through the door. Nevette rose to meet him. She gave Tre to his grandmother and rushed over to the doctor.

"How is he? Is he alive?" she said as she braced herself for the worst.

"Mrs. Goodfellow he survived the surgery, but he is by no means out of danger. His situation is still critical. We were successful in removing the bullet from his abdomen. The other two went straight through him. I am still amazed that he even made it here in the ambulance. From the amount of blood he lost, he should have been dead on arrival. It was touch and go in there. I have hopes that if he continues to be stable throughout the night, he will get better with each passing day and soon be out of danger. We have done everything humanly possible for him. Now we can only watch and wait Mrs. Goodfellow," Doctor Jackson replied.

"Okay, when can I see him? Nevette replied. She was glad her back was to Tre because she was unable to keep the tears from rolling down her face. She wiped them quickly as she felt Tre grab her leg.

"Mommy—" Tre said. He was close to tears. She had not done a good job at hiding the fact that she was crying.

"Mrs. Goodfellow the nurse will inform you when he will able to have visitors. You can rest assured that he will be well monitored and cared for. You know the procedures of the hospital. You're one of our best physical therapists, if not the best," Doctor Jackson replied.

Nevette shook her head, "I wasn't sure you remembered who I was Dr. Jackson. The minute I saw you come through the door. I was confident that everything that could possibly be done for Derrick had been done and every possible avenue of approach well thought out and addressed. You're our best surgeon."

"Thank you for the compliment. Mrs. Goodfellow, although you understand the technical side of this operation, right now you are not on duty. And we will handle you as we do any other family member. All the proper courtesy, protocol and formats will be followed. There aren't very many Goodfellows around, and so I knew it must be a family member of yours when I saw the name," Dr. Jackson replied.

"Thank you for taking care of him. God has him, and I have confidence and trust that all will be well," Nevette said as she turned to address Tre. He nodded and left. He reminded her that the nurse would be out shortly before he disappeared through the doors of the waiting room.

"Daddy is going to be alright Tre. Pretty soon mommy will go see him. The place where they have daddy little children are not allowed. I will tell daddy that you love him, and I'm sure he will send his love for you as well," Nevette said as she stooped down to speak with Tre.

"But mommy I want to see my daddy," he cried. "I have to make sure he's not in a special sleep waiting for Jesus to take him where Callisha is. Please mommy—please let me go with you to see daddy!"

Those words broke her heart, but she controlled her reaction and said, "Oh sweetheart. Daddy is going to be okay. He is not going to be with Callisha. Later when they move daddy to another room, you will be able to see him then, okay."

"You promise mommy? You promise daddy is going to be okay?" Tre asked in a shaky voice.

"I promise baby. I promise," Nevette replied as she pulled him into her arms. She stood and carried him back to where they sat earlier. She closed her eyes and just held him in her arms. No one said a word.

About forty-five minutes later, Shaundra was just about to go and inquire about Derrick when the doctor walked through the door. Lindsay walked over to Nevette and got Tre as she stood to address him. The fact that he came instead of the nurse alarmed everyone sitting there.

"Is he awake? Can we see him now?" Nevette asked.

"Not quite Mrs. Goodfellow. He has not regained consciousness just yet. He is not responding to the reversal of the anesthesia," Dr. Jackson stated.

"What do you mean Dr. Jackson? What are you trying to say?" Nevette asked in a panic.

"Calm down Mrs. Goodfellow. We don't believe that he is in a coma. His brain activity reads and suggests that he should be awake. But for whatever reason, he remains unconscious," he replied. "He is in his room, however, and we will allow you to see him shortly. The nurse will be out soon. Please only two of you for now and definitely not the little one."

"Okay," Nevette replied as she turned to see who would accompany her into the room to see Derrick.

"Shaundra, I think it's best if you go with Nevette first. The rest of us will wait for further clearance of other visitors," Derrick Sr., said as he hugged her for comfort and kissed her forehead.

Shaundra smiled at her husband and wiped tears that she failed to contain upon hearing the news of Derrick's state.

Nevette patiently waited for the nurse to return to get her and Shaundra. She knew her status as a faculty member could very easily override that of a family member. However, she waited nonetheless. She did not want to see Derrick before he was ready. Shaundra was in private practice but delivered most of her babies at Northside. So she too knew her way around the hospital.

The nurse came a few minutes later, and Nevette and Shaundra followed her to where Derrick was. It took everything Nevette had not to run ahead of her. She stopped at the door and told them they could enter when they were ready.

Shaundra grabbed Nevette by the hand and asked her if she were ready. She replied yes. However, when she walked through the door and saw him lying there with tubes coming out of him and on oxygen, she broke emotionally. Shaundra quickly grabbed her and said, "Okay Nevette, out of the room."

"Oh mom I'm sorry," Nevette declared after they stood outside the door.

Shaundra shook her head and said, "Nevette you're going to have to get yourself together. You and I are both in the medical field, and we know he can probably hear us. He doesn't need to hear that his wife is falling apart, okay. Because all this is going to do is take him back nine months, and he doesn't need that stress. Trust me when I say, it is taking everything I have to keep it together. We are going to have to be strong."

"I know mom. It just caught me off guard. I'm gonna be okay. I need to be near him. I can do this," she replied.

They reentered the room, and Nevette went over to his side. She cupped his face and kissed him. She told him that she loved him.

"Oh baby I love you so much. I'm so sorry Justice. Tre and I need you. So I'm going to need you to wake up, okay baby."

Shaundra looked down at her son and her heart ached. She was helpless as a parent. All she could seem to think of were times when he was a small child. All of his firsts' rushed over her mind. His first teeth, steps and words replayed in her mind like a bad recording that you couldn't find the off button too. "Come on Derrick, wake up son."

Nevette cried out, "Oh God! Justice wake up baby." Tears streamed down her face as she continued to talk to him. "Oh baby I'm so sorry. I love you so much. I need you. You and Tre are the air that I breathe. Please Justice, snap out of it baby. Please fight, fight baby! Fight to wake up. Fight to live!"

She looked over at Shaundra and said, "Mom agree with me in prayer." Shaundra nodded and bowed her head.

Tears ran down her cheeks. Nevette placed one hand on Derrick's chest and raised the other one toward heaven as she declared:

> *Oh God I trust you—I trust you now God with my husband. You're Jehovah Rafah, the God that Healeth. I believe that You are going to mend his organs. I thank You God that You're going to repair him. That You're going to strengthen him and bring him into consciousness. Father in the name of Jesus, I thank You for being Jehovah Shalom. God You're my peace*

in the midst of a storm. Oh God and I rebuke death in the name of Jesus! God I thank You for my husband, and I know that You're going to raise him up, and he is going to pull through, and be okay. I pray that his organs are going to function properly and there will be no residual effects to them at all Lord. He is my husband, and we have a child to raise God. Thank You Lord, I thank You that You're going to bless him. I thank You for bringing us back together, and I thank You for accepting me back into Your family God. I love You and praise You as we seal this prayer in Jesus' name,

Amen

She was running on all Evangelistic cylinders. The thought came to her that maybe the enemy kept him from waking up. She started to pray again:

Lord

I pray that You will encamp Your angels around him to protect and keep him. If there is any dark force that is holding him down, Lord I rebuke it now in the name of Jesus. I bind every enemy and demonic force in Jesus' name. If they have a hold, I command that they release it now. And God I trust You that if that is not the case and if God for whatever reason, You have him sleep. I trust that also. I know that if You indeed have him sleep, then You are able to keep him. Your word says: FOR THE WHICH CAUSE I ALSO SUFFER THESE THINGS: NEVERTHELESS I AM NOT ASHAMED: FOR I KNOW WHOM I HAVE BELIEVED, AND AM PERSUADED THAT HE IS ABLE TO KEEP THAT WHICH I HAVE COMMITTED UNTO HIM AGAINST THAT DAY.

Lord I know the scripture is talking about his soul, but I pray that You will keep his body. God please! I love You and I trust You with my husband. I trust that You're going to allow him to come home with me. I trust You God that You'll grant my petition to raise my husband up and completely heal him. And God, I pray that You will just use me. You can use me. I trust You Lord. You are awesome God. Thank You God.

She wiped her tears as she said to Derrick's mom, "Momma, I was wondering if you can keep Tre for me for a little while."

"Of course sweetie," Shaundra replied.

She looked down at Justice and stroked his face gently as she gave instructions to his mother concerning Tre. "You'll have to go to the house and get him clothes and all the supplies he will need for school. He knows what he needs weekly. He has a very busy schedule, and Teddy will help you as well. If you could bring me enough clothes for about a week, I would appreciate it. I'll just wash them in the physical therapy ward. And hygiene essentials so I don't scare him to death when he wakes up." She chuckled at her last statement.

Shaundra shook her head and she said, "Nevette sweetheart."

"Mom don't," Nevette replied.

"Nevette—," she started to say again but was cut off.

"Mom please can you just do that for me? I'm not leaving until he wakes up. I'm not leaving this room," Nevette replied. She did not take her eyes off Derrick and continued to stroke his face.

"Nevette baby this is not healthy—" Shaundra attempted to protest but was again cut off by Nevette.

"Mom please, I'm not leaving my husband until he wakes up. I'm not leaving this room. Mom please do this for me. I want him to know that I love him, and I'm not here just because he got shot. I'm not leaving this room. Can you please bring my bible? Tre knows the alarm, although I don't remember setting it before Teddy and I rushed out of the house on the way here. I changed it from the baby's birthday to Derricks' because I wanted to think about him whenever I left the house and returned. I just wanted to feel him, you know. I didn't want to forget—I didn't know what I was doing half the time. I'm not going off the deep end this time mom. This time I'm going to fight for life with everything I have. I will not allow the devil to have him." She looked up and shouted, "DEATH ANGEL! I PLEAD THE BLOOD OF JESUS OVER THE DOORPOST AND COMMAND YOU TO PASS OVER THIS ROOM TONIGHT AND EVERYNIGHT FROM THIS DAY FORTH! NO PATIENT WHO ENTERS THIS ROOM WILL BE OVERTAKEN BY YOU EVER AGAIN!" She dropped her head as tears began to flow.

"Okay Nevette," Shaundra replied. She understood and realized by her bold declaration that Evangelist Goodfellow was present, and all would be well. "Alright baby. We will take care of Tre and bring you the items you need."

"Thanks mom," Nevette replied. She turned her attention back to Derrick.

"What do you want us to do when Tre wants to come up here? You remaining here is going to make him want to come all the more," Shaundra added.

"It will be too upsetting for Tre to see him while he is still in the intensive care unit. I'm sure Derrick doesn't want Tre to see him like this. But I'm not leaving this room until my husband wakes up," Nevette stated again.

"Okay, don't worry about Tre. Between us and Teddy, we'll take care of him," Shaundra replied.

"I know you will mom, and I will take care of Derrick," Nevette declared.

"I know you will Nevette," Shaundra replied with confidence in her voice.

"I'm gonna start movement therapy whenever they say that I can. I don't want his muscles to start deteriorating. Soon, I'll start his circulation therapy. I'll be careful with his core area, so I won't interfere with his surgical wounds," Nevette stated not really to Shaundra just in general. "Because God is faithful even when we're not," she said and started to cry again. "I'm so glad that God loves me, because I've been so ugly to everybody!" she exclaimed. She looked back down at Derrick and said, "Oh God please! Please let him wake up, please. I'm not going to leave you baby. I'm going to be in this room when you wake up, and I'm going to love on you. Forgive me baby. I was so wrong with Callisha. I was wrong to lock you out. I was selfish and caught up in my own grief. Feeling sorry for myself instead of trusting God. I didn't allow you to cover me. I didn't allow you to comfort me. And I knew you were hurting the same as I was. In my hurt and my anger, I lashed out physically at you, because I couldn't lash out at anybody else. I was angry with God. I asked for his forgiveness and baby, I ask for yours—please forgive me. I love you so much. I love you Derrick. I feel like I don't deserve you. But I'm gonna nurse you back to health sweetheart. Thank you for giving me a second chance to be your wife. I love you baby, and I'm going to be here when you wake up. I'm going to be right here, okay sweetheart. Fight baby, please fight—Justice fight! Tre is okay. He's fine. You saved his life. That bullet would have probably gone right through our baby's head judging where it hit you as you pushed him out of the way. I don't know if I could have taken that. Oh Justice I can't lose you! I can't lose the love of my life! I trust God that you're going to come out of this, so I know that you're going to. It's not a matter of if but a matter of when baby, so you rest. You get all the rest you need and when you wake up, I'm going to be here, okay. I love you."

She leaned over and kissed him again on his lips, forehead and face. She caressed his face and pulled up a chair. She let the side rail down and grabbed his hand. She laid her head on the bed beside his arm and cried as she continued to talk to him.

Shaundra silently turned and walked out of the room as Nevette sat beside Derrick and wept.

As Shaundra entered the waiting area, Yogi rushed in panicked. They calmed her down for Tre's sake and filled her in on the situation.

~Chapter Two~

The ride home months earlier, the day her husband, Bernard and the two other NCO's arrived from Germany after the attack in Afghanistan was full of emotion for Gloria. So much had happened since that time. She had given her life to God and she and Michael entered into counseling. As she stood in the kitchen preparing dinner, she gazed out the window. She thought of the ride home and the weeks that followed.....

.....Tears rolled down her face as she looked into his eyes. The love that looked back overwhelmed her. Gloria longed to have this love from Mike. She fought the hurt that threatened to ruin the moment. Nothing from their past relationship told her she should trust his actions. But yet here he was, looking at her as though it were the first time he laid eyes on her. Everything seemed so fresh and pure between them.

He smiled and dropped his head then looked back up at her. He longed for the moment when they would be alone. The service van pulled into the parking lot of the company, and the boys helped their father and the duty driver unload his and Bernard's personal gear. He stored Bernard's gear in the commanders' office while his boys loaded his in the trunk of the car.

Gloria was busy taking care of the other families that arrived with them. Soon everyone was settled and released for the day. Mike left the rear detachment NCO's in place for the rest of the week. He informed the Lieutenant that Major Travis would probably not be available for another week or so because of the delivery of the twins. He had him to draw up and email the leave of absence paperwork for him to sign and return if he decided he needed more time with his new family. So for the next thirty days he should expect to remain the acting commander. He also left Sergeant First Class Young as acting First Sergeant in his stead. He placed everyone who arrived with him on the flight on administrative leave for the next two weeks. The rear detachment performed well and did a stellar job. There were no holes that needed to be filled.

A memorial service for the fallen comrades would be held the following week on the base. But individual families already began to make their own burial preparations for their loved ones. Mike knew that he and Gloria would be extremely busy in the coming weeks, attending as many of the individual services as humanly and emotionally possible. He looked forward to the intimate time he would share with her.

His action to place everyone on administrative leave was more for himself than it was his fellow comrades. He knew he and Gloria had much to discuss. He silently prayed to God as he tended to his last duties before leaving the company that God would spare his marriage.

As he stood up from his desk to head out of his office, Sergeant Cathy Moore walked in. He felt instant anxiety and looked past her to see where Gloria was.

"Don't worry Mike. She and the boys just left the building. I think they went over to battalion or something," she said as she walked up to him and attempted to put her arms around him.

Her statement was a lie, because just before she walked into his office, she looked Gloria straight in the eyes and gave her a look that indicated she was definitely in charge. Gloria's heart sank. She was about to head out to the car when she had the strong urge to just go into Mike's office to break up their little reunion. But as she approached the door, she cowered and stood just outside, and out of sight instead.

Mike took a step backward and warded off her contact, "Look Cathy. I thought we established right before the attack in Afghanistan that we wouldn't engage in this kind of activity again. I'm married—"

"Okay and—that never stopped you before. Look Mike. I feel like I'm just as much your wife as she is. From the action between you two or lack thereof the last year. I'd venture to say that she is the other woman," Cathy replied as she took another step toward him.

Mike again stepped to the side and out of her reach as he countered, "On the contrary, Sergeant Moore. There is only one Mrs. Thomas, and her name is Gloria. Now look, I told you earlier that what we had was over. I told you when I got back to the states I was going to beg my wife to forgive and not divorce me. Through God, I realized that I love her more now than I ever have. I couldn't see her because I placed you and my own lust in front of her. Cathy, you will never be what she is to me. You will never care for me the way she does. You will never love me as much she does. I owe you an apology. I should have never allowed myself to get involved with you to the degree that I did. It was immoral and unprofessional. I can only pray that Gloria has enough love for me to give me the chance to show her that I can, and really desire to be a loving husband and father."

He paused and said as he looked up, "Oh God, please help her to forgive me. All I want is my wife." He looked back at Cathy and said, "As your First Sergeant, I am commanding you to cease and desist your pursuit to engage in any unprofessional activity with me. We both have our careers to lose. The crime of adultery is punishable in the Uniformed Code of Military Justice (UCMJ) and won't be any more lenient with you as a Sergeant, as it will be with me as a First Sergeant. Therefore, we will disengage in any activity whatsoever. I will address you as Sergeant Moore and you in turn will address me as First Sergeant Thomas. Is that completely understood Sergeant?"

Tears filled Cathy's eyes. At that moment, she realized she was indeed in love with him. To her, it wasn't just an affair. She really hoped she would one day be Mrs. Thomas. She replied barely above a whisper, "Yes First Sergeant."

Mike struggled as well. He knew his words brought pain to her. He realized what he thought he felt for her as love was merely lust, and he had no genuine feelings whatsoever for her. All he could think of at the moment was his wife Gloria. He shuffled papers on his desk as he said, "In the interest of everyone involved, I will speak with Major Travis upon his return to have you reassigned. I feel it will be quite uncomfortable for the both of us to remain in the same unit."

"Yes First Sergeant," she replied. "First Sergeant, I am fully aware of the UCMJ, and I have no desire to disclose our past relationship with anyone. As much as I love you, I love being a soldier more. My career is all I have now. I would like to have the privilege of choosing the gaining unit. I feel that it would be better if I left Robbins altogether. Before I met and became involved with you, I was trying to get assigned overseas to Italy. I would appreciate it if you and Major Travis would consider calling the branch to assist in getting me on assignment there." She spoke with a shaky voice. Everything in her wanted to break down, but she held her military bearing.

Mike nodded and said, "Sergeant Moore you have my word. I will do everything I can. Major Travis knows a lot of people at the branch, and I'm sure he will assist in the matter. He is the only person on this base other than my wife who knows about us. That is unless you have—"

"No I haven't," she replied. "Like you said First Sergeant, I know the UCMJ concerning adultery. We are both NCO's and we would both lose everything," Cathy interjected. "Is that all First Sergeant?" she asked. She wanted to get away to be alone so she could cry.

"Yes Sergeant Moore, that is all. You are dismissed," he replied.

The look on her face when he said she was dismissed told the story. She was not only dismissed from his office as a form of protocol, but also from his life as his mistress. A pleasure she had grown to love. She turned to leave.

"Cathy," he said as she took a step to walk out of the office. "All ranks aside for a moment. I'm sorry. I should have never engaged you. I was wrong on every hand. Please accept my apology. Major Travis introduced me to Jesus. Everything I'd done in my life seemed justified until that point. Including being with you. But now my life, my thinking, everything is different. I pray that you will give God a chance to bring you the peace that I have found in Jesus Christ. Again, I am sorry, for everything. I love my wife. I love her. I can only pray that she will stay with me. I don't blame her if she slaps my face and heads straight to the divorce lawyer in the morning. I don't have any right to even think I deserve to be her husband. She is the only woman in the world that I want to be with. I will pray that God will bless you with a mate that will be faithful and loving to you. One that will be available to love you and only you. Again, I'm so sorry Cathy."

Tears rolled down her face. She smiled through a deep breath and said, "Wow. I knew this day was coming. I mean, you broke it off and started to distance yourself from me the last few weeks we were in Afghanistan. I figured you just wanted to lay low for a while, and we would pick up where we left off once you got back home. I knew there was something different about you. I just couldn't pinpoint what it was. It's me that owes the apology. Not so much to you," she paused to swallow; hard to talk through her tears, "but to your wife. For the first time, I feel ashamed of my actions. I gloated when I was around her. I knew she knew that I was sleeping with her husband. We had some silent power struggles over you. Then she just stopped fighting over time. I thought, yeah. I won—I took her man. And there was nothing she could do about it. I thought she was weak to just allow me do what I did, mostly in her face at that."

"Yes, at first that was my thought too. I used it as justification to continue doing what I was doing," he said and then paused. He looked down and sighed. "It takes a powerful, graceful and elegant woman to be able to save face in front of everybody all while she knows her husband is sleeping with some green NCO half his age. She continued on with her duties with the other wives as though everything was wonderful at home. I saw it as a weakness. But now I understand it was pure strength. My wife is amazing. I had everything I ever needed or wanted in her. I couldn't see it because I was driven by lust."

"Don't worry First Sergeant, our secret is safe with me. I will never approach you again unprofessionally," Cathy stated. "Ahhmmm, can I ask you to pray for me that God will forgive me for what I did to your wife? I think I'm going to start going to church again. I was raised right, and I know better. My grandmother would be so disappointed in me if she were alive. She took me to Sunday School with her every summer when I would visit. Well, I had better go before your wife comes looking for you and misunderstands why I'm here."

Gloria was in tears outside. She had not heard her husband speak well of her or compliment her in any way for nearly two years. At least, not any compliment that wasn't staged for show when they were out in public. She walked across the hallway into the restroom as Cathy left Mike's office. Her heart raced, and she was unsure what to do. She was indeed prepared to go to divorce court in the coming weeks. However, now she wasn't sure how she felt. She knew the hurt and pain she suffered the previous two years would not fade away at sunset. She—they, would have to deal with the hurt of the affair. She dried her eyes and proceeded across the hall to Mike's office.

He shut down his computer and was prepared to leave when he looked up and saw her walk through the door. A smile graced his face at the sight of her. He was overwhelmed with the love that flooded his heart for her. She looked absolutely stunning to him.

"Hey sweetheart, I was just finishing up. We can finally go home. Where are the boys?" he asked. His tone was soft and inviting.

She cleared her throat after the first attempt to get a word to exit out of her mouth failed, "Uhmm, they are outside by the car. Probably messing around with some of the soldiers. I told them to wait outside while I came to get you. I wasn't sure if you would be busy, and I didn't—"

"Shhhh," he said slowly and lovingly as he walked up to her. "You don't have to do that anymore. You don't have to create a diversion, or preview the surroundings before allowing the boys to enter my space. She is not going to be there anymore. Her or any other woman for that matter." He started to breathe heavy and erratically. Suddenly, he burst into tears.

"Oh Mike!" she exclaimed.

She walked over to the door and closed it. She thought for a moment, then turned back and locked the door so no one would happen into his office and see him in his present state. She had become so accustomed to covering for him. She stood unsure what to do. She realized she had no idea what it meant to be his wife anymore.

He walked over to her, embraced her and cried, "Oh God Gloria I am so sorry! I don't even know how to begin to apologize to you. Baby—I—please forgive me! Please, I beg you to give me a chance to show you that I can be a real husband—your husband. I don't deserve you. I hurt you so bad. I disregarded you on every hand. I treated you like yesterday's news. I showed you no real affection whatsoever. I flaunted her in your face like a trophy. But you continued to pretend that all was well in front of everyone. You allowed me to continue looking like the perfect husband and father. You showed so much elegance and grace toward me. You covered me even when I didn't want to, or care about being covered. How can I ever expect you to forgive me? I was so stupid and selfish. I was driven by my lust. Baby it's all about you from now on. You and our boys. Gloria I—oh God baby I love you!"

"Wow," she whispered as tears rolled down her face. "I don't know what to say. I don't know what to do. The things you're saying I have longed to hear. I feel like I'm dreaming. I don't know Mike. There's just so much hurt."

"I know baby," he replied.

He still held her in his arms. He was afraid to let go of her. "I know we will need help. Major Travis has blessed me. He got ahold of me in Afghanistan and—wow—I got dealt with by God concerning you, our marriage, my life—everything. I can't undo the last two years. I can't undo the pain and suffering I caused you. I failed you in every way. I don't have any right to ask you to stay with me. To give me another chance. But Gloria baby, I'm begging you. Please don't leave me. Let me love you. Let me love you the way I'm supposed to love you. Let me love you the way Christ loved the church."

"Mike I—I don't know. I—" she started to reply. She was so overcome with emotion she could barely talk. She had no idea what to say. All she ever wanted was to be his wife and own his heart.

He placed his hands on the sides of her face and kissed her. "I just want to love you. You and only you." He paused and chuckled, "I mean other than God of course. Gloria—" he paused again. This time the sound of her name as it escaped through his lips overwhelmed him. "Please—please give me—I'm begging—let me show you that I can love you. Don't go back to the lawyer. I want to be your husband. I want to spend some time getting to know the real you baby. I want to satisfy you—to be what you need in a husband. What you desire. I love you."

He didn't wait for her to reply. Partly, because he was afraid of what her response would be. He knew he didn't deserve a second chance. He just kissed her over and over.

Finally, she was able to get a word in, "Mike, the boys are outside waiting on us. We need to go."

"Yeah—yeah, let's go home baby," he replied. He looked into her eyes and the love he had was genuine. It was so powerful that she had to look away from him. She dropped her head only to have him touch her ever so gently on the chin and lift it back up, forcing her to look into his eyes. She had never felt so engulfed by him before. She couldn't think of the last time, other than earlier on the ride back to Robbins from the airport, he had looked into her eyes with love and passion.

She was just as afraid to give him a second chance as she was to divorce him. She wanted to believe that this was real. She forced the thought out of the back her mind and smiled at him. "Yeah—let's go." She managed to say.

They walked outside where the boys were. They were just outside the car in the field throwing a football around with a few soldiers. They saw their parents and rushed over to them.

"You finally ready to go home dad?" Mike Jr., asked.

"Yes son, I'm ready," he replied and he mushed his head.

"I belong to mommy and you guys the next few weeks. I mean other than the services for the fallen soldiers that mom and I will have to attend," Mike interjected.

She marveled at him. She felt so complete. This was the family life she longed for. The one everyone assumed she had already. They laughed and talked on the ride home.

After they ate dinner and finally got the boys settled down enough to go to sleep, it was well after midnight. Gloria was extremely nervous. She had no idea what to expect from Mike. She hadn't physically made love to her husband in well over a year. Mostly, because she refused him. She was determined that he wouldn't have his cake and eat it too. After a while, his interest and attempts toward her stopped all together. Everything inside of her wanted to make love to her husband. She felt like she had on her wedding night with Mike. She was a virgin and super nervous.

He sensed her anxiety when he walked into the bedroom. He smiled as he took off his shirt. She had forgotten just how fine and chocolate sexy her husband was. They hadn't paid much attention to each other before the deployment. He walked over to where she stood and touched the side of her face.

"I want to make love to you so bad. But, I'll understand if you don't want to be intimate with me. And I promise. I won't be angry about it," he said as he played in her hair. He smiled at her, "You are so beautiful."

Try as she may, she couldn't get one word to exit out of her mouth. She dropped her head and wept.

"Oh baby no—don't cry. Don't cry. Ahhh, let me kiss those tears away," he declared as he started to parade her with gentle kisses.

All she could do was cry. She couldn't stop herself. Her emotions took over her. He kissed her over and over and held her in his arms for over half an hour before she calmed down.

Although she kept having to stop to wipe tears and clear her throat, she finally started to speak, "Michael—"

He interrupted her, "I always loved it when you called me Michael. It was always so soft and sweet. Especially when we made love. I don't want to be Mike anymore, not with you. I just want to be Michael. Michael Thomas, the man you married."

She was so unsure about everything. She continued, "For the last two years. I've wanted you to want me. I kept wondering what I was doing wrong. Why wasn't I enough for you anymore? Even before you started having an affair with Cathy you weren't happy with me. I mean we have four boys, so obviously we were having sex. But that's all it was, sex. You weren't loving me. I always felt like you were in my bed out of obligation. I never thought you wanted to actually be there. After about thirteen years of marriage things changed, you changed. I don't know, maybe I changed. But something changed, and you stopped looking at me. By that time I'd had our fourth baby. You barely even touched me anymore. I was actually glad when you made First Sergeant because I had purpose again. I knew I would have to head up the wives groups for the unit, and I would feel special again. I talked to Talinda and her mother in the airport before you landed. I was so ready to go to the divorce lawyer in the morning, so I could finally be free from the hurt of watching you give another woman my life. After hearing Talinda's testimony, I realized I still have some love for you. After everything, I still had love for you. I wasn't sure what I expected from you when you walked into the room. I certainly didn't expect you to kiss me. But it felt so good to be in your arms," she paused and wiped tears, "and for the first time, you acted like you wanted me there. I didn't care if it was for show or just for a minute. But I realized then, that I wanted my life back. I wanted my husband

and my life back. I'm hurt Michael. I'm so hurt. And I know it's not going to go away overnight. But I'm willing to try if you are."

At those words, his face lit up and a smile graced his lips. "Really baby—I promise you. I will ne—"

"Shhh," she said as she touched his lips with a finger. "Don't promise me you'll never hurt me again. Promises are made to be broken. Just love me Michael—just love me," she declared.

"I will baby. I will. And I promise I will never go outside our marriage bed again," he replied.

"Michael don't promise me that," she declared again.

"Baby look at me," he said as he gently stroked her hair. "I will never go outside our marriage bed again. It will be undefiled, and it will be honorable. Sunday morning you, me and the boys will find a church to go to. We're going to be a family that prays together and stays together from now on."

She looked into his eyes, and she saw the genuineness of his heart toward her. She nodded her head in agreement. She knew she had been just as intrigued with Talinda's God as she had the story of her love with her two husbands.

He didn't say another word. He scooped her up in his arms and carried her over into the bathroom. He undressed himself and her and led her into the shower. As the hot water ran down over their bodies he stood behind her and kissed her gently on her back and shoulders as he washed the front of her body. After they got out of the shower, he dried her off and once again scooped her up and carried her back into the bedroom. He laid her down on the bed, lit a candle and found the slow jams station on the radio. He climbed into bed and made soft sweet love to her. They both cried and declared their love for one another as the sweet aroma of love went up in a flame of passion all night.

Within the next few weeks, they found a church there in Warner Robins with loving pastors that ministered to them as they recovered from the infidelity that plagued their marriage for years. They expressed some of their hurts, concerns and issues with the pastor and his wife. Gloria wasn't one hundred percent comfortable with the pastor. But that was of little concern at the moment. She was just glad that she and Michael were more in love than ever before. They learned together what it meant to be in a marriage designed by God and His Holy Word. Michael led their home and Gloria quickly learned and understood her role as a helpmeet. The boys took everything in stride. They had no idea what happened behind the scenes of their family. To them, their mom and dad had always been happy and that's the way it stayed.....

.....She was jarred back to reality as he kissed her on the neck and said, "What has you so engrossed in thought this morning?"

She smiled and said, "Why you of course. You consume me."

He smiled and shook his head, "It's hard to believe we've been back from deployment over nine months. The time has flown by. I am so grateful God gave me grace and favor with you. And now that we are a saved family, it's even better. But you know. I really miss having Major Travis at work every day. Since he chaptered out, it's been different. I talked with him yesterday. He asked us to lift Raymond up in prayer. He left the house bound and determined to kill the guys who killed his mom and Bernard's cousin.

"Oh no!" Gloria gasped.

"Yeah, I told him we would be praying about it and to keep us posted. Well baby, I'm off to formation for physical training. I'll see you this evening," Michael replied as he kissed Gloria goodbye.

She walked him to the garage door and kissed him again before going back into the house to get the boys ready for school. "God is good," she thought as she closed the door and headed upstairs to the boys' bedrooms.

~Chapter Three~

Reginald took a deep breath as he saw Sarah approach the door. He didn't bother to ask her how she was doing. Her puffy eyes and tear stained cheeks told him all he needed to know.

"I am so sorry Sarah. This is all my fault," Reginald said as he stepped into the doorway.

"It's not your fault Reginald. It's our fault. It takes two people to make a baby," Sarah replied. "Who would have thought the virgin couple among the teens would be the ones to get pregnant?"

"I know," Reginald replied. "I figured Jessica and Jonathan would be the ones who ended up teenaged parents. Those guys are going to let me have it. I used to give them such a hard time about always allowing their hormones to drive them. I prided myself on being this 'have it all together virgin' who was God driven instead of loin driven. It's just like Minister Travis said, once you open Pandora's Box you can't close it. Have you told your aunt yet?"

"No, I can never seem to find the nerve to," Sarah replied. "Anyway I'm not so sure that I am going to have this baby Reginald."

"Sarah no! Two wrongs don't make a right," he declared. "Look. It's bad enough we fornicated. But Sarah we are not going to commit murder!"

"Murder?" she replied in bewilderment.

"Yes Sarah. You must know having an abortion is like committing murder," Reginald stated.

"Wow, I never even thought about it that way," Sarah replied. "I mean, not in the crime type of way. But yes, I guess it is murder. You're right. I guess I better get ready to tell my aunt, and we better get ready to become parents."

"Yes, I guess we better," he replied with a sigh.

"Well, she's upstairs in her room. She was taking a nap. I'll go talk to her after you leave," Sarah said with a sigh as she looked up at the ceiling.

"No Sarah. We had sex together, and we are going to do everything else together. We will tell her, together. So ask her to come down stairs please," Reginald replied.

"Okay," Sarah said as tears formed and rolled down her face. She was so relieved that Reginald was going to be a part of this pregnancy with her. This was the point that most teenage boys would distance themselves from their alleged girlfriend. She remembered the day at the skating rink in Germany, how one of the local teens shunned his girlfriend after she told him she was pregnant.

Sarah went to get her aunt. She and Reginald together told her that Sarah was pregnant. To her surprise, Veronica already had an idea. She reminded her in jest that she was a nurse on the OB ward. She told her she could tell by the fact the she slept a lot and looked nauseous most of the time. She did, however, express that she was thoroughly disappointed in them, and this by no means gave them legal grounds to have sex over the next nine months.

They both agreed. She allowed Sarah to leave with Reginald so they could tell his parents. Neither of his parents was saved. His mother cried, but his father seemed almost happy about it. They both stated in a stern manner that he would be an involved father to this child and take full responsibility. That he would have to remain in Atlanta to go to college so he could live at home where they could assist him in caring for Sarah and the baby, instead of heading out of state as planned. He respectfully agreed.

Reginald drove Sarah back home and they sat in the living room and talked about what their next plan of action would be. Reginald told her he wanted to know about her scheduled appointments once she made them. They decided to tell the youth pastors and teens in the youth group Wednesday night at bible study.

The news about Minister Goodfellow getting shot hadn't hit all the members of the church. As they sat there talking, they received texts about the shooting, and they prayed with Veronica that all would be well with Derrick. She also prayed for them and the baby Sarah carried, that God would guide them. In the midst of them praying, Talinda also called about Raymond and Bernard's altercation. After prayer, Reginald said goodnight and left to go home. It would be the following morning that Raymond went missing.

*****

They were finally able to convince Tre to leave the hospital without being able to see his daddy. Some of the adults decided not to go in as well. That way, Tre wouldn't be the only one not visiting with his father. They all agreed that even if they did allow children his age to visit patients in the intensive care unit, he shouldn't see Derrick as long as he was unconscious and hooked up to the machines. He was breathing on his own. But because he hadn't regained consciousness, they wanted to closely monitor his vitals and keep him on oxygen to insure his body and brain remained functioning properly.

The nurse stated that they would make an exception for Tre because Nevette worked at the hospital and Derrick's mom was a doctor as well, but they politely declined. Yogi went in after everyone left. She cried and prayed with Nevette over Derrick. She said she would be back the following day. She told Nevette not to worry that she would help her out with Tre. She was glad to hear that they had reconciled. Derrick had called everyone with the news Friday evening as he and Tre moved his belongings back into the house. Yogi made the comment that it looked like their family had begun to become a magnet for tragedy. Nevette didn't respond. Her thoughts were solely on Justice. Yogi said goodbye and Nevette was alone with Justice.

Justice lay there unable to speak or move, but was fully aware of everything going on around him. He had no idea why he couldn't make himself open his eyes. He was in so much pain. It was almost unbearable. He fought to wake up, to escape from the invisible restraints that held him captive. Nevette leaned over and kissed him and expressed her love. When her lips touched his, she felt intense heat. She called for the nurse's station.

"Yes Mrs. Goodfellow, how may we help you?" Nurse Howard asked as she entered the room.

"It just occurred to me that the doctor said my husband had normal brain activity and there was no physical reason why he shouldn't be awake. I would like for him to receive pain medicine every four hours as though he were awake and asking for it. Justice is really warm. He may be able to hear and feel everything that is going on around him. If that is the case, I am sure the effects of the anesthesia are starting to decrease if they haven't already worn off," Nevette declared.

"Well ma'am, that's highly irregular, and I will have to get permission from the doctor and your signature as well," she replied.

"That's fine, please make it happen," Nevette responded.

Inside Derrick was shouting for joy. He knew the connection between him and Nevette was mending, because she could feel him. He was also relieved that his pain would be addressed shortly. The nurse soon reentered the room and after Nevette signed the release form, administered pain medication to him. By the wee hours of the morning, Derrick was feeling little or no pain.

Nevette came out of the bathroom and sat back down in the chair beside the bed. She stroked the back of Justices' hand and began to cry. Through her tears, she began to express her true feelings to him, "Justice, I missed you so much over the last nine months baby. My life was so incomplete. I wanted so many times to call you and tell you to come home. But with each passing day, it just got harder and harder. Baby, I was so ugly and irrational about Callisha. I was worried about you after her graveside service. At the funeral even before you left to go throw up, I could tell you were sick. I was stuck in my hurt, and it controlled me. It was like Satan was literally on my shoulder controlling every thought and every word that came out of my mouth. I didn't know if I was coming or going most of the time. I did the exact opposite of what I wanted to do every time I saw you." She paused and then cried out in tears, "Oh God! Justice baby, please wake up! I'm so scared! I'm trusting God—I am. But—Justice please wake up!"

"Baby please don't cry. I'm going to be okay," Derrick thought. He fought all the more to open his eyes and mouth. He strained with all his might to move his hand just enough to let her know that he could hear her. But he felt like his body was a magnet lying on a metal bed.

It was as though she could hear him, because the next words out of her mouth echoed his thoughts, "Okay, okay, okay, stop crying Nevette, he's going to be okay." She looked down at him. She picked up his hand and held it in hers. "You're going to be okay. I love you and I'm going to take care of you until and after you wake up. I'm going to be right here Justice."

She smiled as her mind went back to Friday night when Justice came to get Tre for the weekend. She was so nervous to see him again. Even though he was unconscious, she found herself still somewhat nervous even now. All the way home earlier that morning, she had an uneasy anxiety. She began to repent for not following her instincts when Derrick had asked if he and Tre should skip the game. She chalked it up to being nervous about being intimate with him again later that night.

"Wow Justice, after eight years I'm still sexually intimidated by you. I was just as much afraid of you coming home from the game today as I was excited. Well, yesterday now considering its two in the morning. I felt twenty-two again and nervous about making love to you for the first time in over nine months," she chuckled, "oh Nevette—girl quit it. God—I love this man!"

Derrick couldn't help but laugh at her in his silent and controlled world as he thought how innocent she still was after all these years. "You'll never get used to me," he thought.

"I just want to curl up in this bed with you. But I know I can't, so I'm just going to say goodnight now baby and curl up in the recliner instead. See you in the morning sweetheart," Nevette said as she kissed his forehead and then his lips.

"Goodnight baby. Thanks for ordering the pain meds for me. I love you," he thought. "God, why can't I wake up or move?"

*****

Her thoughts often trailed off in expectation of the next time they would again be together. She hadn't lost hope that they would reunite soon. But as she watched the evening news, her heart sank at the recap of the day's events. "He needs me!" she said aloud. She just had to see him. The love she had for him was worth the risk. She rocked back and forth on the couch wringing her hands and deep in thought. She searched her memory to recall anyone who would be able to help her. She longed to be in his arms again.

*****

"I knew he didn't look right last night. Why didn't I get up earlier to check on him? It didn't feel right. I knew it didn't feel right!" Talinda exclaimed. "I know—I'm always telling the kids to go with their first instincts. I knew something just didn't seem right with him when he went to bed last night."

"Come on baby don't do this to yourself," Bernard replied. "He is obviously very good at faking how he feels. He has had all of us fooled the last few months."

"But I'm his mother," Talinda replied in tears and said again, "I'm his mother Bernard. A mother always knows. There is just a feeling she gets when something is not right with one of her babies."

"Let's make some phone calls to see if any of the youth have any idea where he may be. Then we need to head down to the hospital to see Derrick and pray with Nevette." Bernard said as he placed his coffee cup in the sink.

"Yes, Nevette just rededicated her life and ministry back to God," Talinda replied.

"Teddy called. He informed me that Derrick was still unconscious, and the doctors couldn't figure out why. He said Nevette is there in the room with him. He's going to head back down to the hospital later. I told him we would call him when we were heading that way. He said Nevette appeared to be handling it totally differently than when they lost the baby. He said she seemed stable," Bernard said and put his hand on Talinda's shoulder as she stood at the sink.

Talinda turned to face him and said, "Well that's a relief. I was really worried about how she might be handling it. I talked with mom after we realized Raymond was missing. She and dad are going to come spend a few weeks here so she can take care of the twins. That way, we don't have to drag them all over town dealing with Raymond and back and forth to the hospital to minister to the Goodfellows along with everything else that is going on in the ministry. If I weren't nursing them still in the morning and at night, we could have just taken them to Athens to them. I hope that was okay baby. I know I probably should have asked you first."

"Oh sweetheart that's an excellent idea. Besides, you know Aunt Helen, she would have probably suggested it herself," Bernard replied with a smile.

"Yeah," Talinda replied with a sigh.

He pulled her into his arms and said, "Come here baby. We'll find him. It's going to work out. Deep inside Raymond loves God. He is going to have to struggle to do this. When I held him in my arms yesterday outside, he was angry, but mostly he was distraught and confused. He was like a five-year-old that had no idea how to handle what was going on inside of him."

She pushed off of him like she had just received a revelation straight from the throne, "I am going to go see Quavis—"

"Talinda no! You will not go see him anymore. You visiting him was part of the problem with Raymond," Bernard replied.

"Sweetheart, I have to. Quavis is still the leader of the Knights. He may be the only one who has any idea where Raymond may be, or who he may be talking to. Besides, he needs to know that Raymond is about to put a hit out on him. I need to go plead for my son's life. Once he finds out, he can have Raymond killed with one phone call."

"Wow, yeah, I hadn't considered that. Okay, we will go see him," Bernard replied.

"Thank you," Talinda replied as she nestled back into Bernard's arms for comfort. "After we leave the prison talking with Quavis, we need to swing by the hospital to see Derrick and pray with Nevette."

"Yes," Bernard replied. He sighed and said, "Everything seems so crazy right now. Derrick's shot, Raymond is missing with a death wish—ugh—what next Lord?" He paused and laughed before he said, "I'm shaking my head and laughing because all I can hear is Brandon's voice saying to me, *'Ministry is always required'*. I feel so inadequate to be your husband and Raymond's father right now. Brandon would know exactly what to do in this situation. He would know where to look, where to go, who to talk to—I don't have a clue." He looked up and said, "Why did you chose me Brandon—why did you chose me?"

Talinda looked up at Bernard and cupped his face, "Sweetheart don't. Brandon chose you because he knew he could trust you to take good care of us—all of us."

"Oh yeah, I'm doing a real good job at that. My son is missing and on a revenge mission. Other than you thinking of going to see Quavis, I don't have a clue what to do," he replied sarcastically.

"That's not fair baby," she replied. "You just took over the job of being Raymond's father less than a year ago. You don't know about Raymond's past contacts. That hasn't been a part of your life with him. Outside of knowing Quavis, for obvious reasons, and the fact that he was a member of the Knights, I don't know much either. Brandon mostly dealt with Raymond. I was just the loving and supportive mother. They kept me in the dark about a lot of things. Neither of them wanted me to worry. Your life with Raymond consists of the youth at the church. None of whom he will contact right now. He won't involve them with this. So baby don't do this to yourself. Because you are a wonderful husband, lover and father."

Bernard sighed, "I just want to find him baby. I just want to find him."

"And we will," she replied and kissed him. "Come on, we need to get dressed because mom and dad will be here soon. I want to nurse the babies before we leave so they will be calm for her. They usually only nurse in the morning and at night now, but it always seems to sooth them every now and then throughout the day.

"Yeah—okay," Bernard replied.

After Helen and Roger arrived, they were soon on their way to visit with Quavis.

*****

Nevette awoke as Nurse Howard checked in on Justice. She lay back in the recliner watching as she took his vital signs. Something about her unnerved Nevette. She was there the night before when Justice arrived via ambulance and cared for him until shift change. Here she was, bright and early this morning. She hadn't noticed that Nevette was awake and went about her normal duty, except for the fact that she was little too touchy feely with Derrick. Nevette could have sworn she heard Nurse Howard moan slightly and caress his chest as she checked the dressing on his abdomen. She knew her husband was naked under the sheet other than the hospital gown. She decided to make Nurse Howard aware that she was awake before her hand went too far south.

Inside Derrick was screaming, "Where are you Nevette? Wake up baby, before this woman exercises immoral liberties with this job!"

Nevette cleared her throat and sat up slightly.

"Oh, good morning Mrs. Goodfellow. I was trying not to wake you," Nurse Howard said as she removed her hand from under the sheet as though she was adjusting Derrick's dressing. "His wound looks good this morning. No sign of infection so far."

"Good morning to you," Nevette replied. "You didn't wake me. Yes other than waking up, he appears to be doing just fine." Nevette's tone suggested that she was well aware of her shenanigans with her husband just now.

She checked a few more things in an attempt to throw Nevette off before she left the room.

"Good morning baby. I know I probably sounded a little jealous just now, but I don't trust her," Nevette said as she kissed him, fluffed Derrick's pillow and placed his head in a more comfortable position.

"Baby you have every right and reason not to trust her," Justice thought. He smiled inside at the fact that even with nonverbal nor physical interaction, they were indeed communicating. They were once again becoming one.

Nevette stroked the side of his face, "Okay baby, I'm going to go jump in the shower. Your mom will probably be here soon. I'll be right here in the bathroom Justice. I'm not leaving the room."

Just as she came out of the shower Nurse Howard reentered the room. She had a tooth brush with children's edible toothpaste, bowl, sponges and antibacterial soap. "Okay Mr. Goodfellow, it's time for your sponge bath."

"Oh, I'll take that," Nevette said as she closed the bathroom door behind her. "I'm sorry Nurse Howard but ahhmmm, I'm a bit of a jealous wife. I'm a physical therapist, and I understand the procedure. Once I finish, you may come back in and check the wound area, but there is no way that I am going to allow you to touch my husband to bathe him. Can you please leave a note at the nurses' station to inform them that no one is to give him baths except me or his mother, Dr. Shaundra Goodfellow?"

"Oh, why certainly ma'am, I understand. I'll just leave you to it. Ring for me once you're done, and I'll check the wound and remove the bed dish. I'll make sure to note your request in his records," Nurse Howard replied.

She hid the fact that she was somewhat irritated with Nevette. She looked forward to getting her hands on Derrick's body. She returned to the nurse's station and made the note in Derricks' file. Not because she was willingly obedient to her request. She figured Nevette was the type of person that would actually check.

Inside Derrick was amused and relieved that Nevette was in his room around the clock. He realized he would have definitely fell victim to Nurse Howards probing hands in more ways than one. He did, however, look forward to the soft gentle touch of his wife.

"Well, I guess we had better get you ready for visitors Justice," Nevette called out from the bathroom as she filled the dish with warm water. She was suddenly very nervous about the thought of bathing Justice. She hadn't seen him naked or touched his body intimately in over nine months.

"Okay Justice why don't we start with brushing your teeth first. Don't want to get any cavities in those pearly whites," she said amused with herself. She carefully brushed his teeth with as little paste on the brush as possible. She wiped them down with a wet cloth several times to remove all the paste.

Inside Justice was overwhelmed by the care she took with him. He strained to open his eyes or to make a movement of any kind. She started to wipe his upper body first. She took a deep breath and lifted the cover to reveal the bottom of his torso. She replaced the cover and decided instead to do one leg at a time to keep his private area covered until last. She could feel her hands start to shake and she laughed out loud at herself, "You've been married to him for eight years Nevette. Why are you so nervous? Just give the man a bath for heaven sakes! It's not like you haven't seen him naked. Why am I so embarrassed?" She finished his legs and folded the cover down to just below his abdomen and begin to bathe his private area. She chuckled as she said aloud, "Mmmm, boy you really need to wake up. I know she didn't think I was actually going to allow her to put her hands all over this. Especially after that stunt she pulled earlier this morning. I'm going to have to keep my eyes on her."

Derrick laughed within himself at the innocence of his wife. Her touch was soothing to him. He thought, "Thank you for not allowing her to touch me. Trust me baby. I am trying hard to wake up."

Just as she finished bathing Justice and called for the Nurse, Shaundra and Derrick Sr., walked through the door. They dropped Tre off at Teddy's house on their way to the hospital so he could spend the day with Josephine. They decided to keep him home from school for a few days. They told Nevette that Tre appeared to be doing well after she had inquired about him. They prayed with Nevette and Derrick. Both Teddy and Lindsay called them and requested prayer for Talinda and Bernard. They explained the situation with Raymond that had taken place around the same time that Derrick had been shot the day before. Nevette noted that she would call Talinda later to check on her. The nurse came in to retrieve the bath dish but left the supplies in the room. After she left, Nevette and Shaundra discussed possible long term treatment for Derrick if it came to that.

*****

Talinda was anxious as they pulled into the state penitentiary. She hoped they would have favor with the warden and be granted an unscheduled visit with Quavis. She never had any issues earlier when she came to visit him. But until today, she had always prescheduled her visits.

"I just pray they allow us to see and speak with him," Talinda stated as they parked and exited the car.

"All we can do is ask baby," Bernard replied.

After going through the proper protocol, they found themselves sitting in the booth staring through the glass waiting to see Quavis. He grew quite favorable of Talinda's visits. When she first began to come see him, he had apprehensions about seeing her. Although she pled for his life from the death penalty and won the bout to lessen his sentence, he was still unsure of her motive and feared facing her. His shame and guilt of his actions concerning Pastor Brandon Travis were at times overwhelming to him. He declared that he would do whatever God desired of him to make right by everyone whose blood was on his hands. He decreed that he would do whatever it took to disarm and dissipate the Knights for good. Or at least turn their mission in a different and less harmful direction.

But today Quavis was uneasy as to why Talinda was there. The word from the streets was already out that there was a bounty on his head. He was well aware that Raymond was the originator of the bounty. When he rounded the corner and saw Bernard sitting beside her, he stopped in his tracks. The color drained from his face, and he shook his head from side to side. He said aloud, "No, I killed you. You're dead—you're dead."

He began to breathe heavily and erratically. The guard walked over to him and asked him if he wished to proceed with the visit. He shook his head without taking his eyes off of Bernard. Talinda watched him with concern. He had never reacted this way before, and her heart began to race. She wondered if it meant that Raymond was in grave danger. Then it hit her that he was staring at Bernard.

She turned toward Bernard and said, "It's his first time seeing you. He must be slightly confused. I remember my inner feelings the first time I laid eyes on you. I thought I had seen a ghost, and I had been married to Brandon for over seven years. I can't imagine that he can tell the difference between you at all, after only one live meeting with Brandon."

Talinda gestured for Quavis to come toward them and sit, in which he obliged. He picked up the phone and held it to his ear but was silent. His eyes were still fixed on Bernard, who had mixed emotions about him as well. Forgiveness was easy when the issue did not literally stand in front of you. He repented within himself for the brief moment that he sided with Raymond to end the nightmare of their lives. However, he quickly dismissed his thoughts as he thought of Talinda and the twins. What stood in front of him was the reason behind him being their father and husband rather than a cousin and uncle. The peace of God entered the room and arrested his thoughts. The silence was interrupted by Talinda.

"No Quavis, you haven't seen a ghost. This is Brandon's cousin Bernard," Talinda said.

Quavis smiled slightly and looked down shaking his head and then back up. "Wow, the resemblance is remarkable."

Talinda smiled and said, "Yes it is. He had the same effect on me when I first saw him too. Pastor Travis appointed him to care for Raymond, the twins and I. We married just shortly after his death."

That statement caught Quavis by surprise. He looked at Bernard again. Bernard placed his elbows on the counter top and clasped his hand together and positioned them just in front of his nose and mouth, as though he contemplated what he would say. He struggled much more than he thought he would with his first encounter with Quavis. He hadn't accompanied Talinda to any previous meetings, and since there was no trial, he had prayed to never actually have to encounter him at all.

"Speaking of Raymond," Talinda spoke again to break the eerie silence, "he is on a revenge vendetta to have you killed for the death of his mother. Quavis he was told that you ordered the hit on her. He feels you had taken Brandon's life for his, and therefore, no more blood was required to get him out of the gang. He disappeared from our home during the night vowing he would take care of it the "Knight" way. He's been planning this for weeks from what we have found out so far. Quavis, please, is there is anything you can tell us about where he may be and who he may be entangled with? We would appreciate it."

Quavis looked back and forth between Talinda and Bernard for what seemed like an eternity before he finally spoke, "Pastor Travis, I have to be honest with you. Everything you just told me, I already knew. I mean—everything about Raymond that is," he paused and looked at Bernard with curiosity after hearing that he was married to Talinda.

Bernard knew that he and Quavis played a silent chess match with each other. Bernard decided to remain silent at the moment. He breathed heavily slightly elevating his nose, mouth and chin above the level of his crossed hands that blocked them, exposing his expression to Quavis, before he lowered himself back down to his original stance.

His actions placed Quavis on alert. He sensed that Bernard didn't share the same merciful attitude toward him as Talinda. He continued, "I have known for a few weeks now that Raymond was after me. Pastor Travis, Raymond is correct about one thing. The hit on his mother was the work of the Knights. But the order did not come from me. The person that the order came from has already been dealt with and sadly, is no longer with us. That too, was not the work of my hands.

My outside leader took a few matters into his own hands that he has since had to answer to me about. I summoned him a few weeks ago, dealt with him and gave him instructions concerning Raymond."

"What do you mean by that?" Talinda asked in a panic.

At that statement, Bernard leaned back in his chair, and his hands went back down to his side and he all but glared at Quavis. Talinda placed her hand on Bernard's thigh to calm him. Because of the height of the table, her action was not seen by Quavis.

"Nothing like that Pastor Travis," Quavis answered. "I placed a protection order over Raymond. I firmly commanded that he not be harmed in any way. I am holding my outside leader responsible for his safety. I also made it impossible for him to make contact with any informants who would be able to assist him in getting a weapon through security when he comes to visit. Because I know that a visit from him is inevitable. If he tries to come through security with a weapon, he will be exposed. He has a Knight tattoo, and he would most likely be arrested and spend some time in jail. So the word is out to protect him while disabling his efforts." He paused for a moment, "Pastor Travis, I understand fully why he wants to kill me. He understands how it works. Normally, the order for a hit would have come from me. This is exactly the reason why I informed Mr. Goodfellow that we could not go to trial. Raymond's mothers' hit went forward without my order. I know what you are thinking. How can I stop them concerning Raymond? Don't worry, my outside leader will not chance crossing me a second time. As it is, he is wondering why he is still alive now. Pastor Travis, I cannot undo what happened a year ago. Trust me there is not a day that goes by that I don't think about the incident between me and your husband that day at your church. Not because I don't want to be in here, but because for the first time, I realized I had been taking innocent lives. I know that being incarcerated, is more protection for me than anything else. I no longer desire to be a Knight much less the leader. But I know the cost of exit and there will be no more bloodshed at my hand. By remaining in prison and their leader, God is using me in a tremendous way. So rest easy sir—ma'am. Unless he does something extremely stupid and uncharacteristic, all will be well with Raymond."

Bernard sat in silence. This time not so much as he was playing out a strategic chess move. He was in awe of and speechless with Quavis' true transformation.

Talinda breathed a sigh of relief as she said, "Thank you. Where do you think he may be?"

"Now that Pastor Travis, I cannot help you with. I have no idea where to find him. He has a Knight tattoo still, so I don't believe that he will solicit help from a rival gang. He knows they will kill first, without asking any questions later. He will not risk them seeking his family should things go south. All the Knights have been instructed not to assist him in any way, but to protect him with their lives. So I imagine by now he realizes that his quest to kill me will not come to pass. I assume, however, he will probably come to see me. To finally, face to face, disclose his displeasure with me concerning his mothers' and Pastor Brandon's death. To say man to man how he feels about me."

Talinda breathed a sigh of relief at Quavis' words. She wiped tears from her eyes as she again thanked Quavis for his actions concerning Raymond.

Bernard finally spoke, "I too am grateful Quavis. I made a promise that I would take care of my cousin's family. That I would love and protect them with my life if need be. I must confess. I didn't want Talinda to come here today or any other day to talk with you. I didn't want her to have anything to do with you. But I knew she had to finish what Brandon started. When Derrick told us of your change, I allowed it. I didn't know how I was going to feel seeing you face to face for the first time, and I have sat here struggling with my feelings the entire time. But listening to the sincerity in your voice, and the passion you have to serve God and do His will despite any discomfort it may bring you, I am ashamed of my apparent attitude toward you today. Please accept my apology."

"Wow, you even sound just like him," Quavis replied. Bernard only smiled and Talinda slightly laughed. "You don't owe me any apology Mr. Travis. Your attitude towards me is totally understandable. It's me that stands in need of your forgiveness."

Bernard shook his head as he said, "You're forgiven—wow. God is—remarkable at how He is ever present in our lives."

"Thank you sir. Pastor Talinda, should Raymond show up here, I will inform you through my lawyer Mr. Goodfellow," Quavis replied.

"So I guess you didn't watch the evening news," Talinda said.

"What do you mean? Has something happened to Mr. Goodfellow?" Quavis asked. He thought maybe some repercussion concerning his case. Raymond was far from his mind concerning Derrick.

"I just figured that one of your leaders would have reported to you there was a gun fight between two gangs, one believed to be the Knights, at the stadium after the game yesterday. It occurred in the parking lot and Derrick and his son were there. He was shot multiple times in an effort to protect his son from running through the crossfire," Talinda replied.

The expression on Quavis' face indicated he indeed had not heard of the incident. But it also made Bernard shutter, because he read his demeanor. He knew that Quavis was withholding something.

"Sorry to hear that. I will pray that he will be okay. I am also grateful that his son wasn't injured in the crossfire," Quavis replied.

Before Bernard could say anything, the guard tapped on the door to indicate that their time was up. It was an unscheduled visit, so they were not allowed the normal full hour.

"Well, that's my cue. I have to go," Quavis said looking over his shoulder toward the guard who appeared in the doorway. "Pastor Travis, as always, it's a pleasure speaking with you. And Mr. Travis, it was nice to meet you."

They both nodded and thanked him again before the guard came to escort him back to his room. Talinda and Bernard thanked and praised God for favor to be able to see Quavis and also to learn that he was protecting Raymond, as they exited the prison. They discussed some possible places Raymond may be hiding as they headed toward the hospital to see Derrick and pray with Nevette. Bernard did not tell Talinda about the concern he felt with Quavis' reaction to the incident at the stadium.

*****

Teddy was there with Nevette when Bernard and Talinda arrived at the hospital to see Derrick. Nevette was over joyed to see them. She and Teddy filled them in on all the details concerning Derrick up to that point. And they in turn, told them everything concerning Raymond.

Derrick wanted so badly to open his eyes. Bernard accompanied Teddy to the cafeteria to get some fruit for Nevette. This gave Talinda and Nevette time for girl talk.

"So how are you really Nevette?" Talinda asked.

"I'm not going off the deep end if that's what you mean," Nevette replied with a smile. "You know Talinda, as I sat here the last twenty-four hours watching Justice, everything I was so angry with him and God about seems so meaningless. All I want is for him to open his eyes and tell me that he loves me." She sighed and wiped her tears.

"Yes. Life has a way of putting things into perspective," Talinda replied. "You realize just how fragile life is, when the thought of it coming to an end slaps you in the face. You just never know from minute to minute when a loved one will be snatched from this side of existence. Brandon's death taught me to never take any day for granted. And to love hard no matter what. To forgive—and forgive quickly. That way, we give no room for bitterness to set into our spirit man. Unforgiveness is a disease that eats away at your insides and leaves you empty."

"Don't I know it," Nevette added. "Talinda I was in such a dark place. It was my voice that I heard whenever I encountered Justice after Callisha went missing and then died, but the words weren't mine. I kept trying to figure out who was talking. I played out in my head on several occasions how our next encounter would be. That I would ask him to come home, and he would kiss me. But when I would come face to face with him, it would go just the complete opposite. I gave in to grief and anger. They overtook me. The more the unconditional love I had for Justice would attempt to rise up, the voice of Satan would speak to me. Reminding me that this was all his fault, and I shouldn't trust, love or forgive him. He kept saying you're better off without him." She paused and shook her head before she continued, "When I went to Myrtle Beach, I didn't have any intentions on coming back alive. The pain was so unbearable. The devil almost talked me into it. I know the only reason I didn't, was because Justice and everyone was praying for me."

"Those were the scariest two weeks of my life baby," Justice thought.

"Talinda. I lined those pills up on the dresser and just stared at them. For days, I didn't move or anything. When the phone rang that day Tre called me, I knew it was God. Because my phone was on silent. I hadn't packed any clothes, yet clothes were in my backpack. Everything around me was pointing to grace. From the room number I was in, to the cross that Tre made for me when he was five. The devil was screaming at me, just take the pills already! I don't even know what made me answer the phone that day. When I heard Tre's voice, life came into the room and chased away death. I never used to understand how anyone could ever think their life was so bad they could ever think of ending it. I would call them weak minded and weak in faith. But the truth is, the force against you is so strong, that the only reason you don't take your life are the prayers of the righteous. Because at that point, you are powerless. Intercessors need to know just how powerful they are. When God wakes them in the middle of the night to pray for someone, they need to rise to the occasion. Lives usually depend on it. But I had only climbed halfway out of the pit, and I was stoic on the drive home. I felt nothing. It's an indescribable feeling. Inside, I was pounding on the walls of my chest trying desperately to escape the prison of my mind."

"Most of the miracles God works in or lives daily go unnoticed by us," Talinda responded. "We take a sound mind for granted. The perfect chemical balance of our brains. There is so much going on in the supernatural around us. So many thoughts of the enemy that God shields us from, by keeping them from entering into our gates. If we encountered everything the enemy suggested and threw at us without God's grace and protection, we would literally go insane. What a mighty God we serve."

"Amen," Justice thought.

"Yes. What a mighty God," Nevette repeated. She looked down at Derrick and lightly stroked his face as she said, "I don't deserve Derrick."

"Don't say that baby," Justice thought.

Nevette continued, "I turned my back on him, God and everyone. I've been saved as long as I can remember. I've ministered to countless people on almost every subject imaginable. In actuality, most of the time, I was out of touch with them. But never one time Talinda, did I ever pray or consider, *'but for the grace of God, go I'*. It's so easy to develop a holier-than-thou attitude toward people that seemingly go through all the time. That have a hard time grasping the promises of

God. My faith failed me. I felt so sifted. Everyone who could or wanted to help me, I pushed away. The crazy thing is, I couldn't pinpoint why. Callisha's death caught me by surprise. I blamed God way more than I actually blamed Justice. I asked, how could He allow this to happen to me—TO ME?" She pointed to herself and patted her chest. "Everything in my life up to that point was about serving Him and His people. I felt as though I had His back, but He didn't have mine. I felt betrayed by Him. The devil is so cunning. Same old tricks since the garden. Once he places doubt, he has you. He takes off running, and drags you behind like an animal tied to the bumper of a moving vehicle. It's impossible to keep up. You have to be rescued!"

"Wow," Talinda replied. "Your experience and testimony are going to bless so many."

"Oh my God baby, you were in such turmoil. I had no idea the extent of your torment. I am so sorry," Justice thought. He struggled to no avail to open his eyes. "God! Why can't I open my eyes?"

"Nevette let's pray," Talinda said as she grabbed Nevette by the hands and bowed her head:

Father,

We just bless your name today. We thank You for who You are, and we thank You for what You have done in our lives. We say right now to You God that we are available. Use us like never before. We thank You for Your many blessings. We pray that You will bring Derrick out of his sleep God. That You would raise him up in the name of Jesus. We thank You that You're mending him even as we speak Lord. That You are ministering to him in that secret place. Father I thank You that the three strand cord of their marriage isn't easily broken. God, I thank You for being in the midst of Derrick and Nevette and for keeping them even when they didn't want to be kept. God You are awesome. We love You for the ministry that will come out of this. We will all rise out of the ashes like the Phoenix and go forth against the kingdom of darkness more powerful than before. I thank You for this dear sister that You have placed in my life. Truly, this is a divine appointment. Thank You for true sisterhood, friendship and ministry. Bless Derrick God with a speedy recovery. Lord, wherever Raymond may be, protect him Lord. Minister to his anger and bring him home to us safe and sound. We ask a special prayer for Tre. He has truly experienced everything that we have. Give him peace in his spirit concerning his father. He is resilient Lord because You are with him. We thank you for the comfort that You constantly surround him with.

In the mighty name of Jesus I pray,

Amen

"Amen," Nevette replied. She wiped the tears from her eyes and smiled. She looked down at Justice and said, "You're going to be okay baby. I'm going to love you to the other side of through." She looked back up at Talinda and thanked her and God for the anointing on her life.

Teddy and Bernard re-entered the room and they all talked for a bit longer before Bernard and Talinda left. They promised they would keep each other up to date on both their circumstances, and lift each other up in prayer.

*****

Bernard and Talinda returned home and filled Helen and Roger in on the details concerning Raymond and Quavis. Helen had prepared dinner, for which Talinda was truly grateful. They prayed with them and sat down to dinner. They continued to discuss the situation with Raymond and Derrick when Talinda's cell phone rang. She jumped up from the table and made a beeline for her purse. It was Raymond's ring tone.

"RAYMOND BABY WHERE ARE YOU? ARE YOU OKAY?" Talinda said in a panic before she even heard his voice on the other end.

Raymond cried out almost in fear, "IT WASN'T ME MOM. I SWEAR. I NEVER PULLED MY WEAPON. IT WASN'T MY BULLET THAT HIT MINISTER GOODFELLOW. MOM, PLEASE TELL ME THAT HIM AND TRE ARE ALIVE? PLEASE MOM! OH GOD PLEASE LET THEM BE ALIVE!"

"OH MY GOD RAYMOND! WHAT ARE YOU SAYING?" Talinda replied in a panic.

Helen, Bernard and Roger rushed into the living room. Everyone's heart raced in anticipation of what had Talinda in such a panic.

Raymond swallowed hard as he replied in a calmer tone, but it was clear he was anything but calm, "Mom. I was there. At the stadium Sunday. I was supposed to be meeting with some guys who were friends of mine before we all ended up in rival gangs."

"Wait son, wait, wait, wait. I'm going to put you on speaker phone so your dad can hear. Your grandparents from Athens are here too," Talinda said and hit the speaker button on the phone. "Okay Raymond, now start over."

Raymond started over, "I was at the stadium Sunday. I was supposed to meet with some guys who were friends of mine before we all ended up in rival gangs. I was walking toward them in the parking lot. Then it all just went bad mom! They pulled their guns and I wasn't sure why. I held my hands up to show I was friendly. Then I realized they were looking past me. I turned and there were five Knights following me. They assumed I set them up! But mom, when I turned back toward them, I saw Tre. He spotted me and started to run toward me right in the path of the gunfire. I don't think Minister Goodfellow saw me. I pulled my gun to protect Tre, but I never fired because shots went off everywhere before I could. I started to run toward Tre, but then I saw Minister Goodfellow. I realized he would get to Tre before I did. However, as I turned to run away, I saw him and Tre go down—" He stopped talking and broke down.

"Oh my God!" Helen cried.

"Son what were you thinking conspiring with a rival gang?" Bernard all but yelled.

Talinda placed a hand on his chest to calm him. She didn't want to send Raymond more over the edge than he already was.

"Tre is fine Raymond. Derrick was shot three times. He reached Tre just as the shots were fired. They got the bullets out, and he is recovering." She didn't want to load him down with all the details about Derrick. Raymond baby, where are you? Please come home sweetheart. We can work this all out," Talinda said in a nurturing but pleading tone.

Raymond cried out, "No! I'm going to get him mom! He will not continue to hurt the people that I love! Everything would have been fine if the Knights wouldn't have shown up. Quavis obviously sent them after me!"

"No son you're wrong. Your dad and I went to see Quavis. The reason the Knights were following you was because he put out a protection order on you. Five knights were ordered to locate and protect you. So they must have heard about the meeting. Raymond they saved your life sweetheart," Talinda replied.

Raymond was silent for nearly a minute.

"Raymond baby, are you still there?" Talinda asked.

Raymond replied barely above a whisper, "I—I have to go momma. I'm sorry. I'm so sorry—"

"Raymond!" Talinda cried. "Raymond!"

"Son—Raymond—," Bernard called out. "He hung up baby."

Talinda leaned into his chest and cried. "Oh God can this get any worse? God please no!"

"We'll find him baby," Bernard said as he kissed her on the top of her head at her hairline.

"Let's pray," Roger said. They gathered in a small circle and Roger began to pray:

Father,

We come before You with our hearts heavy Lord. We're at our wit's end. We seek your peace God, especially for Raymond. Wherever he is Lord, we pray that You will continue to protect hm. Father speak to his spirit and minister to his anguish. Ease the yoke the enemy has placed on his neck. Because of his actions, he now carries a heavy burden. Subside his anger Lord, and dissipate his need for revenge. And give us peace God, that he will arrive home unharmed. We pray that You will begin to raise up forgiveness in the hearts of all involved. We pray for the minister who was shot and lies unconscious still. Give his wife the peace that passes understanding and comfort their son. God we are sometimes stumped with the hand that life deals us. But we will be faithful to You and trust that You will guide us as we play out that hand. God we thank You for Quavis and his regeneration. You truly have him in the right place at the right time. We trust Your perfect plan to play out in our lives. We know that the end of a thing is better thereof than the beginning. So Lord we rejoice in knowing that all will be well with everyone concerned and involved. God we ask again for Your peace.

In Jesus' name,

Amen

*****

"I don't know Reginald. With everything that's happened, maybe we should wait to tell Pastor Travis and everyone about the baby," Sarah said and plopped on the bed with a sigh. She took the phone off speaker mode and held it to her ear as she laid back on the bed and looked up at the ceiling.

"That's just putting off the inevitable Sarah. The response and disappointment aren't going to be any less intense with time. With everything that's going on, this may actually be the best time to reveal it. The strong focus is obviously on Raymond and Minister Goodfellow right now. It may not be as bad as we think. We can't put this off. We need to tell Pastor Travis and the youth on Wednesday night like we planned," Reginald replied.

"My aunt took it better than I expected so I guess you're right Reginald. She is going to set appointments up with Dr. Trevor Johnson because she works with him," she said and then paused. "This doesn't seem real. I can't believe I'm pregnant. This is the one place I didn't think I would ever be. Sex has always been so taboo for me. But through tender love and understanding God that used you and Pastor Brandon, the scars of my father's molestation were all erased."

"Yeah, considering the predicament I got us in. It's safe to say that I erased them a little too much," Reginald replied.

Sarah laughed at his comment as she replied, "It feels good to laugh. I haven't felt like laughing since I looked at the home pregnancy test results. It's not your fault Reginald. Sexual intercourse is the way God designed mankind to multiply. When you have unprotected sex, a baby is supposed to happen. We knew what we were doing. Half the time we used condoms the other half we didn't. We knew the risks, and we jumped in with both feet."

"That may be. But the one useful thing my dad taught me was it's the man's responsibility to protect the relationship from everything. Including unwanted pregnancies," Reginald replied.

"Wow. Are you sure your father isn't an undercover Christian?" Sarah asked.

"Well, I know he reads the bible, because there's always one on the table where he sits. And it's usually on different pages. But I don't know where he stands with Jesus. He has never really said. And doesn't really show a lot of interest in going to church. But he has never said I shouldn't go. I don't know. Some of his principles are dead on, and others are very liberal. When I told him you were pregnant he all but cheered. I really do think he thought I was gay," Reginald replied.

Sarah laughed out again, "Well, I gotta go Reginald. I'll see you at church tomorrow."

"Okay babe, bye," Reginald replied as he hung up the phone. He was super anxious about the look of disappointment that he knew would be on Bernard Travis' face when they shared the news with the youth at bible study. He shook his head and headed downstairs to have dinner with his parents. They asked him how Sarah was doing and talked with him about his, in the near future, responsibilities as a teen father.

*****

"—Come on Raymond, please call me. I miss you and I need to talk to you," LaNiesha spoke into Raymond's' answering machine just as the time ran out.

She sat and sighed. She felt like she was in a bad teen movie. "Give your virginity away and then get the silent treatment from the boy you gave it to," she thought. "Well, what did you expect LaNiesha. Man, why did I do it? Why did I have sex with him? Why do we girls do that? Be so afraid we are going to lose the boy we think we love so we give in. I mean, he did say we didn't have to, and I forced the issue. But God it was only because I figured he would find someone else who would put out the next time he strongly desired it, if I didn't. I wanted him to know that I was willing to be whatever he needed me to be," she exclaimed as she looked up toward heaven. "Who am I fooling? God you know the truth. I wanted it just as bad as he did. The ministers in Germany were right. I should have stayed a virgin. Now I feel cheap and used up." She plopped down in the bed, grabbed a pillow and gathered her feet up to cradle the pillow in the fetal position. She sighed and moaned.

When her cell phone rang she sprang from the bed and was across the room in three steps racing toward it. "Yes it's him!" she squealed in delight before answering the phone. She took a few quick breaths to calm her tone before she answered her phone. She answered with a nonchalant hello, as though she wasn't anxiously awaiting his call.

"Hi LaNiesha," Raymond replied. "I'm sorry I haven't called. But my life hasn't exactly been normal the last few weeks as you know. The last few days have been nothing short of a nightmare."

"Tell me about it. You went missing. Since you didn't call me, I figured you blamed me for telling our parents that you were going after Quavis. Then my aunt tells me that Minister Goodfellow was shot Sunday after the football game. Thank God Tre is okay but Minister Goodfellow is still unconscious from what I understand. I'm not sure how serious it is, but they are not allowing anyone but the adults to see him. So it must be pretty bad. And since he hasn't woke up yet, I think they may not be sure whether he will pull through—"

"What? What do you mean may not pull through? They didn't tell me—" Raymond replied as though having a conversation with himself.

Raymond your mom is worried sick about you. You need to go home, or at least call her and—"

"I already spoke with her yesterday LaNiesha," Raymond replied cutting her off. "I'm not going home. I can't go home." His voice began to quiver.

"Why Raymond? Sure you can. Just go home. Pastor Travis is your mother. She loves you no matter what," LaNiesha said.

"You don't understand LaNiesha. It's my fault. It's all my fault. Oh God please don't let him die!" Raymond exclaimed.

"Raymond what did you do? Is Quavis dead?" LaNiesha all but yelled.

"No—not Quavis! Minister Goodfellow. It's all my fault LaNiesha. They were trying to kill me. I didn't know he and Tre would be there. I went to meet some members of the rival gang. We were friends before we all got mixed up in—ughhh! I swear I didn't pull the trigger—it wasn't my bullet! Oh God please—please!" Raymond cried out.

LaNiesha was silent. She had no idea what to say. This was the side of Raymond she always feared in the back of her mind. She knew the gang mentality existed, but he always seemed so in control and grateful to the Travis'. That world always seemed so far away. Her mind thought back to the night she gave him her virginity. The rage in his eyes as he was demanding her. She was afraid of him then. And slept with him to ensure she would always have a special place in his heart and prayed she would never be on the end of his anger. She wasn't sure if she should continue her relationship with him. But she knew that now was not the time to bring that thought to the table, because if what she felt were true, they had bigger eggs to fry. She knew he needed to go home so everything could be sorted out.

After a moment of silence, she finally spoke, "Raymond just go home. You know your mother loves you unconditionally—"

"No LaNiesha, I can't," he replied. "I did everything I promised I wouldn't. I became what I promised my dad and mom I would never be again. I disrespected Bernard the night before I left. I aimed a gun at him with my mom and the twins in the room. And now, I'm the reason that Minister Goodfellow is lying in the hospital fighting for his life."

"Oh my God Raymond!" she gasped.

"Yes exactly. Now do you see why I can't go home? I can't LaNiesha—I just can't!" he cried.

"Sure you can Raymond," she replied. "Okay then, at least come to see me. I want to see you. I miss you."

"I miss you too. I want to see you too," he replied. "But if I'm being trailed by the Knights, everybody I come in contact with could very well be in danger. Mom says they are following me to protect me, but what if Quavis just told her that to throw her off? If I go home or come see you, then everyone that I love may end up dead. I can't take that chance. I have to go—I have to leave."

"And go where Raymond? How will you support yourself? What will you do? Go to another city and join another gang?" she asked in frustration.

"Ughh," he replied and rubbed his fingers through his hair and down his face. He put his hand on his hip, looked up and sighed. He whispered to her, "LaNiesha I'm scared." He cleared his throat to get the lump out of it so he could speak clearer, "I don't know what to do. I was there LaNiesha. I was there! The police are probably already looking for me. My life is over!" He started to have a conversation with himself, "*Vengeance is mine. I will repay saith the Lord.* GOD I'M SORRY! OH JESUS I'M SORRY! LORD JESUS, PLEASE FORGIVE ME!"

LaNiesha cried out, "Oh Raymond baby, please just go home! Go home Raymond!"

"I can't," Raymond whispered in a defeated tone.

'Okay then at least meet with me. I need to see you," she replied.

"Are you setting me up LaNiesha?" he asked.

"What are you talking about Raymond?" she asked.

"Nothing. I miss you. Where do you want to meet?" he replied.

"Our favorite spot of course," she said with a slight chuckle. "About an hour?"

He chuckled and shook his head, "Okay. I'll be there in about an hour. I miss you."

"I miss you too. See you in an hour. Don't stand me up Raymond," she replied.

"I won't. I'll be there. Just don't set me up LaNiesha," Raymond replied hesitantly.

"Never babe," LaNiesha said and they hung up. She said a quick prayer before she grabbed her coat and headed out.

Raymond pondered in his mind if he should meet LaNiesha. He

tried to pray but felt as though his prayers hit the ceiling and fell back to the ground. "Why would You listen to anything that I have to say right now anyway?" he said as he looked up toward heaven.

*****

He watched her for an extra fifteen minutes just to make sure she was alone before he approached her. He also had to ditch the trails of Knights that he noticed in his near vicinity from time to time. He didn't want to take the chance of another gun fight. He was so reluctant to approach her. Her feared for the lives of everyone he loved. But he needed to hold her. He needed to feel any kind of love he could right now. He was so broken spiritually. She was about to leave when she saw him in the distance. She smiled and began to walk down the trail toward him. He picked up his paced to lessen the ground she had to cover to reach him. They sat down on the bench in the far reaches of the east side of Stone Mountain Park. There was such a beautiful vantage point of the city from that location.

She stopped just short of touching him and said, "You ignored me for nearly two weeks Raymond Travis."

"I ignored everyone LaNiesha. Don't take it personally. I made a mess of my life. A total complete mess," he sighed.

"Raymond I'm late," she blurted out. She hadn't figured out how she would tell him that she thought she was pregnant. But he of course had no idea what she meant.

"Late for what? Where are you on your way to? I knew you were setting me up," he said as he stood to leave.

She grabbed his hand and said, "I didn't set you up, and I don't mean that kind of late. I mean—I'm—late." She made a hand gesture toward her stomach as she spoke.

"Oh," he replied as he sat back down on the bench. "Ahhh—MAN! This cannot get any worse! What did I expect? I knew better. I knew BETTER! We didn't use protection. It's not like I didn't know. Oh LaNiesha I'm sorry—I'm sorry. I just—oh God I can't take another thing. Lord please—just end—oh Jesus—wow. I'm going to take care of you—okay. I won't leave you out there by yourself to deal with this."

"We don't know yet Raymond. There's a chance—there maybe another reason I'm late. I was seriously stressed over you. It could be that," she replied.

He shook his head and asked, "How late are you?"

"Just a day late. It could still start anytime Raymond. I don't feel sick or anything, so I'm hopeful," she replied.

"Okay well there is no need to tell our parents about this until we are sure," Raymond declared.

"Definitely—I agree," she replied and looked up toward heaven. She sighed, "My parents are going to kill me. I mean my mom didn't even think or know I was still a virgin, so she won't be surprised about that. She always said get on birth control and practice safe sex. For whatever reason, I just never said I was a virgin. Probably, because whenever I did decide to have sex, I wouldn't have to be afraid of what she would think because she already assumed I was. I mean all the girls I hung with were considered the fast group, so everybody just assumed I was too. I'm usually like clockwork with my cycle. But Raymond you have my hormones in overdrive right now. I don't even want to face your mom if I am."

"You don't want to face her," Raymond replied sarcastically. "I've broken every single vow I made my father. I had sex again before I got married. I told him I would never hold another gun in my hand with the intention of hurting somebody. Not only did I hold it in my hand. I pointed it at my dad Bernard. I told him to get out of my way, or I was going to shoot him."

"Raymond!" LaNiesha replied.

"Yeah. We fought over it. He got it out of my hand. I said some pretty cruel things to him concerning Pastor Brandon and my mom. I yelled at him that he was not my father. He just kept telling me that he loved me and he wasn't going to let me go," his voice began to crack. He wiped his hand across his face to dry his eyes. "I broke and we went inside to talk about it, and I left the house the next morning before they both woke up."

"Oh my God Raymond. You need to go home," LaNiesha urged.

He replied as though she hadn't just told him to go home, "On top of all of this, I am about to be a father. I haven't figured out how to be a son yet. There is no way I'm ready for fatherhood. Can this get any worse?"

"We don't know for sure that I'm pregnant Raymond. I could be making myself late. Stress will delay your cycle. I probably shouldn't have said anything until I had taken a test and was sure," she replied as she dropped her head.

He stood and pulled her up into his arms, "No. You did the right thing. You shouldn't go through the fear alone. You didn't get here by yourself. And to think, my father put money away for me to go to college. That ain't going to happen now."

"Now you know better than that. You know baby or not, your mother is going to make you go to college. And baby or not I'm still going to college. I'll just have to go local instead of out of town to Athens with you," LaNiesha replied.

"I'm not just talking about the baby. I mean everything else. Our baby is the least of my problems LaNiesha. I'm probably about to go to jail," Raymond replied.

"No you're not Raymond. You said you never pulled your trigger. You're not going to go to jail for standing in a parking lot," she replied.

"I wasn't just standing there. I coordinated the visit. It's like when you plan a robbery. You don't mean for anyone to die, but if they do in the midst of the robbery and you masterminded the plan for the robbery. You are liable and responsible for any deaths that occur during the robbery. LaNiesha, I chose the meeting place because it was so public, I never figured in a million years that a gun fight would go down there," Raymond sighed.

She was silent. She hadn't considered the possibility of Raymond facing charges for Minister Goodfellow's injuries.

He sensed her fear, mustered a smile and said, "Hey, it will work out. Once you take the test, let me know the results, okay? I am going to be here for you if you're pregnant. You won't go through this alone. I promise. God, I've been so crazy these last few weeks. I made so many mistakes."

"Raymond please just go home," she pleaded with him again.

"LaNiesha I can't. My mom and the twins were only about fifteen feet away across the room from us when we were fighting over a gun that very easily could have gone off at any minute and killed anyone of them," he replied. "Then I find out that all while I have plotted and planned to kill him, Quavis had a protection order out on me. I know my mom probably had something to do with that. She had been visiting him off and on for a while. I know my dad Bernard wasn't anymore crazy about her visits than I was. I plotted and brainstormed every possible way I could get into the prison with a weapon, and no doors of opportunity opened until I thought of the rival gang. I don't know LaNiesha," he replied with a sigh. "She is so forgiving though. She just forgave Quavis for killing dad. Just like that, no strings attached."

"And so did you Raymond. You—," LaNiesha started to say.

"I've been pretending LaNiesha, okay! I never forgave him. Not one day was an ounce of forgiveness ever in my heart toward him. I wanted him dead from the first day. I just said all the right things that I knew my mom wanted to hear. Because I knew she needed to hear it, but I've been angry from the beginning and I still am," he replied and turned and took a few steps away from her. The uncertain look in her eyes that she had toward him, pained him. He placed his hands on his hips and continued, "All while we were in Germany I thought about it. I never said anything I just thought about it. I stood up there in that pulpit and laid hands on people all while I had un-forgiveness in my heart. God could have struck me dead, and I would have gone straight to hell. I knew better."

"Raymond you are being way too hard on yourself. You had every right to harbor resentment toward the man you knew killed your father, and at the time, thought killed your mother. No one would have blamed you for being just a little salty with him," she replied.

"That's no excuse LaNiesha. God is not going to alter his word to accommodate my so-called justified anger, and we both know it," Raymond answered.

"Okay, so you screwed up, now what are you going to do about it? Are you going to keep running or go home and face the music?" she asked. "Your mom is afraid she is going to lose her baby boy."

"I'm not her baby boy. BJ is," he replied helplessly.

"You're her first son and first baby boy Raymond," she replied and walked up to him. He still had his back to her. She turned him around as she said, "Turn around and look at me Raymond. Do you still have that gun?"

"No, I got rid of it. I never should have bought it in the first place. Neither of them. The one Bernard took or the replacement. I guess I at least owe Quavis an apology and thanks for his protection and keeping me from making another stupid mistake by trying to sneak a gun in through security to kill him," Raymond replied.

"And after you leave from seeing Quavis, go home Raymond Travis—go home," LaNiesha said sternly.

He smiled, chuckled slightly and looked at her, "We'll see." He paused and then said again, "We'll see. As soon as you find out if you're pregnant or not, you call and let me know."

"You act like you're not going to be around Raymond," she said nervously.

He smiled again, kissed her, then turned and walked away. She dropped her head and breathed deeply. She decided to give Raymond time to go see Quavis and go home before she disclosed their conversation to anyone.

~Chapter Four~

"I can't believe we have to call and tell Nevette that Raymond is partially to blame for what happened to Derrick and Tre," Bernard said with a sigh as they sat at the breakfast table.

"But Bernard! He said he never took a shot!" Talinda exclaimed.

"Talinda his actions are not the issue. His intentions are. You heard him. By his own admission, he set up the meeting that resulted with Derrick getting shot. He is going to be just as responsible as if he pulled the trigger himself," Bernard replied.

"Bernard no, please! Oh God please—my baby," Talinda cried.

"We're going to have to get a good lawyer for him. And because of conflict of interest, we won't be able to get anyone at the Goodfellow and Goodfellow firm," Bernard stated.

"This is a nightmare. God please let me be dreaming!" Talinda exclaimed.

Bernard grabbed her hands and began to pray:

Lord,

We come before You in desperate need of Your comfort. You are the righteous judge, and we humbly stand in Your court room on our son Raymond's behalf. Father we understand the judicial system and pray for favor with the earthly judge should the situation take that course of action. God we thank You for Quavis and the love You showed our family through his protection for Raymond. God wherever Raymond is, we pray that You will keep his mind in perfect peace. Bring him home to us Lord. Let him know that our love for him is unconditional. God we pray that Derrick will awake out of his slumber and have a full recovery. God we pray that there will be no residual effects to any of his organs. God give Nevette and Tre the peace that passes understanding. God we pray for the gang members that were involved. God we believe You are able to change their mindset, that they will first begin to value their own lives. And in turn value others as well. You said in Your Word that all things work together for the good of them that Love You and are called according to Your purpose. We are called Lord, and we rejoice in that fact that we can expect a great end to what the devil designed to be a disaster in our lives. We thank You in advance for Your divine intervention in his plans. You hold our lives ad destinies in the palm of Your hands and we are fully persuaded that You are able to bless and mature the plans You have for us. To God be all the glory.

In Jesus' name,

Amen.

"The peace of God is overwhelming," Talinda said as she wiped tears from her eyes.

"Baby, I trust God that all will be well," Bernard replied.

"Well, I think I will stop by and talk to her later today. This is something that needs to be done face to face. A phone call seems a little cheap and wimpy. Besides they are our close friends. Mom and dad have the twins, so we can head over there after lunch to speak with her," Talinda said as she stood to take their breakfast dishes to the sink.

"That's sounds like a plan," Bernard replied.

*****

Raymond pulled up in front of the prison. He sat in the car looking through the barbed-wire fence. He was overwhelmed at the thought that he may in the near future be an occupant and not a visitor. He turned the engine off and exited the car headed to the front gate. He had mixed emotions about facing Quavis. His anger no longer had a mission and the taste of the humble pie he consumed over the last twenty-four hours lingered on his palate. He checked in and went through the appropriate security procedures. He sat down at the window and waited for Quavis to walk through the doorway. He was suddenly unsure what he would say.

Quavis stopped just inside the doorway when he saw it was Raymond to visit him and not Talinda. He saw the name Travis and never bothered to look at the first name. He was used to his only visitor with the last name of Travis being Talinda. He never got visits from his biological family members; only his gang family. And even then, it was out of obligation because they had been summoned by their leader. God intentionally isolated Quavis, and was doing a great work in him while he was on the back side of the desert. He sat down in the chair and motioned for Raymond to pick up the phone.

"Before you say anything Raymond just listen. I understand exactly where you are coming from. If this situation were reversed, I would have done the exact same thing, if not more than you did. I would have made alliances with whoever I needed to in order to get to you. I would have been on the same revenge kick that you were on. From your point of view, it looked as though I had taken the two lives for your exit, instead of the customary one. I understand your motive and your mission. Therefore, you do not owe me an apology."

Raymond shook his head and looked down. Nothing that had just come out of Quavis' mouth was even close to anything he ever expected Quavis to say to him about attempting to have him killed. He raised his head but before he could say a word, Quavis continued.

"Listen Raymond, go home. I know what you are thinking, and normally you would be correct. Lay low and attempt to let the heat pass over before being seen in the public," he stated.

Raymond looked at him in curiosity and confusion. "Yes, I know what happened Sunday after the football game in the parking lot. Before your mom even came to visit me, I had already put out a protection order on you. I pretended to be surprised when she told me about it. I wasn't sure of your whereabouts, and I wanted to be sure of your complete involvement. Five Knights were charged to find and protect you at all cost. They located you Sunday and learned about your meeting with the Aces. Two Knights are in custody now and have already written sworn statements about the identification of all the Knights that were present and involved. Your name was not mentioned. As far as the city of Atlanta knows, you do not exist as a member of the Knights and was nowhere in the vicinity. Both the members of the Aces were killed in the cross fire. One on the scene and the other quietly and un-broadcasted at the hospital. Raymond there is absolutely no one available to put you on the scene—"

"Yes there is," Raymond interrupted him. "There is. A seven-year-old little boy who thinks the world of me, saw me. I ran toward him to intercept him. Him seeing me, was the reason he started to run in the midst of the gunfire. He ran toward me just as the Knights were discovered by the Aces. He was caught in the cross fire and his father Minister Goodfellow—"

"I know Derrick Goodfellow. He's my lawyer," Quavis interjected. "Those are your parent friends Raymond. They are not going to want to see you in prison. Just go home Raymond. Listen, you have a family that loves and cares for you. They create a loving environment for you every day. They pray for and minister to you. There is nothing they wouldn't do for you. Go home Raymond—go home man—go!"

"You don't understand Quavis," Raymond replied.

"I do understand Raymond. For once in my life I do understand. Before I stood in the back of the gymnasium the day of your fathers' funeral, I had never, ever felt any remorse whatsoever in taking a life. But that day, all I felt was an overwhelming presence of shame. To the point that I was suicidal. I looked forward to getting caught so I would have a reason not to kill myself out on the street. I couldn't understand the love he had for you. Never had anyone offered their life to get a member out of the gang before that day. But he loved you enough. I looked into his eyes the day we came to the church rally. I saw God in his eyes. I saw Jesus, and it terrified me. I wasn't trying to kill your dad. I was trying to kill the fear I felt when I looked into his eyes and saw the power of a living God. It was terrifying and I just wanted out of His presence at all cost. Something I now know is an impossible task, to be out of God's presence that is. I was angry at your father, because no man had ever shown that kind of love to me. At least not positive love anyway. He loved you Raymond and gave his life for you. And I am not about to allow you to blow it. It was because of your father Pastor Travis, that I ordered your protection at all cost. His blood was shed for you Raymond, the same way Jesus shed His for all of us on Calvary's cross."

Raymond was stunned at Quavis' words. Quavis smiled and shook his head as he read Raymond's thoughts, "Don't be so surprised. I have nothing but time in here, and I have become an avid reader. Your mother brought me a bible. And I'm guessing it was one of your fathers, because it has a lot of hand-written notes by him in it."

"Yeah I know," Raymond replied. "Her giving you one of my dad's bibles was one of the things that sent me over the edge. The one she gave me was his main bible. Almost every page is full of words of wisdom. There are also hundreds of very intimate things about my parents and their relationship. There was on in there about the day I received Christ."

Quavis interjected, "Yeah that is in the one I have too. He must have been in the process of transferring notes from one bible to the next, because I too have his thoughts about you on that day. I read them and I cried. I have always wanted a father in my life to love and honor me like that. To speak of me being his son and talk of the pride he had in me. Raymond listen. I'm twenty-one years old and the leader of the most notorious gang in the greater Atlanta area. And at twenty-one years old, I'm in prison. Raymond, I have a hundred young teens under my command and the only advantage I have is they are all easily influenced by me. I have two and a half years to persuade them that they need to do something different with their lives. From what I understand, some of them are taking advantage of the fact that the leader is in jail and attempting to get out without paying the blood sacrifice. I told my assistant Shawn to just allow them to leave. I told him to inform them that this would be their one-time only chance to walk away with no strings attached, and no blood required. That I needed devoted killers for the direction I was taking the knights into. At first, he said they were reluctant. But when one or two got the nerve to walk past the door arms and weren't shot, others gained courage and left. At the end of the meeting only about fifty-five teens were left. I'm hopeful that they will never show up again and will go home to their families. The ones remaining don't realize that the killers I'm leading them toward becoming are demon killers. I have formulated a letter to send to each of their parent's certified mail informing them of my intentions to dissipate the gang and give them control of their sons back. That way, the teens who walked away will not end up in a rival gang. Parents are going to have to step up and parent their children to keep them straight. I have told them they cannot share the contents of the letter with anyone. It has to remain a secret to work. It states the importance of their secrecy. If the information gets out I'm a dead man. And if I die, the gang goes on with new harsher leadership, and they will never get control of their sons again. The only way the gang dies is if I live. I can dissipate the gang over time. And the crazy thing is, that after all this time I find out now that my right-hand man Shawn is a narc. All this time I'm thinking this kid is nineteen, and he is twenty-three and on the police force. He was good. He slipped through and passed all the initiations. He managed to stage every death he was involved in. God had a plan all along Raymond. I need you on the outside, assisting me. Don't blow this Raymond. Go home. I doubt very seriously that the Goodfellows will press any charges against you. You didn't pull the trigger. You just happened to be in the wrong place at the wrong time."

"You and I both know that is not the truth Quavis," Raymond replied. "You know everything else, so I'm sure you already know I planned that meeting with the Aces. I might as well have pulled the trigger. We both know I am responsible for what happened to Minister Goodfellow."

"That's not altogether correct Raymond," Quavis replied. "The Aces only drew and fired because the Knights showed their faces. They were supposed to follow and protect you. They should have stayed out of sight and monitored the meeting only. But they didn't follow the orders as instructed. They saw an opportunity to oust members of a rival gang and prematurely advanced and drew on the Aces. If they had stayed hidden, and just watched as they were told, not a single shot would have been fired that day."

Raymond thought back on the details of the incident. He remembered walking toward them in unarmed surrender fashion. They drew, and he realized they were not focused on him but looking past him. Quavis was correct. The Knights initiated the conflict. He still felt guilty of the outcome. He knew that had he not chosen the location, Derrick Goodfellow would not be in Northside's Intensive Care Unit fighting for his life.

"That's just geography Quavis and you know it," Raymond replied. "My shoulders are not light in the blame for Sunday's events. If not legally, then morally I am definitely guilty."

"Let me ask you this and be honest Raymond. I don't want a 'super saved, saint, always do the right thing' answer. I want your natural instinct response," Quavis stated. "If the person shot had not been Derrick Goodfellow, a good friend of your family. Would you be so apt to plead guilty for the crime?"

Raymond was silent. He knew Quavis had made a checkmate move. He was driven mostly because of his and his parent's relationship to the victim, and he knew it. Had it been a stranger, he would have struggled in connecting himself as the one responsible.

He sat there shaking his head unable to speak. He had his elbows on the table with his hands crossed and rested his head in his hands.

"Look Raymond. I didn't want Minister Goodfellow to get me off, or get me any kind of parole. The minute I walk out of this prison, I am probably a dead man. Because I will denounce the gang. I'm not afraid of death, because now I know to be absent from the body is to be present with the Lord. But I'm on a mandate from God to change the mission of the Knights, and I am going to be on that mission until they change or God relieves me of it. You have your whole life ahead of you. I know what you are thinking, and your family is not going to be in danger. The leader of the Aces had no idea JoJo was there to meet you or have an alliance with a rival member. He never told Lucky about the meeting between you too. I know this because Lucky sent word asking why the Knights broke the truce and ambushed his boys while they were at the game. He never knew about the meeting. I assured him it was unscheduled and individual acts with a few members who were taking matters into their own hands because of my position, that they assumed was weaker. I told him they had been dealt with, and the two live Knights will take the fall for the incident. The police has them in protective custody, and they will probably only serve a few months unless Minister Goodfellow doesn't pull through. Their records are spotless and there are no witnesses willing to come forward to testify against them. So Raymond I say again—go home and talk to your parents and the Goodfellows about what I have shared with you. They will not place you at the scene, and the little boy will have no idea why you were there unless you tell him. You will still be his knight in shining armor, no pun intended, haha." Raymond continued to shake his head. "Look Raymond, God has given you grace and favor in this situation. Now accept it and walk in it," Quavis added. "Look Raymond, I'm unworthy of freedom. Two and a half years Raymond. Two and a half years. That's what the court system is saying your dad's life was worth. I'll be eligible for parole in two and a half years. Because I have never been convicted or even accused of murder before and the fact that your mom pleaded my case, I received a light sentence. You know beyond a shadow of doubt, how many people have died at my hand Raymond. Way too many to count. And the system decided your dad's life was only worth a lousy two and a half years."

"No Quavis that's where you're wrong. The court system didn't decide what my dad's life was worth. God did. It was worth my life out of the gang. And it was about your salvation and countless others to come as a result of you surrendering your life to Jesus Christ and accepting His blood sacrifice. My dad wouldn't have wanted you to spend one day in prison. That's the kind of person he was. He gave everything for youth freedom in Christ Jesus. That was his mission. That was his mandate, and he knew he was going to die fighting for it. If it had not been that night, then it would have been another. It was just a matter of time." He paused and shook his head, "He gave everything for me, and I messed this up. How am I supposed to face my mother after I ruined the sacrifice her husband made for me? I broke every vow I made to my father Quavis. I broke every single one."

"The woman who comes to visit me is not a woman you need to be afraid of. She's full of the same kind of love Pastor Brandon was full of. She is not going to judge you. She's just going to love you. Okay listen, you're right. This is about your dad's sacrifice. So now what? You're going to just let it be in vain? The price he paid for your life and freedom, you're going to just give away because of shame and a mistake? I've never had anybody—ANYBODY fight for me before your parents came along. Your mother pleaded with the judge not to kill me or leave me to rot in jail forever. She studied my record and found every loop hole in it to plead her case. I stabbed and killed her HUSBAND RAYMOND! And what? You're going to walk anyway from that kind of love! Are you freakin' kidding me? Minister Goodfellow tried to talk me out of this life years ago, and I didn't listen. I didn't walk away from it. I ran full steam ahead further into it instead. GO HOME MAN—go—home. When you walk out of this prison today you better go home. I don't what to hear anything on the street about you doing nothing—NOTHING. Do you hear me Raymond? Or I'm going to deal with you myself. RAYMOND TRAVIS—go home!"

Quavis looked over his shoulder because the guard had signaled that his time was up. He nodded his head in the guard's direction indicating he understood. He stood with the phone still in his hands and said on last time, "Go home man—please. Just go home." He shook his head, looked up toward heaven and back down to Raymond, "Go home." He hung up and walked away.

Raymond sat there for a minute after Quavis left the room. His words penetrated deep into Raymond's soul and spirit. Tears fell from his eyes, and he wiped them before he stood and walked away. He got into his car and drove toward Athens, Georgia almost blinded by the hot tears that streamed down his face. He went to his father's grave and sat down beside his headstone. He sat in silence for the span of about a half an hour. He looked up and then back down at the inscription on his fathers' headstone of his favorite quote, *~Ministry is always required!~* He shook his head and thought again of his conversation with Quavis. He spoke with wisdom and authority. Raymond could tell that his conversion was genuine. Nothing about it appeared to be a ploy to gain an advantage. He sighed and with a shaky voice, began to talk to his father:

Dad,

I don't know what to do. I failed you. I broke every vow that I made to you. I feel like everything you did for me is in vain. My freedom is in jeopardy at my own hand, and LaNiesha may be pregnant. Oh God dad, I made a big mess of this, and I know it stinks to high heaven. My heart aches, and I am afraid to face mom and Bernard. Not to mention how will I ever be able to face the Goodfellows again. Tre thought the world of me. How will he feel about me after he realizes I am the reason his father is shot and fighting for his life? That should be me in the intensive care unit, not him. IT SHOULD BE ME DAD! It should be me. How many times does God have to sacrifice blood for my life? First Jesus, then you and now Minister Goodfellow—

He swore he could feel the ground quake beneath him as the Lord spoke directly to his spirit:

RAYMOND,

YOUR DESTINY AWAITS. YOUR PATH HAS ALREADY BEEN CHOSEN AND PAID FOR. THE BLOOD OF OTHERS HAS INDEED PAVED THE WAY. MY GRACE IS SUFFICIENT. GO HOME MY CHILD.

Raymond looked around terrified. He searched to see who had spoken to him. He was the only person in sight. He looked up and said, "Yes Lord." He returned to his car and began the drive home. He had no idea what he would say when he stood face to face with his parents or the Goodfellows. But he trusted God that they would have an understanding heart, and God's grace would prevail. As he got closer to the turn off leading to his house, his heart raced. He looked down at his cell phone that lit up and saw that LaNiesha left him a message. Instead of turning to go down Main Street, he went in the opposite direction.

"Oh God," he thought. "This is it. I guess I had better face the music with her first before going home. She probably took the test." He sighed and headed toward LaNiesha's house.

*****

Talinda and Bernard pulled in the visitor's parking lot, parked and headed to the intensive care unit to speak with Nevette. The smile on her face faded when she saw the heaviness they carried on theirs.

"Oh my God what is it? Is it Raymond?" Nevette asked in a panic. She couldn't think of any other reason Talinda and Bernard would be so solemn.

"No Nevette it's not Raymond. Well, in a way I guess it is. You may want to sit down for what we need to tell you concerning the incident with Derrick and Tre yesterday," Bernard informed her.

She looked and Talinda, who was already wiping tears from her eyes. She whispered, "No. I think I'll stand."

Bernard and Talinda proceeded to inform Nevette of everything that Raymond and Quavis shared with them that they did not disclose or know earlier. Nevette was silent. She stood in disbelief shaking her head from left to right.

Finally, after what seemed an eternity, she spoke. "Oh God, where is Raymond? He must be terrified and overrun with guilt. You have to find him Bernard. The spirit of suicide will challenge even the strongest mind. But one filled with guilt is easy to manipulate. You both know I know all too well about that, and what he must be going through. Oh Talinda I can't speak for Justice, but I don't hold Raymond responsible for this any more than the kids who actually shot him. The devil is the only enemy in this situation, in my opinion. He motivates, manipulates and orchestrates these young kids' minds, and they're powerless against him without the power of the Holy Spirit and Spirit-filled parents. You have to find him. Before the vice of the enemy begins to infiltrate his thoughts and take over."

"Oh God thank you!" Talinda cried out. "I wasn't sure how you would react. I mean, you could easily require recompense from Raymond for Derrick's condition. And you would have been justified."

"Talinda the only thing I would have done successfully by holding Raymond accountable and placing him behind bars is breaking his spirit. Now when Justice wakes up, I will inform him of the details you just shared with me. But as far as I am concerned, we will never have this conversation again. And Tre will never know Raymond's plans or involvement concerning the incident."

"Well said baby," Justice thought. "I will not give the devil another youth to destroy."

Talinda wept, and Bernard thanked God and Nevette for the agape love, grace and mercy she extended Raymond on behalf of the Goodfellows. They prayed together then left to go home to make phone calls in another attempt to locate Raymond.

*****

"Hey, I got your message. I was driving so I couldn't reply," Raymond said to LaNiesha as she opened the door.

She practically jumped into his arms as she all but shouted, "I'm not pregnant Raymond. I'm not pregnant!"

"Thank you Jesus!" he shouted. "Girl, you could have texted me that. You had me in a frenzy all the way over here that you were pregnant. I figured if you weren't, you would have just said it in the text."

"Oh I'm sorry," she said and laughed out loud. "I guess I could have just texted you that my cycle started."

"Yes that would have been good of you. Girl, I am not touching you again. We dodged the bullet big time!" Raymond declared.

"Oh don't worry. I will not let you, protection or not," she replied.

He took a deep breath and let out a sigh of relief. He sat down on the couch as he said, "I went to see Quavis today."

"Oookay, how did that go?" she asked.

"Not at all like I thought it would. LaNiesha he is so different. It's like he has blown by me spiritually. I left there thinking I need to play catch up. He is on a mission. He's driven, and he is sincere in God. I could feel the anointing coming off him through the six-inch glass that stood between us. It was almost like listening to a young Pastor Brandon Travis. He is driven to save and dissipate the Knights. He was doing way more for me than protecting me. I was ashamed of my intentions toward him by the time I walked out of there, and somewhat intimidated spiritually," Raymond replied.

"Wow. There is nothing too hard for God," she declared.

"Yeah, guess not," he replied. He sighed and said, "Well, I guess I had better quit putting off the inevitable. Eventually, I am going to have to stand in front of Bernard Travis and give an account."

"Maybe it won't be so bad. They will probably be too happy to see you to be angry about anything," LaNiesha replied.

"Don't count on that. I fought my dad over a loaded gun with my brother, sister and mother only ten feet away in the same room. He will definitely give me the business for that, and I don't blame him. I would do the same thing. Okay LaNiesha, I am going to go home. I'll see you at bible study tomorrow night," Raymond replied as he stood and walked to the front door.

He kissed her goodbye and headed home to face his parents for his actions over the last few days. They decided they would tell their parents about having sex later after things were calmer.

Talinda and Bernard were sitting in the living room telling Helen and Roger about the visit to see Nevette when the sound of the front door opening caught their attention. Talinda jumped from the couch and made a beeline to Raymond.

"Oh my God, my baby!" Talinda exclaimed as she rushed toward Raymond. "Are you okay? Let me look at you," she declared and she turned him every which way as though thoroughly inspecting him for injuries.

"I'm fine mom really. Nothing is physically wrong with me," Raymond replied. He did not look up nor make eye contact with his father or grandfather.

Talinda continued to fuss over him as Helen asked, "Raymond sweetheart, why didn't you come home when everything first happened? We are family baby, and we love you no matter what."

"I don't know grandma," he whispered. "I'm sorry—" he paused to wipe tears and looked down to the ground.

Bernard did not say a word. Roger watched his reaction and understood completely all the emotions that he knew had to be bargaining for room inside of Bernard. He touched Raymond on the shoulder and said, "We are glad you finally decided to come home son. Raymond we love you unconditionally. We don't condone nor agree with your actions as of late, but love is unconditional. Adversity is not the time to run from those who love you."

"Yes Sir," he replied barely above a whisper. He still had his head down. He knew Bernard was not about to dismiss his actions as easily as everyone else had.

"Come with me son. We need to talk," Bernard said to Raymond. He turned to walk downstairs to the basement.

Before Raymond could reply Talinda interjected, "Bernard baby please—"

"Shhhh, Talinda sweetheart—no," Bernard stated and gave her a look, which told her that he was indeed going to deal with Raymond man-to-man. "Raymond—come."

"Yes Sir," he replied as he followed Bernard downstairs.

Helen placed her hand on Talinda's shoulder as tears fell from her eyes. "Dad please go down there," she begged.

"No sweetheart. I can't interfere. This is Bernard's house, and he needs to reestablish himself as the father and head of Raymond and this house. Although we are glad he is home safe. Absolutely, nothing about what Raymond did is okay baby girl."

Bernard turned to face Raymond once they entered the game room in the basement. Before he could get a word out, Raymond declared, "Dad, I'm sorr—"

"Oh, so I'm your father today?" Bernard declared sarcastically. Raymond dropped his head and looked at the ground. "Raise your head and look at me!" Bernard commanded. "We are going to establish some things in this house today. And after we establish them, we are never going to visit this place again. I am the head of this house, and I am your father. Now I will treat you with the respect of a man, if you earn it. If you don't, then I will treat you like the little boy you have been portraying the last few weeks. It's not so much that you pointed a loaded gun at me. But you pointed it at me with my wife and babies less than ten feet away from me in the same room. That gun could have gone off and killed anyone of them in the struggle. Everything about what you did was stupid, careless and thoughtless! You've done one smart thing over the last few weeks. And that was making the decision to walk back through the door today! Your mother was in a total frenzy the last few days not only wondering where you were, but if you were alive or dead! Brandon gave his life so you can live, and you made the decision a few days ago that his sacrifice was worthless—"

"That's not true dad—" Raymond interjected.

Before the words could fully leave his mouth, Bernard was on top of him and had Raymond against the wall with his feet barely touching the floor. "YES IT IS TRUE! YOU TRAMPLED ON THE GIFT BRANDON GAVE YOU. HE DIED FOR YOU! YOU PUT YOURSELF, AND EVERYONE WHOM YOU CLAIM YOU LOVE IN A DANGEROUS POSITION BY YOUR

ACTIONS. LIKE YOU SO ELOQUENTLY PUT IT, YOU'RE A KNIGHT. IF YOU KNOW THE WAY OF THE GANG. THEN YOU SHOUD HAVE THOUGHT OF THE DANGER YOU WOULD PUT MY WIFE AND BABIES IN BY GOING AFTER THE LEADER, AND CONSPIRING WITH A RIVAL GANG TO DO IT. THANK GOD DERRICK WILL PROBABLY SURVIVE AND THAT HE GOT TO TRE IN TIME. EVERYTHING ABOUT THIS COULD HAVE GONE THE OPPOSITE WAY. IF YOU EVER—"

Raymond dropped his head at those words. They could hear Bernard yelling upstairs, and Talinda was in tears. She asked Roger again to go downstairs. He stated that he felt Bernard was in control of his emotions and would not interfere unless he thought otherwise.

"—LOOK AT ME!" Bernard yelled. Raymond raised his head. He was about to spontaneously combust inside.

Bernard continued, "IF YOU EVER PUT US IN THE SITUATION THAT YOU DID THIS WEEKEND AGAIN, I WILL BOX YOU OUT LIKE THE GROWN MAN YOU ARE TRYING TO BE. I WILL NOT LET BRANDON'S BLOOD BE IN VAIN FOR YOU. DO YOU HEAR ME SON? I WILL NOT ALLOW THE DEVIL, THE KNIGHTS, ACES OR ANYONE OTHER THAN GOD, JESUS, AND THE HOLY SPIRIT TO HAVE YOU!" He dropped his head for a minute because he was about to lose the battle of his emotions. He lowered his voice to a normal tone and continued, "I love you. Raymond—I love you. You're my son. I felt helpless this weekend. I felt unworthy of Brandon's gift, because I couldn't keep nor protect it. I saw the signs, and I didn't want to be hard on you the last few months. But I see that I can't be your friend. I have to be your father. I am your father. I love you—"

Raymond cried out, "OH GOD DAD I'M SORRY! I'M SO SORRY. I'm so sorry."

Bernard pulled him in his arms and hugged him. He held him as Raymond continued to cry out apologies to him. Bernard apologized to him as well for yelling as he reassured Raymond that he loved him. After they gathered their emotions. They sat down and discussed his visit with Quavis and what the next plan of action should be for Raymond and them all as a family.

Before they prepared to go back upstairs, Bernard turned to Raymond and said, "I'm not angry with you son. I'm grateful. Grateful that you are alive. I love you."

"I love you too dad. And I'm grateful to have you as my father," Raymond replied.

Talinda stood and went to the kitchen to pour them a glass of juice when she heard them coming up the stairs. She was relieved earlier when the shouting stopped, and Bernard began to console Raymond. She smiled at them as she handed them the glasses. Raymond took a sip and placed his glass on the counter. He addressed everyone with a heartfelt apology for his actions and thanked them for being there for him through it all. They prayed and sat down to talk about some of the things that Bernard and Raymond had discussed downstairs.

*****

It was Wednesday afternoon and Nevette, Shaundra and Yogi were all in the room with Derrick. They stopped in to visit and get an update on Derrick before getting ready for church that night. Everyone was in prayer for the situation. Nevette finally voiced her concerns about the nurse who took it upon herself to have a constant watch over Justice.

"Mom, Yogi. I'm glad you're here. Y'all can watch Justice while I go jump in the shower," Nevette said and she stood and gathered a change of clothes.

Shaundra looked at her puzzled, "Nevette dear, why do you need us to be here to take a shower? Just let the nurses station know you are—"

"No mom. No way!" Nevette replied.

"Why not?" Shaundra asked.

"Look mom, at first I thought I was just being jealous. But I'm sure that Nurse Howard has a thing for Justice. The first night I stayed here she got a little too close and personal with him. When she came in that next morning to check on him, I guess she didn't realize I was in the room. I caught her rubbing on his chest and moaning. She was about to lift his cover to take a peak, when I cleared my throat to let her know I was in the room," Nevette said she adjusted the blanket over Justice.

"Nevette dear maybe your perception was—" Shaundra began to say.

Yogi interrupted, "No, mom I'm with Nevette on this one. I have an uneasy feeling about her as well. When I was here yesterday and Nevette was in the shower. She came in to check on him. And I guess she didn't see me either, because she had her hands all over him and was about to go south of his belly button when I cleared my throat and walked over toward the bed. She about jumped out of her skin with some sorry excuse about checking the muscle structure around his wounds. But inside I was going, "uhnn huh, I bet you were." She is not going to put her hands on my big brother like that. What's below his belly is not harmed, and you don't need to tend to that. She gave me a look like I foiled her plans."

"There! You see mom. I'm not exaggerating. This nurse has a thing for Justice. I asked at the nurse's station if she was the only nurse who could come to check on him. They said she was the head nurse and made all the decisions on room assignments. I don't trust her at all mom. So if I can help it, I'm never leaving Justice alone with her!" Nevette exclaimed.

"Yeah, I stood there while she finished checking him. But I'm sure she got her little feel in before I walked over to the bed," Yogi said with a sarcastic tone.

Derrick thought, "Yeah Yogi. Her hands got a little too friendly that day. And yes baby, you're right for not trusting her."

"You two are overreacting," Shaundra declared. "She is not going to risk her career like that."

"Whatever mom—please. She's got a thing for Derrick. And we ain't having no more Suzette Timmons's up in here," Yogi interjected in sista girl fashion with a snap and point of the finger and roll of the neck.

"I know that's right Yogi," Nevette replied as they high fived and laughed. "Yesterday, she and another nurse came in to reposition Justice in the bed. She tried everything she could to get his blanket to fall below his waist. I finally told her I would have my family assist me in doing that from now on, and that I will take responsibility of anything that happens as a result of us repositioning him. Oh, and that hot mess wanted to bathe my husband. Like I really was going to allow that to happen. I can only imagine what she did while he was still in recovery before they let us see him on the first day. Mom, I'm not making the same mistake I made with Suzette. I'm going to be a jealous wife from now on. I'm not leaving her alone with my husband."

Yogi added, "I'm going to do some research on her to see if she had any complaints with any other male patients' families."

"Oh honestly, you two are way past paranoid," Shaundra declared.

Derrick smiled and laughed on the inside as he thought, "The women in my life are amazing and something else. But you're right baby. Her hands are a little too friendly at times. Mom, Yogi and Nevette are right on this one. Oh God please, let me wake up. Right now, with all three of them here. Please God!"

He could hear the Lord speak softly to his spirit:

REST MY SON. IT'S NOT TIME YET.

"Yes Lord," he thought.

Nevette went to shower, and Shaundra and Yogi continued to discuss the nurse situation. Suddenly, Shaundra grew very quiet and looked down at Derrick. She sighed and shook her head.

"I know mom," Yogi said.

"Sometimes it's hard to trust when it's your baby. It doesn't matter how old they are, whenever they hurt it crushes a parent's heart. You felt helpless. I know God is able to heal and deliver, but—," Shaundra said as she began to cry.

"I know mom. It's going to be okay. I keep praying that any minute he is going to wake up and say something kooky to me," Yogi said with a laugh. Her statement drew a smile from Shaundra.

"I love you mom—Yogi. It will be well," Derrick thought.

Nevette rejoined them, and they spent about another hour or two talking about the nurse, Friday when Derrick came home, and Suzette for a while longer.

Yogi and Shaundra kissed Derrick on the cheek as they prepared to leave. Nevette walked over to the door but didn't accompany them to the elevator.

*****

Reginald and Sarah said a quick prayer before they entered church for bible study. Sarah headed for the teen girls and Reginald in turn went over to where the guys usually hang out before bible study begins. They decided they would tell their friends first, before they announced it to the youth ministers at the beginning of bible study.

Reginald walked over the guys. They greeted him as he walked up. He didn't return the greeted but instead blurted out, "Sarah is pregnant."

"What!" Jonathan declared. "Mister virgin. Mister no fornication. Mister always getting on us about our hormones being out of control. Mister—"

"Stop guys," Reginald said as his voice cracked. "I need y'all."

Troy said, "Man, what happened?"

"I happened. Life happened," Reginald replied. "To be honest, I don't know what happened. It just—happened! I mean it was so easy for me when I was a virgin and had never really had a serious girlfriend to talk about how out of control y'all hormones were. I kept myself busy and prided myself in being holier than thou. But I had never *really* been tempted or tested. At least not strongly. Sarah didn't try me. She didn't tempt me. It was me. I was all over her. It's different when you have a girl that you're looking at every day. You're ministering to her about what's going on in her life. All of a sudden you find yourself alone, and you're holding her in your arms looking at her. Everything inside of you is out of control. I had no idea how all of you guys felt. I couldn't even relate to you, and I was hard on y'all. I thought of myself more highly that I ought too. After I had her once, it's just like Minister Travis said when we were in Germany, you can't just stop. Now Sarah is pregnant, and I am so afraid and ashamed to tell Pastor and Minister Travis. He is going to light me up like a Christmas tree. I just know it. I told my parents about it, and my dad was half glad about it. Now he says he is sure I'm not gay. All I could do was shake my head at his response. My mom cried and said I was going to do everything with her. Every appointment, everything. I planned on doing that anyway. Her aunt also took it better than we thought. Man, y'all. I am dreading the look on Pastor Travis' face."

"Guys look. We have to make ourselves more accountable. We are not doing anything we said we would do in Germany. We all still just kind of end up on our own little dates alone. It's like the conversation was out of sight out of mind," Troy added.

Reginald continued, "That's right. I started spending too much alone time with her. It started out innocently enough; talking to her, ministering to her. Helping her go over the bible and deal with her past. She went to go see her mom for the first time, and I went with her. I kept telling myself, Reginald you're spending too much time with her. But I also kept telling myself that I could handle it. But I couldn't handle it. It was a very emotional visit to see her mother, and after we left the prison, her aunt went back to work, and I went to her house. I knew I shouldn't have been there. I justified going to her house because she was still somewhat emotional about the visit with her mom. I held her in my arms. Next thing I knew, we were kissing. Then I was just—inside of her. We were both losing our virginity. I don't even remember getting undressed guys. The first thing I remember was telling her how sweet she was. After that, I was—it was like I couldn't stop. Not one time did I ever think about buying a condom. It never entered my mind. I think I just assumed that she was probably on birth control because we were having sex. But I never asked. I've been sitting in church that last few months so convicted. I'm actually relieved we decided to just spill the beans. The secret and silence was killing me. I don't think I could take one more day of Minister Travis bragging on me about still being a virgin as a young male in a tempting and trying world. I turn eighteen in less than six months, and I'm about to be a father. This is going to be a long senior year of me."

Jonathan shook his head as he said, "Wow, never in a million years would I have guessed you and Sarah would—wow man this is crazy. Testosterone is a beast y'all. That's why we have to be accountable to each other, and our youth leaders. We can't handle the strength of testosterone at this age. The devil knows that. He uses it against us to make decisions that we are not mature enough to make, or ready to handle the consequences of at our ages."

"Tell me about it," Raymond replied. He shook his head, but not for the same mind boggling reason everyone else did. He knew he and LaNiesha could have just as easily be in the same predicament right now.

On the other side of the room, the girls were having a similar discussion. "Hey Sarah. What gives girl? You look like someone just ran over your cat and took all nine lives at once," Michelle said in an attempt to break up the serious look on Sarah's face. Everyone laughed and Sarah just stood there. Tears formed in her eyes.

"Oh God Sarah what's wrong?" Lisa asked.

Sarah dropped her head and whispered, "I'm pregnant."

"Oh my God Sarah, really? Please tell me you're kidding," Jessica replied with compassion in her voice.

All Sarah could do was shake her head from side to side as the tears fell.

"Are you sure Sarah? I mean absolutely sure?" Michelle asked as she touched her on the shoulder. "Sarah is there any way you could have read the test wrong?"

Sarah shook her head no. "I'm probably about two months already. I never thought I would be here. Sex wasn't anything I was looking forward to. That is, until I met Reginald. He ministered to me about a lot of my insecurities. He went with me a few months ago to visit my mom. Auntie Ronie went back to work, and he came to the house because I was still upset about the visit with my mom. The next thing I know it was happening. He was climaxing inside of me telling me that he loved me. For some reason, I felt complete at the time. Like he was the only one I could have given it to. I don't even remember when our kisses turned from date level to sex level. I thought my aunt would go through the roof when we told her. But she was surprisingly calm. She said she had a hunch but wasn't sure. She said she heard me throwing up a few mornings ago and that sort of sealed it. I think she was waiting for me to get up the nerve to say it. Reginald has been nothing but supportive. I suggested that maybe I should have an abortion. I thought he was going to come unglued on me. I never really thought of abortion as murder. Birth control never crossed my mind. We were hot and heavy for like a month straight. I went obliviously right through not having a cycle. If I wouldn't have had morning sickness, I wouldn't have thought about being pregnant for months."

"Wow," LaNiesha replied. Her heart raced because she knew this could just as easily been her. She fought the urge to blurt out that she and Raymond had a scare. She knew Raymond wasn't ready to talk to his parents about it yet, so she remained silent.

"Okay everyone let's get started. We have a lot to cover tonight," Talinda said as she, Bernard, Trevor and Lindsay entered the room.

Reginald walked over and stood beside Sarah. He looked into her eyes, and she had to drop her head and look away to keep from bursting into tears. Lindsay saw the interaction between them and nudged Talinda so she would take notice.

"Oh boy. From the look on Sarah and Reginald's face, I would venture to saw we have two teens in trouble," Lindsay said.

"Oh God please no," Talinda whispered.

Veronica entered the room. She wanted to be there to support Sarah. She knew they would be informing the youth ministry tonight. Veronica's entrance and eye contact with Talinda and Lindsay confirmed their assumption.

Reginald cleared his thought and said, "Pastor Travis—youth ministry team. Before we begin tonight, there is something that Sarah and I need to say."

He paused to swallow and attempt to force the lump that formed in his throat down to his stomach. Sarah was silent. She did not want not to make eye contact with any of the youth leaders.

The room was silent and Reginald continued, "As you know Sarah, and I have been dating since we came back from Germany almost a year ago. Uhmmm—okay—ahhhmmm," he paused again then said to himself out loud, "Just say it Reginald."

At that statement, Sarah looked up at him. She prepared to speak, but he gestured for her to remain silent.

"Sarah no. I was trying to be a man months ago. I am going to be a real man now and finish it."

Bernard shook his head and rubbed his hand from the front of his head to the back. He knew the next words that would come out of Reginald's mouth.

"A few months ago we both gave into temptation and lost our virginities. Pastor Talinda, Pastor Bernard, Youth leaders Trevor and Lindsay Johnson, we would both like to formally apologize to you for breaking the vows we promised not only you all, but to God. We went against everything that you taught us."

He looked down and breathing heavily. The room was silent. Everyone had the feeling that Reginald was not through with his confession. He looked back up, glanced at Sarah and continued, "We found out earlier this week that uhmmm—that Sarah, ahmmm—is—is pregnant."

Bernard replied, "What!"

Talinda did not respond because her attention was elsewhere. At his last statement, LaNiesha and Raymond shared a look that did not go unnoticed. They eyed each other several times during Reginald's confession.

"Uhmm," Talinda thought to herself. She shifted her attention back to Reginald and Sarah because everyone was waiting for her response.

"Well, Reginald and Sarah, I won't lie and say that I am not surprised. You two were the last ones we thought we would have to worry about becoming teen parents. The look on Veronica's face when she walked in told me that you had informed her. Reginald have you told your parents?" Talinda asked.

"Yes ma'am. I told them a few days ago," he replied barely above a whisper. He was on the verge of bursting into tears.

Bernard rubbed his eyes and then said, "Germany—Paris! Did you guys not learn anything? Come on Reginald—really?"

He sighed and regrouped. He could see that Reginald was about to lose complete control of his emotions. He walked over to him, but before he could say anything else Reginald fell into his arms and wept. He repeated the apology "I'm sorry" over and over as he wept in Bernard's arms. The women and girls all gathered around Sarah to comfort her.

Talinda wiped her eyes and said, "Well, looks like we need to have more talks about dating and fornication. It appears, we have been, and obviously are, somewhat ineffective."

"No you haven't Pastor Talinda. You, Pastor Bernard and the other youth workers do an excellent job ministering to us on all subjects. Just because you teach it, and we get it, doesn't mean we are still not going to be tempted by it. Or still fall prey to it. We have to do our part," Troy replied.

The teens all agreed with Troy's statement. They loved and enjoyed the relationship they had with their youth leaders.

They realized they would not get to the lesson planned for the night. Instead, they sat down and began to discuss the warning signs and the circumstances surrounding the temptation that Reginald and Sarah found themselves in. The youth all joined in with the discussion about some of their own temptations and struggles. LaNiesha and Raymond were noticeably silent. Talinda continued to observe their non-verbal activity between each other.

At the end of the night Bernard and Talinda updated everyone about the situation with Derrick. They told everyone to keep him in their prayers. They decided that now was not the time to disclose Raymond's involvement in the situation. Talinda sensed that he was not in the right frame of mind to discuss it. She wanted him to minister it as a testimony, and she knew he was very much still struggling with the test.

They gathered in a circle to pray and close out bible study the same way they did every Wednesday night. But this time, many hearts were heavy and sorrowful. Bernard began to pray:

Father

We come with our hearts lifted up to You. As leaders, we don't always have the answers. We also don't always handle each and every situation with the grace and mercy that You require. Help us to be mindful of our own shortcomings when we were teenagers, when we are faced the hardships our youth find themselves involved in. Father, as Reginald and Sarah begin to enter the adult world of parenthood. We pray that You will lead and guide them. As their spiritual coverings, give us the wisdom, knowledge, guidance and understanding when dealing with their shortcomings. Help us to minister to them and not at them. Help us to grow with them and not lord over them. Lord we love them unconditionally. Let us always be mindful of that fact when we find ourselves disappointed with their behavior. God help us to understand they are still but babies living in an adult world where they are daily faced with and forced to make adult decisions. Father, we continue to pray for Minister Derrick Goodfellow and his family as they continue to learn what it means to give thanks for all things and to trust that all things do indeed work together for our good. We thank You for protecting Tre. Father, I pray that the spirit of heaviness that has entered our space this evening be chased away by Your warring angels. And that Your peace that passes understanding, fall upon us like the dew in the morning. That it will gently rest upon our hearts and minds. Father lastly, we thank You that Raymond is home and safe. We leave him in Your hands, and trust the decisions You will make and allow in his life. God, we pray that You will grant him favor and overshadow him with fresh mercy flowing from Your throne. We love you Lord and we will forever praise You.

In Jesus' name,

Amen

*****

After she closed the door behind them, Nevette prepared to settle in with Justice for the night. She leaned over and kissed Derrick as she said, "Okay baby. I'm getting ready to lay down for the night. I love you. See you in the morning. Get some sleep." She looked down at him, and tears filled her eyes as she lost it and cried out, "Oh God Justice I need you! Please baby wake up! Oh God Justice! I am so sorry baby—I'm so sorry! My reasons for being angry seem so meaningless now. Baby please! Ahhhh—okay Nevette stop it," she said to herself in an attempt to pull her emotions together. "I love you baby—okay—I can do this! I can do this—*He won't allow you to be tempted above that you are able to bear*! I can do this—I can do this. I love you baby—I can do this." She began to shower him with kisses as she declared, "I love you baby. I'm going to be here when you wake up. I'm going to take care of you, and love you. I'll be submissive Justice. Whatever you ask me to do, I'll do. Justice please wake up baby."

Derrick lay there struggling to move, make a noise or do anything to give her hope that he was indeed with her. That he could hear and feel everything. "Oh God please! Don't cry baby. I'm here—I'm right here. I hear you sweetheart. I'm trying to open my eyes Naythia. I'm fighting with everything I have baby. I love you Naythia. I promise you baby. I will come out of this. I will come home to you and Tre. Oh sweetheart please stop crying. God, please—please allow me to move, something—anything Lord!" he thought.

She wiped her tears, cleared her throat and spoke to God:

Lord,

Whatever You're doing. I trust You. I'm grateful he survived. I trust You with my husband. I trust You with his life, my happiness, future and family. I trust You God. I will not turn my back on You or him Lord. I love him God, and I place his life in Your hands. I will minister to Your people no matter what. Father, please give our little boy peace. Send Your angels to protect and minister to him. He has been through so much. Comfort him Lord. He is afraid for his father.

Lord we need Your peace. Oh God we need Your strength. Jesus pray that my faith fail not. Shine Your grace and favor upon us Lord. Father, I pray for the youth involved in the shooting. Father, I choose to forgive and not hate. Lord, I pray that You will begin to change their heart and give them a sense of respect for life. Help us to be effective ministers of the gospel. Help us to reach them Lord.

In Jesus' name I pray,

Amen

She kissed him again and said, "Sleep well my love. I'm about to get in the recliner and go to sleep. I'm pulling my chair closer to you, so when that Nurse Howard comes in, she will see me. I'll see you in the morning baby. Sleep well my beloved—sleep well."

"Goodnight Naythia. I'll be waiting for the sound of your sweet voice and your soft touch to wake me in the morning baby," Derrick thought.

~Chapter Five~

The ward was quiet for the night, and there was only about twenty more minutes before her shift ended. Nurse Howard stepped outside the intensive care unit to answer her cell phone. She didn't want to take the chance of being overheard.

"This isn't going to be easy. He has been unconscious for nearly four days, and she is yet to leave the room. Other family and friends come and go, but she has not stepped foot outside that room at all. Because she works here at the hospital, it makes it easier for her. She orders his breakfast lunch and dinner meals, and that's what she eats. But—just hold on. Eventually, we'll figure something out. She showers in the room too, so maybe I can sneak you in while she is in the shower. Well, I have to go. My shift is ending and I need to get off this phone and get the shift changed before I leave for the night. I promise I will figure out a way for you to get in to see him soon."

Suzette Timmons sighed, "Okay little sister. Just get me in the room. I'll take care of the rest and her too, if it comes to that."

They said their goodbyes and hung up the phone. Nurse Howard sighed. She knew her older half-sister Suzette wouldn't take kindly to the fancy she had developed for Derrick. She studied Nevette's routine with Derrick very carefully over the next forty-eight hours to see when the best time would be to sneak Suzette in. She figured early morning before visiting hours would be best. They would most likely catch Nevette in the shower when someone else was in the room. Someone she might be able to persuade to leave the room on a call, or something that required their presence at the desk. Anything that would give her big sister Suzette a few minutes alone with Derrick.

She called Suzette back the evening of the sixth day that Derrick had been there in the hospital and shared her observation and plan with Suzette. She figured that while Nevette was in the shower, she may be able to talk Derrick's sister or mother out of the room for a few minutes to distract them so Suzette could enter unnoticed.

Suzette's heart raced with the thought of seeing and being close to Derrick again. She spent the five days prior, watching Derrick's parents and their routine with Tre should the need arise to hold him as bait to get Derrick to her. But reconsidering the outcome with Callisha, she decided against it. Besides, Tre wouldn't be as easy a snatch as a toddler. Callisha's death sent her into hiding, and she was forced to be away from her beloved. She didn't want to take that chance a second time, so she decided Tre would be a non-factor in her plan tomorrow. In her mind, she figured Derrick had to miss her just as much as she missed him. She just knew he longed to see her as much as she longed to see and be with him. She laughed out loud and jumped for joy over the thought that she was only about twenty-four hours away from being with her man again.

*****

ROSES ARE RED, VIOLETS ARE BLUE,
YOUR HANDS ARE ALWAYS SWEET AND SOOTHING,
WITH A GENTLE TOUCH THAT SAYS, I LOVE YOU.

Enjoy the roses BEAUTIFUL,

Hugs and kisses xoxoxoxoxoxoxo

Lindsay sighed with dreamy eyes as she read the note and smelled the roses delivered by her husband Trevor to the Falcons training facility. She fully enjoyed wedded bliss, and her life was now complete. The love she and Trevor shared was powerful and sensual. He had been hinting around about having a baby, so she figured the flowers were part of his "butter her up" plan. She was surprised he was so formal with the note. He usually hand wrote his notes to her because he wanted them to be very personal. She made a mental note to call and thank him at her next break.

She had quite a few players to work with today, so she wouldn't get another break for about three hours. She headed back into the therapy room on cloud nine. She was so in love with Trevor. She'd always envied Nevette because of the love she shared with Derrick. In a good way, of course.

Finally she had a minute to sit. She closed the door to her office and dialed Trevor. She sat down at her desk and she smelled the roses again while waiting for him to answer.

"You're so awesome baby. Hope you're having a great day. You have certainly made mine wonderful. I love you and thanks. They're beautiful," she said with a soft tender voice.

Trevor smiled but was somewhat perplexed as he replied, "Hey baby, your voice is a welcome break. I've been swamped all day. I think every pregnant woman in the greater Atlanta area, had issues with her pregnancy today. I'm grateful for the rank of awesomeness, but what are you thanking me for?"

"As if you didn't know," she replied.

"Really sweetheart. I don't," he said with a hint of hesitation in is voice.

She sighed and replied, "Ahhh—for the beautiful flowers you sent to me today—a dozen roses sprayed with my favorite scent. Usually you hand write your note instead of typing it. But it was sweet nonetheless. I really love—"

"Whoa, whoa whoa—flowers?" He asked bewildered. "Baby, I didn't send you a dozen roses today."

"Of course you did Trevor. The note is so you," she replied.

"Sweetheart, I think I would have remembered sending my wife a dozen roses," Trevor replied.

"Then who—" Lindsay said as she allowed her thoughts to trail off.

She was interrupted by Trevor, who asked, "What does the note say?"

She read the note to him. This time she looked inside and out to see if there was any evidence of who wrote it. "Come on Trevor. Quit playing around," she said nervously.

"Lindsay baby, I'm telling you. I did not send you the flowers today. But somebody sure as heck did," Trevor replied.

"You really didn't send them?" Lindsay replied as though stating a question to the obvious.

"No baby," Trever answered. "I know you said the note itself was typed. But do you recognize the handwriting on the outside of the envelope?" Trevor asked.

"It looks like one of those pre-stamped envelopes. It just says, *'To An Elegant Lady'*. I thought it was weird that you would be so formal in typing it. This makes me nervous Trevor. If they are not from you, then who are they from?" she replied.

"Well obviously someone who knows your favorite scent. Maybe Nevette sent them as thanks about the situation with Derrick on Sunday," he replied not believing that himself.

"No Trevor, why would it be endearing and intimate? It talked about my hands being soothing and sweet. That's not Nevette. She would have said something about being thankful that I had her back. It would have said "friendship". The note said, "I love you" Trevor, and not in the friendship kind of way. Trevor this makes me nervous," Lindsay replied.

"Let's not jump to conclusions Lindsay. There must be a reasonable explanation. Maybe it's from someone dear to you. A relative of something," Trevor replied.

Lindsay sighed and said, "I don't think so Trevor. I'm not close to my family at all. Trevor only a man would say my hands are sweet and sensual. Trevor I don't—"

"Don't worry baby. There is probably a logical explanation for this. Maybe an over sensitive client that you have helped. Or a sister from the church or something," Trevor replied. He didn't believe a word he just said. He didn't want Lindsay to worry. But he was more than a little unnerved by the note and flowers.

When he hung up from speaking with Lindsay, he called in a favor from one of his colleagues. Dr. John Ramsey was one of the physicians on the team for the Falcons. He paced the floor as he dialed his number. "Hey, John I need a favor from you."

"Sure Trevor. What can I do for you?" he replied.

Trevor checked his pager as he replied, "I'm pretty sure one of the Falcons has a thing for Lindsay. She received a dozen roses today with a very intimate note on them. Whenever you're at the facility on therapy sessions with her, just kind of keep your eyes open to how the guys are reacting to her. I have never liked the fact that she worked so close with nothing but men. But it's her career so—"

"Yeah, I got you Trevor. I'm due to be over there Monday and Thursday of next week. I'll take more notice of the ones flirting a little more than usual," John replied.

"Thanks John. I'm sure it's harmless. But considering what happened to our friends the Goodfellows this last year, I don't want to overlook or minimize this. Look, I've been called into delivery. I have to go," Trevor added.

"No problem Trevor. I'm sure it's nothing," John replied.

*****

"Hi Reginald," Sarah said after she answered the door. She walked back toward the kitchen to get some ginger ale and crackers. Her aunt told her it would help with her morning sickness.

Reginald walked over to her and said, "Hey baby. Awww—not feeling well today huh?"

"No, I'm not," she replied.

"I'm sorry," he said as he touched her face.

She smiled and said, "It's not your fault Reginald."

"Oh but it is," he replied. "It's the man's responsibility to take care of everything in the relationship."

She shook her head as she said, "We both knew what we were doing."

"Yeah but," he sighed. "I don't know."

"I've been meaning to thank you," Sarah said as she took a sip of the ginger ale and started to nibble on the crackers.

"For what? Getting you pregnant," Reginald replied in sarcastic humor.

She smiled first at his comment but then turned very serious as she replied, "For not forgetting about me. For standing up and taking responsibility when we shared the news on Wednesday night. For not acting like you don't know me, or that it wasn't yours. I couldn't help but to think about the girl in Germany at the skating rink. Her boyfriend—"

"Yeah—total jerk." Reginald said finishing her sentence. "Have the fun and then leave when the responsibility starts."

"Yeah—well thanks for not doing that to me," she replied.

"I would never do that Sarah. We got in this together, and we are going to deal with it together. Even if I wanted to, neither my parents nor our youth leaders would allow me to. The one thing my dad said was, he would ensure that I take care on my responsibility. But no one has to make me Sarah. Because I want to be there for you. The last year I've been with you has been special. You were my first real girlfriend. I mean, not that a lot of other girls didn't try. I just wasn't feeling how pushy they were. I wanted a girl I could chase, not one that would chase me. I felt like you needed me. We got so close so fast, and I couldn't control where my feelings for you were going. After a while, the cold showers just weren't working anymore. The devil used my testosterone against me. The truth is, teens are not capable of making a sound decision about sex. He takes advantage of the fact that we're probably not going to talk to a responsible adult about our feelings for fear of repercussions," Reginald responded.

"Except for in our case, our youth workers are very approachable and wouldn't have judged us. The truth is Reginald. We just wanted to have sex. My estrogen was just as out of control as your testosterone. Most of the time girls give in to guys so their so-called boyfriends won't dump them and go to another girl. That wasn't the case with us, but it usually is," Sarah replied as she sat down. She felt like she would throw up again at any moment. She rubbed her eyes with one hand and her stomach with the other. She sighed, "Pregnant my senior year. Well, I should be able to stay in school for the first semester before switching over to the alternative school. Some girls choose to stay at the regular school. I haven't really thought of what I'll do yet." She sighed again.

"I wish you would stay at school. I mean I want to see you every day. When you start to get bigger is when you'll need me to be there for you the most. We're in this together. I already asked my boss if I could bump up from part-time to intermittent. I'll go in to work right after the last bell, after I drop you off at home," Reginald stated as he slightly caressed her shoulder to comfort her.

Sarah looked up at him and stated, "Thanks for truly being there but Reginald you can't go to work right after school. What about football and basketball practice. Then after that, track begins in the spring—"

"Sarah, all of that went out the window when I counted myself an adult and had unprotected sex with you. The only thing that matters now is taking care of you and our baby. That won't happen because I wish it to. I have to work and save so when the baby comes the finance of it is not all dumped on us at one time," he paused and breathed heavily. "Look Sarah, ready or not we're about to be parents. Everything about our lives is about to change. It's not about us anymore. We're about to be responsible for another life. So football, basketball, and track won't happen this year. At least not for me."

"But Reginald this is your senior year. The scouts will be out. You'll miss out on scholarships. Neither of our parents are rich, and we're both depending on scholarships to get to college next year," Sarah declared. "You have to play sports. I mean I obviously can't. But I still plan on being in the math and debate clubs. My scholarships leaned toward academics anyway. I played sports for fun. I didn't have scouts all over me."

"Sarah, that's part of taking the responsibility for my actions," Reginald replied.

"What is? Giving up on a dream?" Sarah declared. "No Reginald. Me being pregnant doesn't have to ruin our lives."

"Sarah look. Our parents both have health insurance, so I'm not worried about the medical bill side. But my parents are going to make me buy clothes, pampers, bottles, milk the whole nine yards. Those things are not going to fall out of the sky. I have been thinking about everything the last few days. College may be out for me," Reginald replied.

"No Reginald!" Sarah exclaimed. "It doesn't have to be that way. Our parents will help us. Okay, so we go to school here in the Atlanta area like we discussed. That saves on dorm fees so our parents can help us with the baby. You don't have to, nor am I going to allow you to give up on your dream because of me and the baby. We can both work until I have the baby. In between practices and meetings and extra on the weekends. But Reginald you will get that scholarship. If you end up having to pay your way through school, then it will be out for sure. You're taking this to the extreme Reginald. I know you are going to be there for me. You've proven that and I'm grateful. But you're going to play sports this year, and that's that."

Reginald shook his head, "Wow. You're way more mature than most girls your age."

"I had to be Reginald. I didn't exactly have the textbook life growing up. I know it won't be easy. It's going to be a struggle. But we can do this. We can finish our senior year and go to college with a baby. We're not the first teen parents to accomplish it and sadly, probably won't be the last."

After her last statement, she bolted for the bathroom. She lost the battle to hold down the rest of her dinner from the night before. Reginald comforted her, and they continued to talk about how they would deal with school and everything else once the baby arrived.

*****

"Thanks again Yogi for coming over early to sit with Derrick before heading to school so I can shower," Nevette said as she gathered what she would need in the bathroom.

"Sure thing big sis," she said as she walked over the bed and touched Derrick's hand and said a hearty good morning to him. "I don't trust little "Miss Touchy Feely" any more than you do."

Nurse Howard called Suzette to inform her that Derrick's sister had just arrived. "Okay Suzette his sister is here. It's all going according to our plan. It should be easy for me to get her out of the room. Nevette will be in the shower soon. I'm not sure how much time you will have with him. Probably no more than a few minutes. I will try to get you in again if this works."

"GREAT! Thanks little sister. I owe you big time," Suzette replied. I'm on my way up now. Goodbye." Suzette was super excited.

She practically ran into the hospital barely waiting for the elevator to come. If she had to wait even one more minute, she would have headed for the stairs. When she got to the intensive care unit, her sister Nurse Howard, put her in the supply closet that was located across the hall from Derrick's room. She stood outside Derrick's door listening for when the water would come on to indicate that Nevette was indeed in the shower.

She hurried back to the nurses' station, went to her office and took the phone of the hook. She headed back to Derricks room. She opened the door and greeted Yogi.

"Oh you're here. There is a phone call in the office for Mrs. Goodfellow. I think it's about insurance," she said with a straight face.

"Okay. I'll tell Nevette when she gets out of the shower," Yogi replied.

"Oh they are on the phone at the nurse's station. I kept trying to send it through here to the room, but for some reason, it wouldn't go through. So I came to get her. If you follow me, I'll take you where you can get the phone call. They said something about dropping them off the plan if no one answered their call this time. His bills will be astronomical without insurance. You may want to talk to them for a second. At least maybe you can explain the situation to them or possibly answer a question considering you're family," Nurse Howard replied. She appeared professional and genuinely concerned.

"Okay. I know most of the insurance information. Which way?" Yogi asked.

Yogi followed her. She figured as long as Nurse Touchy was with her, it would be alright to leave the room for a moment. As soon as they rounded the corner headed to the nurses' station Suzette came out of the supply closet and entered Derrick's room.

She walked over to the bed and just stared at him for a moment. She placed her hand on his chest and whispered, "Hey baby. Sorry it took me so long to come see you, but I couldn't chance it earlier. I'm also really sorry about the baby. It's not too late for us. When you get out of here, we can move forward with our plans to be together. No one will get in our way. I don't want to, but I'll kill her if I have to Derrick. I will not allow her to keep us apart any longer. You look so helpless, lying here unconscious and fighting for your life with tubes everywhere. Don't worry baby, I'm going to take good care of you."

Derrick's heart raced. He couldn't believe his ears. He strained with all his might to wake up. "GOD PLEASE!" he thought. "OH NEVETTE BABY, PLEASE TAKE A LONG SHOWER. OH GOD PLEASE DON'T LET HER HURT MY WIFE. OH GOD! NEVETTE BABY PLEASE STAY IN THE BATHROOM. OH GOD YOGI—NEVETTE! DON'T LET HER DO THIS GOD PLEASE!"

Nurse Howard showed Yogi the way to the office where the phone was. Yogi picked up the phone, "Hello—hello. There is no one here."

"Really?" Nurse Howard replied as though she were surprised as she took the receiver from Yogi and repeated, "Hello. Mmmmm, I wonder why they hung up? I told them I would be right back. I'll hang the phone up, maybe they will call back in a minute. You may as well stay for a second. By the time I come back down there to get you, they may hang up again."

Yogi eyed her curiously. But figured if she were here with her. She couldn't be with Derrick at the same time.

"We're all hopeful that your brother will wake up soon," Nurse Howard stated.

She seemed overly anxious to Yogi for some reason. Her small talk seemed rehearsed and distracting. Yogi decided she would head back to Derrick's room.

"Well, I really need to get back. If they call, just get the name and number, and I'm sure Nevette will get in touch with them," Yogi replied as she walked past her and out the door.

Nurse Howard knew she had no reason to try to keep her there. It had been nearly five minutes. She told Suzette five minutes at the most and hoped that she was out of the room already. She was about to follow Yogi down the hallway when another nurse retrieved her for a serious situation in another room. She breathed heavily. She knew she couldn't neglect her duties as a nurse, "You better not still be in there Suzette," she thought as she followed the other nurse to the patient in room 316 in the opposite direction.

Nevette was out of the shower, dried off and getting dressed. She could hear a voice in the other room that didn't sound like Yogi. However, since the person was not speaking loud enough for her to make out the voice, she assumed they finally got a different nurse to come in to see about Derrick. She hurriedly put on her shoes to meet with her before she left the room.

Yogi had never seen Suzette, because right after Callisha went missing everything went haywire between the two families. It never came up nor crossed her mind to know who Suzette was. It really didn't matter to her. She figured whenever they caught her, she would see her soon enough.

Yogi walked back into the room just as Suzette was about to take a trip below Derrick's waist line with her eyes and hands, "Excuse me. Who are you?"

"Oh excuse me. I'm new here. I was sent to check on Mr. Goodfellow," Suzette replied in an attempt to cover the fact that she'd been caught in the act of attempting to take her liberties with Derrick.

Yogi rolled her eyes and declared, "Uhnn uhnn! Does every nurse on this ward have a touchy feely fascination with my brother—REALLY! Y'all are the most unprofessional—"

Inside the bathroom, Nevette couldn't believe the voice she was hearing. She burst out of the bathroom with one shoe on and one off before Yogi could finish her sentence screaming, "SUZETTE!"

Yogi looked at Nevette then back at Suzette and said in a soprano 'I'm about to rearrange the floor with you' tone, "SUZETTE? WHAT THE—OH HE—"

"Whatever!" Suzette said holding a hand up to Yogi as though indicating she needed to shut up. "Don't play with me little girl. Because I will take both of y'all out to get my man!" Suzette pulled a revolver from under her shirt and pointed it at Nevette. "Now I only came here to get him and kill her if she got in the way. But if you want some too little girl—" she shouted at Yogi without even looking in her direction. She was fixated on Nevette and began to squeeze the trigger.

Before Nevette could respond, Yogi jumped on Suzette, they hit the floor and wrestled over the gun. The thought that Yogi would jump her, never entered Suzette's mind. She totally disregarded the fact that Yogi stood right beside her as she aimed the gun directly at Nevette.

Derrick was screaming inside, "GOD NO! JESUS PLEASE NO, NO! NEVETTE—YOGI! GOD PLEASE LET ME WAKE UP! MY FAMILY—GOD PLEASE! OH JESUS PLEASE—PLEASE GOD!

As soon as Yogi jumped Suzette and they hit the ground, Nevette like a flash, screamed as she pounced on Suzette, "YOU KILLED MY BABY! I'LL KILL YOU! I'LL KILL YOU WITH MY BARE HANDS!"

Yogi pounded Suzette's hand against the bottom of the bed rail until the gun went flying across the room. Nevette had the upper hand at this point. She was already on top of her. She had Suzette by the hair and began to pound her head to the ground while Yogi pulled from underneath her and Nevette and went for the gun. If it had not been for the fact that they were on top of a cushion mat that was beside each bed so the nurses didn't stand on concrete all day when checking patients, Nevette would have been pounding Suzette's head into the concrete floor.

Nevette screamed as she fought with Suzette, "YOU KILLED MY BABY YOU WITCH! YOU TRIED TO STEAL MY FAMILY, AND YOU HAVE THE NERVE TO COME HERE!"

Suzette swung upward at Nevette in an attempt to get her to let go of her hair. But Nevette was enraged and continued to pound her.

A candy striper entered the room. She left the nurses station after being told to watch the monitors when Nurse Howard followed another nurse to a room on the opposite end of the hall. But when she heard the screaming coming from Derrick's room, she left the station.

"Call the police! This lady is wanted for the murder of my niece!" Yogi shouted as she got to the gun.

The candy striper bolted out of the door and back to the nurses' station. She hit the button for hospital security and then ran in the other direction to find Nurse Howard.

Back in Derrick's room Yogi reached for the gun but suddenly stopped in her tracks. She grabbed a paper towel to handle the gun, so Suzette's finger prints would be the only ones on it. She pointed the gun at Nevette and Suzette, who were still on the floor and yelled, "Okay Nevette stop! I have the gun and so help me, I will blow her brains out if she makes another attempt to swing at you!"

Those words fell on death ears. Nevette continued to pound Suzette. She was out of control. Suzette could barely get a punch in edgewise. She was all talk and gun when it came to fighting and was failing to land any serious or harmful blows to Nevette. Yogi feared that Nevette would hit her head against the ground one time too many. "Nevette please! You're going to kill her! PLEASE NEVETTE!" Yogi finally screamed, "NEVETTE THINK ABOUT TRE!"

Derrick was about to explode in a blaze on the inside. Try as he might, he could not move, make a sound, nor open his eyes. Every fiber in his being strained as he desperately attempted to force his way out of his God imposed sleep.

The security team and the nurses all reached the station at the same time. Nurse Howard panicked, "Darn you Suzette! I specifically told you five minutes!" she thought aloud.

Yogi could hear them coming as they rushed down the hall. She went back over and quickly put the gun down across the room where she found it. She went over and attempted to pull Nevette up off of Suzette as the security team entered the room.

"POLICE! EVERYBODY STOP WHAT YOU ARE DOING NOW!" the head of security yelled.

Yogi stopped and stood up as though she were under arrest. The other security member went over and grabbed Nevette by the shoulders under her arms and began to pull her off of Suzette. Nevette kicked and screamed at Suzette as the security officer pulled her up and off of her. "SHE KILLED MY BABY! IT'S HER! IT'S SUZETTE TIMMONS! LAST YEAR, SHE KIDNAPPED AND KILLED MY BABY. SHE HAS A FATAL ATTRACTION WITH MY HUSBAND!"

Suzette stood and lounged at Nevette only to be intercepted by the head of security. "Yes! I recognize you!" He said and handcuffed Suzette as the other security member took Nevette over by the door to calm her down.

Yogi pointed to the gun that was over in the corner by the window as she said, "There, I managed to knock her hand against the bed rail as we tussled over the gun, and it went flying across the room. She had it pointed at my sister. She was going to kill her like she killed my niece last year. The police never found her. She must have heard about Derrick's accident on the news. What I don't understand is, how she got past the nurses' station without me seeing her. The big glass window allows you to see everyone that passes by. Either way, I wouldn't have recognized her anyway. I would have assumed she was a nurse who worked here."

As the head of security went to retrieve the gun, Nurse Howard turned to head out of the room. She was intercepted by Suzette, who was not going to go down alone. "Tell them! Tell them little sister that there must be some mistake!" Suzette said to Nurse Howard.

Nevette shook her head, "I knew you looked familiar. How could I not see this? You act just like her. Well, Suzette you'll be surprised to know that your little sister here has a thing for Derrick as well. I caught her several times attempting to take liberties with him that were more than inappropriate."

"Little sister?" Yogi exclaimed. "So that's why! There was no phone call. You distracted me long enough for Suzette to get into the room where Derrick was. If I wouldn't have come back into the room when I did, she would have killed Nevette! When I jumped her, she was about to pull the trigger."

The head of security looked at Nurse Howard. She looked down. He cuffed her as well and began to read both her and Suzette Timmons their rights.

"Oh Jesus thank you! Thank you—thank you—thank you," Derrick thought. He was worried that Nevette and Yogi would actually get arrested for assault as well. But since Suzette was the aggressor and pulled the gun on them. It was considered self-defense.

Suzette complained of her head and neck hurting in an attempt to have evidence to present a case against Nevette at a later date in hopes to use it to her advantage, because she was now sure she would be tried for the death of Callisha Goodfellow. She was handcuffed to a gurney and taken to be examined before the Atlanta Police Department came to retrieve both her and Nurse Howard to take them into custody.

They came to the room to get Nevette's and Yogi's statements. Nevette was forced to leave the hospital to go to the station to sign the necessary paperwork. Yogi called Teddy and her parents, and they stayed there with Derrick while she and Nevette were gone. Nevette reluctantly accompanied Yogi to the police station.

When she and Yogi returned. Nevette asked them to stay so she could take another shower to get the day and the smell of Suzette's cheap cologne off of her. After she came out of the shower, they all sat and talked about what happened. Shaundra made a comment about Yogi and Nevette being correct in their assessment of Nurse Howard. Teddy was on the phone with his wife, brother and dad during the discussion, filling them in on everything.

He also called the Travis's and Lindsay to inform them as well. Everyone was blown away by the events of the day. It was well after visiting hours but because of all the turmoil, no one from the nurses' station dared to mention that fact to them.

Shaundra looked at her watch and said, "Okay everyone. We are way past visiting hours. We'd better get out of here and let Nevette and Derrick get some rest."

"Yeah, I'm exhausted. Suzette was strong. I saw a side of Nevette I thought I would never see and don't care to ever see again. Girl, you surprised me. I figured you a little girly princess, who couldn't fight her way out of a paper bag," Yogi exclaimed as she laughed out loud.

"Well, growing up, I was a scary cat. But then Jason got ahold of me when I was ten and made me toughen up. He taught me how to defend myself. But what you saw had nothing to do with what he taught me. What you saw was out of control rage Yogi. I don't even remember half of it," Nevette replied.

"If it wouldn't have been for the mat underneath her, you would have busted her head wide open. I was yelling for you to stop. I thought, you were going to kill her and then what?" Yogi said as she shook her head breathing heavily. "I was glad the hospital security came in when they did."

"Wow," Nevette replied.

"Well, like Momma G said. It's way past visiting hours. Nay Nay, I was going to ask if you're going to be okay here by yourself. However, hearing how Yogi said you wailed away on Suzette. I don't think you need me to stay," Teddy laughed. But as he went to hug Nevette, he said, "Princess this could have been ugly. I'm so relieved you're okay. If you need me to stay, I will."

"Guys, I'll be fine. Suzette and Nurse Howard are both over at the jail. I'll probably finally sleep like a rock," she replied.

They said their goodbyes and all walked out together. Nevette walked over to the bed. She leaned over and kissed Derrick. "I love you baby. Wow—what a day. You know Justice. A person never knows what they are capable of, until they are placed in a critical or desperate situation." She exhaled and continued, "I'm so glad it's all over and Suzette will finally be charged for Callisha's murder. We can now have true closure with it. I mean—it's not going to bring my baby back. But at least it will all finally be over. Justice I need you to wake up baby. This is day seven. Hmm—seven. The issue with Suzette came to an end on day seven of you being unconscious. Seven—the number of completion. Truly, God has completed the issue with her. We can finally have true closure now Justice. Well, tomorrow is day eight and definitely holds a new beginning for us. It's the beginning of the rest of our life. One we can live without looking over our shoulders and wondering where she is. I love you baby. Sleep well."

"I love you too baby," he thought. "Thank you Lord for taking care of my family today. I trust you Lord. I trust you. As always, I'll be listening for your sweet voice and gentle touch in the morning sweetheart."

Nevette prayed and thanked God concerning the events of the day. She repented for losing every ounce of self-control she had when she attacked Suzette. Everything spiritual went out the window and all she felt was rage toward Suzette. She understood exactly how someone could plead temporary insanity after a tragedy in their life. Or in the case of catching a loved one in the act of adultery and killing both parties in a fit of rage. She knew had the security not entered the room. She could easily be behind bars right now for the death of Suzette Timmons. She prayed and thanked God. She also as always, for Justice and his state of being. She drifted off to sleep still praying.

*****

Lindsay waited anxiously for Trevor to enter her office. He told her he would drop by her office before she went home. He wanted to take a look at the flowers. After they had a conversation about them. She threw them in the trash and she and Trevor left for home.

~Chapter Six~

Nevette rose the next morning, greeted Justice as she did every morning with a kiss. Today for the first time, she felt confident that she could take a shower without worrying about an over indulgent nurse taking advantage of her husband's state of being. She planned to jump into the shower before the new nurse came in to check on Derrick. But decided to wait after all. She still was a somewhat hesitant and decided she would wait until the initial morning check with the new nurse. She knew after that, she would probably be out of the shower before the nurse would need reenter the room for anything.

Nurse Long was quite professional with a charming personality. She was brought up from the intensive care recovery room to the ward to take over until a permanent replacement could be found for Nurse Howard. She spoke briefly with Nevette about the events of the previous day. She was careful not to appear too interested or prying. After she left, Nevette leaned over and kissed Derrick again before she headed to the bathroom to take a shower.

"Ahhh, there's my baby's touch and voice," Derrick thought. He stayed awake listening for any unfamiliar sounds in the room long after Nevette had drifted off to sleep the night before. An act that he laughed at himself about, considering that fact that if he had heard anything, he would have been absolutely powerless to do anything about it. With all the chaos surrounding Suzette Timmons and Nurse Howard the day before, the fact that all of Derrick's vital signs were off the chart had gone completely unnoticed by the nurses' station.

Nevette emerged from the restroom and pulled her chair up beside Justice. However, she didn't sit. She began movement therapy on his limbs. She talked to him and expressed her love as she went about the therapy. She talked with him more about Suzette and Callisha. She poured her heart out and apologized to him for her hateful heart toward him. As she finished the last movement of his leg, she could have sworn she felt resistance. She stood at the foot of the bed and looked up at him and watched for any facial movement. She was silent, and she could hear her heart beating with anticipation.

"God please let me," Derrick thought.

His heart leaped for joy as he heard the words, *"ARISE MY SON!"*

And so it was. He felt as though scales had lifted from off his eyes and the restraints that had him bound were removed. He felt as light as a feather. He was afraid to move for fear that he assumed he heard what he wanted to hear. He decided to give speaking a try before he attempted to move or open his eyes.

He moaned slightly, "Mmmmm."

"Justice!" Nevette all but screamed as she rushed back up to his side. "Justice—baby, open your eyes. It's me baby. It's Nevette. Open your eyes Justice."

He whispered, "Naythia."

"Yes baby, it's me!" she cried. Tears rolled down her face. "Come baby, try to open your eyes."

He started to open his eyes, but the glare from the lights forced them to shut, and he moaned again.

"What? What is it baby?" she asked him.

"Lights—light," he whispered.

"Of course!" she exclaimed as she turned the overhead light off and pulled the curtains partially closed.

Derrick batted his eyes a few times and said, "Tre" as he opened them.

Nevette was ecstatic, "Tre is fine baby. He is just fine. Oh God thank you! THANK YOU JESUS! OH JUSTICE! OH GOD THANK YOU! YOU ARE AN AWESOME GOD! YOU ARE A HEALER! GOD YOU'RE A DELIVERER! I WORSHIP YOU LORD! I MAGNIFY YOUR NAME! YOU'RE THE KING OF KINGS AND LORD OF LORDS! YOU'RE THE GREAT I AM! MIGHTY KING! MASTER AND SAVIOR! RULER OVER ALL THINGS!"

He lay there listening to his wife praise and magnify God. He slowly turned his head in her direction. As his eyes came into focus, he smiled and whispered, "Hey—hey baby."

She looked down at Justice and said, "Heeyyy baby. I love you baby. I love you so much. Oh God Justice I was so afraid. How do you feel? Are you hurting?" Nevette exclaimed. She kissed him and placed her hands on the sides of his face. She was beside herself. She didn't know whether to scream, jump, run or fall to her knees in prayer. She dropped her head in his chest and wept, "Oh God thank you!"

He slowly moved his hand opposite the side she lay across and stroked her hair as he said in a stronger voice, "Baby don't cry. I'm okay."

All she could do was weep. The emotions of the last eight days overtook her, and she shook under the power of them. He continued to caress her as he said, "Its okay baby, please don't cry. Come on Naythia baby, look at me. I'm alright baby. I'm going to be alright. Nevette Naythia Goodfellow—look at me."

He slightly chuckled. She smiled and looked at him. He wiped her tears as he said, "Baby, I'm going to be okay. It's alright baby. It's going to be okay—it's going to be okay."

"Yeah, it is," she replied. "I better get the doctor in here to examine you." She pushed the button and told the nurse that Justice was awake when she answered the call.

The doctor and nurses were soon buzzing around Derrick. Giving him a thorough examination. They ran tests and sent him downstairs for a magnetic resonance imaging (MRI) to check for any problems.

Nevette accompanied them as they took him from area to area of the hospital to run all the tests needed for a patient who had been unconscious for a period of time. She made phone calls to all the family and church members. His mother, father and Yogi were all excited and soon on their way to the hospital. Along with Teddy, Lindsay and Trevor as well. Raymond wanted to stay behind with his grandparents. He made up an excuse about something he needed to do. But the truth of the matter was. He did not want to face Derrick in a crowd of people.

"No son. You're coming with us. You're going to apologize to Minister Goodfellow and pray he has mercy on you," Bernard declared.

"But dad. I can't face him," Raymond exclaimed.

"You can and you will son. There is no sense in putting off the inevitable," Bernard replied.

Talinda was silent. She was unsure how she felt about Bernard's approach. But she wouldn't dare usurp authority over him. He needed to reestablish himself with Raymond. She knew he struggled lately on being the head of the family. He was feeling substandard to Brandon and unworthy of being over the family.

"Your dad is right Raymond. Putting it off won't make it any easier. You're eventually going to have to face him. It might as well be today," Talinda said as she put her arm around Bernard. She stroked Raymond's head with her other hand and then pulled him in for a group hug. "Mom—dad, we shouldn't be gone long. I just fed the twins, so they should be good and full for a while. You know where everything is anyway. It's just so hard to believe they're nearly a year-old already,"

"Don't worry Talinda. You all go ahead. I know you're anxious to see your friend. We're glad he is awake and things are looking better," Helen said as she walked over to Raymond. "Don't worry too much sweetheart. It looks like the Goodfellows are nice people. If they were going to hold you accountable for anything, their family would have already done it. Goodfellow and Goodfellow is the most prestigious and well known law firm in the city."

"I guess so grandma," Raymond replied with a smile.

"Well, I know so grandson," Helen countered.

He hugged her and turned toward his parents. "Okay mom—dad I'm ready to go."

Raymond smiled outwardly but he was terrified inside. He was so ashamed of his actions and involvement. Both Derrick and Tre could have been killed. No matter how they attempted to comfort and reassure him. He knew Derrick's plight was a direct result of his planned meeting with the Aces. He sat quietly in the backseat of the car on the way to the hospital. Bernard began to second guess if this was the appropriate time for Raymond to see Derrick. He kept eyeing Raymond in the rear-view mirror, and he looked as though he would lose it any minute. They pulled into the parking lot and parked.

Bernard turned the car off and turned slightly in his seat to face Raymond.

"Son, I've been thinking as we drove to the hospital. If you want to stay in the lobby area and no go up, that will be fine. This may not be the best time after all. Everyone's emotions are probably at an all-time high. Especially with Suzette coming yesterday and the events that took place with that," Bernard said.

Talinda smiled and lightly touched Bernard's thigh but remained silent. She didn't want to influence Raymond's decision one way or another. He always looked to her for direction. It was time that she started to back off and allow him to be nurtured more by Bernard and make decisions according to his own heart's desire and not hers.

"Dad, I'm just so convicted about my involvement. He could have died. They both could have. I wouldn't have been able to live with myself if they had. I just—I'm not ready to see him dad. Especially not Tre. However, I was going to be obedient if you insisted. I just don't want you to be upset with me. I don't know what to do—" he lost the battle and began to cry.

Bernard sighed and said, "Son, yes I was very disappointed. But disappointment has nothing to do with the fact that I love you. You're my son, and nothing that you could ever do would stand in the way of me loving you. Children do things to upset their parents. It's the "things" we struggle with because we love you so much. Every parent desires that their child is able to skip over the mistakes they made in their own life. Sometimes, we are so busy attempting to keep you from those mistakes that we forget that some of those mistakes are what it takes to help build your character. I love you Raymond. Don't ever forget or doubt that. You came home to face me and the issue. You could have easily kept running and been perfectly fine on the streets. You know all too well how to survive. But instead, you came home son—you came home. That says a lot to me about your true character."

"Thanks dad. I needed to hear that," Raymond replied as he wiped his tears. "I'm not going to hide out in the lobby. You, mom and grandma are right. The sooner I face the Goodfellows the better. I remember a very important teaching from dad about spiritual warfare. If I avoid them, it will just be more stressful for me. I will open myself to all kinds of torment from the enemy. It will give him too much time to influence my thoughts."

Talinda smiled and winked at Raymond. She wisely chose to be a silent partner in the conversation. This was a father-son moment, and she watched with love in her heart for the both of them.

She touched the side of Bernard's face as she said, "Have I told you lately that I love you?"

Bernard smiled and shook his head. "Everyday Mrs. Travis, and twice on Sundays."

Raymond smiled at Bernard's response. Talinda turned to him and said, "And I love you too sweetheart. I'm so proud of your decision."

They exited the car and headed for the hospital entrance.

Upstairs, Derrick had been moved to a room off the intensive care ward now that all his tests were concluded and other than the obvious wounds from the shooting. He was stable enough to be downgraded from intensive care. The eight days he laid in sedation proved to be a blessing. He was able to begin to heal without the interjection of normal activity that would have hindered the process had he been awake, especially for the last twenty-four hours. If infection is going to set in, it's usually within the first forty-eight hours. They pumped him full of a new synthetic antibiotic because of his and Callisha's allergic reaction to penicillin. A new drug that proved to be very beneficial.

Shaundra Goodfellow arrived with Tre, who was finally going to be able to see his father. Nevette spoke with him over the last eight days and saw him briefly while either Shaundra or Yogi stayed inside the room with Derrick. His father Derrick Sr., called saying he would be over soon. He was called into a meeting just after he got the call from Shaundra that DJ was awake.

Tre ran into the room and was intercepted in thin air by Teddy as he went airborne toward his father to leap into his arms.

"DADDY!" Tre yelled as he entered the room.

"Whoa, whoa, whoa, Tre," Teddy said. "You have to take it easy. You can't jump up on daddy remember. He's still sore from when the bad men shot him."

"Sorry daddy!" Tre exclaimed as he continued to Derrick's bedside after Teddy put him down.

"Hey Tre. It's okay man. You're a sight for sore eyes. Daddy is so happy that you're okay," Derrick replied. "Climb on up here, carefully though, so daddy can get a hug."

"Justice are you sure?" Nevette asked.

"It's fine baby. Let him up," Derrick responded.

Teddy picked him up and placed him on the bed, so he could sit beside Derrick. He placed him on his right side because the worse injury was on his left. Tre leaned over, and Derrick hugged him tight. "Oh God Tre. Daddy is so glad that you're okay."

"Me too daddy. I'm glad you didn't go to live with Callisha. I was afraid you would choose to be with her because she's so little and all alone with God!" Tre exclaimed.

"Oh Tre man you don't have to worry about Callisha. And neither does daddy. Besides, God can do a much better job of taking care of her than daddy can. She's not alone though remember, because great-grandma Graham, great-grandma and great-grandpa Goodfellow and other Goodfellow and Graham family members are there with her too."

"Yeah, that's right. I forgot about that daddy," Tre said as he hugged his daddy.

Derrick winced slightly but gestured to hold Nevette off before she could tell Tre to move. He held his son, and tears rolled down his face. "I love you little man," Derrick whispered. Nevette, Teddy,

Shaundra and Derrick's younger sister Yogi, all stood and watched. It was a tear jerker moment.

"I love you too daddy," Tre replied.

Derrick was on the phone with Teddy Sr., and Jason when the Travis's entered the room. Nevette greeted Talinda, Bernard and Raymond with a hug, and they all chatted while Derrick was talking on the phone. Tre still faced his dad and didn't see Raymond enter because he stood off the side and close to the door.

Derrick saw them enter and waved is hand. About five minutes later he told Teddy Sr., he would talk to him later because some visitors had come in. He hung up and handed the cell phone back to Nevette.

Bernard walked over to the bed and said, "Man, it's good to hear your voice and see you awake. God is great and greatly to be praised!"

"Amen to that!" Talinda added.

"Hello everyone," Derrick replied. "It was crazy the last eight days. I could hear and feel everything happening around me but was powerless to respond. God spoke to me, and I learned so much during that time. The scripture is so true that, *"All things work together for your good".* This is a new beginning for Nevette and me. I don't think Suzette would have emerged from hiding when she did, if I hadn't been shot. We would have been looking over our shoulders wondering where she was all the time. The last ten months have been crazy. I had as tight a reign on Tre and Nevette as I could, from the distance I had to maintain from them. I was terrified when I heard her voice and felt her touch my chest yesterday morning. I feared for Nevette's life. It was just—crazy."

"Wow," Bernard replied. "I have an idea how you feel. Our life hasn't exactly been peaches and cream the last two weeks either. But nothing in comparison with yours and Nevette's last eight days though."

Raymond dropped his head at Bernard's comment. Derrick noticed him standing there for the first time since he got off the phone and engaged in conversation with everyone. "Hey Raymond, how are you doing? I understand you've had a pretty tough time of it the last week."

"Yes Sir," Raymond replied. He looked up momentarily and then back down, but did not make eye contact with Derrick.

Tre saw him and yelled, "RAYMOND! Where have you been? I missed you! I haven't seen you since the day the bad men shot my daddy."

He jumped down and ran to Raymond. He bent down to give Tre a hug. "Were you at the game too? You were there in the parking lot. You were running to me and yelled for me to run to you, but my daddy knocked me down before I could get there."

Raymond swallowed hard to fight off the tears before he replied, "Yeah Tre. I was there, but I wasn't at the game. You see Tre. It was my—"

"Intention to make sure you were okay Tre. Raymond and daddy were both trying to make sure you were okay," Derrick interjected. He shook his head "no" to Raymond.

Raymond made eye contact with him for the first time. Derrick declared, "We're not going to do this Raymond. Me and my family love you. Look Raymond, everything happens for a reason. God uses every circumstance in our life and makes good out of it. Did you not hear me earlier? We may have never seen Suzette again, had this not happened. I'm sure nothing about the situation was condoned by your parents. If I know Bernard, he has already dealt with you about it. I will not hold you in bondage because of it or allow the enemy to torment your mind. All is well in the Goodfellow household concerning you."

Raymond couldn't hold it together any longer. He released Tre, broke emotionally and crumbled to the ground. "I DON'T DESERVE YOUR FORGIVENESS!"

"And I don't deserve God's forgiveness either. But I have it. We all do," Derrick replied.

Teddy said, "Hey Tre, let's go raid the vending machine down the hall and get daddy a candy bar. I bet he's hungry."

Nevette mouthed "Thank you" to him as they left the room.

"What's wrong with Raymond, Uncle Teddy?" Tre asked as they were leaving the room.

"He just feels bad that he couldn't get to you, and the bad men shot your daddy. He thinks that maybe if he would have gotten to you first, then your daddy wouldn't be sick," Teddy replied.

"But it's not his fault the bad men shot daddy," Tre replied.

"Yeah, but he feels that it is Tre, that's why he's sad," Teddy replied.

"I'll remember to pray for him tonight that he won't be sad any more Uncle Teddy!" Tre exclaimed.

Teddy smiled and said, "You do that Tre."

Back in Derrick's room, Talinda bent down and pulled Raymond into her arms. "Oh my baby. My poor baby. Raymond sweetheart please don't do this to yourself. Sweetheart just accept the grace and mercy that God is extending to you."

"Mom—" Raymond cried as she held him in her arms. He'd longed for his mother's comforting arms since he first walked back into the house a few days ago. He felt unworthy of every hand to receive any comfort from anyone. All he felt he deserved was penance."

"It's going to be okay baby," Talinda replied.

Derrick gestured for Nevette to sit him up a little straighter in the bed. He winced slightly as the bed raised. "Bernard, get him up and bring him to me."

Bernard went over to where Talinda and Raymond were on the floor. Talinda wasn't sure that she wanted to hear what was about to be said. But she trusted God and Derrick that he wouldn't wound his spirit. She released him, and Bernard stood him up. They took a few steps and were at the bed.

Derrick looked Raymond square in the eyes and said, "Okay, listen to me carefully Raymond."

Raymond breathed heavily and started to sit in the chair that Nevette had at Derrick's bedside.

"No Raymond, don't sit—stand," Derrick said. He didn't want to look down at Raymond when he spoke to him. He didn't want him more intimidated than he already was at the moment. "Okay Raymond listen to me. Right now, I'm not acting as Minister Goodfellow. Derrick Goodfellow II, the lawyer is speaking to you. Since you won't receive the forgiveness that has been extended to you and have decided to hold your own personal trial, and convict yourself without a jury. I'm going to play the role as the judge in your case. Let's state the obvious first. You just turned eighteen years old. This means you will be tried as an adult in this courtroom today. These are the charges against you as you stand in front of me. FACT & CHARGE #ONE: You pointed a loaded gun at your father and fought over said loaded gun, with three people in the room. Not just any three people, but people whom you love and would die for on any other given day. FACT & CHARGE #TWO: You left your mother and father's home in the middle of the night on a vengeful campaign to plot to commit a murder. FACT & CHARGE #THREE: You communicated and conspired with a rival gang to accomplish the said mission. FACT & CHARGE #FOUR: You arranged the meeting that resulted in the shooting death of two teens with another adult male left in critical condition. Not to mention the hundreds of people that were traumatized while caught in the path of the gun fire. Do I have all the charges against you correct Mr. Travis?"

Raymond whispered, "Yes Sir."

"You're going to have to speak a little louder Mr. Travis. The court cannot make out whispering," Derrick replied.

"Yes Sir," Raymond replied a little louder, but still just barely above a whisper. He was on the verge of tears again.

Talinda's heart ached for what was most assuredly going through his mind. But she held her peace.

"Now, Mr. Travis, if all the charges laid out against you were all served concurrently, you are still looking at well over twenty years in prison. But of course, you would be eligible for parole after serving about three-fourths of that sentence. Now son, my next question to you is, how do you plead? Guilty? Or not guilty?" Derrick asked.

"Guilty," Raymond replied, again barely above a whisper. He wasn't sure what Derrick's intentions were.

"Excuse Mr. Travis, but the court will insist on you speaking at an audible decibel," Derrick replied. "I ask you again, how do you plead?"

Raymond cleared his throat and replied, "Guil—guilty as charged Sir." His voice cracked.

"You are correct in your assessment Mr. Travis. You are by FACT guilty. But we don't deal in FACT in this court. In this court, we deal in TRUTH. And Mr. Travis the TRUTH of the matter is this. We will use for our argument, the story of Jacob when he wrestled with the angel of the Lord all night. Now bible scholars will argue the point on the amount of time they actually fought, but that's not our debate nor concern in this case. The meat of the principle God implied in Jacob's story is this. The bible says the angel of the Lord asked him what his name was. He answered that his name was Jacob. Hebrew word study tells us the Jacob means "trickster or surplanter". After he confessed that his name was Jacob, then and only then did the angel of the Lord bless him. He changed his name to Israel thereby changing his nature. The angel Jacob wrestled with was none other than Jesus Christ himself. Because only Jesus Christ and His shed blood, can change a man's nature. But that man must first admit to his faults and his old nature to receive the grace, and the mercy God desires to extend to his creation daily. Mr. Travis, by your own admission you have claimed the nature of all the facts presented about you today by a plea of guilty. So the sentence that the court will lay out to you today is this. We the court, with the power vested in us by the authority of Jesus Christ hereby release you from all charges and counts against you today. We decree and declare the blood of Jesus over your life, which now runs through your veins. That said blood releases you from the curse of once a Knight always a Knight, thereby freeing you from the sentence that a Knight would receive in the said trial and charges. This court is now adjourned! DO NOT, bring this matter before this court again Mr. Travis."

"Yes Sir," Raymond replied. He was overwhelmed under the power of the Holy Spirit that guided and rode on every word that came out of Derrick's mouth. He fell to the ground and began to speak in tongues. The first time he did so in many months. His life had been riddled with guilt, pain and suicidal thoughts from the enemy.

Talinda was in tears, and Nevette was blown away by how powerful the ministry of her husband was. Derrick's mother Shaundra, beamed with pride and Bernard just stood shaking his head at the brilliance of mind and insight God poured onto Derrick to minister to Raymond.

Talinda knelt down beside Raymond, praised God and spoke in her own heavenly language. She had been secretly more afraid than she expressed about Raymond's state of mind. She feared he would become depressed over the situation.

"Thank you Sir," Raymond managed to say after he calmed down and he and his mother were both helped up of the floor by Bernard. Talinda buried her face in Bernard's chest and started to weep again. She was simply overwhelmed with God's grace and favor in their lives.

Shaundra declared, "Won't He do it!"

"Yes He will mom," Nevette replied.

They settled back down into normal conversation. As he stood outside the door, this was Teddy's cue that it was okay to bring Tre back into the room. He heard the direction that Derrick's conversation with Raymond was headed and distracted Tre in the hallway until he heard signs of all clear.

Tre went back over to his father and climbed back up in the bed with him. He brushed Derrick's side, and Nevette was about to retrieve him but Derrick wouldn't hear of it. He endured every accidental poke and motion of his son. No amount of pain could have made him stay away from his family. He wanted them both underneath him.

Derrick Sr., joined them about twenty minutes later. He fought the tears as he greeted and semi-embraced his son. They enjoyed a wonderful time of fellowship. A smile finally graced Raymond's face, and Talinda was overjoyed.

About an hour later Bernard led them in prayer. He thanked God for the explosion of the Holy Spirit that mended, repaired, renewed, strengthened, delivered, rebuilt and set in order hearts, minds and lives that day. Everyone said their goodbyes and Nevette began to prepare Derrick to settle in for the evening. She had him to reposition himself in the bed so she could get ready to lay him back down flat to sleep. But he beckoned for her to sit beside him instead.

"I know its late baby. But please, sit and talk with me for a while," Derrick said as he played in her hair after she sat down.

Nevette smiled as she sat down beside him. She was as close to the edge as she could get without falling off. She didn't want to agitate him anymore than he already had been by Tre earlier. She looked at him and said, "Derrick, Tre sat here all day today brushing up against you and hurting you. I watched your face. You tried to hide it every time he touched you, but I saw it. I don't need to sit here—"

"Shhhh—Mrs. Goodfellow. I have heard and spoken enough words today. Kiss me," Derrick replied.

She gave him a look, as though she were about to chastise him as she said in a mother's tone, "Justice—"

"Kiss me, Naythia. You've kissed me every day for the last eight days, and I was powerless to reply," Derrick replied and pulled her in closer and kissed her. She melted as she always did whenever he kissed her. He always undid her emotionally with his passion.

At his release, she gingerly pulled away from him and stood to let the bed down and fluffed his pillows. She was busy making a fuss over him and adjusting his covers as she said, "Mr. Goodfellow, you and I both need to lie down. It's getting late," Nevette replied. "It was an exhausting day for you emotionally and spiritually sweetheart, and you need to—" she looked up at him and saw that Justice was fast asleep. She smiled, kissed him, and curled up in the chair under her blanket and was soon resting peacefully herself.

*****

Over the next few days, the doctors were preparing Derrick to go home. He had received all the antibiotics there were going to give him. The eight days he laid unconscious proved to be very productive in his healing process. Although his was still extremely sore and was commanded to lift no more than ten pounds and refrain from any strenuous activity he was set to be released the next morning.

Nevette finally left the hospital so she could go home to prepare the house for Derrick. Nevette rearranged the living room and had the recliner in the basement brought upstairs to the living room to keep Derrick from having to go up and down the stairs. She brought the television from the guest bedroom into the living room as well.

Teddy helped her the night before to rearrange the house and was scheduled to meet her at the hospital the next morning to retrieve and aid her in getting Justice home as painlessly as possible. Tre was super excited that he would finally be going home with his mom and that his dad would be there as well. They were finally going to be a family again.

Shaundra would drop Tre off at home after school. The game that he and Tre had gone to the day he was shot, was the season opener, so they were only a few weeks into school.

She was beyond excited as she pulled into the hospital parking lot bright and early. She brought clothes for Derrick to wear home with her. When she got to his room, the doctor was already there giving Derrick last minute instructions. The nurse ordered his outpatient prescription from the pharmacy, and everything was set as soon as the meds came back.

Derrick smiled when Nevette entered the room. She kissed him, greeted the doctor and sat down so he could finish giving Derrick and Nevette instructions to complete his care at home.

Nevette assisted Derrick in getting dressed while they waited for the prescription to be filled. Teddy entered right on schedule to carry Nevette's luggage to the car. The nurse brought in the prescription and scheduled his follow-up appointment for two weeks later. They placed Derrick in the customary wheelchair that patients had to exit the hospital in, while Teddy retrieved the car and pulled up to the entrance of the hospital.

*****

Justice and Naythia lie in bed, after they finally got the hyper and very excited Derrick Justice Goodfellow III tucked in for the night. Justice was overjoyed to finally be in his own bed so he could hold his wife in his arms.

He beckoned for Nevette to come over to him. She was just about to climb into his arms when Tre burst into the door. "Daddy I—oh I'm sorry daddy. I remember you told me I'm was supposed to knock because you may be acting like the husband and you and mommy may be making love."

Derrick looked at Nevette, who had a 'we are definitely going to talk about this' look on her face. "Yeah little man, what is it?" Justice asked Tre.

"I just wanted to say, I love you daddy. I'm glad you're home with me and mommy. I'm glad you didn't go be with Callisha. Are you sure you're going to be here when I wake up in the morning daddy? You're not going to leave while I'm sleep are you?" Tre asked.

"Ohhh—Justice," Nevette replied barely above a whisper.

"Come here man. No Tre. Daddy will be here when you wake up tomorrow okay." Justice replied. He hugged Tre and said, "Now you need to go get some sleep."

"Okay daddy. I'm sorry. You can make love to mommy now," he said and bolted back out the door.

"Make—love Derrick?" Nevette asked him in an inquiring tone which suggested that he had some explaining to do. She propped up on her elbow and looked at Derrick with that 'you're in trouble' sista girl look.

"Baby he flat out asked me a few months ago. He actually saw us making love over a year ago. I guess because we got so close during our separation, he finally got the nerve to ask me about it," Justice said. He shook his head and smiled, as he recalled the conversation.

"Oh my God. What did he say Justice?" Nevette asked with an incredibly embarrassed look on her face.

"He said, that one day he saw me on top of you. He opened the door one night, and we must have been going at it hard. Because he said I had your legs in the air, and I was moving up and down on you. He asked why I was putting my peepee inside of your peepee..."

"OH MY GOD!" Nevette gasped.

"It's okay sweetheart. I told him everything," Justice said. "He asked me was I hurting you, because you were moaning, and it sounded like you were crying. For a moment, I was quiet. I didn't know what to say. Then I figured, if he's old enough to ask, he is old enough to know. Besides, I couldn't discount what he saw. He saw us baby. So I told him it was called making love, and that was how a man and a woman make a baby. But it's also how to express love to each other as husband and wife. I told him the part that boy uses the bathroom with is called a penis, and the part that a girl uses the bathroom with is called a vagina, and they are two different parts. But God designed them to fit together. When they come together the way you saw mommy and daddy, it makes a baby. I told him there is a special seed inside of mommy called an egg. But if it's not fertilized by the seed from the husband, it doesn't become a baby. But if it is fertilized, then it becomes a baby. That's how mommy and daddy got you and Callisha. But also, they make love to enjoy each other and express love, not always to make a baby. That's part of what husbands and wives do."

"Oh God Derrick. You did not tell him all of that," Nevette replied.

"Of course I did. What was I supposed to do?" Justice asked. "Baby he really understood it. Because then he said, *"Oh I get it, it's like the eggs we eat from a chicken, sometimes they make baby chickens, and sometimes they don't"*. I was blown away when he said that. I wouldn't have thought to relate it to that. Then he asked was he going to make love someday. I said yes, when you grow up and get a wife. You can't do it with a friend or girlfriend. You have to be married for God to approve of it. Then I said, okay Tre, this is the deal. When husbands and wives make love it's a private thing. They don't want anyone to watch. So you can't just burst into mommy and daddy's room anymore okay. You have to knock and wait for us to tell you to come in. Because if we are making love, then we don't want to be disturbed. Mommies and daddies don't like for people to watch them making love. Then he asked me again was I sure I wasn't hurting mommy."

"Oh God, my son has seen me making love. Justice you didn't tell my seven-year-old all of that," Nevette said. She shook her head in disbelieve.

"Baby he saw us, and he kept asking questions. What was I supposed to say? That it was a new way to go to the bathroom? That would have been disastrous the next day at school. I can imagine the phone call from the principal now," Justice said with a laugh.

"I guess you're right. I'm glad he asked you and not me. I don't know what I would have said," Nevette replied.

"Tre is so observant and discerning. Because then he said, well you and mommy aren't acting very much like a husband and a wife anymore. I was thinking to myself— "wow"! All I could say was no man we're not. There is no lying to him about stuff. We saw that the morning after you came back from Myrtle Beach."

"Wow, yeah, I guess so," Nevette replied.

"Enough talk about Tre Mrs. Goodfellow. Let's talk about us. Now come snuggle in close to me," Justice said.

She asked, "Justice sweetheart, are you sure it's not going to hurt you baby?"

"I'm fine sweetheart. I just want to hold my wife," Justice replied.

"Are you sure? You're still really sore baby," Nevette declared.

"Yes I am. Those bullets ripped through my muscles quite a bit. Every move I make feels like someone is inside my body having batting practice. However, rumor has it. I'm sleeping around with the best physical therapist in town," Justice mused.

She chuckled, "Oh Justice."

"You know we've come full circle baby," he said.

"What do you mean?" Nevette asked as she gently nestled into his chest.

"I met you after an injury and we fell in love as you nursed me back to health. Now we are starting our love over after an injury, and you have to nurse me back to health," he replied.

"Yeah, I guess you're right," she replied with a smile.

"I love you baby. I never want to be apart from you again. It was unbearable not to be near you. You were vulnerable, and I wasn't able to do my job as your husband, and that devastated me. You also know I'm struggling with the fact that I can't make love to you," Justice said as he gave her a light squeeze and kissed her on the forehead.

She lifted her head slightly to kiss him and said, "We have plenty of time for that sweetheart."

He sighed and said, "Like I said earlier, the eight days you all thought I was unconscious in the hospital. I was aware of everything that was going on around me. I couldn't open my eyes, but I wasn't unconscious. I could hear you talking to me. You were pouring your heart out to me, and I wanted to tell you that I loved you. I tried so hard to open my eyes, but it was like something was keeping them closed. I was yelling on the inside that I love you. I kept saying, please baby its okay. I'm okay, don't cry baby. You were kissing me and caressing my face, and my soul magnified the Lord because I had my wife back. Everything in me wanted to wake up, but I just couldn't. Then all of a sudden, just as strong as the hold was, it was gone, and I could speak. Baby, I missed you so much. It was the hardest and longest ten months of my life. I prayed to God every day for you. You were so hurt. I punished myself when I would work out every day for allowing our baby to be lost. It was so hard baby. I am so sorry."

"Oh Justice please don't. I am the one who should be sorry," Nevette replied. "I shut you out. I blamed you and God. I was so selfish and hurtful. The whole time I loved you, and I missed you. But for some reason, I just kept lashing out at you. I would cry myself to sleep every night because of the baby, but mostly because I missed you and wanted you home. But I just didn't know what to say. I felt like I didn't know you anymore. That day you came and brought the divorce papers, I wanted you to kiss me. I was screaming at you with my eyes to make love to me. When you turned and walked away, my heart sank. I closed the door and would have fallen onto the floor crying, but Tre entered the room. I thought I had lost you forever. You used to be able to read my every emotion and gesture. You used to be able to read my eyes. I thought maybe I had pushed you to the point of no return. You had never in our entire relationship, ever raised your voice toward me."

"I wanted to kiss you that day, but you're right. I couldn't read you, and I felt so lost that I couldn't. I used to know every inch of you. I used to be able to feel everything you felt and sense your every need. Tre would tell me when I had him on the weekends that you would cry a lot, and that hurt, because I wasn't there to hold you. You wouldn't allow me comfort you when we lost Callisha. It crushed me that I couldn't be your covering. I punished myself for breaking the trust that we had. I never even saw it coming. I should have listened to you. I didn't have any attraction to her whatsoever. I couldn't see past ministry. Truly, we men need helpmeets to keep us out of trouble."

"That may be sweetheart, but wives have to be balanced. To sanctify our emotions. I didn't think about anyone else. I was lost in my hurt. I was insensitive to the fact that you lost your baby too. Everything was my, my, my—my baby, my hurt, my loss, my pain. One day, it came to me that I had said to you that I didn't care that you were hurting. Justice that was a horrible thing to say to a father. You had to put your grief on hold because I was being selfish and evil. I shut you out of everything, including the funeral arrangements. I kept telling myself I was wrong, but I wasn't listening. I was too caught up in my own hurt to see that my husband was dying on the inside. Some helpmeet I was. I failed you Derrick. I sat in that hospital room looking at you every day. I thought I was going to lose you. I chastised myself for wasting the last ten months of our lives. Being angry, silly and foolish when I could have lost you forever. It doesn't matter what you're angry with someone about, in eternity it doesn't matter. At any time, they can be gone from you. Then all you have is regrets. I learned that the last two weeks. They didn't know why you weren't waking up. I prayed to God over you every day and cried out to God telling Him that I wasn't going to turn my back on Him this time. That I wouldn't stop loving Him. I told Him that I was trusting Him with you. I am so sorry," Nevette said as she wiped away tears.

"Sweetheart, we were both on uncharted ground and made terrible mistakes. Ultimately, the man is responsible for every error in his house. Therefore, I failed you greatly," Derrick exclaimed. "I was screaming inside the day I heard Suzette's voice lying in that hospital bed. She touched my body, and a cold chill went all through me. I was terrified she would harm you. I was screaming for you to stay in the bathroom. Then I heard Yogi's voice, and I thought, this is about to get real ugly. I tried with everything I had to wake up. God kept saying, not yet. I was literally about to explode on the inside. I felt like I was about to lose you. I wasn't sure what she was capable of, or what she would attempt. All I could do was lay there and listen as everything unfolded. During the struggle, y'all were up against the bed, and I could feel the intensity of the fight."

He paused to get his emotions under control before he continued, "Then I heard Yogi say *"Nevette stop, you're going to kill her"* and a different fear griped me. A lifetime with you behind bars for murder. It didn't matter what she did, Suzette's life wasn't worth your freedom. There were so many times that I imagined myself choking her to death upon the first time that I would lay my eyes on her again. I spent a lot of days thinking about it. I figured if she was still fascinated with me, then she would contact me but she never did. I was always worried about you and Tre if she decided to finish what she started with Callisha."

"I couldn't believe my ears when I heard her voice," Nevette replied. "I couldn't get out of that bathroom fast enough. I have to be honest at first, terror gripped me. Insane people tend to be extremely strong. Then an uncontrollable anger rushed over me as I thought of Callisha and all our family had been through because of her. From the beginning, I had an issue with Nurse Howard. I couldn't figure out why she looked so familiar. Suzette was the farthest thing from my mind. My whole focus and concern was you. I'm glad Yogi was there that day instead of mom. Mom wouldn't have attacked her. She would have tried to talk to her. But Yogi saw that she was getting ready to pull the trigger and rushed her. Justice she would have shot me if Yogi hadn't been there. I'm just relieved it's finally over. You're awake, and we're home as a family again and that's all that matters."

He squeezed her slightly pulling her in tighter as he kissed her forehead, "Yes—a family again."

"I'm so grateful to God that you remained faithful to me in my foolishness. I practically pushed you away. Any other man would have easily been in another woman's arms and bed," Nevette said.

"I'm not any other man. I'm your man," Justice replied.

She smiled and kissed him.

The pain medication he had taken was kicking in, and she could feel his whole body relax. He sighed and said, "When I was laying in the hospital bed. God dealt with me about everything that had transpired in our lives over the last ten months. I made so many mistakes. You were pouring our heart out to me. You were being so hard on yourself. I kept thinking, baby stop—don't." He sighed again and said with a hint that he was holding back, "there was just so much."

She noted the hesitation in his voice. She knew she would have to initiate the conversation that they needed to have. A conversation that was put on hold because of the incident. She breathed heavily and said, "Derrick—"

He answered as though he were on the verge of falling asleep, "What's this Derrick stuff?" He breathed in and turned his head as if adjusting for a long nights sleep after making love, "You know I don't like when you all me Derrick."

She smiled, "I know Justice. You have been Derrick for the last ten months. We were so formal with each other. It just became a habit I guess."

"Yeah, one you're going to break starting today," he replied and slightly stretched to readjust her position on him to get more comfortable.

"Derrick I'm hurting you," she replied but made no move to get out of his arms.

He replied in that voice that you have just as you are about to drift off into a blissful sleep, "You're fine baby. But you're still calling me Derrick."

She chuckled, "Justice, I love you." The conversation would have to wait until in the morning. She sighed and closed her eyes.

He mumbled that he loved her, kissed her on the forehead and was out like a light.

~Chapter Seven~

She was propped up on one arm and lightly caressed his chest with her opposite hand. She was always somewhat intimidated by him in bed, even if they weren't engaged in physical intimacy. She lay there watching him sleep and silently thanking God for mending her family back together. She had already been up earlier to get Tre ready for school. She usually drove him on her way out to work, but today he would have to catch the bus. She kissed him goodbye and stood in the driveway watching until the bus came. She headed down the hallway and climbed back in bed beside the man of her dreams. As she watched him sleep, she realized how powerful the medicine must be for Justice to sleep through all the movement in the house. He was usually a very light sleeper.

Just then he stirred and turned slightly. He felt for her and opened his eyes. He smiled at her and said, "Good morning Mrs. Goodfellow, what are you doing?"

"Watching you sleep," she replied as she gave him a light kiss.

He moaned, "Mmmm—that's my job."

"I know," she replied. "Just laying here watching you. Like I'm afraid you're going to disappear or something."

He smiled and chuckled. "I was half afraid that I would wake up back in my room at mom and dad's house, and the last few weeks would have all been a dream. I'll take getting shot, to be here where I am right now with my family back in my care."

She closed her eyes for a quick moment, then opened them with a sexy smile as she said, "I love you."

"I love you too," he replied.

She kissed him again. He moaned as he always did to let her know it's about to go down. She felt his body tense, and tried to pull away from him, but he had his arms around her now and his kiss turned passionate. "Justice you know we can't do anything. You heard the doctor. Nothing strenuous."

He sighed and dropped his head back down on the pillow, "Yeah—I know." He breathed heavily and smiled at her. "Back at home with my wife and I can't make love to her. You know Naythia, before I came to get Tre that Friday that we got back together, I asked God for a wedding night experience for when we finally make love again."

"Justice I was a virgin on our wedding night. If you have to break my hymen again after almost eight years of marriage and two children, you are so going to get it," she replied in a teasing manner.

He laughed, "Well obviously there is nothing God can do about that. I meant the fact that we conceived Tre. I wanted us to have another baby right away."

"Ahhh—Justice, God can do all things. Anyway, you're probably going to be granted the baby portion of that prayer. I haven't been on birth control since the week Callisha was kidnapped," Nevette replied.

He chuckled, but then sighed and in a defeated tone said, "Yeah."

"Baby—Justice stop. Stop crucifying yourself," Nevette replied as she kissed him again.

"I'm trying to baby—it's hard. Everything I touched this last ten months just fell apart in my hands," Justice replied. He was on the verge of losing control of his emotions

She moved in closer to him, being careful and mindful of his wounds and said, "Please Justice don't—"

"NAYTHIA, I AM SO SORRY!" he exclaimed as he lost the battle.

She held him tight, and they cried together. He kept apologizing to her about Callisha. She kept reassuring him that they were both to blame saying that neither of them handled the situation correctly. She realized at that moment that she and Justice had never mourned Callisha together, other than that brief moment at her memorial. They were overcome with emotion and held each other as they mourned the loss of so many things in their lives over the last ten months.

She wiped her tears and stroked his head as she said, "Justice, I need to get some food into you. It's time for your medication. Our breakfast is in the warmer. I'll be right back."

He allowed her to maneuver out of his arms, and she disappeared to the kitchen to retrieve breakfast. After they finished breakfast, she placed the dishes in the sink and went back into the bedroom. She knew they needed to have an unemotional conversation about Callisha, their marriage, Suzette and everything involving their lives the last ten months.

She sat at the end of the bed Indian style and just looked at him.

He smiled and said, "I know that look."

"What?" she replied with a smile as she let out a playgirl sigh and looked down as though she were embarrassed. She looked back up at him and said, "You do know me." She paused then said, "We need to talk. I need to ask you something Justice. And you need to be honest with me. I mean we need to be honest with each other."

He looked her with an inquisitive expression and replied, "Okay. What is it baby?"

"What happened? I mean, I need you to be honest Justice. What got us there with Suzette and your need to minister to her over respecting my feelings about it? You were driven to minister to her even if it meant alienating me and our marriage. I need to know what it was that I did, because I don't want to ever be there with you again," she replied.

He sighed, "Baby it wasn't you—"

"No Justice. You need to tell me," she interrupted.

He sighed again, "Okay sweetheart. It wasn't so much what you did, as it was how you made me feel." He paused and looked at her. She looked as though she would cry any minute. "You weren't doing it on purpose. At least, I don't think you were."

"You're right, maybe I don't want to hear this after all," Nevette sighed.

He smiled and beckoned for her to come closer to him, "Come here. I want you in my arms." She moved closer and snuggled up into his chest, being careful of his injuries. He continued, "Naythia I have always been spiritually intimidated by you. From the first day I saw you, I knew spiritually you were out of my league. I was never sure that I could lead you. On our wedding night when I received the baptism of the Holy Spirit, I told myself that I was ready. But the truth of the matter is, I always felt like I was in your shadow spiritually. At Shiloh Tabernacle, I finally felt close to being your equal. The pastor licensed me and was preparing me to be his associate pastor. It just went to my head. I thought, finally, someone sees me, and not my wife."

"I think I've known about it for a while Justice. I just didn't know what to do about it. I definitely didn't know that it was affecting you so much. I didn't know how to turn it off," Nevette replied.

"Sweetheart you couldn't and can't turn off being who you are. I understand that now," Justice replied.

"Yeah, but sometimes Justice I take advantage of you allowing me to have my way. Sometimes when you would say that something wasn't open for discussion, I would just keep going to get my way like you didn't say anything. You just let me Derrick," Nevette declared.

"Yeah baby because it didn't matter. I wasn't going to argue with you about it. I just wanted to love you. I didn't want to dominate you," he replied.

"You should have on some things. Because it gave me authority in the home that I should have never had. Tre would always come to me for approval instead of you. When you would say no, he would come to me to get a yes like I was the final say so in this house. But baby, you're the final say so in this house, or at least you should be. Then when you started making mistakes it just got worse for you," Nevette countered.

"Baby, God is the final say so," he chuckled.

"Well yeah, you know what I mean," she replied.

"Sweetheart you're right. I let you lead. I shouldn't have. It's my fault just as much as it is yours. The truth of the matter is, I was afraid to attempt to lead you spiritually. You couldn't have usurped authority that I didn't surrender to you. A lot of times you were right. And yes it did get worse. I started feeling like I couldn't lead the home or make sound decisions for us. I insisted on us attending Shiloh when in my heart, I knew it probably wasn't a good decision. But there I had a voice over you for the first time, and my ego went flying through the roof. I knew I wasn't ready to become an associate pastor. I hadn't too long before that become a minister. I tried so hard to play catch up that I made a lot of mistakes. I felt so far behind you. I was doing crash courses in God to play catch up. But I realized later, that it takes time and relationship to get there. Instead of allowing God to minister and work on me, or grow me up in His time. I ran full steam ahead. It was all a part of the enemy's plan to shut you out and lift me up, and I fell for it. I tried to force feed the issue, and Suzette happened. I didn't want to admit that you were right. Then when she kissed me, you were right again. I drove home that Sunday that we argued in church over her thinking, there is no way I should be the leader of this family—I suck! I beat myself up pretty bad all the way home. If I would have listened to you, Callisha would be here and our family wouldn't have gone through the last ten months."

Nevette touched his face as she said, "No Justice, I don't think so. I think that long before we realized it, her attraction was fatal. She was just waiting for the perfect moment to make her move. She wanted to kill me. She took Callisha as bait to get you without getting her hands dirty in the process. That day we argued at church crushed me. You were defending her. And outside of the thought that you had possibly been intimate with her, I couldn't understand why you were. I was—stunned. I mean—I don't even have a word to describe how I felt about it. What you didn't know because I didn't share it was, she gloated in my face several times before that day. Justice she would send her little gestures to insinuate that there was more to what she had with you than counseling."

"WHAT!" Derrick interjected. "Baby, never did anything physical happen between us, other than the last day I counseled her at church and she kissed me. Wow, all this time I never knew that. I really feel unworthy now. This woman alienated my wife. Then kidnapped and killed my baby—"

Nevette reached up to touch his face to calm him, "Baby don't. I don't feel that Callisha's death was intentional. She was her bait to get you, why would she intentionally harm her? She had no way of knowing Callisha was allergic to penicillin and what would happen. I think at some point reality kicked in, because she took care in wrapping her in a blanket and leaving a note. Justice what I'm trying to say is, Suzette was just as much my fault, as she was yours. I had you in a place where you had to prove yourself spiritually. I opened the door for Suzette to walk right through it. I should have never demanded anything from you. I should have let you handle her. I hadn't stepped in to be there during the counseling, but I wanted to be there during the dismissal to gloat. It was going good until I butted in. As long as you were having contact with her, everything was okay. But when I forced you to stop counseling her. That's when everything went crazy. I think it would have been okay if I would have just allowed you to wean her off you, but I was desperate, angry and silly about it. I didn't want you to let her down easy. I wanted you to slam dunk her because I was jealous, and I didn't know how to handle that. I had never been in the situation where I had to compete with another woman for time with you. No one has ever had your attention like that other than me."

Derrick shook his head and said, "Baby she didn't have my attention. It was always about ministry to me. She may have had my ministry, but she didn't have my attention. Not like that. I wasn't remotely attracted to Suzette. I can't imagine another woman ever being in my arms. I don't even see other women like that. I see them, but I don't see them. To me, they are just female human beings. There is no woman in this world that satisfies me, or will ever satisfy me but you. You can be confident in that. I was totally oblivious. All along I knew she was attracted. I just didn't think it was an obsession, and she was out of her mind. I wanted to prove my point that I was ready for higher ministry so bad. I was willing to take a chance. That chance cost me my baby girl, and almost my family altogether."

"I need to give you authority Justice. There were a lot of times that I kind of knew I was taking over. You just sort of let me. But that doesn't make it right. I was dead wrong. I'm supposed to be a helpmeet. I'm here to help you make decisions not make them for you. I'm here to nurture you and support you. If you say something is not open for discussion, then that should be the end of it. I shouldn't keep going until I get my way. I'm spoiled, but I need to know when to stop Justice. I didn't know how to turn off being an evangelist," she replied.

"Baby going too far in a conversation is one thing, but you can't turn off ministry because your husband feels inferior to you. You never disrespected me Naythia. You always honored me, especially in front of others. And for the most part, I made the decisions for our home. I have to admit. I allowed you to go too far sometimes when I should have said enough is enough. But I didn't want to lord over you. All I ever wanted to do was love you. Baby, I love you so much," Derrick declared.

"I love you too Justice. And sometimes a man has to lord over his woman. Besides, it turns me on. I don't want to be in charge of anything. A woman likes a man who *respectfully* dominates her. It's a turn on and sexy as heck," Nevette replied with a laugh.

"Oh really Mrs. Goodfellow," Derrick replied smiling like the cat that ate the canary. "Well then listen to this, and you listen good. We will not travel down this road ever again. Although we will continue to make all major decisions together, you need to respect my final decision on the matter. Then next time we have an issue we will stay together and discuss it. I don't care how angry you are with me. We will work through it together. I will not leave this house, and you do not have the authority to put me out. We will not argue in front of Tre. I will spank your tail the next time you even think about trying." He paused and smiled, "And while I'm talking about spanking tail, you do not have the right to ever refuse to make love to me as long as you are my wife. Do you understand me Mrs. Nevette Naythia Goodfellow?"

"I'm sorry," she replied with a sad puppy dog look that usually won him over.

He smiled and shook his head as he said, "Get that little 'five-year-old my daddy just scolded me' look off your face. It's not going to work this time."

"Well, I feel like I'm five and my daddy just scolded me, so the look is appropriate," she replied.

"I still can't believe you served me divorce papers," Derrick said as he played in her hair.

"I can't believe you signed them," Nevette replied.

"I didn't know what else to do. I allowed my anger to speak that day. Mom tried to stop me. Your attitude toward me and the situation with Tre that morning after you came home from Myrtle Beach took me over the edge. I realized that the love I had for you wasn't enough to hold our marriage together. Love just doesn't make it work by itself. I mean Eros love doesn't. It takes agape love and God right smack in the middle of it," Derrick declared.

"Yes, it does. It was a crazy time for me. The devil was on my shoulder, literally talking to me and influencing me. Evil Nevette took over and pushed the regular Nevette out of the way. You and Tre are my world. I did the exact opposite of everything my heart felt for you," Nevette replied.

"I love you baby," he said softly as he stroked the side of her face. He had an endearing smile on his face.

"I love you too. I'm sorry Justice," she replied.

"Oh baby we were both wrong. Like you said, neither one of us handled this well. We did not do a good job with this," Justice said as he pulled her into his arms.

She felt him wince and attempted to back away slightly giving space between them. He pulled her in closer and bared the pain.

"Justice, I feel and hear you. You're hurting. I need to move," she said as she attempted to move away from him again.

"Don't you dare move Mrs. Goodfellow," Derrick replied.

They spent the day with her nurturing and caring for him. They continued to talk about everything that transpired in their lives the last ten months. All the things that she wanted to discuss the Sunday morning she came back from Athens on the day he was shot.

*****

The following weekend after Derick returned home. Bernard, Trevor and Teddy came over for a visit. Derrick spent most of his time in the living room in a recliner because Nevette was extremely over protective. Besides, going up and down steps was extremely painful. She figured she would take the time that the guys were there to run some errands.

"Okay baby, I'm going to pick up mom and we're headed to the store okay. Justice don't you go down those stairs. You know what the doctor said," Nevette said as she leaned over to kiss him.

"I know, I know baby. I'm going to be good," Derrick replied as he returned the kiss.

She waved goodbye to everyone and was out the door.

"Well, you can't go downstairs Derrick. So I guess watching the game on the big-screen today is out," Teddy said with a hint of sarcasm in his voice.

"Whatever man," Derrick replied in an 'I'm the head of this house' tone.

Bernard smiled and said, "Man, you don't have to try to be the big man on campus with us. You better do what the doctor and your wife said."

"Really I'm okay. Now come on let's go," Derrick said he hit the remote on the small 36-inch TV Nevette brought into the living room from their guest bedroom to keep Derrick from having to go downstairs. He eased up out of the chair. He tried to hide the sharp pain that ripped through his abdomen that usually accompanied every core movement that he made.

Trevor interjected, "Derrick man, you look like you're in a lot of pain. It took everything you had to get up out of the chair. We can just watch the game here in the living room."

"No man, nonsense. Let's go downstairs. If I need it, then later on Nevette can lay hands on me and anoint me," Derrick insisted.

Teddy said, "Okay, but when Nay Nay comes back and asks us why we allowed you to go downstairs, I'm going to need you to speak up *'Mr. In Charge of Things'.*"

Bernard and Trevor laughed at Teddy's comment as they head downstairs. Going down the steps proved to be extremely painful. His body jarred on every step, and he already regretted his decision to brave the stairs. He prayed that coming back up them would be an easier task. He was more than ready to have a seat once he finally made it to the last step and crossed the room to the TV area.

He eased into the other recliner and breathed heavily, "Whew. That was harder than I anticipated."

They smiled, and Teddy plopped down on the couch with remote in hand. He began searching through the channels for the Georgia vs. South Carolina game.

"So how long does the doctor think it will be before you get back to normal?" Bernard asked.

"He estimated about another four to six weeks before I should even think of going back to work," Derrick replied.

"That sounds about right. You were hit three times man. With five wounds all together. Two went straight through you. Tearing up everything in their path," Trevor added.

"I need to mend man quickly. It's killing me that I can't make love to my wife," Derrick said with a heavy sigh.

"Well at least you had that Friday night with Nay Nay before you got all shot up," Teddy joked.

"No I didn't Teddy. She left for Athens remember? She came back Sunday morning. Tre and I were on the way to the game. We only had time to all eat breakfast together," Derrick replied.

"Ahhh man that's foul," Bernard said shaking his head and blowing air out of his mouth as though he were attempting to whistle.

"She climbs into bed every night with these silk silhouette gowns on. I'm like, baby please. You are driving me crazy. Sexy—man SEXY!" Derrick exclaimed.

"So when are you going to be able to ahhhh—" Bernard asked.

"I don't know. We were at the doctor yesterday for a follow-up, and I asked him about making love. He said he didn't advise it. I may pull something, plus it would be extremely painful since you use a lot of core muscles to have sex. I dropped my head and shook it side to side. She had on some nice fitting jeans and a sexy as heck shirt and vest. I told her she was teasing and playing with me, doing it on purpose," Derrick replied smiling.

"Wow that's too bad Derrick," Trevor replied. "I can't imagine not being able to have Lindsay."

"Yeah, well, I can't have Nevette. Not yet anyway. So let's just find the game okay," Derrick replied and they all laughed.

"Derrick man I can't believe you let her leave and go to Athens that night. You should have told her she couldn't go," Teddy said.

"Are we still talking about this? Anyway, I couldn't do that Teddy. She had already given her word she would be available. Some other instructor's mom was dying or something," Derrick replied.

"Whatever man, that's part of your problem now Derrick. You let Nay Nay have her way to much," Teddy said in matter of fact tone.

"I know you didn't just say that to me Teddy. I'm just picking up where y'all Graham men left off with the *"princess"*. You personally know Nevette is spoiled rotten," Derrick replied with full sarcasm.

"Yeah, yeah, you're right. We created that monster. No argument there," Teddy laughed.

"That's okay because I love spoiling her. Bottom line, Nevette knows what I say goes. When I say baby, it's not open for discussion, she usually backs down. Every now and then, she keeps going because she knows if she does, she'll get her way," Derrick said. "Anyway, I just need to heal so I can make love to my wife. You know what the doctor said to me? He said if I had a lot of belly fat, it wouldn't be hurting so much, and I probably would be healing faster."

Trevor added, "Yeah that's correct. The bullets really ripped through your muscle and tore them all up. It has to mend, and that takes time. Think about it this way, when you work out what gets sore?"

"You're muscles!" they all replied as though Trevor's statement was the revelation of the century.

"Exactly you never hear people say, boy my fat sure is sore from working out," Trevor said jokingly.

"So if I were a big boy, I would be doing much better? I can't believe that being in shape is making me feel worse," Derrick said shaking his head.

Bernard added, "I couldn't believe that not one of your organs were hit. God is good Derrick."

"Tell me about it. The doctor said it was as though the bullets went through them without touching them. Damage was on both sides of my organs, and you could see the path the bullets took. They should have gone through my liver, spleen and pancreas and kidney," Derrick replied.

"What a mighty God we serve. He uses everything that happens to us for His glory," Teddy declared.

"Exactly," Trevor interjected.

They watched the game and laughed and joked about what had been happening around town, work and church. About two hours later, they heard Nevette come through the door upstairs. She called Derrick's name to see where they were.

"I know he didn't—" she said aloud as she walked over to the top of the stairs that lead to the basement. "Derrick are you guys down stairs?"

"Yeah baby," Derrick replied.

Down the stairs she came. "Uh ohhh, here she comes," Bernard declared.

"Derrick Justice Goodfellow the SECOND! I know you did NOT come down these stairs," Nevette said she entered the room.

"Oooooo man, she called your whole name with emphasis on *"the second"*. You're in trouble," Bernard teased.

Derrick only smiled and shook his head at Bernard's remark.

As she reached Derrick, she shook her head and said, "You are NOT downstairs—Justice—baby?"

"Hey baby," Derrick replied.

"Don't hey baby me Derrick Goodfellow. You know you are not supposed to be climbing up and down stairs yet," Nevette replied in an irritated tone. She turned toward Teddy and said, "Teddy why did you let him come down these stairs?"

"Let him? He's a big boy Nay Nay," Teddy replied.

"Come on baby," Derrick interjected.

"Don't come on baby me Derrick. You're gonna pay for coming down these stairs," Nevette replied almost as though she were pouting.

Bernard chimed in, "I thought you were in charge. The head and not the tail. You know, above only and not beneath. Head man in charge. My wife know I run this—"

Derrick laughed out, "Ohhhh, so that's how it is? Y'all just gonna throw a brother under the bus like that huh?"

"I don't want to hear that. Because all of y'all could have just watched TV upstairs. Justice—," Nevette said as she gave him a playful 'you're in trouble with your mom' look. "Okay, you'll be hurting later on. You'll barely be able to move and don't talk about baby lay your hands on me."

He started to say, "Baby come on—"

"Uhn uhnn—no. I can't believe you guys. I'm going to go start dinner. Tre went with mom Justice," Nevette replied as she headed back upstairs shaking her head.

Derrick shook his head smiling, "I can't believe y'all straight threw me under the bus."

"Man, I told you to stay upstairs," Teddy reiterated.

"Whatever Teddy. Just help me upstairs. I'm hurting pretty bad," Derrick said as he struggled to get up out of the chair.

Teddy helped him up as he said, "You better listen to Nay Nay Derrick. Besides, all you're doing is hindering your progress. If you know what I mean?"

"Yes and boy she is looking *good* today. And a brotha' can't do nothing with that," Derrick replied.

"Well you better follow the rules so you *can* do something with that soon," Trevor added.

"Okay y'all have your fun. But I won't be hurt forever. This too shall pass. We'll settle all this on the court," Derrick replied.

Going back up the steps wasn't any easier than descending them. By the time they got to the top of the steps Nevette had him some warm green tea and ice packs ready.

She smiled at him and said to them, "I need y'all to go so I can take care of my baby."

He smiled and kissed her. Then he turned to the guys and said, "Okay guys. I'll talk to y'all later."

They said their goodbyes and left. Nevette assisted Derrick into the bedroom and got him settled in bed. She placed the ice packs on him and gave him his hot green tea and a blanket.

He looked up at her and said, "Have I ever told you how much I love you?"

"Yes. But tell me again," she smiled.

"I love you Mrs. Goodfellow," he replied and kissed her.

*****

A few weeks later Derrick and Nevette were going to Teddy's house for dinner. Teddy had picked Tre up from school that Friday since Derrick had another doctor's appointment. It was his first time other than going to church on Sunday, and a return doctor's visit, that Nevette had allowed Derrick to leave the house. At church the previous Sunday, Derrick gave part of their testimony and thanked everyone for their prayers.

The doctor cleared him, and he was finally able to get in the shower. He stayed in there for about twenty minutes enjoying the hot water running over his body. His stitches had dissolved, but he was still extremely sore. Derrick got out of the shower and gingerly made his way back to the bedroom. He still had just a towel wrapped around his waist as he emerged from the bathroom.

Nevette looked up and smiled. Inside she quivered at the sight of him. Even laid up for over a month with three bullets ripped through his abdominal area, he was still washboard ripped and out of this world fine. She sighed and thought, "God, *please* mend him quickly. She laughed slightly, which made him look at her.

He smiled and said, "Ahhh, I know what you're thinking Mrs. Goodfellow."

"Stop reading me Derrick," she teased.

Derrick smiled and replied, "Don't worry baby. I'm going to take good care of you when I fully heal, and the soreness is gone." He stood beside her at the bed.

"Do you need me to help you lotion your legs or help you get dressed before I go jump in the shower?" she asked.

"Nah I got it baby. At least, I think I do," Derrick said with a smile. Truth was he didn't have it. To his dismay and surprise, other than the stitches dissolving, he didn't feel any better than the first day he came home from the hospital.

Every time he said "baby" to her, she got weak in the knees. She wanted so badly to make love to her husband. She smiled and headed toward the bathroom.

He attempted to move and grimaced with a heavy sigh.

"Are you okay sweetheart?" Nevette asked as she moved back over by his side.

"This is crazy. Why does it still feel the exact same way it did the first day I woke up in the hospital? I should be feeling better by now. Every time I go to make a step or move a certain way, it stops me in my tracks. It feels like someone is doing a million man march on my abdomen. I can take a lot of pain, but this is about to do me in baby."

"Okay you know what. Enough is enough. Sit down Justice," Nevette instructed.

"What baby?" Derrick asked perplexed. Nevette had a determined look on her face.

"I'm tired of you hurting. Lay down. I'm going to anoint you and pray for a healing," Nevette said she directed him to lay down. She had been praying for him every night that God would mend him quickly. But she had never commanded an instantaneous healing in his body.

He was in much too much pain to resist. Besides, he loved having his wife's hands on him in any capacity. He laid down and placed one arm across his forehead and the other across his chest as Nevette went to retrieve the anointing oil from the living room.

She returned and anointed his forehead and abdomen as she said, "Justice, I am going to pray that God heal you right now and that your muscles regenerate. I'm believing God that all soreness and stiffness will dissipate."

He smiled at her and shook his head. She blushed and said, "Not just for me. But for you. I'm tired of watching you in so much pain. Barely able to move most of the time. I'm believing that God is going to heal you right now Justice."

Father,

In the name of Jesus. I lay my hands on my husband. I pray that You send the Holy Spirit to mend his muscles God. To repair all the damage done by the bullets. Restore him completely Lord to function normally. I thank you now God, and I praise You for mending him. The Holy Spirit is the Spirit of Regeneration. Father regenerate his muscles, remove all stiffness and soreness and replenish any muscle mass he may have lost in the process.

In Jesus' name,

Amen

Derrick moaned as she prayed because he could feel intense heat in the areas where his wife had her hands on him. He could feel the heat moving through his abdominal area to the point that it was almost unbearable.

"Baby, I think I'm going to be okay. I felt God's healing power as you touched me," Derrick said.

"I know you are. Because God is faithful," she replied and kiss him. Not realizing that the healing had indeed been instantaneous when she laid her hands on him, she left to go take a shower.

He knew he needed to get up and get dressed. He braced himself for the pain that usually accompanied every core movement he made. But to his surprised as he sat up, he felt absolutely no pain at all. He stood up and bent over—no pain. He did a couple of side straddle hops—no pain. He did about ten pushups, and again—no pain. He went over and looked in the mirror. The scars from the gunshot wounds were there. All present and accounted for, but the pain was completely gone. He jumped shouted and praised God. Nevette yelled from the shower and asked was he okay. He yelled back that he was fine. He said he was giving God glory for His goodness.

He went back over to the bed, picked his cell phone up off the night stand and called Teddy.

"Hey Teddy, Naythia and I are going to skip dinner. Can you keep Tre with you this weekend? We'll pick him up at church on Sunday," he asked.

"Sure Derrick. What's wrong? Pain too much to get out man?" Teddy asked.

"Just the opposite Teddy. I feel great. Nevette laid hands on me and man I have no pain at all. Absolutely none! It's as though I wasn't shot. That's why I need you to keep Tre. Because he doesn't need to hear the sounds that are about to come out of his mother's mouth."

Teddy laughed. "Ooookay! Yeah. We'll see you Sunday. Take it easy on her man."

"Are you kidding me? Man, I am about to tear her tail up! Then again, you might see us Sunday, if I let her out of bed by then!" Derrick exclaimed.

Teddy shook his head and laughed, "Poor Nay Nay."

"Teddy you know I'm going to be sweet to her—after I TEAR HER TAIL UP!" Derrick replied laughing.

"Alright Derrick. I have Tre. We have more than enough of his clothes over here to make it through Sunday. I can take him to school Monday if I need to on my way in to the office," Teddy replied with a hint or sarcasm in his voice.

Derrick laughed, "You're kidding, but I'll let you know. Hey, the shower just stopped. Talk to you later man. I'm about to enjoy my garden."

"Bye man," Teddy replied and hung up the phone. He shook his head, smiled and went to inform Josephine that Derrick and Nevette wouldn't be over for dinner.

Derrick wrapped the towel around his waist, climbed back onto the bed and waited for Nevette to come out of the bathroom to get dressed.

She emerged from the shower with a towel wrapped around her talking about looking forward to getting him out of the house. She saw that Derrick was still in his towel lying on the bed.

"Hey sweetheart you're still in the same spot I left you in. What's wrong, still hurting?" Nevette asked.

"No sweetheart nothing is wrong. On the contrary, everything is right," he replied.

She looked at him with a puzzled look on her face. She came over and sat down on the bed. She was about to speak when he pulled her down into his arms and flipped her, so he was now on top of her.

"Justice! What!" Nevette exclaimed.

"Baby when you laid your hands on me, an intense heat went all through my body, and God healed me. I feel absolutely no pain whatsoever. It's as though I didn't even get shot," Derrick replied as she kissed her.

"Oh my God!" Nevette exclaimed.

"Yeah, exactly—God," Justice replied.

"God is so faithful!" Nevette shouted.

"Yes He is. And I'm about to make love to my wife," Justice declared.

"Justice, we can't. Teddy and Josephine are waiting for us. And we have to get Tre," she explained.

He started to shower her with kisses as he said, "I already called Teddy and told him we wouldn't make it. I also asked him to keep Tre for the weekend. You belong to me this weekend Naythia, and you're not leaving this room."

"Oh God, something tells me I'm in trouble," she said.

"Yes you are. You have been a very naughty girl. Santa is going to have to spank you," he said as he maneuvered her out of her towel.

"Oh God. Now I know I'm trouble. Justice you have always intimidated me in bed. Take it easy on me. It's been almost a year," she said as she prepared to receive her husband. She was trembling inside.

"No way Mrs. Goodfellow. Take it like a woman and give it up, because I am about to make you climb the walls!" Justice exclaimed.

"Mmmmmm—Wheeeew—" Nevette replied and took a deep breath. Her body tensed slightly underneath him enough that it got his attention. And she could feel herself start to shake just as she did on their wedding night.

"Okay baby, what's wrong? I can feel you tense up, and you're shaking," Justice asked.

"I'm nervous," she replied.

"Nervous?" he replied. "Baby we've been married for eight years and have had two children."

"I'm always nervous before I make love to you Justice. You are so much man. I just don't ever know if I satisfy you," she replied.

He propped himself on his elbows to ensure his weight wasn't rested on her. "Nevette baby what are you talking about? Why would you question whether or not you satisfy me?" he asked.

"Justice I was a virgin on our wedding night and terrified. I shook half of the night. You have all kinds of experience, and I didn't know anything. I always wondered how I measured up to the women you had before me," she replied.

"Measure up? There is no measurement baby. I had sex with them. I made love to you. It was a new experience for me too on our wedding night. I had to throw out everything I thought I knew about having sex and make love to you. I knew I didn't want to treat you like every woman I had been in bed with. I wanted the first time you made love to be special. So baby there was no measuring up because we were both experiencing something new on our wedding night," Justice explained.

"Wow," she replied with a chuckle. "I love you baby. Make love to me."

"Oooo, I thought you'd never ask Mrs. Goodfellow. Hold on for the ride baby. I am so going to enjoy this. But don't worry, I'm going to make sure you enjoy it too," Justice said as he paraded her with kisses.

The fragrance of love filled the room as Justice served *justice* to

Nevette.

*****

Bernard and Talinda were excited that their friends from Germany were being reassigned to Robbins Air Base in Warner Robbins, Georgia. They flew in late Friday night. They planned on spending the weekend with the Travis' prior to going home to visit family before they had to report in for duty at Robbins. Bernard called Michael Thomas and invited him and Gloria to church on Sunday so they could meet Terry, Stacy, Tasha and Jaison since they would be stationed there with them soon. Michael was due to transition from the Air Force in the next six months or so. He and Gloria were considering moving to the Decatur/Atlanta area for retirement. Michael and Gloria were quite excited because they had heard so much about the church.

Tasha and the gang kept out of sight until Sunday and surprised the youth at Sunday School. Michael and Gloria went to the youth Sunday School class with Bernard and Talinda.

Since Derrick and Nevette arrived late, and Derrick hadn't returned to teaching since the incident, they attended the adult Sunday School class. They stood in the foyer before entering the sanctuary.

He kissed her and said, "Mmmm—I love you baby."

"Justice you're kissing me in the middle of the church," Nevette replied.

"What? The bible tells me to enjoy the wife of my youth," Derrick replied and smiled.

"Well, you enjoyed your wife all weekend. Now it's time to give God some time. You can give Him the next few hours. Come on now Minister Goodfellow, share and share alike," Nevette replied sarcastically and laughed.

He kissed her again as he said, "Yeah, I guess I do have to share with God huh?"

She smiled and said, "Yes you do." As she returned his kiss, she chuckled and said, "I love you."

"I love you," he said. He touched her stomach and said, "You be good in there Zoé, take care of mommy alright. Minimum amount of morning sickness."

"You don't even know if she's in there or not yet," Nevette replied.

"Oh baby, after this weekend. She's definitely in there," he declared as they entered the sanctuary.

The pastor saw them and came over to greet them and see how everything was going. Derrick asked him if he could have time after the review to give a testimony and then they sat down and enjoyed the lesson. It was an open forum with several opportunities for audience participation by way of questions, answers and interjections.

The adults wrapped up their lesson as the youth department headed upstairs at the close of Sunday School. Everyone always came together towards the end to give a review of the lesson from each classroom. They sat in the back to the far right of the half sections on the last four rows. The leaders were on the first two rows with the teen's right behind them on the other two rows. Derrick was usually with the teens, but since he was still in recovery and had only been back at church about a month, he was still sitting in the main sanctuary during Sunday School. He looked forward to returning to help teach the youth. He usually learned so much from teaching them.

After they called the last class up for review, the pastor beckoned for Derrick to come forward to give his testimony about his miraculous healing. He looked back at Nevette and said," Come on baby go with me."

"No Justice, go ahead," she replied shyly.

He grabbed her by the hand and guided her up to the front with him. She reluctantly but obediently went with him.

He began to talk about the events that transpired on Friday with Nevette praying for him. He ended it with the statement, "—and pastor, she laid her hands on me, and I could feel the power of the Holy Spirit go through my body. It was a burning sensation that was almost unbearable. She went on to take a shower. I prepared myself for the pain I always endured to rise from a sitting position. But this time I felt nothing. I started doing calisthenics to test myself. I looked in the mirror and there were three tiny scars where the bullets entered my body. And two on the back where two of the bullets exited. But they are the only evidence that the incident ever occurred. I feel great and God is good—HALLELUJAH!" He continued on with praises and exhortation of God about how He blessed him.

Meanwhile, as they gave their testimony, the youth leaders drew and discussed their own conclusions about the Goodfellow weekend. They attempted to keep their voices down as they laughed at Derrick and Nevette's expense.

Bernard leaned over toward Teddy and said, "Man you know it was wild up in the Goodfellow house this weekend."

"You see who Tre came to church with," Teddy replied and they both shook their heads smiling.

Bernard leaned backwards slightly so Terry, Jaison and Mike could all hear, "He got that look on his face like he tore that tail up y'all."

Talinda nudged Bernard in the side as she said, "Bernard! You are not sitting in church talking like this."

Bernard smiled and said, "What? Baby you know Derrick tore that—"

"Bernard Alexander Travis! You will cut it out right now," Talinda exclaimed as she attempted to keep a smile from gracing her face.

Lindsay couldn't resist getting in on the fun. She said, "You know she is probably doing everything she can to walk straight right now." At her comment, they all laughed and then everyone started joining into the jesting.

"Yeah, I think you're right Lindsay. She is definitely walking with that, 'I just got tore out the frame' walk," Tasha chimed in.

"You ought to know," Jaison replied. She gave him a playful punch on the shoulder to everyone's *ooooo's.*

"You walked right into that Tasha," Bernard replied.

"Guys stop! We are not sitting in church having this conversation," Talinda exclaimed.

Bernard smiled and said, "What baby? We are all adults here. Besides the bible tells me to enjoy the wife of my youth. It also says every man should drink out of his own cistern. And don't forget about Song of Solomon, *Let my beloved come into his garden, and eat his pleasant fruits—*"

"Bernard Travis!" Talinda replied.

"What? I tell you what," Bernard stated in a matter of fact manner. "You go on a ten-month rampage, shut me out of your life, and see what happens when you come back. You're going to get it. Nobody will see you outside for about a month. This brother been without his wife for almost a whole year, if you count the recovery time from him getting shot. Oh please, she got it this weekend, and she got it good."

"And she earned it," Lindsay added in sarcastic flare, and everyone cracked up laughing at that comment.

"Okay guys maybe he did. And yeah she earned it. But we're not going to sit in church and talk about it," Talinda replied.

"Girl please, God ordained marriage and sex. He does not have a problem with us talking about it in His house. Girl your goody-two-shoes act ended when you became Mrs. Bernard Travis. Let's not forget when you came to Germany with the youth last year. Travis put that tail down for the count. We thought we were gonna have to come get you. You slept through breakfast, lunch and almost dinner," Tasha replied as she gave a girlfriend flick of the wrist in Talinda's direction.

Talinda gave her a sly look, as she shook her head and smiled.

Lindsay laughed as she said, "Mmmm, Talinda, I think you need to quit while you're ahead."

Teddy added his comment, "Y'all, Derrick called me Friday evening and told me he needed me to keep Tre for the weekend. He said Tre don't need to hear the sounds that are about to come out of his mother's mouth. Then he said we're not going to make it to Tre's game tomorrow. We'll see y'all Sunday."

They all but lost it on Teddy's comment.

"Oh yeah he definitely gave her the business," Terry added.

Bernard said, "Man, y'all know it's on for dinner at the house later. We gonna have to get him good."

Lindsay said, "Oh yes, and we will definitely give her *the business* too. This is going to be fun."

The youth sat behind them snickering at the comments of the adults. Bernard brought out a different side of Talinda that the female teens enjoyed. She was more relatable since she married Bernard. They were also excited to have Tasha and Stacy there visiting. With Stacy, Terry, Tasha and Jaison all headed to Warner Robbins Air Force Base, they knew they would see them more often. They squealed in delight when they popped into Sunday School earlier that morning.

Their fun time of talking and teasing about Derrick and Nevette's weekend came to a close as everyone began to clap at the conclusion of the testimony Derrick gave about his healing that weekend. As they returned to their seats so Sunday School could close out and church could begin, Nevette's eyes met Lindsay's.

Lindsay gave her a look and Nevette mouthed, "Stop it Lindsay."

Lindsay mouthed the reply while shaking her head no, "Uhn uhn, you know you're going to get it later."

Nevette smiled and shook her head as she took a seat.

Derrick glanced at the men and shook his head with an uncontrollable grin on his face. He could only imagine what they had been talking about. He could see them in the back while he and Nevette stood in front of the church giving his testimony.

Gloria and Mike sat and enjoyed the fellowship and teasing of Derrick and Nevette. They didn't really know them well enough to comment but was excited that Christians were so much fun. The people were a little more traditional in the church they attended in Warner Robbins. They thought just maybe it was worth the hour and a half drive every Sunday to come to Grace Tabernacle. They were enjoying the freedom they all had in the Lord. They could still go to mid-week service there locally. With Mike due to go on terminal leave soon, the commute would only be for a about six or seven months. They decided to move to the Atlanta area. Mike had a few interviews at Fort Gilliam, and since he was friends with General Kenneth James, he was a sure to get one of them. Talinda and Bernard were delighted that not only did God save their marriage, but now they would soon be closer to them.

~Chapter Eight~

Bernard stood in the basement in front of the television as though he were about to make an announcement. He looked at Teddy and smiled as he cleared his throat and said, "Yes pastor, and then my wife laid her *hands* on me—"

All the guys burst out laughing.

"Ahhhh—man, okay y'all got jokes. I saw y'all in the back of the church earlier. I can only imagine what was being said," Derrick replied laughing.

Jaison interjected, "Oh you don't have to imagine, we're about give you round two."

Suddenly, in a really serious tone Teddy yelled, "Wait, wait, wait, y'all hear that?"

Bernard replied almost in a panic, "What?"

"I hear something outside. A weird sound. Y'all don't hear that?" Teddy said as he walked over to a window and looked through the curtain. "Oh never mind. I recognize that sound. It's just the aftershock of them Goodfellow mating screams that came out of Nay Nay's mouth."

The room erupted in "Oooh man's" and all out laughter.

"Teddy you're wrong. You're supposed to be my big brother!" Derrick exclaimed. He laughed as he said, "I tried to get all ten months' worth in one weekend. I didn't let her tail get no sleep."

"Yeah, I'm with you there. I told Talinda the same thing because she was telling us we were wrong for teasing about it in church. I said, go away from me if you want to trippin' for ten months. When you come back you're gonna get it," Bernard replied. They laughed again.

"But all jokes aside guys. This has been the longest and hardest year of my life. There isn't a day that goes by that I don't think about Callisha. It was so hard not being able to cover Nevette. Not being able to comfort her. She was hurting so bad, and I was the cause of it. Teddy I promised you, dad and Jason that I would protect her with my life—"

Teddy interrupted, "It's not the same thing Derrick. You didn't have an affair, and you didn't kill Callisha. Heck, Suzette didn't intend to kill her either for that matter. Callisha's death was an accident. You couldn't foresee that happening. There is no way you could have protected Nay Nay from the series of events that transpired. Things happen—life happens."

Derrick shook his head. He continued as though Teddy had not said a word. "I couldn't relate to Nevette. It's like we were on two different planets. I couldn't read her anymore. Guys, listen to your wives. Don't walk down this road. Having to bury my baby girl—that thing took everything my wife had. It almost took her life." He had to pause to gather his emotions. "I couldn't even imagine. As hard as I hurt, the thought of ending my life never entered my mind. With Tre—I didn't realize everything I was saying to him was damaging to her. Everything I did this past year hurt her. I couldn't do anything without hurt being the end result. Everything I touched fell apart and dissolved. It was crazy. The two weeks she was missing, I almost went insane. I think that hurt worse than losing Callisha. But in those two weeks, I understood her hurt with Callisha. The bible says in marriage two flesh become one. I understood more fully how it felt for her with the loss of the baby. Nevette is a part of me, just like Callisha was a part of her. I know she had my DNA too, but Nevette had a connection with her and with Tre that I will never have. A mother's bond with the baby growing inside of her is one of the most powerful forces on earth. If she would have gone through with ending her life, I don't know if I would have been able to take it. Guys just—listen to your wives when it comes to another woman. Women know the hidden motives of other women, just like we know when a man is running game on a girl." He paused to run his hand from the front of his head to the back. He looked up toward heaven and said, "I just have to have another daughter. I just pray that Zoé is in there."

Jaison said, "Yeah me and Tasha lost a baby. But it was a miscarriage. It doesn't even compare to having a baby for almost a year and then lose it to a trauma."

"Jaison, if it weren't for Teddy and Bernard, I don't know if I would have made it through. I was beside myself with guilt most of the time. Thank God they were their brother's keeper," Derrick said as he gave Bernard a pat on the back.

Terry sat and listened carefully to every word Derrick said. He stood, grabbed a soft drink, took a deep breath, and said, "I think a lot of times, in ministry we in general are ineffective because, first of all, we won't be transparent. No one has any idea what we have gone through. They view ministers as super saints, not realizing we all put our pants on the same way. We don't wake up out of the bed fully dressed and smelling fresh. We have to go by way of the shower just like everyone else."

He paused pondering if he should continue, which in fact, proved his previous point. "We're so afraid of the ridicule or rejection that may come, that we sit on our testimony. By doing that, we keep someone else in bondage. Stacy and I have gone through a lot. When I say a lot guys, I mean a lot. Some stuff Bernard knows about. But because he was single, some stuff I only shared with Jaison. I didn't want to influence him in any way when it came to marriage. But mostly, I was just too ashamed, because he sort of looked up to me. About six months into Stacy's pregnancy, I had affairs with more than one woman."

Bernard had a look of astonishment on his face. He glanced at Mike and then looked back at Terry.

Terry continued, "She found out about it right after she had the baby. I think if she wouldn't have had the baby, she probably would have left me. The crazy thing is, if you would have asked me at the time why I did it, or were the other women prettier or better than Stacy, I wouldn't have had an answer to the first question. And they definitely weren't prettier or better. I just didn't have any idea why I did it. I was happy ay home so it wasn't that. I had a wife who loved and satisfied me. Stacy is awesome in bed, so it wasn't that. My guilt eventually made me stop. But even after she found out, my desire for both of the other women was still there."

He had Michael Thomas's undivided attention. He knew all too well how Terry felt. Even though he had not touched Cathy since they were deployed a year ago, nor thought of her. He knew the desire to roam outside of his marriage still lingered. He chastised himself often for allowing his thoughts to go to a place that would surely condemn his marriage forever. He hung on Terry's every word, because he knew his true deliverance was in Terry's testimony.

Terry continued, "But last year when the teens came over, and we ministered to them in Paris, God was yelling at me in my spirit-man. *"THIS IS WHY YOU DID IT!"* Guys, there were too many different women in my spirit. Too many for me to ever be happy with just one. I had too many soul ties. I talked to Stacy about it after everyone left to go back to the states, and Bernard left for Afghanistan. We prayed and there was a power in our bedroom as I denounced all the women I had slept with. It was almost overwhelming. I could feel the separation taking place in my spirit. I felt like I was going through a meat grinder. Afterwards, I felt light. Before that, it were as though all the women I had slept with were hanging on my shoulders, and I carried them with me everywhere, including into my marriage bed."

Bernard studied Michael. He could see the wheels turning and knew Terry had given Michael the tool he needed for total deliverance. He wasn't sure how Michael felt about his affair being exposed, so he didn't say a word to him.

Terry continued on, "The mistake I made, was thinking that getting married would force me to settle down. If you're not saved, what makes you think that getting married will make you stop sleeping with a bunch of women? It's not going to change anything because your nature hasn't changed. That's why a few years ago I threw myself into God. I knew it was going to take the blood of Jesus and the love of God to cleanse me. I was partially right, but I still had not dealt with the root of my problem and therefore, I still struggled until last year. The thing you say you will never do again. You *will* do again if you don't allow God to deal with every aspect of your issue.

"Wow," Michael thought. He shook his head to himself but didn't say a word. Bernard glanced at him from time to time.

Terry continued, "You have to allow Him to dig out the root of your problem and destroy it. My loins and soul were out of control and the reason why was because I didn't own all of them. Bits and pieces of me were spread all over the world. I went through so many women at the academy that I lost count. Not only there, but every duty station I got orders to. When I met Stacy, she was all that, and I finally decided to settle down with just one girl. I wined and dined her, and she was the one pushing for sex, so I thought I had it under control. The devil had just taken a reprieve on me. He jumped on me so hard in the first year of my marriage. Next thing I know, it was back to the old Terry."

He sighed and continued, "That thing hurt Stacy so bad. I alienated her in the marriage. She would say to me that she no longer knew how to satisfy me. She wondered if I really wanted her or the other women and said that one woman would never be enough for me. She said she didn't know how to be my wife anymore. She lost nearly twenty pounds in about ten days. I don't think she consumed the equivalent of a single meal the whole ten days. It was so awkward between us. We didn't know what to say to each other. I would hear her as she lay in the baby's room in the middle of the floor and cry almost every night. I think if it would have been just one woman, it would have been easier. But I was with two women when she found out. Right there in the unit. It crushed her. Eventually, Stacy told Tasha, so I really didn't have a choice but to tell Jaison. I was so ashamed of my actions. I didn't want anyone to know. I wanted to continue being known as this got it all together minister and fighter jet pilot. But inside, I was everything but together. Bernard, I never told you because you were single. You had just separated from Hayes and jumped into God hard following me and Jaison. Your cousin had come to visit, and you were going strong in God. I'm glad I didn't tell you now, because you were getting set up for Talinda, and you needed to be focused. I didn't want to look in your face and tell you that had I slept around on Stacy. I knew how you felt about my wife and Tasha. They're like your sisters. Every time I looked in her eyes all I saw was hurt. And it killed me knowing that I was the reason for the pain. I couldn't do anything about it. I felt helpless and hopeless. I knew if she was going to be mended, it would take God. I threw myself into the church and stayed on my knees at the altar. I thank God he spared my marriage in spite of me."

Bernard continued to glance at Michael from time to time. Other than having multiple partners, Terry was telling Michael's story. Michael shook his head and again mouthed the word "wow". He knew Michael probably wouldn't say anything in front of the group. But as much as he was shocked, and a little upset with his friend Terry, he was grateful for his testimony. It was just what Mike needed. He knew they would probably have a discussion about it sooner or later.

Trevor shook his head and said, "Wow Terry. Everything you said is—wow. Thank you for sharing. I mean, I don't know you that well, but you're right. In ministry, Because of fear and shame, we hold back what may help another brother out. That's why I'm grateful for the men here at Grace. We usually let it all hang out at the meetings. I mean I haven't had an affair, and it's the furthest thing from my mind, but I sometimes think about past girlfriends and entertain the thought a little longer than what is healthy. And find myself saying I'm glad they are on the other side of the country where I attended medical school, and not here. I know now it's a soul tie that I need to pray to God about and denounce. So I can get them completely out of my system. Wow, thanks again."

Terry nodded. He looked at Bernard for some sort of reaction to what he had just exposed about his infidelity. Bernard walked over to him and hugged him. "I love you Terry. Nothing is going to change that." He released him and continued, "My respect for Stacy just went through the roof. I would have never guessed your marriage was ever in jeopardy. From the outside looking in, it seemed perfect. I even envied it. I remember thinking if Hayes could be half the woman that Stacy was, then we would have been alright. Then Brandon came to visit, and I knew Hayes was definitely not wife material. At least not my wife anyway."

Derrick came back into the discussion and said, "Yeah. I'm with Trevor. I love the men here at Grace. I was broken when I came here. I had zero hope in getting Nevette back."

Trevor out of the blue, said looking in Derrick's direction mostly, "There is this guy who sent Lindsay a note and a dozen roses—"

"Whaaaaat?" Bernard interjected.

"Yeah, that's what I said," Trevor replied. "She thought they were from me and called to thank me. We discussed it, and I could hear the uneasiness in her voice that someone may be stalking her. But also I think she wondered if I thought she was seeing someone. But after a few weeks of her receiving the flowers, she hadn't received another gift, so we chalked it up to an overly aggressive but grateful client who had a poor choice of words, considering she's a married woman. I'm convinced it was someone on the team that sent them to test the water, but backed off after she didn't respond. She was going to bring them home and throw them away. I told her no, after I come check them out, you need to throw them away right there. So whoever sent them will see that you're not interested. So I went up there, and we talked loudly in the hall about them and went out through the locker room and threw them out with a few players watching. I knew it could have just as easily pissed the person off. So I'm not going to lie, I had one of my doctor friends who works with the team as well, keep an eye out on how the guys interacted with her. To let me know if one of them was overly friendly. With what happened with you and Nevette, I'm wasn't putting anything past anybody."

"Exactly man. Don't take any chances with your family," Derrick replied.

Upstairs the girls were teasing Nevette the same way the guys started in on Derrick earlier before the conversation turned serious.

Talinda said to Nevette, "Girl you look happy. I mean happier than you've been since Derrick woke up and came home from the hospital."

Lindsay responded in a school girl tone, "I bet I know why."

"Lindsay! Girl stop it—he is still recovering," Nevette replied in an attempt to camouflage her weekend with Derrick.

Lindsay came back at her, "Not according to what he said in church today. Miss *"laid her hands on me, and I was all better."* She ended with a sarcastic, 'I told you so' gesture. Everybody laughed.

Stacy smiled and winked at Tasha as she said to Nevette, "Girl, those sure are some cute boots you have on."

Tasha leaned over and said, "Yeah, nice and shiny. Mmmm hmm—just like we thought."

"What?" Nevette asked curiously.

Lindsay replied, "*Justice* done knocked the dust off them boots!"

"Oooo stop y'all!" Talinda said as she laughed out loud.

Nevette replied as she gave herself a pat on the stomach, "Well, if all goes as prayed, Justice and I will find out shortly if I'm pregnant. I haven't been on birth control since the week Callisha went missing. Up until this weekend. It's been nearly a year since we were intimate."

"A year? Girl please! His little soldiers are in double time, forget marching. You're probably pregnant so, I'm going to just say congratulations to you now," Tasha replied.

They all burst out laughing and as though he were on cue, Derrick walked into the kitchen to get more ice for downstairs from the freezer in the garage. They looked at him like the cat who ate the canary.

He smiled and said, "Why do I get the feeling that you ladies were talking about me just before I came in?"

Lindsay said with a snicker, "Probably because we were."

Nevette smiled and put her head down. He smiled and said, "Naythia baby, I can't believe you're letting them talk about me. You know you're gonna pay for that later right?"

He winked at her and gave her a knowing look, then turned and walked out to the garage without waiting for a response.

Talinda looked down at her boots again and said, "Yeah, nice and shiny." They all cracked up laughing.

All Nevette could do was laugh. They waited for Derrick to get the ice and return to the basement before they continued their conversation.

"On a more serious note," Nevette addressed Lindsay to get the sarcastic heat off of her. "Lindsay what is it with the flowers some guy other than Trevor sent to you. Remember, you were telling me about a few weeks ago?"

"I don't know y'all. It gave me the creeps. I was looking at every guy on the team differently for a while. Those are generally the only guys I'm around other than Trevor. But then when I didn't receive anything else, I figured the person realized I wasn't going to respond to him and gave up. I haven't heard or received anything since," Lindsay replied.

"That's good," Talinda replied. "But nonetheless. Be careful and watchful girl."

"Yes, I am Talinda," Lindsay replied.

"Yeah girl, take no chances," Nevette said. "One thing I know for sure. You just never know how flipped out someone is until you push the wrong button."

"You mean like Suzette did with you when she walked into Derrick's hospital room? Yogi told me how you beat her down," Lindsay teased.

"Lindsay girl—y'all—I don't know what came over me. I heard her voice from the bathroom, and rage came into the room and took over. She pointed that gun at me and was squeezing the trigger when Yogi jumped her and they hit the floor. I pounced on her. The next thing I heard was Yogi yelling, *"Nevette stop, you're going to kill her"*. By the time we finished struggling on the floor with her, Derrick and his bed were slammed up against the window! You know I never understood how people could plead temporary insanity when they went off and killed someone. But that's exactly what happened to me. All I wanted was to end her life the way she ended Callisha's, accident or not. You just never know what you are capable of until you're thrust into the situation."

Tasha added, "Wow. Some people, with their actions can just take you there, right up to the point of no return and dare you to jump over the edge. They push every button you have and invent some more to push!"

"Amen to that!" Gloria replied. They laughed as they raised their glasses as though in a toast.

"Gloria, I'm so glad you and Michael decided to come up this weekend," Talinda said.

"I have had so much fun. Michael and I are so new to Christianity. The church we attend in Warner Robbins is a little traditional. We thoroughly enjoyed the service today. But more than that, we realized we don't have to lose our personalities to be Christians," Gloria replied.

Lindsay added, "Yeah. I think people have the wrong impression of Christians and their lifestyles. They have the misconception that our worlds are perfect. They don't understand it's not that we don't go through anything, but it's how we deal with it and carry ourselves as we go through."

"Exactly," Stacy replied. "One thing I learned early in my Christian walk, is to be careful what you pray to God about. I used to always admire how graceful and elegantly my pastor's wife carried herself. Nothing ever seemed to ruffle her feathers. She always handled even the worse situations with grace. I remember vaguely praying to God that I wanted to be a woman of grace and elegance like that. Well, I learned that the only way to know that you have been blessed with your desire in the Lord, is to be tested."

Tasha smiled proudly at her friend because she knew what she was about to disclose. She knew that Stacy only shared her testimony when she felt the urging of the Holy Spirit, and it would minister to the audience in her immediate vicinity. She looked around the room and wondered who the message was for. She knew Nevette had handled the situation with her husband Derrick poorly, but she had the feeling that someone else in the room needed to hear what Stacy was about to say.

Stacy continued, "About six months into my pregnancy. My husband was having an affair, and I found out just after I delivered our son. Not just with one woman, but with two." You could hear a pin drop. Gloria stopped midstream of swallowing a nice heaping spoonful of apple cobbler.

Talinda was more than surprised. She shook her head in disbelief and said, "Stacy, the way you loved on Terry and how close you all seemed when I was there visiting Bernard in Germany, I would have never thought—I mean there always just seems to be a little something there with women whose husbands have had an affair. You can tell there is animosity between them. Even when they try to fake it in front of everyone else. But you really love Terry. I mean you're submissive, not snappy. You don't treat him like he owes you the world and better pay you back for what he did. I mean...when I was there the first time you had to be—"

"Still dealing with it. And ohh, I had my moments and still do now. But never in public. It's been just over a year since I found out about it. The one thing my mom taught me was never let everyone know what's going on in your house. Long after you forgive him, others will still be mad at him. The truth of the matter is Talinda; I surprised myself. I wasn't exactly what you called elegant growing up. I was the one sista that would let you know when you made a wrong move. I was so hurt. In my mind, the scenario to bash his head open kept playing over and over like a bad low-budget film. But I didn't yell, didn't scream, and didn't throw vases and lamps around the room or at him. None of the things people assume black women do when faced with this type of situation. I think I was just too numb. I was still battling with denial. At first, the only reason I stayed was because of the baby. Taking care of Terry was my life, and I looked forward to stepping away from cosmetology and being a full-time mom and house wife. It's not like we needed the money. I did it solely because I wanted to be independent still. Then the idea of divorce looming over our heads demanded that I continue to work. I don't think men realize what they do to a woman when they have an affair. They don't understand that everything she is, is wrapped up inside of her relationship with her husband."

She paused to sigh while shaking her head with a conquering

smile on her face. "I didn't know whether I was coming or going guys. I felt like I needed to earn my keep around the house. I was on my hands and knees scrubbing the kitchen floor only to lay down in the middle of it while it was still wet, balled up in a knot screaming. For months I didn't tell anyone. I was too ashamed. Ashamed that I couldn't keep nor satisfy my husband and he had to go elsewhere for satisfaction. I crucified myself on a daily basis. All of a sudden, I looked in the mirror and all I saw was an ugly fat slob who allowed herself to get pregnant and lose her shape. My self-esteem went through the basement. If it wasn't for having to take care of the baby, I probably would have lost my mind. I made love to him because I was afraid that if I didn't, that would be more reason for him to go back to them. I lost nearly twenty pounds in ten days, I couldn't keep anything down. I felt like if I ate more than a few tablespoons of food that I would throw up. Heck, every time I looked at him I wanted to throw up. So my pre-pregnancy shape was back but I still felt like a fat slob. I finally told Tasha because I just had to tell somebody. I felt like I was losing my mind. Before the affairs, we used to go on long drives and just talk. After the affairs, we barely said ten words to each other for days at a time. I think Terry wasn't sure what to say or do any more than I was. It's been right at a year and a half now since I found out, and I still struggle from time to time. I ridiculed myself for not getting over it quickly. I kept saying to myself, it's been a year Stacy, why are you still dealing with it like it just happened yesterday? Well, to me it had. I think people in ministry make a grave mistake by telling people to just get over stuff. Well, if I could get over it, I wouldn't be coming to you *Mr. or Mrs. Minister*! I think that's just a cop out for not wanting to sacrifice the time it may take to minister someone through their issue. So their answer is, get over it. Well, some things aren't so easy to get over. Women have to allow themselves time to grieve their marriage. Because the marriage they knew and loved is now dead. You have to blow up the old foundation and build from scratch. At first, Terry wanted to just pick up where we left off. But I'm grateful to Jaison who told him it's not that easy. What we had before didn't work obviously. He kept saying, it wasn't you baby, it wasn't you. You didn't do anything wrong. You were the perfect wife. THEN WHY IN THE HECK DID YOU GO SLEEP WITH TWO WOMEN! It took me nearly a year to come to grips that Terry's affairs were because of inner issues that didn't have a lot to do with me. We still have our moments of awkwardness, and he still has moments where he tries to buy his way out of it. I tell him, Terry don't try and buy me. Just love me and be faithful to our relationship. If it's going to work, the cheating spouse is going to have to agree to be an open book. Terry knows that he can't have passwords on any of his devices. He can't be on any social media sites. I told him I didn't trust him to be on anybody's social media site where you can have private relationships and conversations with women that I don't know about. If the man truly wants his marriage and wife back, he'll submit to what makes her feel secure in the relationship. If he doesn't, I would question his sincerity in reestablishing trust, moving forward in the marriage and remaining monogamous. I surprised myself with how I handled it. Growing up, I was feisty and usually fought at the drop of a hat. One day during one of my many bouts with tears and asking God why he allowed this, I remembered that I prayed to God about being elegant and graceful and showing mercy no matter the circumstance. I thought, wow, I'm right smack in the middle of prayer 101. How would I know that God had molded me into the person I desired to be without a test? I remember laughing at God and saying, I would have been okay with it if He had taken a much less hurtful route."

Everyone managed to laugh at the statement while wiping tears from their eyes. She ministered to them on so many levels. Gloria was about to totally lose it. She fought to keep herself from dropping to the floor and melting into a puddle.

Talinda walked over to her and placed her hand on Gloria's shoulder. Her touch was overwhelming and Gloria completely lost it. She all but screamed as though having a conversation with herself but with an audience, "YOU KEEP THINKING THAT YOU'RE SO STRONG. THAT YOU CAN TAKE ANYTHING. YOU SUPPRESS YOUR FEELINGS SO THAT OTHERS WILL FEEL COMFORTABLE AROUND YOU. YOU GET THIS SUPERFICIAL COUNSELING FROM PEOPLE WHO HAVE ABSOLUTELY NO IDEA HOW YOU REALLY FEEL. AND SO YOU SMILE—YOU SMILE THROUGH THE HURT AND PUNISH YOURSELF FOR NOT JUST GETTING OVER IT. YOU LOVE HIM. BY GOD, HE'S THE FATHER OF YOUR CHILDREN. BUT AT THE SAME TIME YOU HATE HIM. NOT JUST HIM. YOU HATE WHAT HE DID TO YOU. WHAT HE FORCED YOU TO BECOME. WHAT HE DID TO THE FAMILY, THE RELATIONSHIP, THE MARRIAGE. THE BLATANT DISRESPECT AND DISREGARD TO YOU AND WHAT THE RING ON YOUR FINGER STANDS FOR. YOU SAVED YOURSELF JUST FOR HIM. AND HE TRAMPLED ON YOUR GIFT OF VIRGINITY LIKE YESTERDAY'S NEWS. AND DEEP INSIDE, YOU'RE JUST HAPPY THAT HE EVEN ACKNOWLEDGES YOU AGAIN. SO YOU DO WHAT YOU'RE COUNSELED, AND DISMISS HIS BAD BEHAVIOR. AND YOU START TO JUST—GET OVER IT." She paused and whispered almost exhausted, "I just want to be free from the hurt of his affair. I just want to be whole again."

"Oh my God!" Stacy exclaimed. "I knew it. I could feel it. The hurt—I could feel the hurt in this room. Even in the midst of the teasing and laughing, I could feel it. I didn't think it was Nevette, so I knew it had to be you or Lindsay."

Talinda knelt down on the floor where everyone else had already gathered, "We need to pray for restoration of your spirit and emotions Gloria. You need God to mend the holes in your body that the affair left behind that you are trying to fill with routine."

"Don't get me wrong guys. He is doing everything he is supposed to be doing. But I realize after listening to Stacy that I never mourned my marriage. I never dealt with my hurt," Gloria replied. "Michael and I decided we were going to drive here weekly for Sunday service until his final out date from the Air Force. That's the real reason we came this week. We are also house hunting for when he retires. I need what you all have. Most of all, I need peace. I need God's peace that passes understanding."

Talinda laid her hand on Gloria's shoulder and lifted the other toward heaven as she began to pray:

Father,

We come before you in the matchless name of Jesus Christ our Lord and Savior. Whose precious blood was shed for our victory. We claim rights to that victory for our sister Gloria. We thank You for the peace that was bought with Your chastisement. We thank you for the healing that was purchased through the stripes You bore on Calvary. Jesus we pray right now for the peace that passes understanding. We pray that You will mend Gloria from the inside out. She is Your creation God and You are well able to repair what You created. As she lies here God bless her. Reward her for her virtue and grace. Give her double reward for the mercy and understanding she extended to her husband during his time of infidelity. Father draw them closer together like never before. Complete that which You have started in her life.

We thank You for Stacy in her obedience to share with us on today Lord. Continue to bless her and Terry Lord and grant them their every petition about their marriage. God we thank You for covering and protecting Lindsay in the situation on her job. God we know that You have her in the palm of Your hand. And Lord we again thank You for blessing Derrick and Nevette. For sparing his life Lord and restoring their marriage. What the devil meant for bad in our lives. You indeed have made it good. Lord we thank You for blessing Tre as well. Through it all Lord he has been an exceptional little boy. Truly, Your word says, All things work together for our good. You didn't say that it would all be good, but that it, however painful, will be used by You to bless us. The end of a thing thereof is better than the beginning. Lord, we await for an expected great end.

In Jesus' infallible name,

Amen

Jaison stood just outside the kitchen on the steps. He was just about to enter when he heard Talinda praying. He tiptoed back down the steps. "Whew, the women are up there praying and laid out in the floor. So we're going to have to wait on more snacks."

"Wow, Bernard you know what that means. Who is in the center of the circle?" Derrick asked.

"It looked like Gloria but you really couldn't tell. They were all just gathered on the floor," Jaison replied.

Michael looked at Bernard and remained silent. He prayed that Gloria was indeed being ministered to. He knew that things were going well between them, but he also knew that Gloria still wasn't whole from the affair. He lowered he head and gave silent thanks to God that Gloria was finally with a group of women who could minister to her. And also men whom he could come clean with and as well. He knew they had come a long way but still had a long way to go. He was looking forward to becoming a part of Grace Tabernacle and the powerful men's ministry they had.

After the ladies finished praying with Gloria, she exchanged numbers with everyone. She was excited to know that Stacy, Terry, Tasha and Jaison would all be stationed at Warner Robbins. She looked forward to the many dinners their families would have together. Finally, she knew God heard her prayer, because he indeed sent Stacy into her life.

The girls soon joined the guys downstairs where more teasing of Derrick and Nevette's apparent intimate weekend filled the air with laughter. Raymond and the teens had the smaller children in the game and theater rooms for most of the evening until it was time to eat. They all sat around in the basement living area, at tables, on couches, chairs and some on the floor in a family gathering type of setting. They enjoyed good fellowship as they ate. Terry stroked Stacy's cheek, looked deep in her eyes and told her that he loved her. Talinda and Bernard watched and smiled.

After dinner, Michael and Gloria thanked everyone for their hospitality as they hugged them and left heading back to Warner Robbins. Derrick and Nevette gathered up Tre and said goodbye as well. Terry, Stacy, Tasha and Jaison were all staying with the Travis' and they stayed up a little while longer talking. Talinda was excited that she would again see Stacy and Tasha on a regular basis now with them both stationed at Robbins Air Base. They followed each other their whole careers with the exception of one or two deployments and permanent changes of station.

~Chapter Nine~

Talinda turned to Bernard and said, "Tasha, Stacy and I are going to go straighten up the kitchen and get the kids all ready for bed while you guys finish putting things away down here."

"Okay babe, that's sounds like a plan," Bernard replied.

Talinda gathered up the twins and Tasha and Stacy both grabbed their kids as they headed upstairs to put them all in the tub and settled down for the night. They bunked their kids down in the twins' rooms.

Raymond was edgy as they picked up around the basement. He went to straighten up in the theatre room to avoid contact with Bernard, Terry and Jaison.

Bernard called, "Okay Raymond we're done. I'm going to head upstairs to help your mom bathe the twins."

"Hey dad—wait—can I talk to you for a second?" Raymond asked.

"Sure son. I get the feeling we need to sit down for this," he said as he walked into the theatre room where Raymond was and took a seat. Terry and Jaison looked at each other, and Jaison said, "Okay we're going to sit out here and give you guys some privacy.

Raymond dropped his head and breathed in heavily. He breathed out with a sigh, "No Uncle Jaison and Uncle Terry. I would like for you to come in as well."

After they sat down in the theatre room Raymond said, "I guess there is no easy way of getting around this, so I should just come straight to the point."

"About what son?" Bernard asked.

"Before I left the house on a mission to go kill Quavis something happened that I think you and mom should know about. You were in Warner Robbins that day at the Air Base. It was the last day you were officially in the Air Force and mom and the twins came down for the ceremony. I made up a lame excuse about why I couldn't make it because I knew I wanted to go try and find out about Quavis. Plus the teens were meeting at the skating rink that afternoon as well. LaNiesha came over, and we were going to drive to the skating rink together. I got the call right before she came about the hit on my mother. I was devastated and angry. I said things to her that I shouldn't have in my anger—"

"Oh so that's the tension between you two," Bernard interjected. "I was wondering why you two have seemed so distant from each other lately."

Jaison read his body language and knew what Raymond was about to tell his dad. Raymond glanced up at them, and he knew

Jaison had caught on to where he was going with this. Bernard was in denial.

"Yeah. But dad that's not the reason we are distant. I was so out of character, and I was acting like a Knight in every way. I made her feel like if she didn't have sex with me, then she didn't support me, and I didn't need her in my life," Raymond replied. He hoped his father would fill in between the lines, but he had no such luck. Bernard was going to make him say the words.

"Oh, so she left upset with you and now you guys are, what? Trying to figure out if you're going to be together? I was wondering why today was the first day I had seen her over here since you returned home," Bernard replied.

"Not exactly dad," Raymond replied with hesitation in his voice. He swallowed hard, took a deep breath and just said it, "We had sex that day. We didn't use any protection. She thought she was pregnant, but her cycle started, and she's not. I found out she wasn't pregnant the same day Reginald told us about Sarah. I am not going to touch her again dad—I swear."

Bernard just starred at Raymond. He sighed and took a deep breath. He let it out. He had his pointer fingers pointed up, and all others pointed down as he nodded sliding his hands up and down his face. He was breathing heavily.

Raymond sat in silence. He waited for Bernard to explode all over him. He was disappointing his father on every hand.

Bernard dropped his head and ran his hands back and forth from the front to the back.

Terry said to Bernard, "Come on Bernard, think before you speak."

"Yeah, and then, don't speak from your disappointment," Jaison added.

Raymond was instantly grateful that his dad's best friends and adopted uncles were present.

Bernard looked at Raymond and sighed, "I'm sitting here thinking. How can a kid, who is not my biological son, nationality, and has only been in my life for just over a year, be exactly like me at eighteen years old?"

He looked at Terry and Jaison as though he needed them as co-signers to what he as saying. He continued, "Raymond you know what we said to you in Paris. You know it's not going to be as easy as you saying, I'm not going to touch her anymore. You do realize that right? I mean, it was different when you took a vow of abstinence with Brandon coming out of the Knights, because you didn't have any feelings whatsoever about the women you slept with. And you really didn't even want to do it. But it's different with LaNiesha. She's your girlfriend. You realize that this will change the freedom you have with her. There is going to be no more sitting in your room talking. And its group dates or nothing for you two for a while. Everything you do with her will be public until you regain your mother's and my trust again.

And it's not going to come easy. I'll tell your mother when I go upstairs. We'll probably talk about it and your lack of responsibility more as a family tomorrow. But not tonight. Go on and take your shower son, and then get ready for bed."

Raymond whispered, "Yes Sir." He had tears in his eyes and looked as though he would blow any minute. "Dad—Uncle Terry—Uncle Jaison. I'm sorry. I broke every vow I made to my father before he died. I told him I would never have another gun in my hand with the intent to hurt anyone, and that I wouldn't have sex again until my wedding night among other things. Dad, I pointed a gun at you with mom and the twins just a few steps away. Then I all but forced LaNiesha to have sex. I don't deserve—"

He couldn't finish his sentence. Bernard stood and walked over to him and said, "Raymond look at me son."

Raymond shook his head no, as tears began to fall to the ground. Bernard pulled him up against his chest and just held him.

"I'M SO SORRY DAD! I'M SO SORRY! I JUST MADE A MESS OF EVERYTHING!" he exclaimed as he allowed his father the comfort him.

"Come on Raymond. You know you're not the first teenager in be in this situation. And sadly, you probably won't be the last. Raymond you can't go back and undo anything. All you can do is repent and move forward son," Bernard declared.

Terry and Jaison said "Amen" to Bernard's words. They knew Raymond didn't need more lectures. He needed the comfort of a father in the midst of his confusion and disappointment with himself. They prayed with Raymond and then Bernard told him to go on to bed. He told Raymond that he would inform his mother once he got upstairs. He met Stacy and Tasha on the stairs coming down as he was going up. They said goodnight and headed on downstairs. Once they were in their rooms their husbands filled them in on their conversation with Raymond.

Bernard entered one of the twin's bedrooms just as Talinda was laying them down for the night. The boys were in BJ's room and the girls there in Latricia's room. He kissed Latricia and accompanied Talinda to the master bedroom. He stopped off by Brandon Jr.'s room on the way to kiss him goodnight as well. They turned on the monitors so they could hear the kids should they wake during the night.

Bernard told Talinda about his conversation with Raymond. To his surprise, she already had an idea that Raymond and LaNiesha had crossed the sex barrier.

"I caught a glimpse of them looking at each other with guilty eyes while Reginald was talking about Sarah. They were very quiet and it was written all over their faces," Talinda replied.

"Why did I think you would handle this differently Talinda?" Bernard stated as though asking a question.

"I think before Reginald and Sarah disclosed their situation. I would have taken it differently. Our teens live in a very tempting world.

Now I'm not condoning their behavior but what they need is understanding and ministry," Talinda replied.

"Okay so Miss Grace and Understanding, are you saying we shouldn't punish him?" Bernard asked.

"ARE YOU KIDDING? GROUND THAT LITTLE JOKER FOR LIFE! HE'LL THINK TWICE BEFORE HE PULLS HIS LITTLE STUFF OUT OF HIS PANTS TO DO ANYTHING BUT GO TO THE BATHROOM WITH IT!" Talinda exclaimed.

Bernard broke out laughing, "Girl, you've been married to me for too long. Don't worry baby. I talked to him about a few things that would change. I told him you and I would discuss it further with him. Sweetheart, he cried like a baby. I don't think anything we can do or say to him would make him feel any worse than he does right now. I don't want him to get depressed over his actions the last few months," Bernard replied.

Talinda smiled and hugged Bernard as she said, "You've been married to me too long."

He smiled and kissed her, "Mmmmm—dang girl. You are so sweet. Let's hit the shower and go to bed."

"Oooo—that sounds great Mr. Travis," she replied as she returned his kiss.

Downstairs after Raymond settled into the theatre room where he was bunking while they had guests. He called LaNiesha and informed her that he had told his dad, who in turn would tell his mom. He told her they would probably have zero privacy for a while which was probably a good idea anyway. He ached for her and didn't trust himself to be alone with her. He knew what he needed most was to get back in right standing with God and spend time in His presence. They talked for a while. He told her that his parents would probably want her to come over so they could discuss their new boundaries and everything soon. He also told her that he was sure his mom would probably call hers in the near future. So if she hadn't told her mom about them, she should. She informed him that she talked to her mom about it a few days ago. She said she wasn't upset by it because she already assumed that LaNiesha was sexually active anyway. She reminded Raymond that her mom wasn't a Christian and didn't have the same values as his parents. They were both glad their secret was out. They said goodnight to each other and hung up.

*****

On the way home, Gloria and Michael drove in silence for nearly twenty minutes before either of them spoke. Michael finally broke the eerie silence that threatened to take over the entire ride home. They knew the boys were in the back asleep, so he said that they would talk when they got home. After they got the boys all settled they went to the living room and curled up on the couch with a hot cup of tea.

"I guess I don't have to wonder what you're thinking Gloria," Michael said.

She smiled slightly, "Yeah. I suppose you guys heard us upstairs when we were praying. Well, they were praying. I was lying in the floor crying uncontrollably."

"Actually no we didn't," Michael replied. "One of the guys went up for something and came back down and told us. They said you guys were laid out praying, and God was ministering. He said he thought you were in the middle of the circle. I just kept quiet because I really didn't know what to say. But I was glad that God was ministering to you. I have long since known that you needed more than what the ministers at our church were providing for you. I was thrilled when Terry said that he Stacy and the other couple would be at Robbins Air Base. It was like a breath of fresh air. I mean, I know we have been doing well the last year. At least, I thought we were doing well. Then Terry said some things that blew me away. It was like I finally understood how you felt about Cathy. The hurt, pain and humiliation of knowing that I blatantly threw her in your face. It was like he thrust me back into the midst of the affair and made me face things I had strategically ignored and forced you to move past without dealing with. Mostly, because of my own guilt and shame."

"I know how you feel," she replied. "Upstairs Stacy was giving her version. It was as if she read my thoughts and verbally expressed how I secretly felt. I was about to explode as she spoke. There was so much I wanted to talk about but everyone we spoke with in Robbins during our counseling sessions, just kept pushing my feelings to the back burner. They were so interested in checking the blocks and bragging on how they saved our marriage that no one ever bothered to allow me to grieve the part of our marriage that died. It was like a death in the family, and I needed you to understand that I needed to grieve it Michael."

"I know that now baby," he replied. He reached his hand over and placed it on top of hers. "I'm so grateful to God that you didn't leave me. I just wanted to it to be over and for us to get back to normal. But listening to Terry, I realized that we can't just have or go back to normal. Normal was broken because Cathy happened. The thought of being exposed plagued me every day. I figured the quicker we put it behind us the less my chance of exposure. Cathy had already left the base, and I just wanted to be done with it. You appeared happy, and I fooled myself into believing that you were. We will sit down and write out funeral arrangements for our old busted marriage, and then we will have a private ceremony and bury it. I will minister to you through the grieving process, and we will build our new foundation through Jesus Christ and His holy word, once and for all."

Tears rolled down her face as she said, "Okay. I love you Michael. I really do. I don't want you to doubt that. I don't want you to think that the last year hasn't been great because it has. I just never dealt with my emotions. Everything happened so fast. You came back from Afghanistan a different man and just threw your love at me. I was spinning in circles but happy all the same that my husband actually wanted me. Yes, we need to finalize things and set the standard on our marriage. Wow, we really are going to make it. We really are going to be healed and happy."

"Yes we are baby," Michael replied. He lifted her hand up to his mouth and kissed the back of it.

They continued to talk as they finished their tea and then went to bed. The next day when she woke, Michael was already at the kitchen table. He had started to write out the details and notes for the funeral arrangements for the affair and their old marriage. Some things about the affair he had never disclosed to her. She joined him, and they talked for most of the day. They boys were out with friends playing so they took advantage of the time alone and just let God lead them. They prayed, and God gave Michael vision for their home and marriage.

After they wrote out all the feelings, emotions, hurts and pains of the affair. They folded the paper and placed it in an envelope. Michael prayed over it, and together they lit a lighter underneath the tip of the envelope and sent it to a crematory death. Michael wrote out the vision for their home and marriage and placed them in two small picture frames after Gloria typed and printed out two copies. He placed them in their bedroom on the night stands beside the bed so it would be the first and last thing each of them saw every day.

He kissed her and began to gently caress her body. She teased that the boys would probably be home any minute, so they wouldn't have time to make love. He laughed as he locked the bedroom door and declared they would be outside for hours but locking the door was just in case, and made sweet love to his wife.

*****

Derrick and Nevette lay in bed when they got home from Bernard and Talinda's house.

"Come here baby. Snuggle up close to me," Derrick said as he pulled Nevette in close to him.

"Mmmm feels so good lying next to you without wondering if I'm hurting you. I missed this so much," Nevette said.

"Baby I don't have words enough to describe how much I've missed you," Justice replied. "There's something I want to talk to you about. I really would like for you to consider staying home with this baby."

"I knew this conversation was coming. I knew you weren't going to want me to work after I had Zoé," Nevette replied as she snuggled in even closer to Derrick.

"Ahhh no, actually I meant I want you to stop working now. I don't want you to wait until after you have Zoé. I don't want you to go back to work at all," Derrick declared.

She took a deep breath as she gingerly asked, "You always did want me to be a stay at home mom. Is it open for discussion?"

He smiled and kissed her on the forehead, "Of course it's open for discussion. Baby, it's your career."

"Well, I would like to keep my certification," she replied.

"Why baby?" he asked.

"Because I worked hard for it. You never know. When Zoé gets school age, I may want to go back to work," she replied in a pleading fashion.

"Yeah but by then, you'll be pregnant again. Sweetheart you know I want at least two maybe three more children. That means we will be having them in the next three to four years. I don't want my children in daycare. I want them home safe with their mother," Derrick countered.

"Justice just because they are with me, doesn't mean they are automatically going to be safe. As we saw with Callisha—life happens honey," Nevette said as she lightly caressed his chest to sooth his spirit.

"I know babe, but that's not all. I want our values instilled in them in the core and most influential learning phases of their lives. It's bad enough that you have to undo what they learn at public school on some issues. But that's not the main reason. When they are not able to express themselves or say this happened at school or that happened, you have to completely trust that the people that have your children are doing the correct thing with them at all times. I know I'm just a tad bit paranoid. But long before Callisha's incident, I didn't want you to work. This has always been my philosophy sweetheart," Justice replied.

"No you didn't," she replied with a smile as she continued to play in his chest. "I remember we had an in-depth discussion about it on our wedding night. And I have to admit. I have enjoyed being home and taking care of you and Tre this last month. I was able to go to school with Tre and be the room mom. He was so excited that his mother was finally able to be there. I really enjoyed doing it, and I realized just how much I was missing out on in his life by having such a demanding job. I thought for the first time, should I be working, or should I be a stay-at-home mom and take care of my children and husband. I was being rebellious and stubborn the first time you asked me. My argument was legitimate, but financially we didn't need then, nor do we now, require me to work outside the home. I admit that I was operating in an independent spirit. I always kind of put stay-at-home moms down a little bit. But I really love it. There are so many fulfillments in keeping the home, setting the tone, and taking care of my family. Most women today can't establish or set the tone in their home, because their husbands arrive home long before they do. I think sometimes women have come too far, and our value in the home has diminished. Well, maybe I can become private therapists, and we can convert a room downstairs."

"Baby what's your insecurity? Why do you feel that you have to work enough to keep this certification?" Justice asked.

"In one word—fear," she replied.

"Fear of what baby?" he asked.

"What if in a few years from now something else happens and we do divorce, or you pass away. Things that were so solid in my life a few years ago, are not so solid now," she replied.

"Naythia baby, you can't walk in fear. If I die, you and the babies won't have to worry about anything, you know I have that covered. We are not getting a divorce. If we made it through Suzette and Callisha, I don't think there's anything we can't make it through. Because we are going to communicate effectively. But God forbid we do, then it's called alimony and child support. Nevette you know I'm going to take care of my responsibility. You forget who my parents are," he replied and chuckled. "But seriously, I really want you to stay home baby. I want to come home to you greeting me with a kiss with a red hot teddy on, because mom and dad have the kids, and it's been a long week, and you miss your man. I want to come home to surprises and bring you surprises. I want to live inside of your creativity for our home. Baby please consider it."

"I don't have to consider it, think about it, or pray about it. Tomorrow I'll go turn in my letter of resignation," she replied and kissed his chest.

"Really?" he replied as a huge grin graced his face.

"Yes tomorrow. I'm going to stay home and be your wife Justice. And take care of this house and your babies. That's what you've always wanted anyway. Plus I'll get to spend more time with Talinda, volunteer at Tre's school and bring you lunch from time to time. Like I said, I've enjoyed the last month," Nevette replied.

"I love you baby. Are you sure? I don't want you to be unhappy sweetheart, or do this because you feel forced into it because of everything we've discussed this last month about our relationship," Derrick asked.

"I'm sure, and I'm happy," Nevette replied as she moved on top of him. She began to kiss him more passionately.

"Mmmm somebody wants to confirm little Zoé's entrance into her womb," Justice teased.

"No, someone just wants to make love to her husband. Like you so clearly put it in church today. With how hot and heavy we went at it all weekend. She is already in there," Nevette replied as she kissed him again.

"Ooooo," he said in between her kisses, "I don't remember using the words hot and heavy. But I'll take it any day."

She chuckled and continued to kiss him. The sweet aroma of love soon filled the air as yet again—two became one.

*****

Nevette sat at the doctor's office Friday afternoon on pins and needles. She couldn't wait for Dr. Yolanda Harrell to return with the official results. From the contents she threw up in the toilet from dinner the night before, she already knew she was pregnant with Zoé. She planned on having a special dinner for Justice that night. She was glad school was out because of teachers planning day, and she had a reason to allow Tre to sleep in or the jig would have been up. She barely made it into the bathroom as Justice walked out the door headed for work that morning.

"Well just as you thought Mrs. Goodfellow. You are indeed pregnant. We need to get you scheduled for prenatal care. Stop at the nurse's station on your way out to schedule your first OB appointment," Dr. Harrell said as she sat down across from Nevette. Nevette squealed in delight, touched her stomach and gave God thanks. "Now I understand that your mother-in-law has been the physician for all your deliveries thus far."

"Yes, although I saw an obstetrician regularly, she performed the deliveries, with the doctor present of course, barring any unforeseen turns," Nevette replied.

"I know Dr. Shaundra Goodfellow very well, so I'm sure we'll work wonderfully together," Dr. Harrell replied.

"Oh thank you doctor! I know you have other patients after me, so I'll stop at the desk to make an appointment," Nevette replied. She thanked and praised God as she walked down the hall to the reception area. As she rounded the corner, she heard the name "Lindsay Johnson" being called. She stopped in her tracks and turned just as Lindsay entered from the triage room. "Oh my God!" she thought.

She made her appointment and sat down to wait for Lindsay to come out of Dr. Harrell's office.

"Yes, I'm here to make my first appointment with Dr. Harrell. I left earlier so excited about the baby, that I forgot to make it," Talinda said as she stood at the reception areas.

"OH MY GOD TALINDA, YOU'RE PREGNANT!" Nevette yelled as she ran over to the desk.

"Yes girl, I found out earlier today. I was so excited I left out without making an appointment," Talinda replied. "Bernard has been a wonderful father to Raymond and the twins. But I know he still wants his own biological child. He just won't admit it. He keeps saying the three we have are enough."

"Girl you will never believe who I saw entering Dr. Harrell office as I was coming down the hallway to the reception desk. She was coming from triage and headed into Dr. Harrell's office. None other than Lindsay Johnson," Nevette replied with much excitement.

"Oh my God, really!" Talinda replied as she covered her mouth as though attempting to hide the smile on her face. "I wonder why she just didn't go to her husband. He's an obstetrician."

"She probably wants to surprise him. She said the other day they were talking about it. Or something like that," Nevette said.

"Wow, I can't wait to see the look on Derrick's face when I confirm that Zoé is safely tucked away. Hey, I was going to plan a special dinner for him tonight. Why don't we wait for Lindsay to come out, talk to her, and we'll tell the guys together tonight?" Nevette replied.

"That sounds wonderful. I mean, assuming that Lindsay is pregnant. She could just be on a women's yearly exam appointment," Talinda replied.

"Oh please. Trevor does those for her. No, she is hiding this from him. That must mean she at least thinks she's pregnant," Nevette said.

"That's true. I'll tell Bernard we're invited to the Goodfellows tonight for dinner. The twins are with Helen and Roger in Athens for a few days, and the teens have something planned. They are all stuck to each other like glue lately with all the fornicating going around in the group. Raymond talked to the teens about him and LaNiesha last Sunday. We told him he didn't have to. He said he and LaNiesha wanted to be accountable and felt they owed the group and youth leader's apologies. So it will just be me and Bernard," Talinda replied.

"Okay, I'll take Tre to his grandmothers, and we can make it a couple's night," Nevette said as she grabbed Talinda's hands like a school girl who just got asked out on her first date.

Just then Lindsay entered the reception area. Talinda and Nevette rushed over to her.

"Judging by the smile on your face. I will venture to say your test was positive Mrs. Johnson," Talinda said to Lindsay.

"Yes it is. Trevor and I are going to have a baby! I'm probably already about three to three and half months. I wanted to be sure. I kept thinking that maybe I was willing myself to be sick and missing my cycles. I have misused my body so much. All I could think of lately was the baby my mom and the deaconesses made me abort. I felt guilty and undeserving to expect God to bless me with another life. I was so scared to come take a test. I allowed myself to miss two cycles before I got the nerve," Lindsay replied. She was so excited she was about to burst.

"Oh my God Lindsay, really! You didn't say a word about it Sunday night. You said y'all were trying," Nevette squealed in delight.

"I know girl. I was too afraid to say anything. I was hoping and praying that I was," Lindsay replied.

Nevette touched her the on the shoulder as she said, "Girl you know that baby you aborted when you were fifteen was not your will or decision. Neither to conceive or to destroy. You are not the one who will have to give an account for that life. You were raped by your pastor and forced into aborting that baby. The people you should have been able to trust abused you."

"Wow, thanks Nevette. I really needed to hear that again. Sometimes you think you're completely over something until your thrust with a different aspect of it. As long as I wasn't trying to be anyone's wife or mother, the abortion part of the abuse didn't plague my mind with wild thoughts. But now I have Trevor, and I'm about to have his baby. CAN YOU BELIEVE IT?" Lindsay squealed in delight.

They filled Lindsay in on the dinner plans.

"That's awesome ladies. So how are we going to spring this news on the men?" Lindsay asked.

Nevette snapped her finger and pointed as she said, "I got it. After dinner, we'll play a riddle game. You know where you have to guess the riddle. After a few rounds, we give them the riddle, *"What's full of life and comes in three's".* They will rack their brains trying to figure it out."

"Trevor is going to be so excited. I can't wait to see his face when he finds out about the baby," Lindsay replied. She was close to tears. "Guys, I am too happy and so grateful to God. There was a time I thought I would never be where I am today. Heck, I didn't want to be where I am today. I was mad at the world. That is, until I met Nevette Naythia Graham—soon to be Goodfellow one hot afternoon in Athens, Georgia."

"Stop it Lindsay! You're going to make me cry," Nevette replied as she wiped the tears that were beginning to form in her eyes.

Talinda wiped her eyes too as she said, "Well, we had better get going. We have a dinner to plan. What's on the menu Nevette?"

"Girl the roast is already at home in the slow cooker. The veggies in cool water waiting to be stir fried. I have shrimp pasta on the menu. The soup will cook up in minutes and the salad is layered in the fridge. A cheesecake for dessert and sparkling cider chilling to celebrate. There will be enough for everyone, so I had this thing covered already. I prepared more than enough because I figured we would have left overs for a few days."

"Okay so Lindsay and I will each bring something for appetizers then," Talinda added.

"That sounds great. What time should we be over?" Lindsay asked.

"I'll call and take Tre to his grandmother's for the night soon as I get home. She is off today. By the time Justice gets home from work and showered it will be about six so let's say around six-thirty?" Nevette stated in question form.

They both agreed that sounded great. They hugged and departed on cloud nine. Nevette went by the store to grab a few additional bottles of sparkling cider and more shrimp, so she could make a larger portion of pasta and headed home. Tre was excited to spend the night at his grandparent's house. He loved playing with the kids in their neighborhood. There weren't a large amount of children his age where he lived with his parents. That was the main reason his mom drove him to school every day instead of allowing him to ride the bus. Not to mention, his grandparents had a game room just for him.

*****

"I can't believe you volunteered the information to your parents Raymond," Johnathan said. "I would have never told my parents I had sex with my girlfriend in my bedroom, unless they point blank asked me."

"I told my dad and he told my mom. But I think she already knew anyway somehow. Besides, I was feeling mega guilty about it guys," Raymond replied. "Of course LaNiesha and I have zero privacy now. We can't even *go* into my bedroom, door open or not. And we have to always be in a group on dates now too. I mean what can you expect? I blew it."

"We blew it," LaNiesha added. "It takes two to fornicate Raymond. Let's not forget who pushed the issue, after you said we shouldn't."

Lisa chimed in, "It doesn't matter who started what. You were both wrong. And we have to be each other's keepers the way we promised we would in Germany." She turned toward Sarah and said, "We're here for you girl. None of us are going to abandon you or Reginald. What's done is done and all that matters now is getting ready to be parents. We decided to go to the classes with you guys. This is all of our pregnancy, and we're going to support you all the way. We're not condoning nor advocating fornication. But we can't punish the innocent child by not supporting its parents and loving him or her to the fullest."

Sarah was in tears, "Thank you. You guys are the best."

"Yeah," Reginald added as he gave the guys a man's only type hug and handshake.

They headed into the bowling alley engaged in usual teen talk and enjoyed the evening. Sarah was surprisingly big for three and a half months, and Veronica had an ultrasound scheduled for her the following week.

*****

The Travis's and Johnson's both arrived at the Goodfellow's at six-thirty on the dot. They greeted each other and the men soon retreated downstairs leaving the women upstairs to help Nevette finish with dinner.

"Girl, it took everything I had not to just tell Trevor when he got home today. I know he noticed how anxious I was. Girl, he was too funny. He thought I had received another gift from my secret admirer again. I assured him I hadn't heard anything since the initial roses and note," Lindsay said as she placed the tray with chips and spinach dip on the counter.

"That was just weird," Talinda added. She took the top off of the hot wings that she brought for the guys to eat.

"Yeah," Nevette said as she checked on the dinner rolls in the oven.

"I'm going to take these downstairs to the guys. I'll be right back," Talinda said as she headed downstairs.

The girls sat around the morning room table eating the spinach dips and chips as they continued to discuss the master reveal about the pregnancies.

The guys joined them, and they ate dinner and enjoyed great

conversation. They discussed, of course, all that was going on with the youth. Lindsay's admirer came up in the conversation as well. They also talked about Michael and Gloria the previous Sunday night at the Travis's.

They settled back into the basement and started to play bible the trivia game as they enjoyed cheesecake. Nevette had sparkling cider on the table. Justice wondered why they didn't have it with dinner but didn't question it.

They went back and forth with riddles. It was the girls against the guys, and so far the guys were leading. It was Nevette's turn to say the riddle to the guys. She looked in the book as though she were flipping through pages. Lindsay was about to spontaneously combust.

"Okay guys. You'll never guess this one," Nevette said as though she found the riddle in the book to challenge the men with.

"You said that the last time Mrs. Goodfellow," Bernard said with sarcastic humor.

"Well, you won't get this one," Talinda added with just as much sarcasm.

They laughed and then Nevette asked the riddle, "What's full of life and comes in three's?"

The men were stumped.

"I got it!" Trevor screamed out. Lindsay about jumped through the roof. "Father, Son and Holy Ghost! BOOYAH!"

Lindsay laughed and said, "WRONG! BOOYAH!"

Bernard laughed as he said, "Trevor that was a good answer."

After about five minutes of the men guessing and the ladies saying no repeatedly. Talinda finally said, "We're going to have to put y'all on a two-minute timer, or we'll be here all night."

The men went into an uproar claiming there was no answer. They playfully yelled that the women made the question up. Bernard demanded to see the question in the book. Nevette smiled at Justice, placed her hand on her stomach, looked down and then at Lindsay and Talinda and back up at Derrick. He eyed her, as though he were extremely curious about something. Then what she did hit him.

He smiled at her and said, "Oh my God! We're about to have Zoé! That's it, isn't it?"

Nevette only nodded. She was overcome emotionally by Derrick's reaction. Bernard and Trevor both said, "Hey congratulations Derrick."

"What do y'all mean congrats Derrick? Nevette only accounts for one of the three. And I didn't pray for triplets." They both still had blank stares on their faces. Derrick shook his head and sighed as he looked at Talinda and Lindsay pointing at their stomachs, "Get it guys. "What's full of life and comes in—*THREE'S*?" He had the 'come on man, y'all are not that slow' look on his face.

Trevor got it. He looked at Lindsay as he said, "W-w-we're g-g-g-gonna—" he couldn't get it all out. Lindsay nodded and all he could do was pull her into his arms and begin to praise God. He was overjoyed and overcome with emotion.

Bernard yelled, "OH MY GOD! TALINDA YOU'RE PREGNANT? WE'RE GONNA HAVE A BABY? MY—I MEAN—OUR OWN BABY. YOU AND ME?"

"Yes sweetheart," Talinda replied.

"Wow you ladies got us good," Derrick said. "So this whole thing. The dinner, the game—it was all to set us up?"

"Yes," Nevette replied. "I love you baby."

"I love you too," he replied and kissed her.

Bernard touched the side of Talinda's face and said, "Thank you baby. For reading my mind. I love Raymond and the twins. I didn't want to appear selfish. Oh God baby, I love you so much!" Before she could answer he just kissed her.

Trevor paraded Lindsay with kisses, and the Goodfellow basement looked like a teen make-out session at a Stone Mountain Park.

The ladies went back upstairs to help Nevette clean before they all headed home. They guys stayed downstairs discussing the babies and their wives.

The next day Justice and Nevette told Tre about the baby. He was overjoyed that he would have a baby sister again. Talinda and Bernard shared their news with their families. His mom Teresa was super elated.

Lindsay was actually closer to four months pregnant than she thought after Trevor gave her an ultrasound. He agreed to allow Dr. Harrell deliver their baby, but he insisted on being Lindsay's obstetrician. Talinda was about six weeks, and Nevette was barely three weeks pregnant.

That Sunday morning the teen class was elated that their youth pastors were having another baby. And that their youth leaders, the Johnson's and the Goodfellow's were also expecting.

Jessica said, "Man, it's going to be baby grand central station in the youth ministry department."

Everyone laughed at her comment.

Derrick and Nevette missed Sunday School all together that morning. She woke up extremely sick and light headed. Against Derrick's better judgment, they headed out for Sunday service.

Nevette took a deep breath as they pulled into the parking lot. Justice looked at her and asked her if she was sure she wanted to go into the building. She nodded, and he got out the car. But before he could get around to her side of the car, Tre had already opened the door for his mother.

"I got the door daddy," Tre said as he opened Nevette's door.

"Okay thanks Tre," Derrick replied as he stood waiting for Nevette to get out of the car.

Tre retrieved his bible case out of the back seat as Nevette was getting out of the car. After she stood up and got ready to take a step, she was lightheaded and started to go down.

"MOMMY!" Tre yelled.

"WHOA, WHOA, WHOA WHOA, baby! I got you baby—I got you," Derrick said as she scooped her up in his arms. As he placed her back into the car he yelled over his shoulder at Tre, "Go find your Uncle Teddy, Tre! Stay with him today. Daddy is going to take mommy to the hospital okay."

"Okay daddy," he replied. He was frightened for his mother. He whispered, "Mommy are you alright?"

Nevette replied in a tired voice, "I'm aright baby."

"Go Tre. Find Uncle Teddy or Aunt Lindsay and go home with one of them. Tell them to call daddy, so I'll know you're with them," Derrick said to Tre.

Just then, Teddy and Josephine pulled up. An extra diaper and outfit change for the baby, due to diarrhea, had them running late. Derrick yelled across the parking lot for him to get Tre because Nevette wasn't feeling well. Tre ran over to Teddy and told him what happened as Derrick drove off with Nevette.

Derrick sped back down the highway toward their side of town toward Northside hospital.

"Justice, slow down baby. I feel fine. I was just lightheaded. It's part of morning sickness sweetheart," Nevette said.

"You weren't this bad with Tre or Callisha," Justice replied.

"Sweetheart every pregnancy is different. Being dizzy is a part of morning sickness. I haven't thrown up nearly as much. This time I mostly just have a nauseous feeling, and I'm lightheaded a lot. Sweetheart really, let's just go home. I promise I'll lie down and take it easy for the rest of the day," Nevette pleaded.

He looked at her, shook his head and smiled, "Okay, but if you have another episode today. We are heading to the emergency room, Nevette Naythia Goodfellow."

"Yes sir," she replied with a smile.

They drove home, and he assisted her into the house. He got her settled in the recliner in the living room that they hadn't taken back downstairs yet, and went to make her some hot cider and a sandwich. She drifted off to sleep with the sandwich still in her hands. He tucked her in and went into the bedroom to pray.

He returned to the living room and was reading through the bible when the doorbell rang. It was Trevor and Lindsay. They came straight there after church was over.

"Hey Trevor, Lindsay, how was church?" Derrick asked as he answered the door.

"Good as usual Derrick," he replied as he walked past Derrick to enter the house. Lindsay made a beeline for Nevette in the living room. "How is she? Teddy and Tre told us what happened in the parking lot this morning. We figured you guys would be at the ER still."

"Against my better judgment, I let her talk me out if it, she insisted she was okay. But I'm going to make her go in to see Dr. Harrell tomorrow when they have walk-ins," Derrick replied.

"Girl are you okay?" Lindsay asked Nevette.

"I'm fine. I just got a little lightheaded," Nevette responded.

"A little. Honey you all but passed out. And tomorrow we're going to the hospital, and you're going to let Dr. Harrell draw blood and check all your levels to make sure that everything is okay," Derrick commanded.

"Honestly Justice—" she started to say.

"Naythia, this isn't open for discussion. You're going to the hospital as a precaution tomorrow and that's all there is to it," Justice stated sternly but lovingly as he cut her off in mid-sentence.

She smiled and replied, "Okay baby, bright and early right after we drop Tre off for school."

Trevor and Derrick head downstairs and Lindsay turned to Nevette and said, "Oookay—this is a new you."

She replied, "Lindsay you know that was part of the problem with Derrick and me. A lot of times I would override him. He would make a decision about something, and I would suggest something totally opposite. I was submissive to him, but not always and a lot of times I bruised his ego without even knowing it. He needed to prove himself with Suzette that he was ready for ministry. And then when that fell apart—just—yeah—anyway I need to allow my husband to lead, even if I don't agree. The final decisions in this house have to come through him. Besides, he is not the same man as he was a year ago. Something happened to him this past year. The way he ministered to Raymond at the hospital he wouldn't have been capable of last year this time. He has flown by me girl. I feel like I'm playing catch up with him spiritually. Lindsay you're just like me—strong willed. Trevor isn't going to dominate you. He is a lot like Derrick was. Take my advice. Make sure you allow him to lead and make mistakes. And when he does comfort and minster to him, not by letting him know in your own way that your choice was better. He knows that already when his falls apart. I wouldn't do it directly but I would send a lot of indirect signals. I would butt up to Derrick because I was spoiled and knew I could get my way. But when Justice says, "it's not open for discussion" that is supposed to be my cue to shut it down girl. Kiss him, say okay and I love you. A lot of times my way proved to be right. And in that, I caused him to have less and less confidence in leading our family. I was killing his ego proving that he couldn't lead or make good decisions without even knowing it. When Suzette happened, that was the cake topper for both of us. I don't mean that I have to, or need to baby him or his ego, but when the man says no, I need to just stop. "

"Wow girl. I guess y'all did discuss everything huh? I know some of that was a bitter pill for you to swallow. I mean Nevette you were never disrespectful to Derrick, but sometimes you would override him. You just did it in a nice way," Lindsay replied.

"Yes, all I was doing was nicely and silently screaming that my ministry was better than his. Lindsay you are just as spoiled and spiritually aggressive with Trevor as I am with Justice. Sometimes you do it too Lindsay," Nevette stated.

"I hear you girl, and I will definitely check myself in the future. I surely don't want a Suzette Timmons in my life," Lindsay replied.

"Amen girl," Nevette said with a gesture of her hand as she playfully swatted at Lindsay.

As the guys came back upstairs the doorbell was ringing. Teddy and Josephine arrived with Tre. He ran in to hug his mommy. He asked her was she okay and touched her stomach and said hello to Zoé. He told Zoé to be a good girl so mommy wouldn't be sick. Everyone smiled at his innocence and purity.

About thirty minutes after they left, Talinda called to check on Nevette. Derrick informed her that she was resting, and they would go to the doctor in the morning just to be sure that everything was fine.

They settled in for the evening and watched movies after dinner with hot chocolate and hot apple cider for Nevette.

Everything checked out okay with Nevette and the baby at the doctor's visit the following day.

~Chapter Ten~

A few months later, Nevette sat at the table with books open everywhere. Talinda finally convinced her to teach at the women's meeting the coming Friday night.

Derrick came in from work. He smiled as he saw the table full of books because he knew what that indicated.

"Hey baby, how was your day?" Nevette asked.

"Mmmmm," he said and kissed her. "Hello sweetheart. My day was wonderful. But it just got better coming home to you."

"Awww you're so wonderful," she replied shyly.

He kissed her again and said, "Where's Tre?"

"He's downstairs and dinner is in the oven. Whenever you're ready, I'll set the table," Nevette said as he kissed her again.

"Okay, what you doing?" he asked as if he didn't know.

She sighed as though she were relieved about something she had been worrying about and said, "Getting ready for Women of Virtue on Friday night. Talinda has me teaching the class."

"Oh really. So Evangelist Goodfellow is finally getting back to work huh," he replied with another kiss.

"I love it. I've missed this," she said as she returned his kiss.

"I know I've missed this too. I used to love coming home finding you here at the kitchen table. You have your laptop out with books sprawled all over the table studying the word of God. I'm always so turned on by that," Justice admitted.

"What? Really? Justice—" she replied.

"Baby you look sexy when you're studying God's word. Because I Know the same way you're giving God everything right now, you're going to give me everything else later," he replied with a sly look.

"Justice stop it boy. You're too much," Nevette replied almost embarrassed.

"Baby, I'm just being honest," Justice replied.

"Justice go downstairs and say hello to your son," Nevette said in a teasing way.

"Okay sweetheart. I'll let you get back to your studying," Justice said as he headed toward the stairs. He stopped and looked back when he reached the door that led to the basement and said, "Mmmm—mmm—mmm."

"Justice stop it," she replied. She couldn't control the smile on her face. A warm tingling feeling rushed through her body.

He headed downstairs. She could hear Justice call Tre's name as he descended the stairs. She smiled as she listened to the excitement in Tre's voice upon seeing his father. The last few months they had once again been a family were precious. She took advantage of every moment. She knew they still had much more bonding to do as a family, and some kinks to completely iron out, but overall they were closer than ever before.

*****

The following Sunday at church Tre wanted to go home with Raymond because he and the teens were taking the younger kids in the youth ministry to the skating rink, after they had hotdogs and hamburgers and the Travis'. But Tre was about to get some bad news from his dad about the festivities for the day.

Tre ran up to Derrick in an excited voice, "Daddy. Raymond is going to take all the little kids skating. We're going to Raymond's house first to eat hotdogs and hamburgers. Raymond said I could ride home with him and you and mommy can pick me up later after we come back from skating. Can I ride home with Raymond please daddy?"

"Now Tre, what did I say when we left for church this morning? I said after church, you needed to come back home and clean up the mess you left downstairs in the basement. Now you would be able to go with Raymond, but you didn't do what you were supposed to last night. I told you to pick up your toys before you went to bed. When I went downstairs this morning, your toys were still all over the floor. I told you that mommy was not your maid. But if you do a good job, and daddy feels like it. He'll drop you off over to Raymond's house later."

"But daddy—," Tre exclaimed before Derrick cut him off.

"No buts Tre. You're not going. Now go back downstairs to the youth center and get your coat. This conversation is over," Derrick said.

Tre turned away in tears and headed down the hallway to go back downstairs. He saw his mother talking to Lindsay and ran over to her.

"Mommy!" he exclaimed through his tears.

She bent down to him and asked, "Oh Tre, baby, what's wrong?"

"Daddy won't let me go over to Raymond's house. All the kids from children's church are going. They're going to eat hotdogs and hamburgers and go skating. Daddy said I can't go. Mommy please ask daddy if I can go. He'll say yes if you ask him mommy."

"Baby—oohh—so why did daddy say no?" Nevette asked.

"I don't know mommy," Tre exclaimed. "Mommy you ask him please?"

She smiled and said, "Ok Tre, I tell you what. I'll go ask daddy and—"

"Good! I'll go tell Raymond to wait on me," Tre said as he hurried down the stairs not waiting for Nevette to reply.

Nevette shook her head as she stood back up. She headed to the front of the church were Derrick and a few of the other brothers and sisters were gathered.

She walked up to Derrick and said, "Hey Justice—"

"Hey baby. Where's Tre? I sent him to get his coat," Derrick replied before she could finish her sentence.

"Yeah he came to me crying. He said Talinda and Bernard where having all the kids over their house and the teens were taking them skating later, and you said he couldn't go," she asked.

Derrick shook his head and said, "That little manipulator."

Nevette smiled and said, "So he told me to come asked you if he could go. I asked him why daddy said he couldn't go. He said he didn't know why you said no."

"He said what!" Derrick exclaimed. "That little lying manipulator. I told him he couldn't go because last night I told him to pick his toys up in the basement and this morning when I went down there, his toys were still everywhere." Derrick turned from a teasing tone to an irritated one. "And I told him, that if he goes home and cleans up, maybe we'll take him over to Bernard and Talinda's before they leave to go skating. However, now since he's come to you lying, he's not going at all. And I'm going to deal with him for lying to you about it."

"Oooh—Derrick please—" Nevette started to say.

"Now Nevette, don't Derrick please me. Sweetheart he's lying, manipulating the situation trying to pull you against me," Derrick replied.

"Now I got him in trouble," Nevette said in a 'daddy pretty please' tone.

"He got himself in trouble Nevette. He has to learn," Derrick replied.

"Derrick—" she replied as she batted her eyes at him.

"Don't Derrick me. And don't bat your pretty eyes at me trying to manipulate me. You and him are just alike. Y'all think y'all have me," he smiled as he kissed her.

"We do have you," she replied as she pulled away from him with a playful punch on the shoulder.

"You do. But I'm just saying," Derrick replied smiling. "Mmmmm, girl, I love you." He kissed her again.

"Derrick you're standing in the middle of church kissing me," Nevette said in between his kisses.

"Uhh huh, sure am—and—," he replied and kissed her again.

"And everybody is probably watching. Derrick don't," she replied.

"You're always so shy when it comes to sexuality," Derrick said as he touched the side of her face.

A couple of the guys who were talking to Derrick before Nevette walked up were in the corner talking.

"Man, Derrick's wife is so beautiful," Vic said.

"I'm telling you. How can a woman be almost four months pregnant and STILL be fine? I bet she'll be just as fine at nine months," Darryl added.

"Y'all need to stop looking at the man's wife like that," Nate said and shook his head.

"We're not trying to get with her. We're not on stalker mode or anything. We just said she was fine. I would have been on the altar crying out for six months for all of that too. I just saying," Vic responded.

"Y'all tripping," Nate said with a laugh and walked away.

The women on the other side of the sanctuary were having a similar discussion about Derrick.

"Girl, I would love to wake up to all of that every morning," Tammy said as she sighed.

"Who you telling? How about a sister was secretly hoping his wife wouldn't have come to her senses and taken him back. Girl, I would have been on him before the ink dried on that divorce decree, mmmm—FINE," Sherry replied.

"Girl who are YOU telling?" Tammy repeated.

"I already had plans for me and him," Tonya declared. "I heard him crying out on the altar for her one day. I was like, oh my God. I would love to have a man like that. I thought, is she stupid, crazy or what!"

They both laughed as Tammy said, "I know that's right. But mmmm—that man know he fine. And little Tre already fine. Girl, how in the heck are you fine at seven years old!"

"I now right," Sherry said as they burst out laughing.

Tre ran up to his parents, "Okay mommy. I told Raymond to wait for me. Did you ask daddy if I can go?" Tre asked full of excitement.

"Well, Tre ummmmm," Nevette started to say.

"Well nothing. Tre you lied to mommy. You knew exactly why I told you that you couldn't go over to Raymond's house. Now we'll deal with this when we get home," Derrick interjected.

"Mommy!" Tre exclaimed.

Nevette adjusted his coat as she said, "Sweetheart, we'll see what happens when we get home. Maybe—"

"We're not going to see what happens when we get home Nevette. He's not going to go, and I'm going to deal with him for lying," Derrick declared.

"Derrick—" she started to say.

"Nevette—we're not going to discuss this okay. You guys go to the car while I go tell Bernard that Tre's not going to be able to make it," Derrick cut her off. His tone indicated that the matter was not open for discussion, and she ceased her engagement on Tre's behalf.

"Okay Derrick," she replied.

As Derrick walked away, she turned to Tre and said, "Okay, come on Tre."

Tre replied through tears, "But mommy!"

"Tre, you lied, okay. You were wrong," Nevette said as she helped him with his gloves.

"Daddy's gonna spank me!" Tre blurted out.

"Probably baby. But you can't lie. Tre you know how daddy feels about lying. Come on, let's go to the car. Maybe by the time we get home he'll forget about it," Nevette said as she stood up to head to the door.

"I don't think so mommy. He's pretty mad," Tre said still crying as he followed his mother out the door.

She sighed, "Yes he is. Come on sweetie, we had better get to the car like he told us to."

Nevette and Tre got to the car and buckled their seat belts just shortly before Derrick arrived. He got in and closed the door. He looked over his shoulder slightly to ensure Tre was buckled in before he put the car in reverse.

Tre sniffled in the back seat. Nevette sat up front thinking to herself, "Tre, please stop sniffling."

No sooner than the thought entered her mind, Derrick said as he looked in the rear-view mirror at Tre, "Tre if you don't stop all that noise back there, I'm going to pull this car over and deal with you before we get home. Now just stop it. I'm not going to drive home for the next thirty minutes listening to you sniffling in the back seat. I have not touched you yet. Just suck it up son."

"Derrick," Nevette said in a soft but pleading voice. "Do you know how hard it is for him to stop crying? Him anticipating your spanking is worse than the actual spanking baby."

He softened his tone, "Look Naythia."

"I know Justice—I know. You have to do this. I understand. But baby don't torture him all the way home okay?" Nevette replied as she placed her hand on his thigh to reassure him.

"Yeah. Alright, let's just get home," Derrick replied.

Tre was still sniffling. Nevette thought, "Oh God Tre. Please stop sniffling."

"Tre if you don't stop it right now!" Derrick said. His tone was louder and harsher.

"Tre baby, it's going to be okay. Calm down," Nevette said to Tre in that soft motherly tone women used just before father's were about to discipline the kids for disobedience.

Derrick shook his head in frustration. "Tre!"

"Yes sir. Okay daddy," Tre replied. He tried with all his might to control his emotions.

At this point, Nevette was a little frustrated herself. The one thing they had always taught Tre, was not to try to control his emotions. Derrick always taught Tre that it was okay for men to cry. And here he was now, telling Tre to suck it up and not cry. But she dare not correct him in front of Tre.

Derrick was slightly nervous about how Nevette was taking his disciplinary actions with Tre. He hadn't had his family back but a few months, and they still took some things day by day. They drove the rest of the way home in silence.

As soon as the car pulled into the garage Tre started to breathe heavily. Derrick got out and walked around the car to open the door for Nevette and Tre. As they entered the house, Tre walked toward the door that led to the basement.

"Tre, don't go downstairs yet. Go to your room and I'll be in there in a minute," Derrick said.

"Okay daddy," Tre replied in a pitiful voice as he walked toward his bedroom.

Derrick headed to the master bedroom to put his bible down and grab the belt out of the closet he usually spanked Tre with. Nevette was behind him.

"Justice please," she pleaded.

"Nevette baby I have to do this. I can't allow him to think that it's okay to lie and manipulate to get his way. Sweetheart he tries to play us against each other. That's not acceptable. Nevette he flat out lied to you. What if it were something more serious, and he lied to get his way and put himself in danger. I can't let him get away with that alright baby? So let me just go in here and take care of this okay," Derrick said as he walked by Nevette to the closet.

She followed him and said, "Derrick."

He turned and said, "Nevette baby, look at me."

"It's just that we've all been through so much. Justice everybody's feelings are so delicate right now," she said with a sigh and dropped her head.

He lifted her head in his hand and said, "Baby I understand that. Naythia I don't want to go in here and spank him. I have to. It's going to kill me to do this. We're just a few months back together, and you're right. We've all been through so much. But we have to start getting back to normal. I can't let him flat out lie and attempt to manipulate us like that. He's always been successful at playing us against each other to get his way. Not this time sweetheart. He has to learn. I did the same thing to him concerning you, and look where we ended up. With you, me, and him all devastated. You to the point of suicide. The spanking is mostly for the lie. He's probably going to be more wounded in his feelings than he is the seat of his pants. I'm barely going to touch him baby."

She nodded in agreement and sighed, "Okay. You're right. You go handle it, I'm not saying anything."

He didn't reply to her last statement but walked past her. He wasn't actually asking for her permission or waiting for her response. She sighed and followed him down the hallway. She went into the kitchen as he headed to Tre's room.

He entered Tre's room. When Tre saw his father, he shifted in his seat and dropped his head. Derrick felt terrible. He really didn't want to spank Tre but knew he had to.

He sighed and said, "Son listen."

"I'm sorry daddy. I'm sorry I lied to mommy," Tre stood and said before Derrick could get anything else out.

"Son, I know you are," Derrick replied. "Sit down and listen to me."

"Okay daddy," Tre said crying again.

"Tre stop crying alright," Derrick replied in a calm tone. He sat down on the bed beside Tre. "Look man, I can't allow you to lie to me and your mother like that. A man's word is his bond. If he can't be trusted by what he says, then he has nothing. I told you," Tre looked down. Derrick continued, "Tre look at daddy. I told you to come home and pick up your toys and maybe later mommy and daddy would take you to Raymond's house before they left for the skating rink. Is that not what I said?"

Tre spoke in a shaky voice through his sniffling, "Yes Sir."

"And what was the reason you told mommy that I said you couldn't go?" Derrick asked.

"I told her I didn't know why," Tre replied.

"But you did know right?" Derrick asked.

"Yes Sir," Tre responded as he fought to keep from crying out loud.

"So you were trying to get mommy to either tell you to go ahead and go or talk me into allowing you to go, right?" Derrick asked.

"Yes Sir," Tre replied.

"And that's wrong isn't it?" Derrick asked.

"Yes Sir," Tre replied.

"So you understand why daddy has to punish you?" Derrick asked.

"Yes daddy," Tre replied.

"After I get through spanking you. You need to go apologize to mommy, and then get your little tail downstairs and clean your toys up like I told you to last night. Do you understand?" Derrick asked.

"Yes Sir," Tre replied barely above a whisper.

"Come on, let's get this over with," Derrick said. He stood Tre up off the bed and began to spank him.

"OKAY DADDY, OKAY DADDY. I'M SORRY DADDY!" Tre yelled out as his dad spanked him.

As Derrick landed the last swat of the belt he said, "Now go do what I told you to. First apologize to mommy."

Nevette could hear Tre crying as his dad spanked him. When she heard Derrick command him to come apologize to her. She wiped her tears and sat down in the living room and waited for him to come to her. Tre was breathing fast and erratic and could hardly catch his breath.

"Tre, breathe baby," Nevette said before he could get a word out.

"Apologize son," Derrick commanded.

"Derrick sweetheart, please let him catch his breath first," Nevette said in a soft tone without looking up at Derrick. She was also trying not to cry in front of Tre.

"Nevette," Derrick replied.

"Okay," she said as she choked back her own tears. She didn't want to upset Tre more than he already was.

Tre looked at his mother and said, "Mo-mo-mo-mommy. I'm sor-

I'm sorry mommy." He tried hard to catch his breath.

"Aww it's okay baby," Nevette replied.

"Nevette it's not okay that he lied to you," Derrick replied.

"Derrick what am I supposed to—mommy accepts your apology okay?" Nevette replied.

"Okay-okay-okay mommy," Tre said as he still fought hard to catch his breath. His body moved and shook with every breath he took.

"Son, I did not hit you that hard. Get yourself together before I give you a reason to be hyperventilating," Derrick replied.

"Derrick!" Nevette exclaimed in a soft tone. She knew this was an extremely delicate situation for everyone.

"Nevette," he replied.

"Derrick please. This isn't normal sweetheart," Nevette replied.

She was correct in her assessment. This was anything but normal for Tre. He was no longer upset about not being able to go the Raymond's house. He could feel the tension between his parents rise in the car on the way home and in the conversation just now. He remembered the last time things got bad between them. His father left the house, and his mother went away. He was afraid that he had hurt his mommy like before. He felt that she would leave and when she came back, his daddy would leave again. He didn't know how to express the fear he felt. He couldn't get his breathing under control. This sent Nevette into a panic and got Derrick's attention as well.

"Tre baby, please calm down. He can barely breathe. Derrick please, let me get him some water," Nevette said to Derrick as she consoled Tre.

"Yes sure baby," Derrick replied as he walked over to Tre.

He got down on his knees, so he would be at Tre's level. He didn't want to stand at an intimidating height above him.

"Da-da-daddy, I'm g-g-go-gonna go do-down-downstairs," Tre managed to get out.

"Oh God. Tre come here son. Let daddy hug you. Listen, calm down okay. Daddy loves you. You know that right?" Derrick asked him.

"Ye-ye-yes Sir," Tre said still breathing heavily.

"Daddy loves you Tre. That hasn't changed. Come on son calm down. Take big breathes for daddy alright?" Derrick replied as Nevette returned with the water.

"Come on Derrick calm down sweetheart. Drink this water for mommy and daddy okay?" Nevette said to Tre. He knew that whenever his mother called him Derrick, she was attempting to get him to focus. He looked at her and took a few sips of the water in between his erratic breathing.

"I'm sorry daddy. I'm so-so-sorry," Tre exclaimed.

"It's alright lil' man, okay. It's alright. I know you're sorry. Daddy accepts your apology alright? Daddy accepts it. Calm down and take some deep breathes. You're scaring mommy and daddy a little bit," Derrick replied. He pulled Tre into his arms and just held him. He whispered, "Oh God what did I do."

Nevette stroked his head and held the glass for him to take a few more sips of water as Derrick continued to console him. He slowly started to calm down, and his breathing eased. Nevette let out a sigh of relief that his breathing, although still somewhat heavy, was returning to normal.

"I'm sorry mommy. I'm sorry daddy," Tre managed to say without stumbling through his words.

"Oh baby. Mommy and daddy both accept your apology," Nevette said as she stroked the side of his face.

"Yes Tre we do okay. Now run on downstairs and put your toys away," Derrick replied.

"Okay daddy," Tre replied.

He was still visibly upset and shaking, but more in control of his breathing. He turned and went downstairs to put away his toys.

"Oh God he was shaking. I'm regretting this," Derrick said. He looked at Nevette to get a read on how she was taking the situation.

"Well it's done now Derrick," she replied as she rose and went into the kitchen to place the glass in the sink. She started to mill around in the kitchen to get ready to prepare dinner. Derrick sighed but decided against attempting to strike up a conversation with her. He missed the cue. She tried to warn him that everyone's feelings were probably still just a little too raw. However, Derrick knew he couldn't allow Tre's behavior to go unpunished.

It only took Tre about ten minutes to gather his toys and put them away. He returned to the top of the steps and then reentered the living room. He stood a noticeable distance from his father in between the kitchen and living room looking down. He didn't look up at his dad as he spoke to him.

He whispered, "I put my toys away daddy."

"Okay Tre. Now go in your room and lie down until mommy calls you for dinner," Derrick replied.

"Okay daddy," he whispered.

Nevette was noticeably irritated. But she said nothing. Tre looked at his mother as he turned to go to his room. She had tears in her eyes. She felt so bad for her baby. She knew what Derrick was doing was correct. And she knew she had to allow him to lead. Even so, neither of them had any idea what was going on inside of Tre's head. Her emotions drew emotion from him as he turned and headed down the hallway to his room.

Derrick thought, "Okay, alright, alright, alright...I have to finish this. I have to follow through." He sighed.

"I've never seen him so upset when you spanked him before," Nevette stated.

"I know me either. I don't' know where that's coming from. Because I barely touched him sweetheart. He was shaking. I don't know maybe I shouldn't have spanked him," Derrick replied as he shook his head, as though he desperately tried to figure out a riddle.

"Well it's a little late for that now Derrick. It's over," Nevette said as she got up and headed back to the kitchen. She silently prayed as she prepared dinner. She knew her tone, and body language had not sent off the best of signals to Derrick. She prayed that everyone would calm down by dinner time, so they could enjoy a nice meal together.

Tre reached his bed. But instead of lying down he knelt beside his bed as he did every night to pray before going to bed. He was crying again and struggling to catch his breath.

G-God,

Pl-please don't let my daddy, l-leave m-my mommy. And m-my-my m-mommy go away again. I don't want her to g-g-go on vacation. I don't w-want m-my mo-mommy and daddy to g-get a di-divorce.

He lay there shaking and cried himself to sleep clutching Mr. Willow, his favorite teddy bear. Derrick went to the prayer room and spent some time with God. He chastised himself for making such a big deal about it. He was nervous because he wasn't sure how Nevette took the whole thing. He thought she was obviously irritated with him about it. About an hour later she called Tre for dinner.

"TRE. Come one sweetie. It's time for dinner," Nevette called over her shoulder in the direction of Tre's room as she set the dining room table. When Tre didn't respond she said to Derrick, "Honey he's probably not going to come out until you call him."

"Okay baby," Derick replied.

He called Tre, but again, no answer came. He decided to walk down the hall to get him. He figured that he may be in the bathroom. When he reached Tre's doorway, he smiled. He found Tre fast asleep cuddled up with Mr. Willow. He walked over to the bed and sat down. He touched Tre on the shoulder to wake him as he said, "He son. Mommy is finished cooking. It's time to eat."

"Okay Daddy," Tre responded as he sat up and rubbed his eyes.

"Okay, go get washed up and come to the table. Mommy is done with dinner, and it's time to eat."

"Yes Sir," Tre replied as he climbed out of bed and headed toward the bathroom.

Derrick returned to the dining room where Nevette was still busy setting the table. "Poor guy. He had cried himself to sleep."

"I've never seen a spanking affect him like this before," Nevette said.

"I know. That was kind of weird," Derrick replied.

Tre came down the hallway and sat down. Derrick prayed, and they began to eat dinner. Tre studied his parents. He watched if they engaged in normal conversation. There wasn't much conversation at the table, and he was terrified that his dad would leave again. That it would all fall apart, and his parents would get a divorce because he made mommy mad.

After dinner, Derrick sent Tre to take a bath while he and Nevette straightened up the kitchen. After they finished they headed to Tre's room and prayed with him before they went to lay down.

Nevette was calm and peaceful. God ministered to her while she cooked and all throughout dinner. She knew Justice had done the right thing concerning Tre. She decided to send the message to him that she was okay and not angry. She got out of the shower and returned to the bedroom still wrapped in her towel. She slipped into the red silhouette teddy that Justice loved and got into bed. He normally wore nothing to bed but decided tonight was probably not going to be a normal night for them. So he put on some boxer shorts and hopped into the bed without even noticing what she had on.

They laid in bed silently, both attempting to figure the other out. After about five minutes, Derrick finally said, "Why are you so far away from me?"

"I'm not far away from you Derrick," she replied.

"And why are you calling me Derrick? You've called me Derrick ever since we left the church today and I was coming home to spank Tre," he said.

"Justice," she started to say.

"Baby look, come here," he said and pulled her closer to him. "I know you're upset with me because I spanked Tre. But baby—"

"Derrick. I'm not mad at you for spanking Tre," she replied. She turned over and propped herself up on her elbows so she slightly hovered over him. "Sweetheart when you came home, I said Tre and I were going to do what you said. I meant that, okay baby. Tre and I are going to do what you say. He was wrong. You have to teach him now at his most impressionable age, that a man has to be a man of his word. I know how strongly you feel about that right now. You probably feel just a little bit too strong about it. He just really wanted to go play with the other kids. But he also has to understand the value of his word and the importance of not lying. What if it would have been something very serious, and he was about to walk into something dangerous? The old Nevette probably would have talked you into allowing him to go with his friends and forsake his responsibility of cleaning up his toys despite that fact that he just lied to me to my face. And you would have allowed me to do it. However, the new Nevette is not going to interfere with the things you need to teach him to become a man of valor and integrity."

"Whether you think I'm right or wrong?" Justice asked.

"Baby it's not a matter of you being right or wrong. It's a matter of knowing you have your wife's support behind you no matter what the situation or outcome," she replied. "I don't think you were wrong about spanking Tre for lying. He flat out lied to me and was manipulating me. He was using the fact that I get my way with you, and because of that, he usually gets his too. He knows that in the past, I've been able to talk you into things. I was wrong for showing him that. Baby I'm not angry with you."

"I was wondering. I was really nervous about that," Justice replied.

"I think Tre probably sensed our tension about it too. That may have been why he took the spanking so hard," Nevette added.

"Yeah, I've never seen him cry and lose his breath like that. School is out for the Thanksgiving holiday this week. I think maybe he and I will do something special," Justice replied.

"That will be nice," Nevette replied. She pulled the cover down to reveal the red teddy she had on.

"Well alright now Mrs. Goodfellow. You come on and climb on board," Justice said as he started to kiss her.

"Maybe I want you on top," she teased.

"Sweetheart I'm a big boy and you're pregnant. You know the drill. Until you have the baby, you're on top," he smiled and kissed her again as he moved her into position on top of him.

"Oh you gonna make me do all the work huh Mr. Goodfellow," she teased.

"Oh I'm definitely going to work you. But not too hard. You know I got you baby. I love you. But you know you're gonna get it for wearing this red teddy to bed right?" he said as he turned it up a notch and landed more passionate kisses on her.

Tre knocked at the door. Derrick answered him, "Yeah Tre. What is it son?"

"C-c-can I t-talk to you and m-mo-mommy daddy?" Tre replied. He was about to hyperventilate. He had sat in his room stewing since his parents left. He thought maybe they were in the room arguing over him lying to his mother.

"Oh God Justice. He's breathing fast again," Nevette exclaimed as she moved from on top of him.

"Yes he is," Derrick said as he sat up in the bed. "Come on in son."

He walked over to the side of the bed, and he was in tears again. Nevette leaned over and sat up beside Derrick.

"Tre are you okay? What's the matter baby?" she asked.

He blurted out, "I-I-I'm really sorry that l-lied to you mommy!"

"Baby—ohh Tre," Nevette exclaimed as tears filled her eyes.

"Son, we already dealt with that earlier today okay. That's already in the past. Mommy and daddy forgive you. That's over. You don't have to worry about it anymore okay. We just have to tell the truth for now on alright," Derrick said.

Tre continued as though his father had not spoken a word. "Daddy I-I'm s-sorry. I'm sorry daddy. T-That I was m-mean to m-m-mommy. I l-lied to mommy. MOMMY I DON'T WANT YOU TO GO AWAY AGAIN ON YOUR VACTION. DADDY I DON'T WANT YOU TO LEAVE. I DON'T WANT YOU TO GET A DIVORCE. I-I-I'M S-S-S-SORRY DADDY."

"Baby—Tre! Oh my God Justice!" Nevette exclaimed.

"Son no, lil' man, uhn uhn. Come here son, come here," Derrick declared as he threw the cover back and swung out of the bed. He pulled Tre into his arms and said, "Daddy is not going to go anywhere okay. Mommy and daddy are not going to get a divorce. No one is mad at you Derrick. Mommy is not mad at you, and she's not going to go away."

"Now sweetheart. Mommy isn't going anywhere," Nevette cried.

Tre cried, "I don't want my mommy and daddy—"

"Oh God son please, listen to daddy. Look at me Tre. Derrick look at daddy," Derrick said in an attempt to get his full attention. "Mommy and daddy are not getting a divorce. We love you. We are a family, and we're staying together. Mommy is having a baby, and she is staying right here and so is daddy."

He finally started to catch his breath again," Y-you promise mommy?"

"I promise baby. I'm not going anywhere, and neither is daddy," Nevette replied.

"Listen son," Derrick said. "Daddy spanked you because you lied. It wouldn't have made a difference if it were daddy, mommy, Raymond or anybody else. Daddy only spanked you because you lied. It has nothing to do with anything else. Mommy and daddy are not getting a divorce."

"Are you sure you're going to be here in the morning when I wake up daddy?" Tre asked, still slightly panicked and breathing heavily.

"I'm going to be here Tre. And so will mommy," Derrick replied.

"Yes baby, mommy will be here too. We're not going to get a divorce," Nevette added.

"You promise mommy?" Tre asked.

"Oh baby I promise," Nevette replied.

"Ever?" Tre exclaimed.

"Not ever baby," Nevette reassured.

"Okay," he replied.

Nevette instructed him to take deep breaths. He was soon breathing normally again.

"Hey why don't you sleep with Mommy and daddy tonight? Would you like that?" Derrick asked.

"Can I Daddy?" Tre exclaimed.

"Sure you can. Tell you what. Go turn your light off in your room and come right back," Derrick instructed.

Tre was back in a millisecond and climbed into bed with his parents.

"You should sleep in the middle daddy. That way, me and mommy can make sure you stay in the bed, and don't go anywhere," Tre declared.

"I'm not going anywhere son. You sleep in the middle okay," Derrick replied with a smile.

"Are you sure daddy?" Tre asked.

"I'm sure lil' man," Derrick answered.

Tre climbed in the middle. He was emotionally exhausted and was fast asleep only after about ten minutes of climbing into bed with his parents. Tre soon found himself lying on top of his father. Derrick shifted over to the middle of the bed so Tre wouldn't fall off of him onto the floor. Tre moved to the other side of Derrick as soon as he maneuvered his way into the middle of the bed. So there they lay, in the exact same position as the night Nevette came home from Myrtle Beach. Nevette on his right side snuggled up and Tre on his left.

He looked down and noticed they had come full circle. He smiled and prayed to God over his family that they would have sweet sleep and that Tre would have stability.

The next morning Nevette rose early and cooked breakfast. Tre and Justice both slept through her getting out of bed and cooking breakfast.

"Alright you two sleepy heads, rise and shine," Nevette declared.

Derrick stirred and then woke Tre, "Hey Tre look. Mommy made us breakfast in bed."

Tre yawned as said, "Good morning mommy. Hey daddy."

"Morning Tre," Derrick said. "Look mommy cooked us breakfast."

"You mean I get to eat in here with you and mommy?" he asked with excitement.

"I guess so Tre," Derrick said. "Go use the bathroom, wash your hands and come right back, okay," Derrick replied.

Tre jumped down and started to run out of his parents' bedroom to the bathroom in the hall.

"Hey Tre, where you going? Use the bathroom right here in mommy and daddy's room," Derrick said.

"Oh okay daddy," Tre replied. He was so excited.

"Baby this smells so good. When did you get out of the bed?" Derrick asked Nevette.

"You guys were sleeping so peacefully. It was easy for me to sneak away," she replied.

"We must have been out, because I didn't feel you get out of the bed," he said as he moved to the edge of the bed. "I didn't realize how fragile he was baby. He was so afraid I was going to leave. I feel so bad now for spanking him."

"Justice no. You can't feel bad about spanking him for telling a lie. We just needed to explain to him a little more in depth. I'm glad he came to us last night and let us know what was going on inside of his little head and heart. He could have walked around in fear for who knows how long, making himself sick before we figured it out," Nevette said to reassure him.

"Now I really am glad you're staying home. That will reassure him more that you're going to always be here," Derrick said.

"Yes. Besides, like I said. I'm enjoying being a house wife. Taking care of my two big men," she said as she kissed him.

Derrick came bolting out of the bathroom, "I'm done daddy. And I washed my hands."

"Okay Tre," Derrick said with a smile. "Daddy's going to use the bathroom now so we can eat breakfast."

"Okay daddy. And don't forget to wash your hands!" Tre replied as he jumped back into his parent's bed.

Derrick shook his head and went to the bathroom. When he returned they sat down on the bed and ate breakfast. Nevette served it up family style. They laughed, fed each other and made plans to spend the day together doing whatever Tre wanted to do.

~Chapter Eleven~

Reginald helped Sarah get onto the table. She was moving very slowly because of all the water she had to drink in preparation for the ultra sound. Today they would find out if she was having a boy or girl. His mother was outside in the waiting room until they got Sarah settled in. Veronica prepared the equipment for Dr. Trevor Johnson. She was his nurse and had insisted that Sarah go to him for all her prenatal care. Her insurance covered the care so money wasn't an issue.

For the first time, Reginald was excited about the baby. He was growing into the idea of being a teen father. It wasn't so overwhelming anymore, now he just worried about being a good father and provider for his son or daughter.

Although Sarah was her niece, since Veronica adopted her, she looked at Sarah's coming baby as her grandchild.

"Aunt Ronie I am so grateful to you and Uncle Jeff. You have both been nothing but supportive. You've never condemned me, and you have used your insurance to care for my hospital visits. I know I'm only your niece, but you love and care for me like a mother and father cares for their daughter. I don't want you to be the great aunt and uncle of my baby. I'm your daughter, and you are both my baby's grandparents. I love you—mom."

Veronica was speechless. She and Jeff had all but gave up on having their own children. She was beginning to believe they would never be parents or grandparents. She had to continue with hooking up the equipment to fight off the tears that formed in her eyes.

"Oh Sarah. If you only knew what those words mean to me, and will mean to your Uncle Jeff.

"He's my dad," Sarah replied as she wiped a tear from her eyes.

"Yes he is baby girl," Veronica replied. "We'll have to make a video for him and take some pictures since he couldn't be here today. When he gets back in town he'll be excited."

"We can take one with our phone to send today," Reginald added.

"That's a great idea Reginald," Veronica replied.

Trevor walked in and greeted Reginald and Sarah as he sat down on the stool and turned the machine on to prepare to look at the baby.

They went to get Reginald's mom as he started. He found the baby and started the video and took several pictures. Before he turned the screen around for them to see, he announced the sex of the baby.

"Well, I think you guys had better start picking out boy names," Trevor stated.

"Wow a boy!" Reginald exclaimed.

"Yes! A boy!" Sarah said in delight.

Reginald's mother and Veronica both cried. Trevor couldn't help but to think about Lindsay. She was nearly seven and a half months now, and they recently found out they too were having a little boy. They were going to wait and be surprised at delivery but decided against it.

He took plenty of pictures for the parents and grandparents and a video as well.

As soon as they left the hospital Reginald and Sarah stopped by the department store and started looking at boy clothes and deciding what theme to make the nursery.

"So—" Sarah finally said to Reginald.

"So what?" he inquired.

"It's going to be a boy. You haven't said if it's going to be a junior or not yet," Sarah replied.

"Reginald smiled, "I wasn't sure if that was an option. I mean we're not married. So I wasn't sure if you would give the baby my name."

"That's silly Reginald. You're his father. Whether we get married or not that fact is not going to change," Sarah replied.

"Okay," he replied with a smile. "Sure, I would love to have a junior." He turned very serious suddenly. She looked at him with curiosity and was about to address him when he continued, "Sarah, I promise you I am going to be a good father. I know we're young, but I'm going to do my best. We have an awesome youth ministry team, and I am going to get all the mentorship I can from them on fatherhood. I'm going to take this responsibility and do the right thing by you and our baby. I love you Sarah. I really do. I know I've just barely turned eighteen, and you'll be eighteen too soon. But I know that I love you. I am going to continue to be there for you."

Sarah was moved by his words. All she could manage to say was, "Thank you. I love you too Reginald."

Tears fell from her eyes, and he wiped them. She smiled and said, "We're standing in the middle of the store and people are starting to look at us."

"I don't care," Reginald said as he continued to wipe her tears.

"Neither do I," Sarah replied.

They finally decided they would go with the pastel Noah's Ark theme for the baby's room. While they were at the store. They went to the store computer and started a registry for people that had been asking her what they could get her. She was overwhelmed at the support she was getting from everyone. Although Talinda and Bernard didn't condone fornication, they were supportive nonetheless.

Michelle and Lisa planned a baby shower for her and got with Veronica and Reginald's mother to iron out all the details while Sarah and Reginald were out shopping. They wanted to have it early so they would have time to help her put the baby's room together. So they set the date for the end of the month. She would be going into her seventh month by then.

*****

The time for the trial of Suzette Timmons for the kidnapping and accidental death of Callisha was at hand. Derrick had mixed feelings about if he should allow Nevette to attend court. She was four months pregnant and was still lightheaded more than he was comfortable with. Every test ran on her had come back negative. He had come too far and endured too much to start doubting God's ability in his life now.

"I want to go Justice," Nevette pleaded. "I want to hear what was going through her mind when she decided to kidnap and kill my baby."

"Sweetheart she is probably not even going to take the stand. I understand that she plans on pleading not guilty by reason of insanity. Baby, dad said her lawyer is trying to cut a deal for her because she recorded all of our prayer sessions on her smart phone. Now I know there was nothing said or done by me that is incriminating or could be held against me in any way. But sweetheart she can splice the tapes and get them to say whatever she wants them to say. By the time the experts examine and tell us the tapes have been tampered with the damage would already be done in the ears of the jurors. Naythia, I have never done or said anything inappropriate or sexual in nature to her. The only kiss we were ever involved in was when she kissed me by surprise on that last day I counseled her. Baby you're going to have to trust me because this could get ugly."

She looked at him and said, "I trust you, and I love you."

He nodded his head and said, "Baby. I swear—"

"Shhhh Justice," she replied and kissed him. "You don't have to do this. I said I trust you. We were separated for ten months, and you didn't touch anybody when you easily could have. There is no way that Suzette Timmons is going to get me to believe with some tape she has played and tampered with, that anything unprofessional ever happened between you two. Now with that being said Justice, I would like to attend the trial, hearing, or whatever it ends up being."

He smiled and said, "Okay baby. It won't be easy. They will no doubt show pictures of Callisha's life, when she was left at the entrance of the ER at the hospital and in the morgue. I'm going to be watching you. And if you look like you're going to lose it. I will limit your attendance. Fair enough?"

"Yes my love. Fair enough," she replied.

"We have Dysan's dad, John Jamison doing all the research. He is working with the prosecuting attorney on this case. I was a little apprehensive at first when dad said John Jamison was handling the research. Dysan told me about how he was at first with his wife Laytoria and their interracial marriage. We watched him for a while, but his performance at work remained stellar. We're a black-owned firm, but we are and never will be an all-black firm. I'm not on trial here, so I'm not worried about anything like that. I just don't want Suzette to get off on a technicality. I know she won't spend any time in a regular maximum security prison. I just want to ensure she's locked up in a mental facility and not free on the streets. I can't, baby—I—just can't take another blow. You know baby? I'm already worried about you. If this were regular morning sickness, it would have stopped already. You're four months pregnant, and you're still lightheaded and the doctor doesn't have any idea why."

"Justice sweetheart. Don't let the enemy play with your mind concerning me and Zoé. She and I are both fine. There is nothing set in stone when morning sickness ends. There are only suggestions but always exceptions to every rule. Some women feel queasy their whole pregnancy. Some women even have been known to have their menstrual cycle, or something that feels like it, for their entire pregnancy. It doesn't have to mean anything that I'm still lightheaded," she replied.

He rested his elbows on his knees and moved his head up and down rubbing it through his hands. He breathed heavily and said, "I know baby. I just don't want anything to come between us. I don't think I can take another thing right now."

She touched his chin and lifted his head to meet her eyes, "Baby, there is nothing that will or can come between what God has joined together. The devil already tried, and he wasn't successful. We came through, and we're stronger as a result. Rest easy baby. Zoé is fine sweetheart—she's fine. All will be well," Nevette said.

He smiled and said, "I love you. You, and Tre are my world. And you too little princess." He touched her stomach.

*****

Almost a month later both Lindsay and Sarah had their baby showers. Talinda and Nevette threw one for Lindsay, and the teens hosted the one for Sarah, both at the Travis' house.

Not soon after she and Trevor had the baby's room together. Trevor called everyone frantic that Lindsay was in labor. Everyone met at the hospital anxiously awaiting the arrival of the Johnson baby. Trevor was a ball of knots. You would have thought he had never been at a live birth the way he carried on. It was totally different being on the father's side of a delivery.

"Trevor would you calm down?" Nevette teased him.

"I know. You would never guess that I do this for a living," he replied.

Lindsay breathed heavily as she prepared herself for the next contraction. It was a doozy and almost lifted her off the table. She managed to laugh at that precise moment.

"Lindsay what in the world is so funny?" Nevette asked.

"Girl, I was just remembering when you were pregnant with Tre. You had a contraction hit you that raised you off the table, and you started calling all kinds of names for Jesus. You looked at Derrick, just as I reminded you that he was the same man you were gaga over a few years earlier in the therapy pool in college," she replied.

They both laughed. Dr. Harrell checked her, and she was right at nine centimeters when Trevor's beeper went off. Sarah was being rushed to the hospital. Her water broke at seven and a half months. There were no other obstetricians on call that night, and Dr. Harrell was busy with his wife Lindsay. He whispered to her stomach, "Don't you dare come out while I'm downstairs junior."

"Don't worry Trevor. Go get Sarah settled. I will call you if Lindsay gets close before you return," Nevette said. "I won't let you miss this little guy's entrance into the world."

He thanked Nevette, kissed Lindsay and declared his love to her and rushed off to assess the situation and get Sarah stable. Reginald was a mess by the time they arrived at the hospital. It was so like God that almost the entire youth ministry was there at the hospital already with Trevor and Lindsay, so her support team was in place.

Trevor assessed Sarah and left her aunt Veronica there with her. He rushed back upstairs. Just as he entered the room Dr. Harrell was checking Lindsay to see if she was at ten centimeters and fully effaced yet.

"Dad you are right on time. We are ready to push," Dr. Harrell said.

Trevor supported her back, and Nevette coached her through the final contractions and the pushing.

One, two, three pushes and little Trevor Jr., let out his first cry. Lindsay cried uncontrollable tears. She couldn't help but to think of the child she was forced to abort at age fifteen. She was so grateful for God's deliverance, blessing and gift in her life. She would never have dreamed she would be where she was at that precise moment. Happily married with a beautiful new baby boy. Trevor was able to cut the cord and hold his son before he had to rush off to go deliver Sarah's baby.

Shortly after everyone saw baby Johnson, they got the announcement that Sarah's baby made it through the birth canal successfully at three pounds and twelve ounces. They rushed him to the neo-natal unit with Reginald and his mother in tow. Veronica stayed in the room to comfort Sarah, who was just at the point of being hysterical. She only got to see her baby once, and was unable to touch or hold him before they rushed him off.

It was Nevette's turn to be the paparazzi, and she filled the role like a professional.

Sarah was soon able to join Reginald in the neo-natal unit. Little Reginald was in an incubator by the time she got there. Between the parents and grandparents, they mapped out the schedule of who would be with the baby, so they had twenty-four hour representation there at the hospital. Sarah would spend most her day sitting right there beside her baby boy.

*****

Suzette's sentencing hearing was put on hold due to unforeseeable technicalities. Her legal team attempted to come to an agreement with the state that if they allowed her to plead not guilty by reason of insanity, they would ensure she would be in a mental facility for the next ten years. However, when she was evaluated for soundness of mind, she was found competent and capable to stand trial for the murder. If found guilty, she would spend her time in a maximum security prison. So now the defense and prosecution needed additional time to prepare their cases.

Nevette was five and a half months pregnant now. And with the thirty-day delay, she would be well into her sixth month by the time the trial even began. Derrick worried about Nevette. She was still to date nauseous and lightheaded.

When Justice shared the news about Suzette, Nevette appeared stoic. She just wanted more than anything, for everything to finally be all behind them one way or another. But she wondered just what the defense had up their sleeves. Because Suzette most definitely would have benefited from the insanity plea.

~Chapter Twelve~

The day started out like any other day. Nevette was right at six months pregnant and Derrick was elated, because for the last week Nevette felt perfectly fine and hadn't had a single incident where she felt lightheaded. Derrick kissed her, rubbed her stomach and then prayed over his family before leaving the house.

"Okay baby, I have to go before I'm late," Derrick said as he kissed Nevette again.

"Okay Justice. Have a great day sweetheart," she replied as she pulled him down to her to kiss him again as he attempted to walk out of the door. She stood in the doorway until he backed out of the driveway and then headed down the hallway to rush Tre along so he wouldn't be late for school.

After she dropped Tre off, she went to the hospital to see Sarah and baby Reginald. He had been in the neo-natal since birth a few weeks ago, but had already managed to gain well over a pound and things were looking very hopeful that he would be home within the month.

She decided to stop in and see Lindsay and her godson before she headed to the grocery store to pick up some salmon and a few other things for dinner.

"Girl, it's hard to believe he is two weeks old already," Lindsay said as she laid TJ down in the bassinet.

"Oh Lindsay girl, you haven't seen anything yet. Next week, he'll be off to kindergarten and won't need you to help him tie his shoes or put on his coat anymore," Nevette replied.

"Yeah, but Tre still lets you help him with his coat," Lindsay added with a laugh.

"He feels sorry for me," Nevette replied still laughing.

They sat, and chit-chatted about Suzette and the trial among other things for over an hour.

Nevette looked at her watched. She stood and grabbed her purse as she said, "Girl, look at the time. It's nearly one o'clock. I have to get going if I'm going to have that house smelling like harbor salmon by the time Justice gets home. He's not done until nearly six on Thursdays, so I still have time after I pick Tre up from school to finish dinner."

"Girl, you are really loving the stay-at-home mom thing aren't you?" Lindsay asked.

"I have to admit girl. I wish I would have quit working sooner. It's way more fulfilling than I ever imagined," Nevette replied.

"I hear you. I must admit. I am enjoying being home with the baby and taking care of Trevor and managing the house. He has hinted around that it would be alright with him if I didn't go back to work after my maternity leave ended," Lindsay replied as she stood to walk Nevette to the door.

They said their goodbyes and Nevette decided to stop by the supermarket to grab the salmon and get dinner started before she went to pick up Tre form school. She smiled as she pulled into the parking lot. This was about the time of her pregnancy when she would have to start modifying everything that was around her to accommodate her belly. She sat in the car for a minute and thanked God again for Zoé. She thought of everything she and Derrick had been through and gave her stomach a quick pat and said aloud, "Sometimes you just have to fight for life. No matter the obstacle, you just have to fight."

She felt strange as she walked through the aisles. She decided to gather the items needed to make a pound cake as well. She had that uneasy feeling. The same one she had just before Justice and Tre left the house for the football game that Sunday morning. "You're being silly Nevette," she thought. She finally made it over to the seafood department and picked up the salmon.

*****

He moved through the super market aisles, taking careful notice of all the female patrons. He was there every day waiting patiently and monitoring the aisles. "Anything worth having is worth the wait," he thought as he rounded the corner headed toward the deli area. There she was, radiant and stunning. He could smell the perfume she was wearing and she took his breath away. She was glowing and full of life. "Mmmm, good things come to those who wait," he said aloud as he moved closer to her. He watched to see if she were alone or with someone. The harsh evil of the unclean spirit that dwelled within him was overjoyed when he noticed that she was alone when she got into the line to pay for her items.

He stood almost directly behind her in line and breathed heavily. Their eyes met once, and a fire raged within him. His manhood stood at attention. He just had to have her. Yes, she would definitely be the next one. The way she caressed her very pregnant stomach turned him on as he watched her place her items on the conveyor belt. Her voice was soft and heavenly as she conversed with the cashier. He couldn't wait to smell her hair and caress her breast and stomach as he mounted her bloody and exhausted body. It had been a while since he was able to quench his desire. He laid low since his last encounter. The leads were getting too close to him. He longed for the hot sweet softness of a woman with child. A woman rendering herself to him to protect her unborn child, gave him an orgasmic high that was unmatchable. His heart rate quickened at the thought of what he was about to have pleasure in.

The person in front of him had a price check, and he panicked. What if she left the parking lot before he checked out? He got out of line and left his basket on the floor. He hoped he still had condoms in his backpack, because he couldn't miss the opportunity to have her.

She was simply angelic as she appeared to glide across the parking lot to her car. He hurriedly got into his truck and watched which direction she was headed in before he pulled out of the parking lot. He didn't want to follow her too closely. His manhood ached with the anticipation of having her.

All the way home Nevette had that uneasy feeling again. She started to call Justice to check on him, but dismissed it and said, "Lord I'm not going to be overprotective of him for the rest of my life. He's okay. I trust you Lord. He's okay. I'm not going to bother him at work."

She spent way too much time at the supermarket. If she didn't get started soon, she would be late getting dinner on the table for Justice and Tre. As she pulled into the driveway, she let the garage door up.

He was excited to see that no other car was in the garage. He stopped his car, slipped on a pair of surgical gloves, donned his face mask, and grabbed his backpack from the back seat. He ran up the side of the driveway, so she couldn't see him as she got out of her car.

Nevette had the strangest urge to let the garage door down before she unlocked and got out of her car. She shook her head and said, "Nevette you're being silly." She exited the car and retrieved her grocery bag from the back seat.

As she opened the door leading into the kitchen and got ready to push the button to let the garage door down, he rounded the corner of the garage and grabbed her from behind. One bag of groceries fell out of her hand and landed by the car the other went in every direction onto the kitchen floor as he hit the button to let the garage door down and forced her into the house screaming.

*****

Derrick sat at his desk shaking his head at the wonder of God. He couldn't wait to give Nevette the good news. At the urging of her attorney, after being deemed fit to stand trial by medical psychologist Dr. Angela Taylor. Suzette Timmons changed her not-guilty plea by reason of insanity, to guilty for kidnapping and negligent homicide. There would only need be a hearing to pass sentence and the prosecution was pushing for twenty to life. Her sister was charged with negligence and aiding and abetting a known criminal, which she has also pled guilty to. He was relieved that neither, he nor Nevette would have to sit through and relive the horror of losing Callisha. With her impeccable career and lack of criminal record, plus her testimony against her sister, Nurse Howard would most likely receive a light sentence or possibly probation. She would most definitely lose her license as a registered nurse.

He tried calling Nevette but got no answer. He made a note to stop by the store on the way to home to grab a couple more bottles of sparkling cider. This was definitely a reason to celebrate. The Suzette Timmons issue would finally be behind them and they could breathe a little easier.

*****

The stench of his breath as he kissed the side of her neck and smelled her hair, made Nevette nauseous. He pushed himself against her from behind, and terror ripped through her. The anticipation of what she knew was coming had every fiber of her being crying out for help. She threw up as he pushed her to the ground. She hit hard on her elbows and knees in an effort to protect Zoé as her body was plunged to the floor. As he went to climb on top of her, she rolled over on her back and kicked up at him connecting with his groin. This was her opportunity to try to get to her cell phone that went flying across the room onto the floor as he forced her into the house.

Rage entered his spirit and he had to control his thoughts. He knew he had to maintain control his emotions to stay on top of the situation. Even within the rage and pain in his groin from her kick, the uncontrollable ache in his loins for her intensified. She was playing her role exactly as she should. She was fighting him off. This was going to be a sweet victory, and he could hardly wait to stand over her lifeless body and have his spoil at his pleasure and leisure. The anticipation of her helpless moans as he entered her kept him focused to make sure he had the full enjoyment of every step along to the way to the sweet prize between her legs.

As she scrambled across the floor, he grabbed a knife off the kitchen counter and intercepted her.

"OH MY GOD, OH GOD PLEASE! NO—MY BABY—DON'T DO THIS—PLLEEEEAAASSSEEEE! Nevette screamed.

His excitement mounted as the blood begin to fly. It was beginning. The first fruits of his orgasmic ride rushed out of her with each tiny jab he made into her flesh. He didn't want to penetrate her too deeply. He jabbed her with the knife on her arms, chest, stomach and legs, just enough to keep her off of him and to ensure she would lose blood without passing out. He wanted her very much conscious when he mounted and entered her.

She fought him, screaming and kicking with everything she had, as he drug her towards the basement entrance. She held onto the side of the doorpost, and her bloody handprints left a trail all the way down the stairway as he drug her.

At the base of the stairs, she knew the lamp would be just to the left on a table. She began to lean towards the left and grabbed it just as he snatched her from the stairs. She swung around and landed a blow to his shoulder and neck, and the lamp went crashing to the ground. This again gave her a moment to gain a foothold because he was forced to regroup. Before she could get back up the steps, he grabbed her.

He thrust the weight of his body on top of her, and she screamed in terror, "MY BABY!", as her stomach was forced into the rise of the steps. He had her around the neck with one arm, and she could feel the tip of the knife at her stomach.

He said, "I will cut it out of you, if you don't quit it."

The calmness of his tone terrorized her. He was enjoying this. Her fear fed his desire, and he began to press against her.

"You are going to be sweet. I can tell because I'm about to climax just thinking about being inside of you," he whispered in her ear as he licked the side of her face.

She screamed, "JUUUSSSSSSSTTTTIIIIIIIICCCCEEEE! OH GOD PLEASE DON'T ALLOW THIS. PLEASE DON'T! MY BABY...MY BABY. OH GOD—OH GOD!"

As she felt her unborn child tighten inside of her, she realized what she just felt was a contraction. She began to reach behind her scratching and clawing at him. She knew she had to get his skin underneath her nails.

He stood and snatched her up. He drug her back down the stairs to the basement. She felt her body grow weaker. She had lost way too much blood. But she also knew she had to continue to fight until her last breath. Her mind raced back to the words she said just a few hours earlier as she sat in the car before going into the supermarket. She realized her fight was not about her surviving. Her fight was to keep Zoé alive at all cost. She would have to relax her body to keep Zoé stable. She prayed silently that after he left, her lifeless body would be discovered in enough time to save Zoé.

"I have to give him what he wants to save you Zoé," she whispered as she clutched her stomach. "Justice, I'm sorry—I have to."

He slung her down to the floor yet again, and she plopped on her side like a rag doll. He stood over her smiling as he unbuckled his pants. She tried hard to maintain consciousness for Zoé's sake, but the room was going in and out of focus.

He smiled at first when he realized she was now too weak to move or put up any resistance. She was exhausted and bleeding from the forty plus stabs wounds all over her body. Most of her wounds were not more than a half inch deep. But to his alarm, some were bleeding more than he would have liked. It wasn't as thrilling a victory when the prey was unconscious. He had never stabbed anyone enough to kill them before. He figured he had better get to his business and leave because she was going downhill very fast.

He left her there and went back upstairs to retrieve his backpack. When he returned he made haste to prepare for his victory. He opened the backpack and took out the small trash bag. To his relief there was a condom in his pack. He opened it and put it on. He took off his gloves placed them in the trash bag and put on a fresh pair.

He smiled, ripped her underwear off and pulled her up off the floor up to her knees, so he could enter her from the rear. But she was too weak to support herself. He yelled, "I don't care about your baby!

If you don't want me to pound you into the ground, you need to support yourself on your knees and make this easy for me. If you don't, I will lay you flat on your stomach and drive you into the floor with the full weight of my body!"

Nevette could only whisper, "Zoé." She knew she had to muster the last bit of strength she had to get on her knees to keep him from thrusting her stomach into the ground. She was contracting, and tears streamed down her face. She was unable to get another sound to exit out of her mouth.

He pulled her over to the couch and shoved her face down into it, so she would be more supported on her knees.

"Finally—sweet victory," he said as he pushed her dress up over her back toward her shoulders. He closed his eyes and a smile of sheer pleasure graced his face as he entered her and enjoyed the spoils of his conquest.

She was helpless to stop him. She supported her body with the little bit of energy she had left to protect the life that grew inside of her.

She could feel herself losing consciousness with each thrust of his body on top of hers. Her body went limp, and her head dropped to the side.

After he finished, her body fell to the floor unconscious. He stood over her as a mighty warrior over his prey. He placed the used condom in his little trash bag, zipped up his pants and once again changed gloves. He gathered everything he brought with him to include the mask he wore and placed them into his back pack.

He bent down and whispered in her ear before he left, "You are so sweet. Thank you for a fulfilling afternoon." He didn't realize she was already unconscious.

He looked around upstairs for a minute to insure he hadn't left any evidence of his being there. He went out the same door he forced Nevette into. He let up the garage door and walked down the driveway to his car hoping he wouldn't encounter anyone who would notice her blood all over his clothes and drove away.

Nevette lay there on the basement floor, unconsciousness. All functions in her body slowed down, and the bleeding stopped.

*****

Two hours later Tre stood outside with the after school attendant waiting for his mother to drive around the corner.

"It's not like her to be late," Mrs. Stewart thought to herself.

After it was clear she wasn't going to come and all the other children had left. She told Tre to follow her back into the school. They went to the office to call his father.

"Hello Mr. Goodfellow, this is Mrs. Stewart the after school attendant at Derrick's school. He is here in the office with me. Mrs. Goodfellow didn't come to pick him up today. I looked in his backpack and there no note saying that he was to ride the bus, so I kept him here. Will you be able to come pick him up or shall I call his grandmother?" Mrs. Stewart asked.

"Really? That's not like her. Ahhhh, no I'll be there shortly," Derrick replied.

He got off the phone and called Nevette. Her phone went straight to the voicemail, and he left a message:

> *"Hey Nevette baby, are you okay? I'm on my way to get Tre from school. You forgot Tre today sweetheart. Are you alright? Is everything okay? Give me a call when you get this message Naythia okay? Love you."*

He called the house phone and left a message there as well, when she didn't answer. He pushed the thought of something being wrong out of his mind as he filled his father in on the situation before he left the office to get Tre. As he drove to the school, he dialed Nevette's cell phone again and left a second message similar to the first one. He entered the school and headed for the office. He spoke briefly with Mrs. Stewart and left with Tre.

As he drove home, he decided to call Teddy to see if he had spoken with Nevette.

"Hey Teddy have you talked to Nevette today?" he asked after Teddy answered.

"No I haven't why?" Teddy replied.

"Hopefully nothing. I'm on the way home now with Tre. The school called, she didn't pick him up," Derrick replied.

Teddy was silent. He took a deep breath and said, "Okay, ahhmmnn—it's not like Nay Nay to forget about Tre."

"I know. I don't want to say too much with little man with me. I'm going to call mom to see if she has talked with her today. Maybe she laid down to take a nap and over slept. She'll probably call me in a panic and apologize any minute," Derrick said to keep the situation in the car out of panic mode.

"Okay Derrick. I'll start calling her phone to see if I can get her. Call me when you get home okay," Teddy replied.

"Alright," Derrick said as he hung up. He dialed his mom, "Hey mom, listen. Have you talked to or seen Nevette today? The school called, she never showed up to get Tre."

"No DJ I haven't seen her. It's not like her to forget Tre," Shaundra said almost in a panic.

"Yes that's exactly what Teddy just said," Derrick replied. "I'm on the way home now. I'll call you when I get there mom."

"Okay baby. In the meantime, I'll call her to see if I can get through," Shaundra replied.

"Okay mom. Let me know if you contact her," he replied.

"Okay sweetheart. DJ I can hear it in your voice. Stay calm baby," his mom replied.

"I'm trying to mom," Derrick said.

He drove a few more minutes, and it popped in his head to call Lindsay. "Hey Lindsay have you seen or talked to Nevette today?"

"Yeah Derrick. She stopped by earlier today to see the baby. She stayed for a little while and said she was going by the grocery store to grab some things she needed for dinner before going to get Tre," she replied.

"What time was that Lindsay?" he asked. He tried hard to keep his voice as calm as possible. But the invasion of terror kept attempting to creep into his thoughts.

"It was about one-thirty or so when she left the house. You sound panicked Derrick," Lindsay replied.

"I am. She never showed up to get Tre. He's in the car with me now. The school called. We're on the way to the house now," Derrick replied.

"Okay Derrick call me when you get home. I'll call to see if I can get her on the phone. Maybe she got caught up shopping or something and lost track of time," Lindsay said in an attempt to ease Derrick's mind.

"Yeah okay," he answered nervously. "Well I'm turning into the subdivision Lindsay. I'll call you back in a few minutes," Derrick replied and hung up the phone.

In the back seat, Tre could feel the level of panic rise in his father concerning his mother. His spirit of discernment was very keen for so young a person.

"Daddy—is mommy okay?" he asked in a shaky voice.

"I'm sure she's fine Tre," he replied.

As he pulled into the driveway, he was somewhat relieved that Nevette's car was in the garage. But as he parked behind her car, he saw that the door leading into the house was open, and a bag of groceries was on the ground by the car. Before he could tell Tre to stay put, he was already out and coming around the car. Derrick took one step into the house, and his heart sank.

He stepped back out before Tre could enter and said, "Tre don't come any closer. Go stand beside daddy's car while I go look for mommy."

"What's wrong daddy?" Tre asked.

"Just stay in the garage Tre," Derrick commanded.

The living room and kitchen area both looked as though a domestic violence tornado had exploded, and blood was everywhere. He raced through the house calling out to Nevette and praying all at the same time. "OH GOD PLEASE NEVETTE—SWEETHEART! WHERE ARE YOU BABY?"

He could hear Tre outside yelling his name and asking where his mommy was. He looked back toward the door to make sure Tre hadn't come any closer to entering the door when he noticed the blood all over the doorpost leading to the basement. His heart raced, and hot tears started to flow down his face. His heart pounded fiercely. The first three steps he took down the stairs seemed to slip from beneath him as he became nauseous.

He could see the blood going all the way down the stairs on the walls. At times, his could make out bloody handprints and the blood on the carpet of the stairs was smeared to indicate someone or something being drug.

Tre slowly began to make his way to the backdoor after his father stopped responding to him. He entered the kitchen and stood there. He heard his father's voice in the basement. He turned and looked over his shoulder at the doorway that led downstairs unable to move a muscle.

When Justice reached the bottom of the stairs, he stopped and terror gripped him. Nevette lay on the floor in front of the couch curled up in a ball with her clothes half torn off of her. Broken lamps were on the floor, and the couch was pushed back and up against the wall with pillows throw around. There was blood on the couch, walls and all over her.

"OH GOD, OH GOD, OH GOD. BABY PLEASE. JESUS NOOOOOOO! PLEASE GOD. OH GOD, OH GOD. OH MY GOD WIFE AND BABY!" he rushed over to her and touched her shoulder.

She screamed, "NOOOOO! GET OFF OF ME! GET OFF! NOOOOO!"

He withdrew his hands from her as though he had just touched a hot stovetop. He could hear Tre at the top of the steps crying because he had heard his mother.

"MOMMY!" Tre exclaimed.

"GO TO YOUR ROOM TRE. DO NOT COME DOWNSTAIRS!" Derrick commanded.

"DADDY—," Tre replied with a whimper.

"Please Tre go to your room. Daddy will take care of mommy," he replied in a calmer voice. He knew he had to keep Tre from coming downstairs.

Tre stood in the kitchen where he was when he first entered from the garage. He didn't go to his room, but also did not advance to the basement. He was still, unable to move from the spot where he stood. His heart raced, and he began to breathe erratically. He just kept looking back and forth from the garage door to the basement door.

Derrick moved over and pulled her up into his arms. She was now barely conscious. He attempted to touch her face as he said, Naythia baby are you ok—"

"NOOOOO, NOOOO!" She yelled and pushed off from him swinging wildly.

"NAYTHIA BABY ITS ME," he exclaimed as he made a move to come close to her again.

"GET AWAY FROM ME! GET AWAY FROM ME!" she screamed.

"Okay, okay. I won't touch you," he replied. He held both hands forward as though saying 'whoa'.

He scurried back and few paces away from her and pulled his phone out of his pocket. As he dialed 9-1-1, he saw her underwear behind her torn as though they were ripped off of her. They were full of blood. Most of her clothes were also almost completely ripped off of her. He could see that she had been stabbed several times.

She moaned and started to speak as her head plopped back down on the floor again.

He whispered, "Baby talk to me—Nevette what happened baby?" Derrick could feel himself getting nauseous again at the thought of what had transpired in his home.

"9-1-1 how may I help you?" the service attendant said as she answered the phone.

"YES HELLO. MY NAME IS DERRICK GOODFELLOW. I LIVE AT 12224 CASTLETOWN ROAD IN ATLANTA, GEORGIA. I JUST GOT HOME. THERE IS BLOOD EVERYWHERE IN MY HOUSE. UPSTAIRS AND DOWNSTAIRS. I FOUND MY WIFE DOWNSTAIRS ON THE FLOOR. WHEN I WENT TO TOUCH HER, SHE SCREAMED AND PULLED AWAY FROM ME YELLING NO. GOD PLEASE. SEND SOMEONE. IT LOOKS LIKE SHE HAS BEEN STABBED A LOT. AND I THINK SHE HAS BEEN RAPED. THERE IS BLOOD EVERYWHERE. SHE'S ALMOST SIX MONTHS PREGNANT!" He yelled.

"Oh my God—him again," the attendant whispered to herself. "Okay Mr. Goodfellow listen to me very carefully. Do not attempt to touch your wife again. Is there a female that your wife trusts that doesn't live too far away, that may be able to get there in time to go with her in the ambulance?"

"Yes her best friend Lindsay Johnson," Derrick replied.

"Okay Mr. Goodfellow. Does your wife appear conscious at the moment? And if not if, is she at least breathing?" she asked.

"Daddy I want mommy—wants wrong with mommy?" Tre cried.

"She's hurt Tre okay. Daddy needs you to stay in your room Tre," Derrick replied as he crawled around the couch so he could see Nevette's face. Her eyes were closed and her mouth slightly open. He took a chance at touching her to feel for a pulse. She didn't move. His heart pounded. He could feel the pulse and that somewhat eased him as he breathed a sigh of relieve realizing she was just unconscious.

"No she is not conscious but she is still breathing. Please get someone here quick. There's blood everywhere!" he exclaimed.

"Sir I have already requested female paramedics and sent them to your home. You need to call that friend to help assist your wife now Mr. Goodfellow. Is there another phone line you can use so I can stay on this line with you until the paramedics arrive?" she asked.

Derrick answered yes as he stood up and walked over to the coffee table and dialed Lindsay's number. He was moving on auto pilot but when Lindsay answered the phone, his emotions began to take over again.

"OH MY GOD LINDSAY, PLEASE GET OVER HERE NOW. I FOUND HER IN THE BASEMENT. 9-1-1 IN ON MY CELL PHONE AND THE AMBULANCE IS ON THE WAY. SHE IS UNCONSCIOUS NOW, BUT SHE WAS FIGHTNG ME EARLIER. THERE IS BLOOD EVERYWHERE LINDSAY. SHE'S BEEN STABBED SEVERAL TIMES AND R-R-RAPED!" he blurted out. He calmed himself and continued, "She won't let me touch her. The lady from 9-1-1 said a female she trusts needs to be here to ride in the ambulance. Plus I have Tre here anyway. I'm going to call mom to come get him so I can follow the ambulance to the hospital."

"OH MY GOD. JESUS—PLEASE NO!" Lindsay exclaimed. "I'm not far from your house. When you first called I could hear the panic in your voice and told Trevor I needed to head your way. I'll be there in about five minutes. I'm turning into the subdivision now."

"Lindsay please just call Teddy and my mom. I don't think I can do this again. I mean, describe this," was all he could manage to say and he hung up the phone.

She said "okay" as the dial tone alerted in her ear. She called Trevor and filled him in. Trevor told her to be careful and to let him call Teddy and Derrick's mom, so she could focus on driving. Trevor called Teddy and informed him. Teddy went into a panic and said he would call his father and brother and then head to Derrick and Nevette's house. He told Teddy it would probably be best if he went straight to the hospital. He told Teddy he would call Talinda and Bernard to meet him there and get the church to start a prayer chain. Shaundra's line was busy. He called Lindsay back to let her know that he couldn't reach Derrick's mother. She said she would inform Derrick when she got in the house. She had just arrived. Trevor called Bernard. He and Talinda were soon on the way to the hospital. Raymond stayed at the house with the twins.

Lindsay arrived about five minutes before the ambulance. Tre was still standing in the same spot in the kitchen looking down toward the basement.

She burst through the door yelling for Derrick. When she saw the scene, she gasped. Her eyes instantly filled with tears.

"Aunt Lindsay my mommy is downstairs and and—and—and she hurt. And my da-da-daddy is with her!" Tre exclaimed. He was crying uncontrollably. His shoulders were rising and falling with every word he stuttered through.

"Calm down Tre, okay. I'm gonna go see mommy. Stay here okay Tre," Lindsay said in a calm voice.

"I WANT MY MOMMY!" Tre screamed.

"I know baby. She'll be okay. Daddy and I need you to stay right here okay," Lindsay said as she hugged him.

After she felt he was stable enough, she went downstairs to where Derrick and Nevette were. When she got to bottom of the stairs. What she saw stopped her in her tracks, and she looked at Derrick. He was crying and trying extremely hard not to scream so he wouldn't send

Tre into a tail spin upstairs.

"OH MY GOD DERRICK. WHAT?!" she screamed.

She went over to Nevette and softly called her name as she approached her from the front, so she could see she was coming.

"I don't think she's conscious right now Lindsay," Derrick said.

"Okay Derrick I have her. You go upstairs and take care of Tre," Lindsay said she crawled closer to Nevette.

"But Lindsay—" he started to say.

"No Derrick. Tre needs you. You can't do anything for her right now. Go to Tre!" she instructed.

"Okay," Derrick whispered as he wiped his tears. He got ready to call his mom when he heard Lindsay engage Nevette. He dialed his mom's number before he headed back up the stairs.

Shaundra answered the phone, "DJ have you heard anyth—"

He cried out but attempted not to shout as he cut her off and said, "Oh God mom! I found her—I found her in the basement. Mom can you come get Tre. I need to—I don't know—I mean—mom—just—I need to you to get Tre. I CAN'T DO THIS GOD!"

"DJ baby you're not making sense. Calm down and talk to me," Shaundra replied.

"Looks like she was stabbed several times and raped momma!" he exclaimed and fought not to fall apart again. "She's going in and out of consciousness. I want to go to the hospital when the ambulance gets here. Lindsay's here. She won't let me touch her mom!"

"Oh my Go—," Shaundra started to stay but despair snatched the last word right out of her mouth. "I'm on my way baby. Hang in there. I'm on the way. I'll call your dad. Where is Tre now?"

"He's upstairs. I'm about to go see about him now that Lindsay is here with Naythia," he replied.

"Okay you go do that. I'm on the way," Shaundra replied and hung up before Derrick could answer. She looked up toward heaven and declared. "Dear Lord how much more can they take!" She called her husband Derrick Sr., as she left the house. He said he would meet Derrick at the hospital since he was already downtown instead of coming that way and possibly miss them in transit.

Downstairs, Nevette allowed Lindsay to touch her and started to scream in her arms.

"Nevette," Lindsay called her name calmly as she touched her. "Nevette honey its Lindsay."

Nevette had a wild look in her eyes as she screamed, "LINDSAY! MY BABY! MY BABY! HE WAS GOING TO KILL MY BABY!"

"Oh sweetheart. Oh God Nevette," Lindsay replied as he pulled Nevette into her arms and started to rock back and forth with her.

"I HAD TO—I HAD TO—I HAD TO. SHE'S NOT MOVING! ZOÉ'S NOT MOVING! I TRIED TO FIGHT. HE WAS SO—" she lost the battle to be able to speak another coherent word. She started to scream things that made no sense, and stuttering and stammering over her words.

Justice was beside himself as he stood in the middle of the stairway listening. He realized that his assumption was correct. She indeed was raped. He forced himself to go up the stairs. He found Tre standing in the middle of the kitchen in the same spot.

He said, "Come here son," as he reached the top of the steps.

Tre stood still. He did not move nor attempt to advance toward his father. Derrick called Tre to him again, but he just stood in the same spot and cried.

Derrick looked down at him as he began to walk over to him. What had Tre frozen in time finally caught Derrick's attention. Tre was standing in the only spot in the kitchen that was not covered with his mother's blood. Derrick hadn't noticed that her blood was almost over the entire floor as he scurried through the house earlier looking for her.

"Oh my God!" he exclaimed as he reached Tre.

He scooped him up in his arms. He grabbed a kitchen towel and put it on the floor to get the blood off the bottom of his shoes before he walked down the hallway toward Tre's bedroom. He realized that his son was probably going into shock. He grabbed the comforter off Tre's bed and wrapped him in it. He sat down on the bed and held his son and cried through a prayer:

> *God,*
>
> *I don't understand. Please God. Oh God. Comfort my son Lord. Give him peace about his mother. Tell me what to say to him Lord. I don't know what to say. I don't know what to say...*

Derrick lost control of his emotions. All he could do was cry and hold Tre tightly in his arms. He desired to be downstairs with Nevette and Lindsay but knew being with Tre was his appointed task for the moment. So he sat there and held Tre as they both cried.

He heard the ambulance coming in the distance. He prayed that his mother wouldn't be too far behind it.

~Chapter Thirteen~

The paramedics arrived. Derrick heard them and left Tre on the bed for a moment to find out what the plan was and to let them know to go down to the basement. Nevette stopped crying and was unconscious again. Lindsay just held her in her arms as hot tears streamed down her face.

Just as Derrick turned to head back into Tre's bedroom his mother scampered through the door.

"Oh mom. Thank God you're here!" Derrick exclaimed.

She embraced him as she told him to trust God. She then told him to go on downstairs, and she would take care of Tre.

"I think he's in shock mom. We are going to need to take him in the car and follow the ambulance," he said to his mother as she turned to head to Tre's room.

"For that matter, DJ, I also believe you're in shock. You've forgotten that your mom is a pediatrician. Let me assess him son. You go with Nevette. If need be, I'll bring Tre," she said and she went into the room. She scooped Tre up in her arms as she sat on the bed beside him.

Lindsay informed the paramedics of the conversation she had with Nevette before she lost consciousness again. One of the females said as she shook knelt down to begin to Nevette for transit to the hospital, "It's starting again. They really need to catch this guy."

Derrick headed back downstairs just as they strapped Nevette onto the gurney. She was still unconscious. However, since she had a pulse, they wanted to get her out of there fast. They would hook up an IV and finish assessing her wounds and call the hospital en route. They instructed Lindsay to jump in the ambulance to be with her, in case she regained consciousness again along the way.

Derrick was beside himself. He grabbed his keys, yelled to his mother that they were leaving and followed the ambulance with his hazard lights on.

*****

The ambulance arrived at the emergency room at Northside Hospital. Derrick pulled in right behind them and parked in the first vacant spot he saw. He sprinted over to the entrance of the emergency room. They were heading into the lobby area with Nevette when he caught up with them.

As they headed to the clinic area one of the paramedics stopped Derrick, "Sir please. Your presence in the room will only be a hindrance. She will not do well with you there. Her friend is with her, and her obstetrician Yolanda Harrell has been called and should arrive shortly. Until then, we will try to talk your wife into allowing the male doctor on call to examine her. Sir, they will keep you informed with everything that happens with your wife. Please just trust them. Trust us, we know what's best right now."

All Derrick could do was nod and rub his head as he turned and started pacing the floor. He was beside himself.

There were three other couples in the ER waiting area. Two of the women were pregnant. One looked to be about four months pregnant. She had cold and flu symptoms. The other was about three months pregnant. She'd been bleeding slightly off and on over the past few days and was about to be taken into the clinic area when the call about Nevette came in and put everything on hold. The other couple present there was the godparents-to-be and were there with them for moral support with the threatened miscarriage. They weren't sure what Nevette had been brought in for. They all sat in silence unsure what, if anything, to attempt to say to Derrick.

Derrick continued to pace the floor and rub his head. He didn't acknowledge the other people in the waiting area. As far as he was concerned, he was the only person in the room.

He finally sat down and dropped his head in his hands. "Oh God please," he whispered. He broke down crying.

Bernard and Talinda rushed in and practically tackled Derrick before they came to a stop at the seat were he sat. Derrick jumped up.

"How is she Derrick? Have they said anything?" Bernard exclaimed.

"They just went in with her Bernard. I don't know anything yet," he replied and wiped his eyes. Suddenly, he lost it and began to scream.

"OH GOD BERNARD WHAT? WHAT AM I DOING WRONG? WHY? WHO? OH GOD WHAT BERNARD—WHAT? WHAT KIND OF ANIMAL RAPES A PREGNANT WOMAN? He paused for a millisecond, nowhere near enough time for Bernard to reply. Derrick wasn't looking for nor desired a reply. He just needed to get it all out before he exploded.

The couples that were in the waiting room area heard Derrick.

"Oh my God!" Sylvia Davis exclaimed. She was the one who was three months pregnant and had been spotting. She grabbed her stomach and placed her hand on her husband's lap. Her husband George clasped his hand in hers and shook his head in disbelief. She empathized with Nevette and Derick and began to cry and pray under her breath.

Talinda went to the desk to see if she could talk to Lindsay to find out if she could go into the examining room with her and Nevette. The clerk went away and came back quickly to get Talinda. Derrick was so hysterical neither of them noticed that Talinda left the room. She knew that what Derrick needed was Bernard. So she went to see what she could find out in order to come back and tell Derrick something positive to calm him down.

Derrick continued to cry out before Bernard could get a word in edgewise. He was borderline hysterical, "GOD PLEASE, WHAT AM I DOING WRONG? WHAT AM I NOT DOING? PLEASE GOD. WHAT DO YOU WANT FROM ME? WHAT DO YOU WANT ME TO DO? GOD PLEASE TELL ME—HELP ME. WHAT! MAN EVERYTHING I PUT MY HANDS TO—WHAT AM I DOING WRONG BERNARD? HUH—WHAT?

"Come on Derrick, this is not healthy. Don't do this to yourself," Bernard said as he touched Derrick on the shoulder.

Derrick continued, "EVERY DECISION I MAKE FOR MY FAMILY ENDS IN DISASTER. WHAT? JESUS—JESUS."

"Come on Derrick look. DERRICK—DERRICK LOOK AT ME MAN. This is not your fault," Bernard declared.

"YES BERNARD. YES IT IS. IT WAS ME...I ASKED HER TO STAY HOME. I ASKED HER TO QUIT HER JOB. IF SHE WERE AT WORK, SHE WOULDN'T HAVE BEEN THERE WHEN THIS GUY BROKE INTO THE HOUSE. OH GOD LORD, PLEASE HELP ME!" He fell to his knees and whispered before he completely lost it, "I just got my family back together. Nevette—Zoé—Jesus please—" he was distraught.

"Come on Derrick," Bernard interjected.

Derrick would not be consoled. Through his tears, he continued, "I just got my family back. I did this. Here I go again! I put her in harm's way. Look what I did to her. I promised her I would never hurt her again Bernard. I did this man—I did this!"

"Listen to yourself. Derrick it's not the same thing. You didn't rape or stab her," Bernard said.

"I may as well have Bernard! I placed her in the position to be there at the house. OH GOD WHY! WHAT ARE WE DOING WRONG? I DON'T UNDERSTAND WHY GOD WOULD ALLOW THIS TO HAPPEN. HE STABBED HER OVER AND OVER. HER CLOTHES WERE RIPPED OFF OF HER. I WENT TO TOUCH HER, AND SHE JUST SCREAMED AT ME NOT TO TOUCH HER. OH GOD THIS IS A NIGHTMARE. GOD PLEASE, SOMEBODY TELL ME I'M DREAMING!" Derrick exclaimed.

"Derrick you are going to have to calm down," Bernard said.

Just then Teddy rushed through the door. "WHERE IS SHE DERRICK? WHERE IS MY SISTER? I NEED TO SEE HER!"

Bernard sighed and looked up toward heaven, relieved as though he had been pleading with God to bail him out.

"I'M SORRY TEDDY. I PROMISED YOU AND YOUR DAD THAT I WOULD PROTECT HER. I PROMISED. I'M SORRY—I'M SORRY—I'M SORRY," Derrick all but collapsed in Teddy's arms. Teddy was more than just his brother-in-law. Teddy was his big brother, mentor and confidant.

His actions jolted Teddy. He realized that what happened to Nevette was over. All they could do now was to remain calm and pray for Nevette and the baby.

"They won't let me see her!" Derrick cried. "She won't let me touch her. She doesn't want me to touch her Teddy!"

"Derrick look at me," Teddy said as he grabbed Derrick by both of his shoulders to get his attention. "It's not you Derrick." Derrick dropped his head. Teddy shook him slightly and said, "No, listen to me. She's just been raped. She is not going to want me, dad or any man to touch her right now. You can't take that personally Derrick. She doesn't trust any man right now. They will get her stable and calm, and then she is going to want her husband."

He shook his head "no" and whispered in a defeated tone, "I just got her back. I promised her—I promised her Teddy. I promised her that I would never hurt her again."

"What are you talking about Derrick? That's absurd. You are not responsible for this any more than you were responsible for Callisha. Come on Derrick don't do this to yourself. This guy could have been watching her for a while. He could have easily waited for her outside her job or in the parking garage or when you and Tre were at practice or something. Derrick you're going to have to calm down. They are not going to allow you to stay in here hysterical like this."

Bernard walked over to the desk and asked the clerk if there was a private room that they could take Derrick too.

Derrick dropped to his knees and cried out, "God—please! How much more can we take? God help me please!" he began to shake violently, and his emotions overtook him.

Bernard rushed back over to him and just began to pray.

Sylvia said to everyone else that was in the waiting area, "Hey everyone let's join them in prayer. We need to pray for him, his wife and their unborn baby."

The other couple that was there with flu-like symptoms stood. The wife said, "We're not Christians. I mean—we don't know how to pray. God's not going to listen to us—is He?"

"You don't have to be a Christian or know the perfect words to pray. God's word says, where two or three are gathered in His name, He will be in the midst of them. It also says when people touch," she paused and reached her hand out to grab hers. This made all of them connect hands as they stood behind Bernard and Teddy, who were on the floor with Derrick. She finished the scripture, "and agree on anything. He will do it. Do you trust that there is a God, and if I pray, He will hear me?"

"Yes, because I believe that you believe. I can see it in your eyes," she replied.

"Then that's good enough. Stand and agree with us," Sylvia replied.

The woman smiled and squeezed her husbands and Sylvia's hand as tight as she could. She closed her eyes and had already begun to cry before Sylvia even opened her mouth to utter the first word.

Bernard looked up and saw that everyone in the waiting room had joined them in prayer. He looked at Sylvia, who had already begun to pray. He could see the Holy Spirit upon her. He quieted down and he and Teddy joined in agreeing with her as they laid their hands on

Derrick. He shook and sobbed uncontrollably:

Father,

We come before You, gathered in Your Son Jesus' name, because according to Your word You will be in the midst of those gathered in Your name. Father, I have no idea who the woman is that lies in the hospital bed on the other side of this wall, but I come to You on her behalf. And on behalf of her husband who lies here on the floor in front of us broken and in despair. Lord You said that You are nigh unto them that are of a broken heart; and saveth such as be of a contrite spirit. So Father, according to Your word we have confidence that You are indeed in the midst of us. Father we ask You for Your comfort for this man and his wife. God we pray that the peace You declare that You shall give that surpasses all understanding will fall on them in a mighty way. Lord every laceration she had God You be the balm in Gilead. Father, You are able to heal our every infirmity; spiritual, physical and emotional. God she will be in need of a complete restoration. We thank You that even as we speak You have already begun the process of recovery. Lord we speak to the womb that houses the unborn child of this couple. We speak strength stability and life to it and the fetus that is within the confines of its walls. God we rebuke a spirit of despair. And come against condemnation because neither of them comes from You. Father Your word says that perfect love casts out fear. God, allow the love that You have for him, and that he has for his wife to overtake and destroy every fear that attempts to attach itself to him about anything concerning this incident. We pray for a healthy fetus. God we pray for the physicians that are caring for his wife. Lord we thank You for guiding them in the knowledge of how to care for her and the steps to take. Lord I pray that this family will draw even closer to You and to each other. God You will get the glory for the testimony that rises like a Phoenix out of the ashes of this tragedy today. God we would not be true Christians if we did not also pray for the predator who committed this heinous act. God we pray that the Holy Spirit will get hold of him and convict him where he stands. There is no place that we can go that the Lord is not there. Even though the authorities may not know where or who he is, God

You know because You are Omniscient and Omnipotent. Justice is in Your hand and vengeance is Yours. But more than that. We pray that he would be totally delivered and set free from the evil spirits that dwell within him. God we don't always see the good at the time of tragedy, but we trust Your word, which proclaims that all things work together for our good. Father give this man peace. Lord...give him peace. And Lord protect everyone who is here in this circle of prayer. Heal every disease, infirmities and illness according to the promise of Calvary that Your stripes paid for.

In Jesus' uncompromising and powerful name,

Amen

At the close of her amen, the Holy Spirit fell like a blanket over the entire room, and a peace overtook each person standing in the prayer. Everyone, including Derrick was silent. Sylvia could feel the presence of God flow through her body, and she knew that she would no longer need to see a physician that night.

She turned to her husband and declared, "God just went through my body and healed me. Our baby is going to be fine."

He declared that he knew that, and they praised God together. The other couple stood in awe of what they had just witnessed. She felt better than she had felt since she first became pregnant. She felt stronger, and she could breathe clear and free from any nasal blockage. She and her husband had no idea what to do.

Bernard shook his head at the wonder of the Lord, and Teddy looked toward heaven and thanked God. Derrick still laid crumpled on the floor, but he was silent and appeared to be at peace.

Inside the clinical area, Talinda and Lindsay could not talk Nevette into the exam. The emergency room technicians needed to administer a rape kit on her. But she would not allow a man to touch her. Lindsay told her they would be sending in female nurses. But still nothing.

She had, however, allowed the nurse to look at her lacerations. They determined that none of them were deep enough to cause any lasting injuries. The reason she bled so much was mainly due to the adrenaline running through her body. Her heart rate and pulse caused blood to flow fast and erratically. The nurse suggested they may have to sedate her in order to administer the rape kit on her. The evidence would be needed to match with any suspects found in the case.

Nevette motioned for Lindsay to come down so she could whisper in her ear, "Lindsay, I'm having contractions."

"What? Oh my God Nevette, sweetheart you are going to have to allow the doctor to touch you to examine you. Dr. Harrell is on the way to the hospital, but she may get here too late. You're going to have to allow him to touch you," Lindsay exclaimed.

Fear came across Nevette's face. The thought of a man having his hands anywhere near her vaginal area was terrifying.

"We're going to be here with you every step of the way. But Nevette," Talinda said as she held Nevette's hand, "You have to let them gather evidence so this doesn't happen to another pregnant woman. I remember this case before a few years ago. They never caught the guy, and he disappeared. For some reason, he just stopped raping women. This has to be the same guy. Please allow them to administer the test, so they can see if it's a match with the other cases?"

"Nevette look at me," Lindsay said. "You said that you were having contractions. You are only six months pregnant. By the time Dr. Harrell gets here it may be too late. Nevette please, you have to allow them to examine you."

Nevette looked at Lindsay. The thought of losing her baby was more terrifying than what she had gone through. She fought hard and long for Zoé's life. She couldn't allow it to end this way. She nodded that she would allow the test. Tears rolled down her face as she made sure that Talinda and Lindsay would stay in the room while the test was being administered, and the OB doctor examined her to see if she had dilated any.

Nevette agreed because she was concerned for her baby. However, when it came time to sign a release to be examined, her hands shook too violently to get a coherent signature on the consent form. Talinda accompanied the nurse out so they could take it to Derrick. They explained that they were about to examine her. They informed him that she was having contractions and that her OB doctor had been called and should arrive shortly.

"CONTRACTIONS! But she's not quite six months pregnant!" Derrick exclaimed as he signed the paper.

"We know sir, and we are doing everything we can to make sure the baby stays put. But your wife is not cooperating with us. This second form also gives us the okay to sedate her, so she will relax during the examination," the nurse replied.

"That's not going to hurt the baby is it?" Derrick asked. He was apprehensive about signing them. He just couldn't bear the thought of making another horrible decision for his family. Talinda assured him that Nevette was in agreement, but her hands shook too much to get a coherent signature. He sighed heavily, shook his head and said, "please God", as he signed the paper.

Derrick asked when he could see Nevette. Talinda looked at him and shook her head slightly, "This isn't a good time Derrick. Just give her a little while longer."

He nodded and turned to go have a seat. He dropped his head in his hands and wept. Once again, in the time of tragedy he couldn't console his wife. He was beside himself. He had a gamete of emotions catapulting around inside of him.

"Come on Derrick the women have her. It's going to be alright," Bernard said.

Derrick wiped his tears and breathed heavily. His demeanor changed, and he went from despair to a different emotion. Anger. He was starting to lose the battle to the old man trapped inside of him.

"She was a virgin when we married. She belonged to me Teddy—she belonged to me, and he took her Teddy—he took her! OH GOD PLEASE HELP ME!" He breathed heavily and regained his composure somewhat and continued, "The house is a mess. She fought him for who knows how long. Blood was everywhere. She was probably calling out to me for help. She had lacerations all over her body. He ripped her clothes off and cut her up!"

He sat in the chair looking straight ahead with a determined look on his face. His elbows rested on the arms of the chair. He had his hands clasped and was breathing heavily between his thumbs and pointer fingers. His shoulders were going up and down with the strong rhythmic movement of each breath he took.

Bernard touched his shoulder and said, "You've got to get your anger under control. You can't let it begin to speak to you or for you. It will take over Derrick."

Inside Talinda held one hand and Lindsay the other as the doctor prepared to examine Nevette. To all their relief. Dr. Yolanda Harrell entered the room just he was in the motion to touch her. Although she was now being examined by a female, Nevette was still very uncomfortable with being touched.

She breathed heavily and erratically as Dr. Harrell administered the rape kit. After that, she checked Nevette to see if she was dilating. When Nevette felt Dr. Harrell's fingers touch her cervix, she panicked and started to scream. She fought them and attempted to get up off the gurney. It took Talinda, Lindsay, Dr. Harrell and the nurse to hold her down. Dr. Harrell did not want to give her a sedative because she knew it would be too much sedative along with the meds she would need to give her to stop the contractions.

Derrick and everyone in the waiting room could hear Nevette's screams, and he rushed over to the desk, "OH GOD PLEASE TELL ME WHAT'S WRONG WITH MY WIFE!"

"Sir, I will go see what I can find out," the clerk replied.

When she stood to leave Dr. Harrell came through the door to address Derrick.

"Dr. Harrell!" Derrick yelled.

"Calm down Mr. Goodfellow. It's okay," Yolanda said. "We administered the rape kit. But when I went to check her cervix, it was too much for her. We are going to move her to labor and delivery—"

"LABOR AND DELIVERY! BUT SHE'S ONLY FIVE AND A HALF MONTHS," Derrick declared. His heart raced. He knew Zoé would not survive outside of Nevette's womb at five and a half months into gestation.

"Mr. Goodfellow please," Yolanda continued. "We are moving her there as a precaution, and to get her out of the emergency room environment. We will be able to monitor her and the baby once we administer the medication to stop her contractions.

"CONTRACTIONS. WAIT A MINUTE—WAIT A MINUTE. OKAY, OKAY, OKAY. Are my baby and my wife going to be okay?" Derrick asked as he managed to get himself under control.

"Sir we are doing everything we can to keep baby Zoé on the inside of her mother. That's why we're moving her upstairs. You all can go to the third floor and wait there for us. We are taking her up in the service elevator to avoid coming through here where everyone is. If all of you rush her, she will go into hysterics," Yolanda stated.

"Okay we know where that is," Teddy replied as he touched Derrick on the shoulder. He stood silent and had a defeated look on his face.

Dr. Harrell returned through the doors, and the men prepared to go upstairs.

Bernard walked over to Sylvia and said, "I looked up at you and the Holy Spirit was all over you. I knew we needed to all just be quiet and allow the Lord to speak to us through you. I pray that God will bless you and all will be well with your baby," he paused and looked at the other couple and continued, "With both your babies. Thank you again for obeying God."

Sylvia nodded and her husband shook Bernard's hand, "Yes. We will be praying for them. You guys take good care of him. Hope they catch this guy."

"Yeah me too. As you all saw, my wife is pregnant as well. I think we'll all rest easier knowing that he is off the streets," Bernard said as he turned to leave with Teddy and Derrick.

The couple that wasn't saved talked with Sylvia and her husband more about God and the situation as they waited for their names to be called. They told them they had never experienced anything that powerful before in their lives. The other pregnant woman cried and said she could feel something moving through her body as Sylvia prayed. The couple that came with Sylvia and her husband, led them both to the Lord right there in the waiting room. They exchanged numbers and told them they would be looking forward to seeing them at their church on Sunday.

They both knew they no longer needed the services of the doctors there in the emergency room, so they signed release forms and left shortly after they prayed again for Derrick and Nevette and themselves. Sylvia and her husband thanked God all the way home as did the other two couples.

~Chapter Fourteen~

They got Nevette to the third floor to labor and delivery. Dr. Harrell gave Nevette a mild sedative to relax her. She knew it would also affect Zoé and hoped if Nevette relaxed, the contractions would soon stop without any further medication needed. After she calmed down the nurse came to treat and bandage her wounds.

Talinda went outside and filled everyone in on what was going on with Nevette. Bernard told her about Derrick and asked if they thought he would be able to see Nevette anytime soon. He told her about Derrick's outburst, the prayer and everything that took place in the emergency room waiting area. She said she would check to see when he would be able to come in when she returned to Nevette's room.

Soon, Nevette could feel the effects of the medication. She knew she would be near to unconsciousness soon, and she wanted to make sure that Lindsay would not leave her alone.

"Lindsay please don't leave me," Nevette cried.

"I'm not going anywhere Nevette," Lindsay replied. "Nevette Derrick wants to see you. Correction—Derrick needs to see you."

"Oh Lindsay I can't! I feel so dirty. I belong to Derrick. I tried to stop him—to fight him off. But I couldn't—he was too strong and so big. Derrick is the only man whom I've ever—and I let somebody else take what belonged to him. I feel so dirty Lindsay!" she exclaimed as tears rolled down her face.

"Nevette he raped you. You didn't *let* him do anything. He is the one dirty not you. Derrick needs to be here for you," Lindsay declared.

Talinda said, "He's blaming himself for asking you to stay home and not work. He's thinking if you would have been at work, you wouldn't have been home to get raped. He is beating himself up with guilt Nevette."

Nevette could fully feel the effects of the medication now. She felt completely relaxed. She said in that 'just about to fall asleep' tone, "It's not his fault Lindsay. Who knows how long he's been watching me? It could have happened anytime—anywhere. It wouldn't have mattered where I was."

"Bernard said, those were almost the exact same words that Teddy said to him, but he needs to hear it from you Nevette. They said he collapsed on the floor in the waiting room crying like a baby. He needs to see you—to touch you," Talinda replied.

Nevette couldn't keep her eyes open. She closed them and went to sleep. Talinda went back out to the waiting room and informed them that Nevette was resting.

Lindsay called Trevor to check on the baby and to make sure there was enough milk in the refrigerator. She filled him in on everything that transpired thus far. He assured her that all was well with TJ. He said he had already called into work for the next day and would bring the baby up the following morning for her to nurse him. She told him she loved him and they hung up.

Teddy Sr., and Jason arrived, and Teddy filled them in on everything. Derrick struggled to face Teddy Sr., and broke down and cried in his arms apologizing over and over. Teddy Sr., assured him that no one blamed him for this.

*****

Back at the Goodfellows the forensics team arrived and Shaundra had to leave with Tre. She packed enough clothes for Derrick, Nevette and Tre to last a few weeks. She also gathered the supplies Tre usually needed for school and headed to the senior Goodfellow residence with Tre. After they got there, she whipped him up some hot cocoa with milk and held him in her arms praying until he finally went to sleep. She laid him in her bedroom and called Derrick to find out how Nevette was doing. Teddy had called her earlier and filled her in on what he knew when he arrived. Derrick Sr., was finally on his way over to the hospital after a new development held him up.

Talinda and Bernard called Raymond to check on the twins. He informed them that they were fed, bathed, and in the bed. He sent his love and prayers to Nevette and Derrick.

Everyone sat and waited. Derrick sat in the chair with his elbows on his knees. His head rested in his hands, positioned as though he were looking at the floor, but he had his eyes closed. Every now and then, someone would pat him on the back to ensure he was okay.

*****

As he watched the news, his eyes darted back and forth reading the headlines that moved across the bottom of the screen. He waited to hear anything about a rape victim that day. He feared as he left the Goodfellow residence that his victim was near death. She was different from the previous ones. She bled more, and he feared he had stabbed her deeper and killed her.

He waited patiently, and his patience paid off. At the bottom of the hour, he saw what he was looking for. The anchorperson reported that a thirty-one-year old, five-and-a-half month pregnant woman, had been brutally stabbed and raped in her home on the Northside of Atlanta earlier that afternoon. There was no news if she or the baby survived the ordeal, and police were gathering evidence and looking for suspects.

He began to breathe heavily. He assumed she and her baby had not survived. He figured if she had, then they would have clearly said so. His heart raced at the fact that he could have committed a double homicide. The feeling caused a stir deep within. One he had never felt before. He feared if the evidence got too close that he would again have to disappear.

His mind and loins were still stimulated from the excitement of the victory of his spoils earlier. He could still smell the sweet scent of her cologne in his nostrils. He closed his eyes and breathed in deeply and let it out with a moan. He turned the television off. He packed his emergency backpack and placed it in his trunk. He couldn't risk attempting his usual five before going back into hiding. "She was as sweet as five," he thought. He was satisfied for the moment, and so he decided that he would disappear the following morning. He went back in the house and fixed himself a sandwich and had a glass of juice before going to bed.

*****

Nevette stirred and opened her eyes. She sat up in the bed in a panic. She swung wildly and yelled, "MY BABY! JUSTICE!"

"Hey, hey. It's okay Nevette. It's over. It's all over, and Zoé is going to be okay. You're safe Nevette," Lindsay said as she gently grabbed Nevette by the arms.

Talinda began to pray, and Nevette calmed down. A minute later the nursed rushed into the room to ensure all was well. In the waiting room, Derrick and the others didn't hear Nevette cry out.

Nevette relaxed and laid back in the bed. She rubbed her stomach and asked if she could have water. They offered her food, but she assured them she wasn't hungry.

Lindsay looked at her and said, "Nevette. Derrick is about to go crazy. He needs to see you."

Nevette shook her head no and said, "I can't face him Lindsay. This is my fault."

"Nevette, what do you mean your fault?" Talinda asked.

She blinked to control her tears as she said, "I think he followed me home from the grocery store. All the way home I felt like someone was following me. I should have listened to the Holy Spirit. I kept feeling like I wasn't supposed to go straight home. However, I was so concerned about the food spoiling in the car if I went somewhere else. I should have listened to God—He tried to warn me. Even when I got home, I felt like I should have let the garage down before getting out of the car. Lindsay I can't look Derrick in his eyes. I let this man—"

"Nevette stop it! A woman doesn't *let* a man rape her. He forces the issue. That why it's called *rape*. It's an act of violence. Girl, I was there today. That house was tore up. It's obvious that you fought him. You just didn't lay down and let him have his way. And it was good that you fought, because they were able to retrieve his DNA from under your nails. They think he probably used a condom because there was no semen present at all in your vaginal area, which is a good thing because if he had any type of sexually transmitted disease, he probably didn't transmit it to you. Even so, they tested you all the same. There was also evidence that he left some pubic hairs on you too. He probably thought he was smart by using a condom," Lindsay replied. She was irritated and angry. This was too close to home for her. Although she couldn't relate to the stabbing violence of the act. She knew how violated and afraid Nevette felt.

"I don't know Lindsay," and then she broke down crying again.

Talinda said, "Listen sweetheart, your husband needs to know that you are not angry with him. He is blaming himself for this. He just wants to see you."

Nevette wiped her eyes as she said, "He is going to want to hold me in his arms, and I'm not ready for him to touch me—I can't—I can't do it! Please—not now! Lindsay please go talk to him, tell him I love him, and it's not his fault."

Lindsay sighed, "But Nevette—"

Talinda stopped Lindsay and said, "Give her more time. We'll go talk to Derrick in a minute."

Nevette said, "I'm afraid Talinda—I'm afraid!" She was crying hard. She grabbed her stomach and said, "Oh my God. I think I'm starting to have contractions again."

Talinda stood and said, "I'll get the doctor."

Lindsay held her hand and began to pray. The doctor came in with an ultra sound machine to look at the baby. Lindsay excused herself while they hooked her up, and Talinda talked with Nevette to keep her calm.

She walked down the hall to the waiting room. Derrick jumped up when he saw her. "What's wrong Lindsay?"

"Calm down Derrick she's okay. She's still not ready for visitors. She woke up in a frenzy. We just got her calmed back down. I need your cell phone," Lindsay told Derrick.

"For what?" he asked.

"Just give me your phone Derrick. I'll be right back," Lindsay said as she took Derrick's phone out of his hand.

Teddy Sr., told her to let Nevette know that he and Jason were there. She said she would as she turned and walked away.

She told Nevette her father and Jason were in the waiting room. They had her hooked up, and they were about to get their first glimpse of baby Zoé.

"Okay Mrs. Goodfellow everything looks good so far. Her vitals are elevated, but that is to be expected considering what she and her mother have gone through," Dr. Harrell said as she smiled. She knew Derrick and Nevette were believing God for a girl.

"Ohhh it is a girl!" Nevette exclaimed. "May I see her, please doctor?"

"Sure Mrs. Goodfellow," Yolanda replied.

Talinda and Nevette watched and tears rolled down her face as she saw her baby.

"Is it okay if I video the baby on the father's phone, so he can see this?" Lindsay asked.

"Sure that would be fine as long as Mrs. Goodfellow is okay with it," the doctor said. She then turned to Nevette and said, "Mrs. Goodfellow, we're going to give you another mild sedative. Since you had another contraction, we want to keep you relaxed. The baby doesn't appear to be affected. She was pretty active. The nurse will be in with it."

"Okay Dr. Harrell if you're sure the baby will be okay," Nevette replied. She turned and asked Lindsay to make a video on her phone for her as well. Talinda also made one and took several pictures. Later after she was sure Derrick had seen the video first, she said would text her pictures to Bernard, Teddy, Raymond and Trevor.

As the nurse came in to give Nevette the medication Dr. Harrell prescribed, Lindsay walked out to go show Derrick the video. He saw her coming and asked if he could see Nevette yet.

"Not yet Derrick, she's not ready," Lindsay replied.

"It's my fault Lindsay. I should have never asked her to stay home," Derrick said and sighed.

"She doesn't blame you Derrick. She said that it could have happened anywhere any time," Lindsay replied as she touched Derrick in the shoulder.

"Then why won't she see me Lindsay?" Derrick asked.

"She feels dirty Derrick. She feels like she let you down by not fighting longer. She feels like she let him take something that was precious to you. She knows you're going to want to hold her in your arms, and she's not ready for that. She described him Derrick. This guy was huge. Much bigger than you, she said. I know all too well how she feels. Just give her some time okay," Lindsay replied.

Lindsay you saw how the house was. They practically destroyed the kitchen, living room and basement. The way she fought him, it's by the grace of God that he didn't kill her," Derrick declared.

"I know that, and you know that. However, she doesn't see it that way yet. But hey, that's not why I came back out here. I thought you might want to see your little girl. The doctor let me video the ultra sound she just gave Nevette to check if the baby was doing well," Lindsay said as she handed Derrick his phone back.

Tears filled his eyes. He sat down in the chair and hit the play button. Derrick both smiled and cried as he watched the video of Zoé.

Derrick whispered, "Wow. Thanks Lindsay. And thanks for being here for her."

"Derrick—she doesn't blame you. This is not like Callisha. She's not angry with you. Not at all. She says it feels almost like she just had an affair. She just feels like she let you down, that she didn't fight hard enough. Just be patient. Because after she calms more, and the baby is completely out of danger. She's going to want you. She's going to want to be in your arms," Lindsay stated in no uncertain terms.

"Affair. That's crazy Lindsay. That's the furthest thing from my mind. I've never thought that. Not once. Please tell her that I don't think that, Lindsay," Derrick said. He thanked her again for the video.

He sat back down and started to watch it again.

Bernard walked over to Lindsay before she left to go back into the room and said, "The police were here. They got Derrick's statement on what he saw when he got home. The lady at the reception desk told them that Nevette would not be available for a statement tonight so they left. Just wanted to you to now so you guys can prepare Nevette. She is going to have to tell them what happened eventually."

"Okay thanks Bernard. I'll let her know. I had better get back in there," Lindsay said and turned to leave.

They all sat back down. They knew this was going to be a long night. Teddy and Jason went downstairs before all the shops that had food closed up and got everyone snacks. Derrick insisted he wasn't hungry, but his father made him eat so he wouldn't have a headache. He also called his wife Shaundra to fill her in on the latest details and to check in on Tre.

She was excited to hear about the video. She informed him that she and Tre were at their home, and he was asleep. The crime scene investigators came and suggested that they leave. They said they were going to have to block the house off until it was cleared. They would let them know when they could return home. So she packed clothes for all three of them and she and Tre headed back to their house. Derrick Sr., said he would inform Derrick. He told her he loved her, said goodbye and hung up the phone.

"Bernard, why do I feel so violated? It happened to her not me," Derrick asked.

"She is a part of you Derrick. So indirectly, it did happen to you." Bernard replied.

"I guess that makes sense," he replied. He shook his head and said. Bernard the more I sit here thinking and wondering what my wife and baby are dealing with in there. The angrier I become."

"You have to control that Derrick. Anger can quickly turn into rage if it's not properly dealt with," Bernard said.

Just then Yogi rushed into the door. Shaundra had finally gotten in touch with her and told her what happened. She was in tears as she rushed to her big brother's arms. Her heart ached for him and Nevette. She wanted to scream out and ask why God had allowed this. However, she knew it was not the time nor place for such an outburst. Derrick held her for a moment, and she calmed down. She went over and sat beside her father and leaned her head on his shoulder.

Dr. Yolanda Harrell came out to talk to Derrick about an hour later. "Mr. Goodfellow we were able to get the contractions stopped, and your wife is resting. None of the wounds were life threatening to her, but she did lose a lot of blood. That was why she was lethargic when you found her. That, along with the stress of the ordeal are what sent her into premature labor. After she leaves the hospital, I want her on bed rest for at least the next month, and it is probably not a good idea for her to return to the home where she was attacked just yet, it may be too much emotionally for her. Stress will affect both her and your unborn daughter. Your wife was able to see her, which brought her a little comfort, but she is still very stressed. We had to sedate her again."

"How is that affecting the baby?" he asked.

"The baby should be fine. It will slow down activity for a while, but they could both use the rest," Dr. Harrell replied.

Derrick Sr., stepped in and said, "Derrick why don't you guys come and stay at the house for a while? You can take a few weeks off from work to be there with her until she feels more comfortable. Your mom said your house is off limits anyway."

"Thanks dad. I think that's best," Derrick replied.

Dr. Harrell shook Derricks hand and said she would be back later to check on Nevette.

The nurse checked the pad underneath Nevette to ensure she was not bleeding or leaking amniotic fluid. Nevette called out for Justice as she was waking up.

Lindsay smiled and said, "Hey girl."

She smiled slightly and said, "Lindsay—is Zoé?"

"Girl Zoé is fine. They stopped the contractions once they got you sedated and calm. They're probably going to keep you a day or so to keep observing you and Zoé to ensure she is out of danger. Plus they want to be sure your wounds are okay before releasing you," Lindsay stated.

"Where is Justice?" she asked.

"He is in the waiting room with everybody else," she replied.

"Everybody else?" Nevette asked.

"All of yours and his family," Talinda said as she snickered.

"Where's Tre?" Nevette asked.

"He's with Derrick's mom," Lindsay replied. "They didn't want him here, but Teddy called and talked to him because Derrick wasn't in any shape and didn't want to alarm him. Shall I go get Derrick?"

"I—" she said hesitantly.

"Nevette he is about to go crazy. You need to say something to him," Lindsay replied in a pleading tone.

"Okay Lindsay, but don't leave me alone with him," Nevette replied as she sighed.

The nurse said, "Mrs. Goodfellow, do you want me to send him in on my way out to make it easier?"

"Yes thank you," Nevette replied and took a deep breath.

Talinda stood and said, "Well, I'm going to go call Raymond and check on the twins." She hoped that Nevette would be able to endure a private moment with Derrick. She figured it would be less obvious if she exited the room before he entered.

"It will be okay Nevette," Lindsay said. She gave Nevette a slight pat on her hand to reassure her.

The nurse left and walked across the hall to the waiting room. "Mr.

Goodfellow?" she called as she looked to see who would stand.

"Yes!" Derrick replied as he raced over to her.

"Your wife is awake and asking for you," she said.

"She is!" Derrick exclaimed with excitement on his face. He started to walk past the nurse when she stopped him.

"Mr. Goodfellow remember, don't make any sudden movements towards her. Let her lead as to when or if she wants you to touch her," she reminded him.

"Okay thanks," Derrick said as Teddy touched his shoulder for comfort.

He smiled at his brother-in-law and walked across the hall to the room. He took a deep breath and entered. As he entered, Lindsay stood and Nevette grabbed her hand sending a private message that Derrick noticed.

Lindsay said, "I'm going to go sit on the other side of the bed so Derrick sit here okay."

Nevette nodded her head giving Lindsay the okay. Lindsay walked to the other side of the bed and sat down.

Derrick carefully and slowly walked to the side of the bed where Lindsay had just left and sat down beside Nevette.

He said, "Hey baby, how are you feeling?"

She smiled slightly and said, "Okay—tired."

She noticed how red and puffy his eyes were. She reached up and touched his face. He remembered what the nurse said, so he dared not attempt to touch her hand with his. He just allowed her to touch him. His eyes filled with water, and tears fell down his cheeks. He closed his eyes and took the chance and leaned into her touch. He couldn't get another word to come out of his mouth. He was overcome with emotion, and his body began to shake from the tears he shed. Lindsay sensed that they needed to be alone got up and quietly walked out of the room.

Nevette called his name, "Justice—baby it's not your fault."

At those words, Derrick completely lost it.

"Oh Justice, please don't cry. Sweetheart we're okay. Zoé and I are okay," she replied as she started to cry herself.

He put his head down on the bed beside her. He made sure he still did not make any unintentional contact with her. She cried and stroked his head. There was no need for words, they just cried together, and she gently continued to stroke his head.

After she somewhat regained her composure, she called his name, "Justice—don't blame yourself for this. Justice—"

He was too overcome with emotion to respond to her. She took his hand that was beside his head on the bed and placed it on her stomach, because at that moment, she could feel Zoé move for the first since she had come into the ER. The movement of his baby seemed to comfort him.

He looked up at her stomach and called Zoé's name. "Zoé—hey

little princess—how is daddy's little girl?"

Nevette once again touched the side of his face. Her contact soothed his soul.

"I love you Nevette. Baby I'm so sorr—," he started to say.

"Shhhh Derrick don't—this is not your fault. I will not let you beat yourself up—please don't—okay—please don't Justice."

He took a chance and turned his face toward her hand and slightly kissed it. She flinched just slightly but took a deep breath and allowed him to kiss her hand. He decided not to try to touch her further and thought maybe he shouldn't have kissed her hand. Nevette started to feel a little uncomfortable, but she didn't want to upset Justice.

She removed her hand, took a deep breath and said, "I'm so tired."

She closed her eyes for a second, opened them again and slightly smiled at Justice in an attempt to reassure him.

"Okay baby," he said. "I'm going to let you get some rest okay. Your dad and brothers are outside along with my dad and Yogi. Mom is home with Tre, and he's sleeping finally. He didn't tell Nevette that Tre was in the house. He didn't want her to worry that Tre was worried and close to shock. She smiled as tears rolled down her face. He wanted to wipe them but dared not touch her.

"Tell them," she paused to wipe her tears, "I'll see them later okay. Can you send Lindsay back in please?"

"Okay baby. I'll be outside when you wake up," he replied. He fought to keep his composure.

"Okay," she said.

She smiled and closed her eyes. She wanted to end the moment because she could feel herself starting to fear his presence in the room. He turned and walked out. Lindsay was talking with Talinda and everyone else in the waiting room when Derrick returned. He walked up to her.

"She's afraid of me Lindsay," he replied. He felt so defeated. "She put my hand on her stomach so I could feel Zoé move. She touched my face but when I leaned into her, my lips touched her hand, she flinched. She's afraid of me."

Lindsay sighed, "Derrick she's afraid of intimate contact from any male. It's not you personally. You're going to have to give her time. Rape is a very violent and emotionally destroying act. There is no trust of the opposite sex whatsoever, no matter who it is."

"We've been through so much Lindsay. How much more can we take?" he said as he looked up toward heaven.

"Derrick, you and I both know that God will not allow you to be tempted above what you are able to bear. So obviously, he knows you're able, so just trust him. All things work together—" she said.

"Lindsay—I know—I know you're right. She's just hurting so much right now. And there's nothing I can do to fix it," he replied.

"Derrick you're hurting too for that matter. Just give it time. She will get more comfortable with you. You're her husband. You'll see. It will be well," Lindsay replied.

"Yeah okay," he replied as he wiped a tear. "Well listen, you better get back in there," Derrick said.

*****

Later, after realizing that Nevette was not going to see anyone else that night, everyone started to leave to go to their respective homes. Her father and Jason went to Teddy's house. They hoped Nevette would be up to the task to see them the next day.

Derrick said goodbye to everyone. He said he would stay a little while longer in hopes of being able to say goodnight to Nevette. A little later, Nevette was sleeping when Justice entered the room. He asked Lindsay if she was sure Nevette was sleep.

She replied, "She's out Derrick."

He leaned over and lightly kissed her and stroked her face. He kissed her again and whispered that he loved her. He breathed heavily, dropped his head and shook it side to side.

"Thanks again Lindsay, for being here for her. Mom said she packed some of our clothes and took them over to her and dads. The doctor suggested she not go home just yet. But of course, I'm going to ask her to see what she wants to do. Truth is Lindsay. I don't want to stay there tonight or any other night ever again."

"I hear ya' Derrick," she replied. "She may think she'll be okay at home Derrick. However, once she walks back into the house, it will be a different story," Lindsay replied.

"I don't know Lindsay. Maybe I should just sell the house and—," Derrick started to say.

"Just wait and see Derrick. Let her decide okay?" Lindsay stated.

"You're right. I'm just beside myself, and I don't know whether I'm coming or going. I swear I'm going to bump into myself pretty soon I'm going in circles so fast," he replied.

Derrick it will get better. She has not one time asked God why he allowed this. She is different this time Derrick and she most definitely does not blame you," Lindsay stated.

"Thanks Lindsay. I am indebted to you," Derrick replied and mustered a smile.

"Oh please as much as you and Nevette have been there for me. Don't mention it at all. Besides Trevor, you guys are all the family I have," Lindsay replied as she fought not to cry. She thought of all the times over the years that Nevette had been there for her.

"We love you Lindsay," Derick replied.

"I know Derrick and I love you guys too," Lindsay said.

"I'm going to go home, take a shower and check on Tre. He probably needs to see my face by now. I hope he's still asleep. I really don't want to face him. He's going to have a million questions about mommy and what happened."

"Just tell him mommy loves him, and she and Zoé are going to be okay," Lindsay said with a smile.

"Okay," Derrick replied. "I will. I'll be back later."

"Derrick go get some sleep and come back in the morning," Lindsay said in the tone a big sister would use when she had been left in charge of younger siblings when the parents left to go out for the evening.

He smiled and replied, "Are you sure Lindsay, not that I'm going to get any sleep." He pondered the idea for a millisecond then said, "I think I'll come back just in case she asks for me. I want to be here."

Lindsay smiled and said, "Okay, see you in a few hours."

"I just had a terrifying thought," Derrick stated with a hint of confusion in his voice. "Lindsay what if she is too afraid to come home with me?"

"I don't think that will be a problem Derrick. She is already ten times calmer than when she first came in earlier. She is going to change from one extreme to another with you," Lindsay stated.

"What do you mean Lindsay?" Derrick asked.

"She is going to go from being afraid of you, to not wanting you to leave her," Lindsay replied.

Derrick smiled, "Well I don't mind the *other* extreme."

She laughed and said, "It will be okay Derrick. Zoé is fine and so is Nevette physically. We just have to help her get through the emotions of it all."

"Yeah. I'm sure the physical will prove to be the easier of the two." He sighed, "Thanks again, see you later Lindsay."

"Okay Derrick," she replied.

*****

Tre woke and screamed, "MOMMY! WHERE'S MY MOMMY?"

Shaundra rushed into her bedroom where she had laid Tre down and scooped him up in her arms. "Shhhh—sweetheart. Mommy is okay. She is going to be okay. I'm sure daddy will be home soon. You'll see. He will tell you that mommy is okay."

Just then she could her Derrick enter the house. She heard his father and him engaged in conversation. Then she could hear him come up the stairs.

"See Tre, daddy is here," she said.

She released her hold on him, so he could get down out of her arms. He reached the doorway just as Derrick reached the top of the steps.

"DADDY!" Tre exclaimed and jumped up into his father's arms. "Where's mommy?"

"She had to stay at the hospital Tre. They want to make sure that she and Zoé are okay. She will probably be there for a few days," he replied.

He wasn't sure how much of the incident he should relay to Tre. He decided to say nothing of what happened. He knew it was something that Nevette would want to discuss with him together.

Tre accepted his answer. However, he would not allow Derrick to leave him. Derrick carried him down stairs to get a glass of juice and back to the bedroom. He realized he would not be able to return to the hospital after all that evening. He called Lindsay, who assured him that would be fine. She told him that Nevette was sleeping, and she was about to stretch out in the recliner in the room. She told Derrick she was glad that Tre wouldn't allow him to leave and commanded him to go to bed. Derrick thanked her again and hung up.

Tre sat with his grandparents in their room long enough for his father to take a shower. Then he and Derrick got ready to turn in for the night. Derrick said a quick prayer with Tre, and they got in the bed in his old bedroom that was now a guest bedroom. Derrick realized that Tre would probably need some professional spiritual counseling, considering everything they had been through the last year and a half.

Tre soon drifted off to sleep atop of his dad. After Derrick was sure that Tre was asleep, he began to pray more earnestly about the situation:

> *God,*
>
> *I'm at my wits end. I have absolutely no idea what to do. I'm devastated. I'm not going to try to pretend that I am in control right now. Or that I know what words to say or speak in authority about the situation, because I don't. All I feel is anger and despair. There is so much running through my mind Lord and I can't keep up with the thoughts. So many emotions that I can't balance them. Nothing inside of me wants to be spiritual or logical right now. God I can't—*

He paused. His emotions threatened to overtake him. He tried hard to control his breathing. He could feel his body begin to shake, and he didn't want to awaken Tre, who was still on top of him asleep. He cried as he continued:

> *"—can't do this. I don't understand what I'm doing wrong. God I'm just—oh please. Please, please, please. God please tell me this is not still about my decision making mistakes concerning Suzette. I'm trying so hard to lead this family you've placed in my care. Please God, tell me what I'm doing wrong? Jesus please— "*

He lost the battle. He was overcome with tears. He slipped from under Tre and left him in the bed. He went to the basement and laid in the floor. He cried out in anguish to the point that he was sure he would throw up at any minute.

A hand touched his shoulder, "Son," his father said.

"Dad," he whispered still in anguish as he cried out, "I feel like I'm about to lose my mind. I don't know what to do. This is worse than Callisha. Dad help me—help me!"

He laid in his father's arms the same way Tre had laid in his just over an hour ago. Derrick Sr., held his son and called on the merciful God of heaven to overshadow him and give him the peace that passed understanding. He rebuked the spirit of despair, suicide, anger and confusion. He prayed for Nevette, Zoé and Tre. He also prayed for Teddy Sr., Jr., and Jason. He prayed until he could feel the presence of God enter the room. He quieted down at the prompting of the Holy Spirit. As he lay there holding DJ, the Lord spoke with authority:

> *BE STILL AND KNOW THAT I AM GOD. I AM SOVEREIGN. I WILL GRANT YOU MY PEACE TO ENDURE MY SON. REST IN ME AND ALLOW ME TO COMFORT YOU. IF YOU FOLLOW YOUR OWN WAY, IT WILL SURELY END IN DISASTER FOR YOU. BE STILL MY SON—BE STILL.*

Derrick sat up and wiped his eyes. He was unsure that he just heard and witnessed what he thought he did. God spoke directly to him in his spirit. He shared with his father the words the Lord laid on his heart just then. They prayed and thanked God for his comfort and went back upstairs.

Derrick found Tre still in the bed asleep. He got back into bed, and Tre quickly climbed back on top of his father. He closed his eyes, thanked God again, and was fast asleep.

~Chapter Fifteen~

Quavis was on fire and effective in carrying out Gods plan for the Knights. He made a lot of headway in dismantling the bulk of the teens originally initiated in a short amount of time. Many had given their lives to God. Several had already joined the youth group at Grace. Some of the teens were skeptical at first, but Talinda reminded them of Brandon's mission. The young ex-Knights teenagers were hungry for God and it didn't take long for them to prove their genuineness in God. They were on fire and actually sparked the rest of the group to step their game up in Christ. Sarah and Reginald announcing her pregnancy, affected everyone more than they expressed.

Talinda and Bernard were up with the twins when Raymond entered the kitchen. He asked his mother if she were going back to the hospital to see Nevette, and if so what time. He expressed that he had planned to go visit Quavis that morning. He wanted to be back in time in case she needed him to stay with the twins. Bernard told him not to worry because he would be home with the twins. After breakfast, Raymond and Talinda both headed toward Atlanta. Raymond to the State Penn, and Talinda to Northside hospital to see Nevette. She wanted to give Lindsay a break. She had already talked it over with Bernard and took an overnight bag in case she needed to stay.

*****

Raymond waited anxiously for Quavis to round the corner toward the booth. Quavis smiled when he saw Raymond and greeted him with a hearty hello.

"Hey Quavis how are you doing?" Raymond asked.

"Can't complain Raymond. I feel freer behind bars than I ever did on the streets," Quavis replied.

"Wow, that's crazy," Raymond replied.

Quavis shook his head and sighed as though he had remembered a childhood fear, "You know Raymond. Secretly, when you hid from the gang, and Pastor Travis found and mentored you, I envied you. I wanted your life. You had a father that cared for you and was there for you. You had a family—a real family. Not a made up one who only hung out with you because they feared the repercussions if they didn't. I was so tired of looking over my shoulders, and sleeping in different places all the time. Never getting into a routine for fear that someone was always watching and waiting to see where my weakness was so they could exploit it. Never being able to have a serious relationship for fear that she would become a casualty of the gang revenge life.

The only reason I really came for you that day at the youth rally, was because it was brought to my attention where you were in front of half the gang, and I didn't want to appear weak. I had to maintain my tougher than life status. I was already getting tired of it. I was surprised when the police didn't come looking for me after I killed your dad. I figured killing a pastor was a different ball game than just another gang member that no one cared about anyway, and that the police were secretly glad you would deal with me so they wouldn't have to. That's when I realized this would be how I would do it. This would be how I would finally be able to get out, without dying myself. I didn't want to kill you, but I knew I had to. When he stepped up in front of you and took the knife in your place, I didn't know what to do. No one had ever volunteered to die to get anyone out before. So I just stabbed him again and again and ran. The truth of the matter was, Raymond, I knew where you were all the time, long before it was brought to my attention in front of everybody. You never really fit in. I knew you had never killed anyone and had taken credit for other hits. I figured eventually you would get the killers edge, but you never did. I wasn't surprised when you went missing. The pressure on me to be hard was overwhelming sometimes. I rarely wanted to be alone. Being alone meant I had to face myself and I never wanted to. But now I can look at myself every day and finally be proud of the face I see looking back at me in the mirror."

Raymond sat silently. He couldn't believe what he was hearing. He finally spoke, "Wow. Quavis I would have never guessed how you really felt. You were so ruthless most of the time."

"It was a front, Raymond. You know, I actually ended up the leader of the Knights by sheer accident," he replied as he remembered the moment. "I was with the former Knight leader when a gunfight broke out. I was just shooting wildly and running backwards. He got hit and somehow, I ended up in front of him. He assumed I was protecting him with my life. Later that night at the hospital as he died, in front of the second man in charge he appointed me the leader. He said that none of them had ever put themselves in harm's way to protect him. He said I had the true heart of a leader. I was too afraid to tell the truth and no one else dared, even on his death bed, to defy him. And so, I became the leader."

"You're kidding right Quavis?" Raymond asked.

Quavis chuckled and said, "No. That's the absolute truth."

Raymond shook his head in disbelief. "Wow—"

"Raymond. You know yourself that most people in gangs are afraid. They are afraid of normal. They are just looking for love and affirmation in all the wrong places because they are not getting it at home. Parents need to understand how fragile their teenagers are and give them unconditional love instead of always condemning them for the least mistake they make. Gangs would be a lot emptier if kids got unconditional, agape love at home," Quavis declared.

Raymond looked down and shook his head. He looked back up and said, "Wow Quavis, God has really transformed you. I mean the youth at Grace have embraced at least fifteen ex-Knights into the ministry. You're doing more for God with the youth on the inside than most of us are doing free on the streets. Imagine what you could really do on the outside. You should really push for a quicker parole. I'm sure my mom and dad will—"

"No Raymond," Quavis said to stop him from even suggesting it. "They wanted to kill me. The prosecution sought the death penalty and your mom rallied to get me twenty-to-life. I would have taken the death penalty for killing your father. I earned it. We both know on the outside I wouldn't be as effective, because I would have to be the active, aggressive, and vengeful leader that I was already tired of being. No—this is the best way for me. I minister to the other inmates as well. God has me right where he wants me Raymond, and I'm grateful. Hey—we're a good team. I'll keep sending them to you. And the youth at Grace will keep ministering to them. It's a win for everyone. And God gets the glory."

"I feel like I have to play catch up. You have blown by me Quavis," Raymond said and paused. He wasn't sure how Quavis would react to his next statement. "My dad's death took a lot out of me. I was angry, not just with you, but also secretly with God. I went to church but wasn't as effective. With each passing day, I grew more and more passive in my relationship with him. I was on fire the first week after his death and even received the baptism of the Holy Spirit. But I extinguished my own fire with my private anger." He paused, looked up and said, "Wow, forgive me Lord." He shook his head and continued, "Then everything happened with LaNeisha and Minister Goodfellow and it was like I woke up from a deep sleep. I wasn't ready to come to prison and I was terrified because I understood that I set up the meeting. I knew that made me somewhat liable for the shooting, even though it wasn't my bullet that hit him. Even if I wasn't legally liable, emotionally I had already tried and convicted myself for it. Quavis I am so grateful to you. I probably should be dead—I would be dead if you wouldn't have placed a protection order on me. Every Knight on the street had grounds to dismiss me for coming after you."

Quavis smiled and said, "Just like God's word says, *All things work together for the good*."

"Yeah, I guess so" Raymond replied.

"So you're doing the right thing by your girl now, right?" Quavis asked.

Raymond smiled, "Yeah. I thought my dad would put me through the wall about it. But he was more understanding than I thought. We don't have nearly as much freedom in the relationship as before. But it's all good. And we're good."

"Alright. Raymond stay focused. Go to college and lead a productive life. Pastor Travis valued your life enough to give his for it.

And it changed not just your life but mine as well. It made me realize that although I was the big man around town. Without God, I was as empty as I felt when there was quiet on the gang front, and I was left alone with my thoughts. We're going to both be okay Raymond. I value your friendship and the visits from you and your family. Please don't forget about me. Because your family and the members of Grace are going to be the only interaction I have with the outside. My biological family are mostly dead and the ones that aren't, won't come here to see me. So don't forget me," Quavis replied.

"Never my brother. We're family now for real," Raymond replied.

Quavis smiled and fought off tears. Not of sadness, but of joy because he finally had acceptance into a real family.

"Well our hour is coming to a close. Please remember to keep the Goodfellows in your prayers. Minister Goodfellows pregnant wife Nevette, was brutally stabbed and raped yesterday," Raymond stated.

"Please tell me you're kidding! He's one of my mentors," Quavis said as he gasped slightly.

"I wish I were," Raymond replied.

"Wow, okay. Man, it's like one thing after another with them. I will keep my ears open to see if anything throughout the jailhouse talk will surface about it," Quavis replied.

Raymond thanked him again for sharing with him. He had been enlightened on so much and left feeling very empowered. He knew that he and Quavis just made a bond he thought he would never have with him. He marveled in the power of a mighty God to make your enemies be at peace with you.

*****

Talinda arrived at the hospital just as Nevette finished forcing down breakfast at Lindsay's command. Justice called and said he would be on his way after he spent a little time with Tre.

"Well look who's up and eating," Talinda said as she knocked then entered Nevette's room.

"Hey," Nevette replied.

"Hi Talinda," Lindsay said as she adjusted the bed for Nevette.

"How are you feeling today," Talinda asked Nevette.

"Tired and sore. I feel like I got hit by a freight train," Nevette responded. "The wounds aren't deep, but every move I make, I can feel all forty-five of them. Needless to say, I don't move much."

Talinda chuckled slightly, "I'm sure you don't. But hey, I have my overnight bag and I came to relieve Lindsay for the day."

"Oh Talinda you're a gem. But Derrick's mom is coming up later and she already said she would spend the night, so Lindsay could go home. My wounds aren't life threatening so they will let me out of the hospital soon. Maybe even tomorrow they said. Most of them did require stitches though. They're the dissolving kind. However, they still want to see me every two weeks up to my eighth month, then every week after that until I have Zoé. I haven't had a contraction since last night but the monitor will be on through tonight just as a precaution," Nevette stated. "Besides Talinda, you're almost seven months pregnant and you need to be home in your comfortable bed at night."

Talinda smiled and said, "Okay if you're sure. But remember I'm just a phone call away if you need me."

"Okay and thanks again," Nevette replied.

Talinda sat and talked with Nevette and Lindsay for a little while longer. Soon Shaundra came in to relieve Lindsay. She said that Derrick would be up later, he was taking care of some things with Tre. Shaundra told Lindsay she was prepared to be there with Nevette until she was released from the hospital. Nevette grabbed Shaundra's hand and squeezed it giving her a silent approval and a thank you for her decision to stay with her. They all talked a little while longer and prayed before Talinda and Lindsay headed out.

About thirty minutes later Derrick called his mother and said that Nevette's father and brothers were on the way to visit. He said he would wait and come later, that way it wouldn't be too many men in the room at the same time. She replied okay and informed Nevette of the visitors coming. She breathed heavily but also looked forward to the comfort of her father and big brothers.

"Just see how you do dear. But if you think it will be too much we will bring them in one at a time," Shaundra said.

"Okay mom. I think I will be okay. As long as they don't all crowd me or touch me too much," Nevette replied.

About thirty-five minutes later the nurse called down to inform them that Nevette had male visitors coming.

"Hey princess," her father said as he, Teddy Jr., and Jason entered the room. They were careful not to come too close to the bed per the nurses instructions at the station when they checked in. It was a private hospital. Therefore rape victim's visitors had to check in before entering the patients' room.

"Hey daddy," Nevette replied. Tears fell down her cheeks as she reached out to touch her father.

Shaundra moved up more toward Nevette's head to give Teddy Sr., room to get closer to her. She appeared to be somewhat comfortable with her father and brothers thus far, to Shaundra's relief. They sat and talked about anything but the events of the day before with Nevette. They mostly talked about the pictures and short video that Talinda sent them all of Zoé.

They knew they shouldn't attempt to stay for a lengthy amount of time. Her father and Jason said they were headed back to Columbus the following day but would stop in to see her before they left town. Teddy also said he would check on her again later the next day.

She allowed and struggled through the moment as they each gave her a very light hug or pat on the shoulder before they got ready to leave. Because of her wounds, no one was sure where to touch her that wouldn't bring physical much less emotional pain to her.

After they left Nevette, expressed that the visit was emotionally draining and she felt exhausted. No sooner than she closed her eyes, Derrick called Shaundra's phone. She informed him that it probably wasn't a good idea for him to come just yet. She told him that Nevette's brothers and father's visit took a lot out of her and she was resting. She said he should wait until later that afternoon to visit. He agreed. He asked his mother to have her call Tre to reassure him that she was okay when she awoke up. Shaundra promised she would.

Although Derrick understood, it was extremely hard for him to stay away. He took Tre out for lunch and tried to get his and Tre's mind off of Nevette. He showed him the video of Zoé and they talked about making plans for a family vacation once she was born.

About an hour later after they returned home. He and Tre were sitting in the basement. Derrick was at the wet bar getting him and Tre juice when his cell phone rang. It was his mother. He shook off the initial panic that tried to overtake him that something was wrong.

"Hey mom is everything alright?" he asked.

"Yes son Nevette is awake and wanted to speak with you and Tre," Shaundra replied.

"Great," he replied. He called over his shoulder as Shaundra handed Nevette the phone. "Hey Tre! Mommy is on the phone and she wants to talk to you."

Nevette smiled when she heard Derricks voice. She closed her eyes and breathed heavily.

"Okay daddy!" Tre exclaimed as he rushed over to the bar area.

Derrick handed him the phone without speaking to Nevette first. He didn't want to monopolize the time or get her stirred emotionally before she had the chance to speak with Tre.

"Mommy!" Tre exclaimed.

"Hey baby!" Nevette replied as tears fell from her eyes.

"You're okay?" Tre asked.

"Yes sweetheart. Mommy is going to be okay. And Zoé is fine too, so don't worry. Mommy will probably be home soon alright. So you be a good boy for daddy," she replied.

"You were hurt really bad mommy," Tre said. His voice indicated that he understood that something terrible had happened.

"Yes baby. Mommy got hurt. But then daddy came and made it all better," she replied.

She wanted to ensure Tre that there was nothing negative going on between her and his father. Derrick could hear her conversation with Tre and tears formed in his eyes when she said that he had made it all better. He knew what she implied by that statement and it soothed his spirit. He knew even though she would require time. That they would indeed recover.

"Okay Tre. We need to let mommy get rest," Derrick said to Tre so he would prepare to end the conversation with his mother. But he was eager himself to speak with her as well.

Tre seemingly read Derricks thoughts as he replied, "Okay daddy," He then said to Nevette, "Mommy, daddy said I have to go. But I think it's just because he wants to talk to you now. Bye mommy," Tre said with child's innocence and logic.

"Goodbye sweetheart," Nevette replied and chuckled slightly.

"Hey baby. I guess I can't get anything past Tre," Derrick said. He was glad Tre gave him an introduction to speak with her. He wasn't sure if she was going to want to.

"No you can't," she replied.

"How are you feeling today?" he asked.

"Really sore. Hurts to move. But the baby is fine. They are thinking I can leave the hospital in the next day or so," she replied.

"I wanted to come for a visit if you were up to it. But if not, I completely understand," he replied and held his breath for her response.

"That will be fine Justice. I miss you and I need to see you," she replied.

His heart raced. He smiled and said, "Okay, well unless you want me to bring Tre, dad ran to the office to get some files for a case he working on. When he gets back, I'll call mom to let her know I'm on the way."

"Okay Justice, and no, please don't bring Tre. I still look a mess. I'll see you soon," she replied.

"You're beautiful sweetheart," Derrick replied. We'll record a video to bring him.

She said okay and goodbye. When she hung up she looked at Shaundra and took a deep breath. When Nevette handed her the phone back her hands were shaking.

"Oh sweetheart, it will be okay. You'll get through it. You did a good thing. He needs to be near you right now. He needs to be a part of this," Shaundra said.

"I know mom, but I'm afraid of Derrick. It's not the same as my brother's and father. And even when they hugged me, I almost lost it. Derrick is going to want to hold me in his arms and be intimate. Not in a sexual way, but in a comforting way. I don't want to reject him or jump when he goes to touch me. I could see it in his eyes yesterday when he leaned in and kissed the palm of my hand and I jumped slightly. I was so afraid. I just said I was tired so he would leave the room. Lindsay said she wouldn't leave me alone with him and then she did. I mean, I understood why she did, but—," Nevette exclaimed.

"Now, now Nevette. Don't beat yourself up. Sweetheart, you were brutally raped just yesterday. If you ask me, you are doing good to see anybody, male or female," Shaundra said as she gave Nevette a pat on the back of her hand.

She didn't answer. She wiped the tears as they formed in her eyes. Shaundra smiled and continued to hold her hand to comfort her. No words needed to be said.

*****

Talinda and Raymond both returned home around the same time. Talinda filled them in on Nevette and Zoé. Then Raymond told them about his visit with Quavis. Talinda couldn't help but to think of the words God audibly spoke to them at the pastor's office the day after Brandon was killed. *"FORGIVE THAT HIS WORK MAY BE COMPLETE".*

"God is so amazing. There truly is nothing too hard for Him. We should never underestimate His power. He is well able to accomplish that which He promises. He is faithful, just and true. Quavis is a living example of His power, glory and majesty. I never doubted from day one what God would do in Quavis' life. When he showed up at the funeral and then followed us to Athens, I knew then it was already done. I knew that God would use Him mightily and that he would also require much from him. It's almost like the Apostle Paul, where God said that He would show him how much he would suffer for Him. What a mighty God we serve," Talinda declared.

"Yes mighty," Bernard replied. "Every morning I wake up beside you, I give thanks to God for the sacrifice that was prepared and made for me. For the blessing that was bestowed upon me through Brandon. I pray for direction and guidance in protecting the gifts I have been entrusted and blessed with."

All Raymond could say was "wow". He shook his head as he again thought of the conversation he'd just had with Quavis. He thought of his father Brandon and the sacrifice that was willingly made so he could live. He was overcome by the power of the Holy Spirit that hovered over them.

Bernard gathered them in a small circle and began to pray and give God thanks for His many blessings and favor on their lives. He spoke into all their lives including their unborn child, and declared God's strength and promises over them. After he said amen, he embraced his family and continued to praise God for His goodness.

*****

"I'm on my way mom. I have one stop to make and then I'll be there, okay," Derrick said to his mom before he hung up the phone. He turned to his dad and said, "Alright dad. I'm going to go see Nevette now."

He looked down at Tre. He picked him up because he looked as though he would burst into tears at any moment. "I know you want to see mommy Tre. Daddy will bring you something special back from mommy. She will be probably home tomorrow or the next day. It's not like when daddy was in the hospital. Mommy talked to you earlier today. She is not going to go be with Callisha. Daddy promises he is going to bring her here to Nana's and Papa's house real soon, okay little man," Derrick declared.

"Okay daddy," Tre whispered. He voice was in the tone that indicated that the jury was still out on whether or not he believed what his dad had just said to him concerning his mother.

Derrick hugged him tightly and kissed him on the forehead before he put him back down. His father told him not to worry. He would keep him busy and all would be well. Derrick thanked his father and left.

He grabbed the cologne that Nevette loved for him to wear and stopped off at the teddy bear factory on the way to the hospital. He made Nevette a teddy bear and named him Mr. Cuddles. He was chocolate brown with a baby pink tie with his name embroidered in dark brown letters. He lightly sprayed the bear with the cologne.

He called his mother as he entered the hospital so she could let Nevette know that he would be coming through the door soon. He didn't want to do anything to startle her. Shaundra hung up and informed Nevette that Derrick was on the way up to the room. She took a deep breath and hunched her shoulders up and then down when she let it out as though her mouth as though she were bracing herself for impact.

"You'll be fine dear," Shaundra said.

"I know mom. He's my husband. Deep inside, I know he is not going to do anything to hurt me. But I just don't—I don't know why—ugghhh—okay—okay Nevette," she replied.

Just then Derrick knocked on the door and waited for Shaundra to tell him to come in. She glanced at Nevette and waited for her to nod her head before she addressed Derrick at the door. Nevette breathed deeply again and nodded.

"Come on in DJ," Shaundra called out.

He slowly opened the door. She wouldn't actually see him until he was about five steps into the room because of the way the bed was situated in conjunction to the doorway. When he approached the bed and she saw the huge soft cuddly teddy bear, a big smile graced her face.

Justice lifted the tie as though he were in show and tell and said, "His name is Mr. Cuddles. I thought he could keep you company for me."

He stood at the base of the bed. He dare not walk directly up to her side without a clear go ahead sign from her or his mother.

Nevette held her hands up and said, "He's beautiful Justice. Thank you."

He took a few steps forward, still being careful to not get too close. He didn't want to make any aggressive or incidental contact with her. He smiled at her delight in the teddy bear. She hugged Mr. Cuddles and commented on how soft he was. She caught a whiff of the cologne. She closed her eyes, sighed and smiled.

"Thank you Justice. This was so thoughtful of you," Nevette declared.

She reached up to touch his hand and gave it a slight squeeze. He smiled but did not attempt to reply in kind. He asked if he could pull up a chair and Nevette obliged him. He sat and talked with her and his mother for a few minutes. Then he remembered he needed to make a video to take to Tre. Nevette agreed and placed the bear almost in front of her to camouflage the wounds that were showing. She said hello to Tre, expressed her love and that she would be home soon. She reiterated that she was okay and blew him a kiss. She excitedly bragged that she also had a teddy bear now and told Tre what his name was.

Shaundra and Justice were both relieved that Nevette was able to converse with him, although his conversation was mostly with his mother. Nevette was still somewhat an active participant.

"So how much longer did the doctor say you would be here?" Justice asked.

"Not many more days. Possibly tomorrow but definitely within the next three days," Nevette replied. "Mom told me that we are at their house for now."

"Yes. None of us thought it would be a good idea to go home. Not that we could anyway. The house is still blocked off by forensics to gather evidence," Justice added.

Nevette started to feel more comfortable with Justice. She started to initiate conversation with him. Zoé was extremely active whenever Justice was in the room.

"Wow she knows when her daddy is here. Every time you walk in the room, she gets very active," Nevette said to Justice.

He smiled and replied in a teasing manner, "I've already promised her world, I would spoil her rotten. She knows her daddy's voice."

She looked at Justice, took a slight breath and said, "You can come closer Justice, so you can feel her moving. It's okay—I mean, it'll be alright."

"Okay," Justice replied.

He stood and moved the chair a little closer. But he made sure that his mother was still closer to Nevette than he was. He waited for Nevette to grab his hand and place it on her stomach. Zoé immediately began to move.

He smiled and said, "Here I am baby girl. Daddy's right here."

Dr. Harrell entered the room to check on Nevette and speak with her about what would happen over the next twenty-four to forty-eight hours. She was glad to see that her husband was not only in the room, but that Nevette allowed him to have his hands on her.

"Baby Zoé must be active today," Dr. Yolanda Harrell stated.

"Only when her daddy is in the room," Nevette said in a joking manner.

"That's right. Daddy's little girl," Justice teased.

"Wonderful. I was going to ask you about her activity today. We considered taking her off the monitor this evening, if she had returned to normal activity. That way you will get more rest tonight. I spoke with the doctors that dressed your wounds. They said that all looked well and they see no reason to hold you for an extended amount of time, as long as you followed the instructions they gave you for home. They are looking to release you as early as tomorrow morning. Pending the outcome of the Victim's Awareness and Abuse team's evaluation on your emotional stability. And of course, as we discussed earlier yesterday, I want to check you and Zoé every two weeks until month eight. Then we'll move to every week. Of course you will be on absolute bed rest for the next thirty days at home," Dr. Harrell stated.

Neither Shaundra nor Justice replied. They both watched Nevette's reaction to Dr. Harrell's previous statements. She appeared calm and responsive toward the idea of going home.

"Okay Dr. Harrell. The sooner I go home, the sooner I can start to put this behind me. I'm just glad that Zoé is okay and my wounds are doing well. If they declare I am okay to go home, then I will be fine with that," Nevette replied.

Justice didn't want to stare at her, but he wanted to be sure she wasn't just on auto pilot and was sincere in her declaration. Shaundra smiled and gave her hand a slight knowing squeeze. Nevette returned the smile. Justice gained more and more confidence from Nevette's actions that all would be well between them. It was just as Lindsay had said, she was total opposite from her reaction and attitude toward him as with Callisha. He let out a healthy sigh and relaxed as he sat back in the chair and smiled. He brought to Dr. Harrell's attention that the next day was Sunday. She assured him that the team counseled seven days a week so that was of none effect. He again, thanked Dr. Harrell for taking care of Nevette and Zoé.

She nodded as she said, "You're welcome". Then turned and left the room. They discussed the possibility of Nevette coming home the next day after she left. Nevette still appeared to be comfortable with the idea.

"Justice, I'm your wife. I know you're not going to hurt me. I have to admit that I am not sure if I will be ready to sleep in the same bed with you right away. But I'm not going to run from this, or you. We're going to face this, deal with it and get through it together," Nevette declared.

All Justice could do was nod. He dropped his head as he shook it side to side. He looked back up at her as he nodded up and down and bit his bottom lip and then released it. He was only able to mouth, "thank you" before he looked back down and breathed heavily.

Shaundra also breathed a sigh of relief and smiled. They spent a little more time talking before Justice prepared to leave for the evening. He was about to burst on the inside. He couldn't wait to get home to prepare the room for her in case she was released to come home the next day. He said he would be there the next morning to see how everything went with the counseling session. He assumed she would want to go through it without a male presence.

"Justice I think you need to be here when they come tomorrow morning. I'm sure you have questions that they may be able to answer.

I'm pretty sure that I won't think of everything we need to know," Nevette said.

Derrick smiled and replied, "Okay, I'll be here early in the morning. It's Sunday so Tre can just go to church with dad. Or maybe I'll drop him off to Teddy's later today, and he can go on to Grace."

Their pleasant visit went south when the police entered the room to attempt to get a statement from Nevette concerning the rape. She started to shake and reached for Derrick instead of his mother to his surprise. He scooted his chair up closer to the head of the bed so she could grasp onto his hand easier, but he still allowed her to control the amount of contact they engaged in. She shook harder and realized she was not ready to talk about it yet. They understood and left their card with Derrick.

"Are you going to be okay baby?" Justice asked.

She nodded and clutched Mr. Cuddles. She whispered "yes" and managed to smile when she looked up at him and his mother.

"Well, I think it might be a good idea for me to leave now. So you can get relaxed for the evening and get a good night's sleep," Justice stated as he started to move his chair.

"No don't leave me! I mean—don't go just yet, Justice," Nevette replied.

Shaundra praised God inside. She knew Nevette had a long way to go to feel secure. But delighted in the huge steps of courage and faith she was taking.

"Okay sure. I'll stay as long as you like sweetheart. You let me know when it becomes uncomfortable," Justice replied.

Inside he shouted for joy at her response to him. He sat back down beside her. Shaundra walked around them and stood at the foot of the bed. Nevette seemed comfortable with her action to leave Justice there by himself beside her. She grabbed Justice's hand and placed it on her stomach because Zoé had begun to move again. Justice smiled and began to talk to his baby girl.

He stayed a few more hours and enjoyed his wife and daughter. He still allowed Nevette to initiate all the contact between them. After a while she yawned a couple of times.

"Okay Nevette baby, that's my cue. You're tired sweetheart. You, Zoé and mom all three need rest. I'll be here first thing in the morning. Prayerfully to take you home," Derrick stated.

Shaundra smiled and nodded. Nevette yawned again and replied, "Okay Justice. You're right. I'm tired. I'll see you in the morning."

He didn't attempt to kiss her goodbye and she made no gesture that she was ready for that type of intimate contact from him. He said goodbye but didn't see her clutch the bear and kissed the top of its head because he had stood and turned to walk out of the room. She closed her eyes and held on to Mr. Cuddles with all her might. He turned around at the door to say goodbye again, but she still had her eyes closed clutching Mr. Cuddles. He smiled and looked at his mom.

She smiled back at him and he quietly left the room.

She lay there cuddled up with Mr. Cuddles, nestled into to him the same way she would with Justice when she was in bed with him. He smelled like Justice and that brought her familiar comfort and security. Before long she was fast asleep and Shaundra hunkered down as well and drifted off.

*****

Derrick drove home very excited about his successful visit with Nevette. He could hardly wait to show Tre the video of his mom. He figured he would put Nevette in Yogi's old room, because it was a suite and was still decorated in a more feminine way than his old room with calming colors. He would stay with Tre in his old room because it was larger and had its own bathroom as well.

When he got home his dad had a look on his face that indicated he had news for him that was anything but pleasant. Tre was downstairs watching television.

"What is it dad? Is Tre okay?" he asked in a panic. He shook his head in frustration at his negative pre-action with getting news of any sort.

"Tre is fine DJ. He's down stairs watching a movie," Derrick Sr., replied. "It's Suzette Timmons."

"Oh God what? Don't tell me she escaped and is on the loose or they found some sort of loophole to get her off or something like that," Derrick replied in frustration.

"No son nothing like that. She is definitely not going to get off. As matter of fact she pled guilty yesterday to all the charges of child endangerment, conspiracy to kidnap and the murder of Callisha, not just the kidnapping and accidental death the defense was attempting to manipulate earlier this week. That was why I couldn't get to the hospital when Nevette first arrived there in the ambulance. You knew she was pleading guilty to the lesser charge but right after you left out to look for Nevette the other plea came though via fax. I didn't want to pile anything concerning Suzette Timmons on top of the critical situation what was already going on. So I told your mom it was non-related work. But that's not what I wanted to inform you of. I just received a call from her defense team. Son, they found her dead in her cell this morning. It appeared that she'd hung herself," Derrick Sr., stated.

"What?" Derrick replied in unbelief.

"There was no note, letter, no nothing. They just found her hanging by her sheets in her cell this morning. Her sister who previously pled guilty to aiding and abetting a criminal with the intent to do bodily harm, was fined. But would also only get probation considering her stellar background as a nurse and the fact that this was her first offense. Plus they took into consideration that she had been manipulated and strong-armed by Suzette and had agreed to testify against her before she killed herself. Just as we thought, her license will most definitely be revoked without the ability to ever work as a registered nurse again," Derrick Sr., stated.

"Wow—that's crazy," Derrick replied. He shook his head and said, "God forgive me for being glad that it's over with her. I'm not glad that she's dead of course. But relieved I don't have to wonder where in the world she is, in conjunction with my family. But now she's replaced with some maniac serial rapist who has a fetish for pregnant women. Dad I just want to get my hands on him. Yesterday, I experienced every emotion imaginable. But as I drove home, the one that took precedence was rage. For Tre, I'm controlling my actions. But dad, what I feel inside is overwhelming. I was supposed to be the one and only man to ever make love to her. He stole so much from me! He stabbed her over and over until she was too weak to continue to fight him off! He stabbed her just enough to keep her off of him, but not enough to kill her. They fought hard, because the house was a wreck. Nevette's blood was everywhere. You can see where he drug her down the stairs. Tre was traumatized standing in the kitchen in the only spot that wasn't covered in his mother's blood. It's one thing after another in his little life. I don't know what made me take him home with me instead of dropping him off somewhere else!"

"Son how were you supposed to know what you would find when you got home. You didn't even expect Nevette to be there. Tre is doing well. I think you and Nevette definitely need to take him to see a counselor to make sure. For that matter, all of you need counseling," Derrick Sr., declared.

"Yeah—yeah that's for sure," Derrick replied as he sighed with his hands placed on his hips. He looked up toward heaven as he breathed out. "I'll tell Nevette about Suzette when I get to the hospital tomorrow morning. I'm not going to keep this from her." He paused and then continued, "One thing is for sure. The police really need to find this guy before I get any kind of idea who he is. I'm sure I won't be able to be in the courtroom with him. Dad all I feel towards him is rage. I feel it every time I think of the image of the house, and what she must have endured. Dad, I want to kill him. I'm going to need help with my emotions and my actions. The only thing that keeps me under control is knowing that Zoé is doing okay and Nevette is well, and also what it would do to Tre. But dad, I don't think our family can take another thing. Not one more thing—please GOD!"

He fell to his knees and began to cry. His father knelt down and began to pray for his son's peace of mind. He prayed God would control Derrick's emotions and bring a swift resolution to the situation.

As they stood Tre entered the room. He was excited to see his father and practically jumped up into Derricks arms. They sat down on the couch and Derrick showed him the tape of his mom. Tre watched it over and over.

"I can't wait to see Mr. Cuddles daddy! He looks the same size as Mr. Willow," Tre exclaimed.

"Well, that may be sooner than you think Tre. It looks like mommy will be home very soon," Derrick replied.

"Really daddy!" Tre squealed.

"Yeah little man. But hey, listen to daddy. When mommy comes home. I know you're going to want to jump in her lap and hug on her. But we are going to have to be very careful with her. She is very sore. She was hurt pretty bad and has a lot of cuts all over her. So it will hurt her for us to hug on her too tight okay," Derrick explained.

"Okay daddy," Tre whispered in a sorrowful voice.

"I know Tre. Daddy feels it too. I don't like mommy being hurt either," Derrick said.

He looked up at his father with tearful eyes. No words needed to be said. Derrick pulled Tre into his arms and just held him and prayed over him as he cried for his mother. He knew what his father spoke just minutes ago concerning Tre and counselling was a definite must. He would discuss it with Nevette once she got home and settled. He wasn't sure how much she wanted Tre to know about the attack. He didn't converse with her about it during his visit. But they would have to discuss it before she came home, because Tre would surely ask her what happened.

Tre fell asleep in his father's arms and he put him to bed. Then he jumped in the shower and laid down with him. As he lay in bed, he began to pray again for his family:

God,

I come before You confused, angry and frustrated. Lord, I feel so helpless and overwhelmed. Everything that I want to do for Nevette is off limits right now. I just want to hold her tight in my arms, and let her cry as I comfort her.

God I'm not going to attempt to hide from you what I feel because You know my thoughts before they form in my mind. God I'm struggling with my anger. I appear fine and in control to everyone, but I'm anything but that on the inside. If it weren't for the fact that I need to be here for Nevette, I'm sure rage would have taken over me by now. What I feel inside I cannot explain with the English language. The anguish in my heart is gut wrenching.

God this man jeopardized and attacked my entire family. Again, I wasn't there to protect them, and I'm battling with the guilt of that as well. I lay here with my son, unsure how to minister to him on his level to make him understand without telling him the total truth about what happened to his mother. Give us the words to say to him Lord.

OH GOD, I'M SO ANGRY! ANGRY WITH HIM, ANGRY WITH MYSELF FOR BEING SELFISH AND ASKING NEVETTE TO STAY HOME FROM WORK. AND YES LORD—ANGRY WITH YOU! WHY DID YOU NOT SEND YOUR ANGELS? WHY DID YOU NOT SUPERNATURALLY PROTECT HER? WHY DIDN'T YOU SHIELD HER FROM HIS VISION? GOD YOU WATCHED AS THIS MAN BRUTALLY RAPED MY WIFE! JESUS PLEASE! I—AM—SO—ANGRY!

He paused and then whimpered, "Help me. Help me Lord!" He was breathing heavily and had to pause to attempt to regain control. His body began to shake from the emotions that he fought to keep inside, and rage was taking center stage deep within. He pulled Tre tighter into his arms and cried. He kissed his forehead and kept saying over and over, "I'm sorry."

Tre continued to sleep peacefully. Completely unaware of the turmoil that threatened to overtake his father. Derrick continued to kiss his forehead and hold him tight in his arms. He lavished on him all the love and comfort he couldn't give to Nevette. His kissed Tre and cried until he drifted off to sleep from exhaustion.

~Chapter Sixteen~

Derrick woke the next morning to the sound the alarm on his cell phone that he was sure he didn't set. He thanked God for the wakeup call and got Tre ready for church. He packed a change of clothes for Nevette just in case she was released. His dad had breakfast ready when he and Tre got downstairs. Derrick declined breakfast. He didn't want to miss the therapy session Nevette had scheduled for that morning. He kissed Tre and told him to be good at church with Grandpa. He hadn't taken him to Teddy as planned the night before. Tre smiled and said okay as he sat down to eat breakfast. Derrick's father convinced him to at least take a sausage biscuit and juice with him to eat on the way. He obliged and was out the door.

Once he arrived, he texted his mom that he was in the lobby of the hospital and on the way up, so she could inform Nevette. He also wanted to ensure that she still wanted him to be in the room when the hospital counselors come to speak with her. His mother assured him that all was well and Nevette actually looked forward to him being there with her. He was elated and said he would be right up.

She reached her hand out for him when he entered the room. He touched her hand but again allowed her to control how much pressure would be applied to the touch. She smiled and greeted him. He returned the greeting with a smile. He gave his mother the bag with a change of clothes for Nevette and sat down beside her. They had idle chit-chat about Zoé. Derrick wanted to feel her out, before he disclosed the information about Suzette to her and his mother.

"I'm glad you're feeling well this morning," he stated.

She smiled and touched his hand again. "Derrick I am not going to allow this to conquer me. I know I am not ready for a lot of things. Even so, I am not going to push you away. I will fight through the sudden urges of fear, and I'm going to discuss everything I feel with you. The devil will not win baby," Nevette declared.

All Derrick could do was nod. He thought of his prayer the night before and knew that God was speaking to him through Nevette.

Before he could open his mouth to tell her about Suzette, the counseling team entered the room. She breathed in deeply as though bracing herself for impact in an automobile accident. She looked at Derrick and squeezed his hand tighter. But this time, she pulled it slightly toward her indicting she wanted him to move closer to her. He shook his head to ward off tears of comfort and relief as he slowly and unaggressively, moved his chair up to her side. Shaundra moved to the opposite side, and they each held a hand as the session began.

To her relief, they didn't ask her to relay the details of the incident. They dealt more with her mental well-being in how she was dealing with it. They wanted to ensure she would feel safe in the environment she was about to enter when she returned home. They informed them that they would be at senior Goodfellow residence. They were satisfied with that arrangement and reminded them that they should not push her to return to the scene of the crime. That it would have to be in her timing, especially considering her condition. Their suggestion was to wait until she had the baby, unless she felt confident and ready before then.

All in all, they had a good session and saw no reason to retain her in the hospital. They would submit their notes about the session to Dr. Harrell and suggest that she be released after the medical issues were under control. They concluded that there was no abnormal emotional stress, considering the type of trauma she suffered. They informed Derrick and Shaundra that there would be some breakdowns and moments of high anxiety, but as long as they felt she was in control emotionally, to just be there for her and take it one day at a time. They wanted to see her again when she returned for her next appointment with Dr. Harrell. Shaundra thanked the counseling team before they left Nevette's room.

Derrick asked Nevette, "How are you feeling sweetheart?"

"Okay. I mean better than I thought I would be," Nevette replied. "They didn't ask any details of the incident. So it was easier than I anticipated it would be. Ask me again after I have to talk to the police about it." She smiled to reassure him.

"Nevette there is something that I should probably tell you, and I'm not too sure how you will feel about it. However, I will not keep it from you," Derrick stated. "First off, Tre is fine so relax," he said after her saw her tense slightly.

She breathed heavily and said, "Okay. What is it Justice?"

He took a deep breath and said, "Well, first off. Suzette was deemed mentally sound to stand trial and changed her not guilty plea by reason of insanity, to guilty on Friday afternoon."

Nevette was about to reply when he shook his head in a way that let her know he wasn't finished. She sat silently and braced herself as she pondered what blow he was about to land concerning Suzette.

He looked at her and then his mom. He looked back at Nevette and said, "Dad informed me that Suzette hung herself and was found dead in her cell yesterday morning. They believe it was suicide pending further investigation of course."

Nevette gasped. He informed her and his mother of all the details his father told him the night before to include the plea of her sister, the nurse and her probable punishment as well.

"I know I should be elated. But all I feel is sadness for her. I can't rejoice in it, because it's a soul lost to the enemy," Nevette replied.

"Even though I wasn't excited about her demise. I had to repent for my feelings of relief that she was out of my life and no longer a threat to my family in any way. I know it was wrong, and I repented. However, sweetheart with everything that is going on right now. Closure with her was a welcomed relief," Derrick admitted.

"While I agree with Nevette. I also have an understanding with you as well Derrick, "Shaundra replied. "I too must expose my immediate relief that the matter is permanently closed. Nevertheless, my heart aches as well, over the loss of life and soul to the enemy. We can only pray that she allowed God to deal with her heart in repentance, before she took her last breath."

Nevette touched the side of Derrick's face as she said, "Justice, your feelings are normal and human. You're the husband, father and head of our home. Our views are not always going to mesh. I don't think any less of you for your thoughts and feelings about Suzette's death. I know deep inside you mourn the loss of God's creation as much as I do. However, as my head, I understand that your main concern is protecting me, Tre, and Zoé and providing a safe environment for us."

He closed his eyes and relished in her touch. He whispered, "Thank you."

Just then Dr. Harrell entered the room. "Well, the Victim's Awareness and Abuse team just left my office. They felt you were under a tolerable amount of stress concerning the rape, and that your mental state was stable enough for you to be discharged. Therefore, the nurse will be in to discharge you shortly. She will give you an out-patient prescription and information about your next appointment. Like I stated earlier, you are to be under strict bed rest for the next month. I want to see you in two weeks, barring any setbacks. The counseling team will speak with you again at that appointment."

"Dr. Harrell are you sure her wound situation is under control?" Derrick asked.

She smiled and replied, "We're sure Mr. Goodfellow. Rest assured, we would not discharge her if we remotely thought there was any cause for concern. She will undoubtedly be sore still for some time as she continues to heal. However, none of her cuts are life threatening. Her perpetrator obviously is very skilled in his attack. Unfortunately, it appears he is not a novice and has done this several times to know exactly how deep to puncture her to keep her in the state she was in. I just pray that the police are able to catch him this time. He went dormant for a few years, and everyone relaxed."

Justice only sighed and nodded his head in agreement. He did not reply to the comment. Nevette noticed his demeanor and touched his arm to get his attention. He was focused and tense as Dr. Harrell spoke of her perpetrator.

"Thank you doctor, and we will ensure that Nevette stay in bed and rested," Shaundra replied. The tension in the room heightened. As she too, noticed Derrick's reaction.

The nurse came into to the room shortly after Dr. Harrell left, to prepare Nevette for discharge. She sent Derrick to the pharmacy for a topical cream for her lacerations and a mild pain reliever. With the pregnancy, they were cautious not to give her anything stronger to take without being under their immediate supervision. They informed her that she would be set to leave after her husband returned from the pharmacy. They also stated that she should return to the emergency room if the pain reached to a level the medication prescribed could not control. She informed them that she would.

They had her sign her release form and gave her copies of her treatment plan and scheduled appointments. They wished her well on her recovery and left so that she could get dressed. They informed her they would return to wheel her down to the hospital entrance.

Shaundra retrieved the bag Derrick brought with clothes for Nevette and got her dressed. She smiled as she thought of Derrick's thoughtfulness that she would not have clothes to wear home from the hospital. She sighed and dreaded the day that she would have to relive her encounter for the police report. She knew they would be calling soon for her and Justice to come to the station.

*****

On the way, they discussed what they would tell Tre concerning what happened to Nevette.

"Well you're not going to get away with saying mommy was just tired or something like that. He stood in the house in full view of all the blood," Shaundra stated.

"Oh God my poor baby has been through so much," Nevette replied.

"You all have dear," Shaundra said. "God is faithful. He saw you through before, and he will be with you all now. Remember, He will never leave you nor forsake you."

"I know mom. I trust God. He will give us the words to say to Tre," Nevette replied.

Derrick was silent. The jury was still out about how he viewed and felt about God's lack of involvement in Nevette's attack. Nevette looked at Derrick and spoke to him to break up the obvious tense meditation he had entered into. Zoé moved, and she placed his hand on her stomach.

"Sweetheart mom is right. We will have to tell him I was attacked and hurt by a bad man. But I don't think we need to disclose the rape portion to him. That may prove to be too much for him to handle at his age," Nevette replied.

"Yes," he finally replied. "I agree. I don't want to have to deal with it, much less force it on a little boy." He smiled at Zoé's movement. She rolled all the way across Nevette's stomach as though she were searching for him. It brought him comfort and soothed his spirit.

*****

"MOMMY!" Tre exclaimed as he made a beeline for Nevette when she entered the house with his father and grandmother.

Derrick intercepted him as he declared, "Hey Tre. Remember what daddy said. We can't touch and hug mommy too tight because of her cuts."

Tre replied in a defeated tone, "Sorry daddy. I'm sorry mommy." He now stood unsure what to do next.

Nevette knelt down and hugged him. "Oh Tre baby, mommy hoped and prayed that you were okay. I was so worried about how you were doing."

"I'm okay mommy. Are you okay? You were hurt really bad at our house," he said as tears formed in his eyes.

"Yes baby you're right. Mommy was hurt," Nevette replied. She looked up at Derrick to get a read on if he wanted to talk to Tre about it. She wanted him to lead in every aspect of their lives. Especially now. She feared that he would once again feel unworthy to lead their family. Derrick nodded in affirmation that it was okay for her to go ahead with Tre.

She looked back at Tre and said, "Well Tre, come sit down in the living room with me and daddy. We want to talk to you about the day mommy was hurt."

When they sat down she looked at Justice and gave him the go ahead nod. He returned the nod and preceded to inform Tre about Nevette's attack. Informing him only about the details they discussed earlier. When he finished he hoped it would be enough to satisfy Tre's very mature curiosity.

Tre looked at his mother when Derrick finished and asked with much compassion, "Mommy does it hurt a lot?"

"Not as much as before. But it feels a lot better now that I am back with you and daddy," she replied as she hugged him slightly again. He returned her hug being careful not to squeeze too tightly. Nevette marveled at the tenderness of his touch.

Justice looked on. When Nevette looked up at him, he mouthed the words "I love you" to her. She replied in kind and reached over to touch him. He didn't make a move to hug her or engage in any intimate touch whatsoever.

Justice and Nevette were both relieved that Tre accepted the details of the incident that they were willing to disclose. The sat down and enjoyed family time. Derrick Sr., went out to get something for dinner because he knew they were all was too emotionally and physically exhausted to cook. When he returned, they sat down to eat dinner. Nevette was surprised that she even had an appetite enough to eat. She knew it was mainly because she was pregnant and Zoé would have to have nutrition now that she was off the nutrition she received intravenously.

After dinner, they prepared to get Nevette settled in Yogi's old room. After she was settled into bed and comfortable, she looked at Derrick and said she wanted him to stay there in the room with her.

Derrick was about to protest when Nevette stated, "Justice, I am just as afraid to be by myself, as I am to be alone with you."

His heart almost went off the chart in both compassion and anger. He couldn't imagine the turmoil she most surely felt. He nodded in agreement but didn't respond to her statement.

Shaundra said that she would give Tre his bath if they needed her too. Nevette thanked her but informed her to allow him to come back into the room to spend a little more time with her before he had to go to bed. Derrick suggested they keep him home from school for the week. He said he would call the school as soon as they got up to speak with the principal. He stated they were concerned when she didn't show to pick up Tre Friday when he spoke with them on the phone.

Nevette knew that meant that Derrick would most likely inform him about the attack. She nodded in agreement and permission. He sighed slightly. He sat in the recliner beside the bed. He decided it was probably best he slept there each night. He was sure Nevette would not be comfortable in bed with him.

Nevette felt a little anxious. She wasn't sure about her decision to have Justice in the room after all. But she was determined she would fight through her fear and conquer it.

Derrick felt her uneasiness. He stated, "Nevette sweetheart. I know this is hard for you. If you rather mom stay with you for a few nights, I'm sure she would be happy to."

"No Justice. I'm not going to—we're not going to allow him to do this. To separate us—you said when you came home that we would never separate again. That we would work through anything that came our way," Nevette replied.

"But baby this is different. My presence is terrifying to you. It's not the same. And I'll understand if you need some time. I already told Tre that we would probably let you sleep here in Yogi's old room, and he and I would be in my old room. That way, we wouldn't touch you and hurt your cuts and bruises in the middle of the night. He understood sweetheart. So you don't have to do this," Derrick countered.

"Justice I need to do this. I have to do this. I have to deal with this fear from day one. I'm afraid that if I don't, then fear will overtake me," she paused. She swallowed hard in an attempt not to cry. His heart flooded for her. He wanted so bad to just hold her. She continued, "Baby. It's not going to be easy. I want to run. Nevertheless, I have to do this Justice—I have to. I will not allow him win. He took my body. I will not allow him to take my joy nor will I give him my soul or spirit by giving in to fear."

Tears rolled down Derrick's face. He couldn't stop them. He dropped his head in his hands. She said as she reached out to touch him, but then pulled her hands back, "Oh Justice don't."

"Naythia I'm so angry. I am so—angry. I almost can't control it," he said as he wiped his tears and shook his head as though he attempted to get his emotions under control. "Okay, okay, alright. Whatever you want to do baby. Just—whatever you want to do. I'll let you lead, and we'll take this slow."

She smiled at him and whispered, "Okay." She quickly wiped the tears from her eyes because she could hear Shaundra and Tre coming back across the hall. Justice stood and walked into the bathroom and closed the door to get his emotions under control.

Shaundra could tell by the look on Nevette's face as she looked in the direction of the bathroom when she and Tre entered that it was a tense moment. Before she could say anything, Nevette gave the bed a light pat to indicate to Tre that he could climb up beside her.

He crawled up in bed beside her, being careful of her wounds just as his dad had instructed. She smiled and shook her head at his concern for her.

"Where's Mr. Cuddles at mommy? I saw him on the video daddy showed me of you when you were in the hospital," Tre asked.

"Yes of course," Nevette replied. "He's in the car. We'll ask daddy to go get him when he comes out of the bathroom okay."

"Okay Mommy," Tre replied.

They talked about a field trip he had coming up at school in a few weeks as they waited for Derrick to return. He opened the door and walked toward the bed, again not making any aggressive movements in her direction. Nevette asked him to retrieve Mr. Cuddles so Tre could meet him. Derrick smiled and told her he would be right back.

As he walked down the stairs, his phone rang. It was Teddy apologizing for not getting to the hospital to see Nevette earlier that day. He explained that both the baby and Josephine were under the weather. Derrick apologized as he told him Nevette was released and was at his parents' house with him. With so much going on, it completely slipped his mind to inform anyone of her discharge. Teddy made a mild joke about letting him off to hook this time.

After he hung up with Teddy he sent a group text out to everyone else that Nevette was home and resting. They all replied with praises to God and said they would be praying for their strength. He replied with his thanks for him and Nevette as well. He retrieved the bear from the car and headed back upstairs.

"He's the same size as Mr. Willow!" Tre exclaimed as he jumped off the bed to get Mr. Cuddles from his father.

"Remember Tre, Mr. Cuddles belongs to mommy. And be careful jumping on and off the bed, okay lil' man," Derrick stated just below the level of a chastisement tone.

"Yes sir," he replied. Tre turned toward his mother and said, "Sorry mommy."

"Alright baby. Just be careful like daddy said, okay," she replied in support of Derrick's statement to Tre.

"Okay mommy," Tre replied as he eased back on the bed beside her.

Nevette smiled at his attempt to be cautious. His action also brought a smile to Derrick's face. They sat and talked for a little while longer. Tre yawned and stretched.

"Somebody's sleepy," Nevette declared.

"I'll put him to bed and get him tucked in with Mr. Willow. Be right back sweetheart," Derrick said as he retrieved Tre from the bed to carry him into the other room. Tre looked over his father's shoulder and gave his mother a sleepy goodnight wave, and they disappeared across the hall. Shaundra offered to allow Tre to sleep with them since Derrick would be with Nevette. Tre squealed in delight and jumped out of his father's arms. He ran to get Mr. Willow and said goodnight to his father as he followed his grandmother down the hall.

Nevette was under the cover already when Derrick returned. He was unsure what to do. He didn't want to intimidate her by getting in the bed. So he settled into the recliner with a pillow and blanket.

Nevette looked at him and declared through teary eyes, "I need you. However, I'm so afraid Justice. Part of me wants to lay in your arms where I know I'm going to be safe. The other part of me is terrified at the thought of being that close to you. I hate this. I hate what this must be doing to you. How this must make you feel. We just got back together just over six months ago and now..."

"Naythia baby don't," Justice replied. "Look, God kept me for nearly a year after Callisha died and we separated. So don't worry about me baby. Sweetheart I just want you—"

He couldn't finish his statement. He dropped his head and covered his eyes with his left hand. His emotions were catapulting around inside his soul. She swung the covers back and threw her legs over the side of the bed. She was directly in front of him. She reached up and grabbed his head and forced him to look into her eyes. His eyes were red and puffy from the barrage of tears that flowed through them the past forty-eight hours.

She touched his face, and he closed his eyes and breathed in like he had just come from under water and took a breath of survival.

"Justice look at me baby," she said. "I know the place where you are, and I know how you feel."

"Naythia this is not the same as with Callisha. With her all I felt was sadness and grief. I was in despair that I had lost my family. But this—baby this is different. All I feel is violated and enraged. It's burning inside of me like an inferno. I'm trying so hard to control it."

He broke eye contact and looked back down. He started to shake his head left and right. He swallowed hard over and over. He felt as though he were an active volcano that would blow at any moment. The acid rose from his bowels to his throat and burned like the worst case scenario of indigestion.

"Justice. You are scaring me. Come on baby...look at me. "Derrick Justice Goodfellow the second—look—at—me," she replied in a matter of fact tone.

She placed her hand under his chin and gently forced his face upward. When his eyes met hers he burst into tears. He didn't know how to express his anger. He had never been to a place called rage before. She pulled his head down into her lap, forcing the fear of him touching her out of her mind. She took both of his hands and placed them on the sides of her stomach. Zoé was moving around in a frenzy. She leaned down and kissed the top of his head.

The kiss of his wife and movement of his unborn daughter brought him comfort. He dare not return the affection. He knew she was fighting through the fear she must have felt at having his head in her lap and both of his hands on her stomach. It was such an intimate touch. He just lay there and let her lead. Through her tears, she began to pray:

> *Oh God,*
>
> *Please—we need you right now. God my husband is so broken. Please Lord, give him peace. God we don't understand—WE NEED YOUR RESTORATION. GOD WE NEED YOUR GRACE AND YOUR MERCY. SHOWER HIM WITH YOUR LOVE. GOD PLEASE COVER HIM. PROTECT AND GOVERN HIS THOUGHTS. I'm grateful that our baby survived and is still thriving in my womb. God we thank You for giving Tre peace. Lord please give us the words in the coming weeks to minister to him and to each other. We need You Lord. We need Your guidance. Father, Your word says You are a Lamp unto our feet and a light unto our path. Lead us sweet Jesus...lead us.*

The presence of the Lord entered the room, and both Justice and Zoé seemed to calm down. Justices' breathing relaxed, and he sat up. He didn't want to remain in her lap for fear that he would touch her the wrong way and she would begin to be fearful.

He sat up and said, "Thank you sweetheart. I feel better. You need to get some sleep. I'm going to camp out here in the recliner. It's pretty comfortable so don't worry. We need to take this slow okay?"

She half smiled and whispered, "Thank you."

She got back into bed and covered up. He did not attempt to assist her into the bed. They were both so emotionally exhausted that it didn't take long for either of them to drift off to sleep.

~Chapter Seventeen~

"MY BABY! MY BABY! NOOOOOO—GOD PLEASE! MY BABY—PLEASE! PLEASE DON'T DO THIS. GET OFF OF ME! SOMEBODY HELP ME PLEASE. JUSTICE! JUSTICE HELP ME! NOOOOOOOO!"

Justice sprang from the chair in panic. Nevette screamed as though she were being killed. He jumped into the bed and grabbed her by the shoulders. He started to call her name to get her to awaken up from her nightmare.

"Nevette baby wake up! Come on sweetheart you're having a night mare!" he exclaimed.

By this time, his mother and father entered the room.

As she came out of her dream, she couldn't determine where the dream ended and reality began. She started to fight Derrick and swing wildly at him, "NOOOO—GET OFF OF ME! GET OFF OF ME!"

"NEVETTE BABY. IT'S ME SWEETHEART. NEVETTE LOOK AT ME!" he yelled.

Nevette continued to fight him off as she screamed. She was fully awake and in a panic. Shaundra rushed to the bed as she screamed for Derrick to let her go, as she jumped unto the bed and gently grabbed Nevette. She began to call her name in a calm manner, "Nevette sweetheart calm down. It's me baby girl, its mom. Come on Nevette. Relax baby—"

Tre was at the doorway. He stood there and silent tears ran down his face. He whispered, "Daddy—Nana—what's wrong with mommy?"

Derrick went over and picked Tre up and went back into his parent's room and sat in the middle of the bed with him. He told him that mommy had a bad dream about the day she got hurt by the bad man. He said they should pray for mommy. They prayed, and Tre appeared to calm down a bit.

"Shhhhhh—yes sweetheart, its okay. It's okay Nevette," Shaundra said as she held Nevette and stroked her temple areas with one of her hands.

Nevette shook under the weight of her tears. She lay in Shaundra's arms and cried. In the other room, Derrick was once again in anguish. He knew they had many more nights ahead like this one.

"Oh God help me," he said under his breath.

Shaundra rocked gently back and forth as Nevette calmed down. "Justice," Nevette whispered.

"He's with Tre," Shaundra replied.

"I—I need him. I just want him to hold me. I just want him to protect me. Protect me from—" Nevette cried.

"I'll go get him baby girl," Derrick Sr., said as he left the room headed down the hall.

"How is she dad?" Derrick asked when his father entered the room.

"She's calmed down a bit. She is asking for you. I'll stay here with Tre," his father replied.

Justice looked surprised by his father's statement. He got up and told Tre to stay there with grandpa. Derrick Sr., sat down with Tre and began to talk to him as Derrick left the room.

Justice cautiously entered the room. Nevette had her back to the door. She was still in Shaundra arms as she steadily stroked her head.

Shaundra whispered to Nevette, "DJ is here sweetheart." She motioned for Derrick to come around to the side of the bed so Nevette could see him without her having to move.

He did so. He attempted to appear as gentle as he could as he approached the bed. Shaundra stopped stroking her head and lifted her chin up. She smiled and released her embrace. Shaundra motioned for Derrick to sit down when she got up out of the bed. He was hesitant at first, but nevertheless, he sat.

Nevette looked at him and declared, "Justice! I'm so sorry!"

"Baby—it's okay," he replied.

She fell into his arms to his surprise. He held her for the first time since everything happened. He was overwhelmed at the comfort he felt by having her in his arms. He fought the urge to kiss her forehead. She cried and nestled into his arms even further. She shook, and he took the chance and held her tight. She welcomed it. She was afraid. Just as Lindsay had said. She'd gone from not wanting him to touch her, to not wanting him to let her go for fear of not being under his protective presence.

He closed his eyes and relished in the moment.

Shaundra took a deep breath and said, "Nevette if you're okay, I'm going to go back to dad and Tre. I'll get him some warm milk to sooth him, so he can get back to sleep."

Derrick replied, "Thanks mom." Nevette did not respond. She lay deep into Derrick's chest, as though she were hiding from the world.

As Shaundra left the room she looked up toward heaven and sighed as she whispered, "Thank You."

Derrick was nervous, and his heart raced. He knew at any moment the momentum could shift, and she would be in sheer panic from him holding her. But that moment didn't come. Instead, she clutched him tighter if he even attempted to ease up on his grasp. He was finally able to comfort her. He pushed his anger aside for the moment.

At the risk of her withdrawing from him, he said, "Nevette sweetheart. We need to get you back into bed all the way. You need to lay down and get some rest."

She eased her grip on him. However, when he attempted to get up out of the bed she yelled, "Justice, don't leave me!"

"Okay sweetheart. Are you comfortable enough for me to get in the bed with you? Or do you want to just sit up. I can just sit here and hold you all night baby. Whatever you want me to do," Derrick stated.

Nevette looked up and realized he sat in an awkward position. She whispered, "It's alright if you lay back Justice."

"Are you sure Nevette?" he asked.

"Yes. But let's just lay on top of the cover," she replied.

"Okay," he replied. He lay back in the bed, and she again nestled tightly into his chest. If she got any closer to him, she would be inside of him. She was still just a bit shaky. He held her tight, and they drifted off to sleep.

Shaundra came into the room about an hour later to check on them. When she saw that they were laying on top of the bed covers, she placed a throw blanket over the top of them. Derrick stirred and whispered "thank you". She smiled and left the room.

Sometime in the middle of the night Nevette awoke. She realized she was in Derrick's arms and started to panic. Her breathing became erratic, and she forced herself not to lose control. She moved away from him and got under the cover, so their bodies would no longer physically touch. She lay there and looked at him as he slept. She cried silent tears because of the fear she now felt lying next to him. She didn't want to wake him nor hurt his feelings in anyway. She prayed that the moment would pass.

Thirty minutes later her anxiety eased, and she could again tolerate lying next to him. She did, however, stay under the covers that separated their physical touch, and she now had him at arm's length. She soon drifted back off to sleep.

For the next week and a half, Nevette and Justice pretty much had the same experience almost nightly. She would wake in a panic, swinging wildly and screaming. But would ultimately end up in Justices' protective arms while she slept.

*****

The time finally came that Sarah nervously anticipated. Today she would finally take little Reginald home from the hospital. Veronica had made such a fuss over her and the baby the last few weeks. Everything was set at home, and she was at the hospital early to get Sarah and the baby. Reginald was already there when Veronica arrived. Sarah inquired how Minister Goodfellow was doing as they went through the checklist to leave the hospital. Trevor skipped most of the formalities with the consideration that Veronica was an OB nurse on his staff.

He had gained almost two more pounds and was well over the five-pound minimum limit for newborns to be able to go home with parents. Sarah was surprised by her excitement to be going home with her baby boy. She didn't have any interest whatsoever in breast feeding. But with the urging of Reginald and the barrage of beneficial facts poured on by Veronica. She decided to give it a whirl. She was surprised at how close it made her feel to Reginald, Jr.

They settled into a routine quickly. Sarah continued to be grateful for Reginald and his support of her and the baby. She had been in the expecting mother's program at school, so she was allowed to do all her homework at home and email it to her class instructors during the time she was in her last few months of pregnancy and through Reginald Jr.'s, hospital stay. But now she would have to head back to regular class, so she, Reginald and Veronica began the interview process to find a suitable babysitter. Sarah and Reginald proved to be good parents and were a good team with little RJ. They often sat together to discuss their plan of attack for when it came time to crunch college into their life of parenthood.

*****

Nevette had been home for a few weeks now, and Teddy and Derrick were downstairs talking as they waited for her to get dressed. Teddy hadn't seen her in a few days and stopped in for a visit.

"So how is it going Derrick? If she doing any better?" Teddy asked.

"Well she doesn't have as many nightmares, and they are not as strong as before. So I guess that means things are getting better," Derrick replied.

"Well, thank the Lord for that," Teddy added.

"Yeah, if you say so," Derrick replied sarcastically. He replied almost on impulse. He thought he had been doing a good job of hiding his anger toward God about Nevette's attack and rape.

"What's that supposed to mean?" Teddy asked.

He completely ignored Teddy's question and said, "I'm not fit to lead this family."

"Don't you start that! Don't let the devil win," Teddy replied.

"Teddy man, he drug her down the steps. You could see her bloody hand prints at the top of the stairs and then smeared all the way down the walls. Her blood was everywhere. They tore that kitchen and basement up. It must have been terrifying for her," Derrick replied with a hint of despair in his voice. "The way she described him to the police, he could have been me. The size, build and complexion was almost identical to mine. She said he was slightly bigger than me. So of course you know that made the police officer give me a look. Man I thought, if you don't get your mind off me or the fact that I could ever do such a thing to my own wife—I knew he was thinking it Teddy. I could read his face. I shook my head in disgust."

"He was just doing his job Derrick. They have to at least consider every option. And unfortunately, sometimes it is someone close to the victim," Teddy replied.

"Maybe," Derrick said as he shook his head at the notion.

"Anyway, back to your negative response to God when I for the situation appearing to get better. What was that all that about?" Teddy asked.

Derrick looked at him then away to the left and back at him before he said, "Teddy, why is God noticeably absent in my life when it appears that I need him the most? Where was He?"

Teddy replied, "What do you mean, where was he Derrick? There is nothing that happens that God is—"

"Really Teddy, really? Okay, where was HE when Suzette walked out of the daycare with my daughter? Where was HE when she gave her penicillin? Why didn't HE stop her? Huh? Why didn't he? And where? Where in the heck was HE when this maniac targeted, attacked and raped my pregnant wife? Answer me that Teddy, huh, answer me that!" Derrick exclaimed. He took a deep breath to settle the rage that continued to grow inside his inner man.

"Derrick man, what's wrong with you?" Teddy asked.

Derrick all but glared as he said, "I'll tell you what's wrong me Teddy. I'm mad as he—"

"Stop! Derrick stop before you go too far. You're beyond mad Derrick. What I hear in your voice and feel coming off of you is nothing short of rage. Don't you let the devil have your mind or emotions like this! Don't let him steal your joy or your peace," Teddy said as he touched Derrick on the shoulder to calm him.

Derrick looked at Teddy. His nostrils flared and his breathing was heavy, "I went back over to the house to get some things that Tre needed. All I could see was Nevette's blood. It was almost worse than the first day I came home. I relived the moment as I stood in the kitchen when I first walked in. One thing is for sure. There is no way I'm taking her back there to live. And I swear to you right now Teddy. The day I lay my eyes on this maniac is the last day he is going to breathe. I'm going to kill him for what he did to my wife, and to me! I'm not going to show him anymore consideration for his life than he did for Zoé's or Nevette's as he stabbed at her stomach, so she would stop fighting him! I swear to you, the day I see him. He's a dead man, Teddy. You hear me. He's a dead man!"

"Oh my God Derrick you have got to get yourself under control. Come on Derrick, calm down," Teddy said.

"Calm down! Teddy I could have buried my wife and unborn child a few weeks ago!" Derrick exclaimed.

"Exactly! And that's where God was. He protected what mattered. He protected life. What doesn't kill you, makes you stronger. You and Nay Nay have an awesome testimony. Together y'all will minister to countless marriages," Teddy said to answer his previous question about God. "Look man, life happens, things happen. They're not God's fault one way or the other. The question we really have to ask ourselves is, was there something God said or did to warn us about it and we ignored it. Man evil is ever present. We don't know why God allows some things and stops others. You and Nay Nay need to just make sure y'all talk a lot and communicate. You both need to know what the other is feeling."

"Yeah we didn't communicate well after Callisha," Derrick replied.

He rubbed his hand across his face and appeared to momentarily get his emotions under control.

"Y'all didn't communicate at all after Callisha," Teddy stated. "Y'all yelled at each other. Well, Nay Nay did most of the yelling."

Derrick sighed and said, "She had every right to feel the way she did. I wasn't any better a protector or leader for her or this family then, than I am now. Every decision I make, falls apart in my hands."

"Derrick you know that's not true. Stop listening to the devil," Teddy said.

Before Derrick could reply, Nevette walked down the stairs where they were.

"Hey Teddy," she said as he gave her a light non-threatening hug.

"Hey princess," he replied.

They talked for a while before Teddy said he needed to leave. Josephine and the baby were still nursing a cold that transferred back and forth between the two of them the last few weeks. He said his goodbyes as he gave Derrick a knowing pat on the back. He looked at him for a moment before he turned to Nevette and gave her another hug. She pondered what could be the meaning of the look Teddy gave Derrick. Teddy sat in the car and called Bernard before he drove off. He shared his concerns about Derrick and his anger. Bernard told him he would pray about it and call Derrick soon.

*****

Nevette woke yet again in the middle of the night screaming. Although she fought him in her sleep less, and they appeared to be coping with the rape and moving toward healing, Justice knew they were still far from it. The fear he saw in his wife's eyes when he would make an unannounced move in her direction kindled the fire that blazed within him.

That morning he skipped breakfast. He told Nevette he needed to take care of a few things and should be back home around noon or so.

He planned on pulling a few favors with the guys he knew on the police force to see if they would leak any information they had concerning the identification of the serial rapist. He secretly planned to exact his own *"justice"* upon Nevette's attacker. He made a few calls and decided to head to the local pawn shop while he waited for them to return his call with the information he requested.

After going over the specifications on all the guns in the case with the pawn shop owner, he decided on his weapons of choice. Of course, his background check went through and came back with flying colors. An hour later, he was on his way back over to his house. He walked in through the garage door. When he crossed the threshold into the kitchen, his mind played out what he imagined the horrific day was like for Nevette. He looked at the details of everything thrown around the room, and a scenario began to unfold in his mind. He could hear her screams and shuttered at the sound of her pleading for hers and

Zoé's lives as her attacker stabbed her over and over. He could hear the thump, thump, thump on the stairs as he drug her kicking and screaming down to the basement. He clinched his teeth as he saw her lying there helpless and exhausted after he raped and left her for dead.

His hand played with the trigger of the gun and the fire inside of him shot sparks of volcanic ash, and it threatened to overflow any minute.

His phone rang, and he answered with in impatient tone as he anticipated finding out any information at all about Nevette's attacker. His police officer friend apologized that he couldn't help him. But the information they had he could not jeopardize sharing. He did, however, truthfully relay that they had no suspects in the case as of yet. The DNA recovered at the scene, although proven to be the same that was found on the other victims, was not a match to anyone in the system. Whoever this person was. He did not have a record. At least, not one in their system. They were sorry to admit that the trail was as cold as it was after the previous victims.

Derrick thanked him and hung up. He sighed and breathed heavily as he stood at the top of the steps that led to the basement. He looked down the stairs at the blood on the carpet, railing and walls. He walked towards the backdoor, opened it and sat down on the step. He placed his head in his hand. He still had the gun in his left hand, and it rested on the side of his face with the other hand on the other side as he tried to force the images of the day out of his mind. He was angry that the cop's trail was already cold. He sat on his back porch for nearly half an hour, in turmoil contemplating his next move.

Thoughts of his family ran through his mind like sting rays and images of the possible scenarios of his premeditated actions displayed with shocks of electricity across the screen inside his head. Each one jolted him, and his eyes darted back and forth as though he were in REM sleep.

"What are you doing Derrick? You can't do this. You can't put your family through another hardship," he whispered to himself.

He got up went back into the house. He locked the door behind him, got in the car and let the garage door back down with the remote. He placed the gun on the seat and pick up his phone. He called the realtor and told them to go ahead with the sale of the house. He had spoken with them a few weeks prior just after Nevette was released from the hospital. He knew they could never live there comfortably again. He called the cleaning and moving teams and asked them to meet him at the house in about an hour.

He went back to the pawn shop where he purchased the gun and sold it back to them. He didn't care of he lost money, he needed that gun out of his hands before he made a decision out of rage that would change his and his family's lives forever. He went back to the house, pulling into the driveway simultaneously with the moving team.

Back inside, he instructed the movers on everything that needed to be packed and stored. As they walked through the home, and he gave instructions, the cleaning team arrived. Derrick told them to stay coordinated with the movers so they would know when to come in to clean the home prior to the walk through with the new owners.

He told the movers their job would be easy because they were to pack no furniture from the house whatsoever. The house would be sold fully furnished. Only to pack all the personal and endearing things he pointed out earlier. He set up a time to come back on the last day of packing to make sure they had everything he wanted to take. He wanted to start fresh with Nevette. He didn't want any furniture from the house to move forward with them.

He told the cleaners the carpets in the basement would be replaced to just clean everything else in the house. He made a note to order carpet on his way out of the house. He gave them both deposits and left heading back to his mother and father's house. He felt as though the thousand-pound weight of anger that plagued him had been lifted off his shoulders. He knew neither of them would ever recover in that house. The knowledge of what happened there fueled his fire. From the first day, he knew he heard the voice of the Lord say to sell it. Even so, he held on to it as a secret gasoline stash. He wanted a reason to be justified with his premeditated plan to exact his revenge.

*****

Nevette felt uneasy about Justice's demeanor as he left the house. She knew they needed to talk about his anger. She didn't want to leave any stones unturned. Unlike with Callisha, she was determined they would communicate their feelings about everything. Today, when he got back home, she would make him talk to her.

Nevette talked to Shaundra about her concerns and wasn't surprised that Shaundra had the same concerns has she did. She told Nevette that she would keep Tre busy when DJ returned so they could talk. Nevette thanked her and went to pray for God's strength, wisdom and guidance.

It was well into the afternoon when she heard Justice coming through the front door. They had already eaten lunch, and Shaundra was already prepping for dinner. Tre was downstairs in the kitchen with Shaundra, and Nevette was upstairs. He laughed and talked with Tre for a few minutes before they both came up the stairs. He called her name as he entered so he wouldn't startle her.

Shaundra came in shortly after they entered the bedroom to get Tre to help her bake some cookies to eat after dinner. He jumped up and ran out the door with his grandmother. Derrick always knew when his mother was either stalling for time or clearing a room so a serious conversation could take place. He looked at Nevette and wondered what was on her mind. He was somewhat hesitant to inquire if anything were wrong, because he knew that everything was wrong.

Nevette took a deep breath and asked Derrick to come sit down so they could talk. He eyed her curiously as he crossed the room and sat on the bed beside her. She was becoming more and more comfortable with him, but was clearly not out of the woods totally. They were nowhere near close to physical intimacy. He figured it would probably not happen before she delivered Zoé.

"Justice, baby I am so worried about you," she said as she looked him in the eyes.

"I'm fine Nevette," he replied.

"No you're not Justice. I can see it in your eyes, hurt, despair and anger," she stated.

He shook his head, smiled and let out a light chuckle, "You know me girl."

"Yes I do. We're going to talk about this Justice. We will not allow the enemy to bombard or control our thoughts and actions concerning the situation," she declared.

He bit his bottom lip, shook his head back and forth and said, "I have struggled so much Naythia." He was at the point of tears. His voice quaked. "I've been so angry. Today I thought my anger was going to take me to a crazy place. I thank God for intervening, even though it's Him I've been the angriest with. Thank God for his unconditional love."

"I could see it, and it scared me. Let me help you baby. What can I do?" she asked.

"Most of it was done today. I spent most of the afternoon going back and forth in my thoughts. But toward the end, God started talking, and he dealt with me. He instructed me and after I was finally obedient to him, I could feel the weight of the anger lift off me," Justice replied.

Nevette let out a sigh of relief. "Thank You Jesus. I need you Justice. If I'm going to get through this, I need you. All of you, mind body and soul."

Her words were bittersweet to him. Because he knew all of her didn't belong to just him anymore. This guy owned a part of his wife he would never be able to get back.

She touched his face and said, "Come on baby, talk to me. There's something else. Just say it Justice." She feared that he would ask her why she just gave herself to her attacker. That had been her fear all along. She braced herself for the question she thought he had longed to ask her.

Justice rubbed his hand through his head and said, "He had no regard to my baby growing inside of you. No value to life whatsoever." He paused then continued, "Baby. I was supposed to be the only man to ever make love to you. You belonged to me Nevette. Your virginity was mine. It was sacred, holy and special. He devoured it. I was supposed to be the only one for you—ever."

"First of all, Derrick Justice Goodfellow II, my virginity didn't belong to you. It belonged to God and me. I presented it to you on our wedding night," she replied with a smile. She touched the side of his face and continued, "Oh sweetheart. You still are the only man who has and will ever, make love to me. What he did to me was not love. It wasn't even sex. It was violent, evil and painful. But it wasn't love Justice. It wasn't love."

He let out a heavy sigh, "Oh God Naythia. I feel so violated. But I'm finally ready to talk about it with the pastor and first lady if you are."

"I am," she replied.

He told her about what happened at the house that afternoon. He neglected to tell her that he had the house prepped for sale, and that he left it fully furnished. He wasn't sure why but felt he shouldn't disclose that information yet. She gasped as she realized how close her husband came to going over the edge.

They started meeting with the pastor and first lady the following week for counseling. They also set up appointments for Tre. Pastor Tills included Talinda and Bernard since they were the youth counselors on Tre's sessions.

*****

As she headed into the seventh week since the rape, Nevette was frustrated with what she considered a lack of progress on how she dealt with it. She had been to the doctor three times since the attack. Yolanda was somewhat concerned with the stress the nightmares had on Zoé even though she knew they were the normal process of rape victims. However, Zoé checked out remarkably well physically and was progressing normally for just over the seven-month point of gestation. She was reluctant to give Nevette anything to help her sleep better, because she knew the effect it would have on Zoé. Nevette was grateful to Dr. Harrell for her honesty about the prescriptions.

She stood in the kitchen as she helped Shaundra rinse and cut fruit to have with lunch. The men were downstairs playing video games with Tre.

Nevette had a faraway look in her eyes and sighed often. "How long am I going to be a nervous wreck mom?" she asked.

"Nevette you were brutally raped and repeatedly stabbed just over seven weeks ago. If you ask me, you're doing well. You sleep with Derrick almost every night, and you don't jump nearly as much when touched. Don't be so hard on yourself," Shaundra replied.

"Don't give me too much credit mom. Half way through the night, I still wake up screaming and beating the crap out of Justice. Then I'm this crazed wife who doesn't want to let him out of my sight. I just keep going from one extreme to the other. Halfway through the night, I wake up and want him out of the bed. I'm terrified and doing everything I can not to panic as the anxiety of him lying next to me subsides. I still struggle with guilty thoughts of what Justice thinks of me. And I still I feel as though I had an affair. We talked about it, but I still wonder if he believes that I fought as long as I could or secretly wanted someone else. I know it's the devil messing with me. I try to keep myself busy because my idle mind almost drives me insane. I think of the moment that I know is coming. I am eventually going to have to make love to Justice and that terrifies me. I don't want to lose my husband. The way I feel right now, I don't know if I will ever be ready to be intimate with a man again. I don't want to live my life afraid. Afraid of every little noise. Unexpected touches from people. Not just men but anybody. I'm in whirlwind even with Tre's touch at times. He's my baby. I can't deny him affection from his mommy. So I wouldn't exactly call that doing well," she replied.

"Nevette dear—" Shaundra started to protest.

"No mom. I can't hide behind the sympathy of the act. Up until Callisha happened over a year ago, my life had been perfect in God. I mean, I lost my mother to cancer. But even in that, everyone rallied around to protect me, and we were prepared. We knew she was going to die. That's why I fell apart with Callisha. Physically, I didn't know how to touch God for myself. I was good at getting everyone else to that place of trust, but I wasn't there myself. I didn't know how to pull on God for myself. Partly, because I was angry with him. I'm afraid that's where Justice is right now. I was squeezing the life out of Justice's hand under the table when I had to give the police the details of the rape a few weeks ago. I fear that he's still angry with God mom. He said he dealt with it, and God dealt with him. But I still think he's angry. I know he is. I know the look—and the signs. I mean he prays with Tre and me, but he hasn't opened a bible since the day it happened. I don't know what to do, because most of the time I'm barely getting through the moment with him," she interjected.

"Yes his dad and I have talked about it as well. But you have to understand his position in this. A man has raped his wife. Violated his life in every way, and there is nothing that he can do about it. No one knows who or where this man is. Men live to protect their families. Anger and self-pity bombards their minds and all but takes over when they fail at the task. He is going to go back and forth with victories and defeats in his emotions for a while the same way you are dear," Shaundra replied.

"Speaking of which, the police called us this morning and confirmed that it's the same guy who raped five pregnant women three summers ago. It looks like he goes on a spree and then disappears after he has satisfied his fetish for the moment. Unless he strikes again and gets caught in the act, I'm afraid this is going to be an unsolved case. That thought has Justice even more on edge and worried. I was afraid we would be right back where we started with that rage thing again. But he seemed to be in control when they told us the bad news. I attempted to trust the bright side forward by saying to him that there hadn't been a pattern of this guy repeating with the same woman twice. Besides, I wouldn't be pregnant but a few more months, then I would no longer be a target anyway. But I'm sure it was of little comfort because Justice doesn't see it that way," Nevette added.

"Of course not dear. He will be on edge for a long time if they don't catch this guy," Shaundra replied.

"I know," Nevette replied. Her voice cracked, and she was suddenly on the verge of tears.

Shaundra rubbed her back in a gentle non-threatening motion. Nevette smiled and then sighed. After they finished lunch, Justice asked Nevette if she wanted to go for a walk. She accepted, and Derrick went to see if Tre wanted to come while Nevette got into her walking shoes. He was busy on a project with his grandfather and declined Derrick's offer.

He informed them they wouldn't be gone long and he and Nevette left. They walked and enjoyed the conversation. The connection between them had been began to feel somewhat normal again. However, she knew she still wasn't ready to be sexually intimate yet, but she welcomed his touch instead of nearly coming out of her skin.

As they walked Nevette said, "I remember when I was single and counseled a woman once after she had been raped. I remember I was trying to say all the right words according to scripture. Now I often sit and think about those words, and I realize how ineffective they really were. Because the thought of the words I said to her, have brought little or no comfort to me. I never reached her emotions. I never reached her hurt. Rape is a life-changing event Justice. You have to rethink everything. You have to reprogram yourself not to walk in fear, and that takes God. No psychologist or secular therapist can help you with that part of it. You have to yield the fear over to God."

"Wow baby. God *is* doing a quick work in you. It's been just over a month and a half, and already you're able to comfortably talk about it. Not to mention that fact that you no longer come unglued when I touch you now. I know we're not all the way there yet, but for the first time, I really feel like it's going to be okay," Justice said.

He reached out and grabbed her hand. She smiled, and they continued to walk and talk. Nevette avoided the one thing she knew would determine where she really was in her recovery. The return trip home. She knew it would happen eventually, and she would almost hyperventilate just thinking of how powerful and intimidating the first encounter with their home since the rape would be. Although she withheld her feelings about it from Justice thus far, he was more than aware of her fear. Partly, because he shared the same obstacle.

But unlike the fear that Nevette was certain would overtake her when she walked back into the house. The only thing it had done to Derrick was enrage him all the more.

He smiled as he thought of how angry he was. He was relieved it was behind him. He wasn't completely past it. But the turmoil to deal with the matter with street justice had passed. Logic and reason took their rightful place in his spirit. Derrick now focused on his relationship with God because one thing was for certain. He would have to trust God concerning Nevette's attacker. Because it appeared that he had once again disappeared off the radar.

They continued their walk enjoying good conversation and each other as they headed back toward the house. He didn't want her to be too exhausted. She was just recently taken off bed rest.

*****

He had indeed left that next morning after Nevette's attack. He rose and ate the second half of the sandwich he made the night before. He hopped in his car and drove out of town headed north. Everything about Nevette's rape plagued him, and he still feared that she may not have survived it. The night before the news only stated that she came into the hospital, but never disclosed her condition as anything but critical. He knew he couldn't chance it. Although he still felt tingly about his encounter with her, and his loins were still warm from the sheer excitement of having her the day before. He decided against attempting a second victim. "He who rapes and runs away, lives to rape another day," he chuckled that day as he drove past the *"Welcome to South Carolina"* sign.

*****

Nevette rose the next morning after she and Justice had gone on their intimate walk feeling empowered. For the first time, she hadn't awaken during the night in an all-out war with Justice as a result of a nightmare. She managed her fear when she rose for a restroom break. It was especially hard whenever he got out of the bed for whatever reason and returned. The intimidation of him getting in the bed was frightening at times, and so he would always get into bed before her. Once she got out of bed for any reason at all, she would often put a layer of sheets in between them. But not this night. She got back into bad and cuddled right up close to him. She felt an overwhelming sense of security with him the last few days. And today she felt like more than a conqueror and for the first time, actually believed that she would be able to make love to her husband again in the near future.

Justice was due to go back to work the following week. Nevette felt it was time to face her biggest fear. She knew they would eventually have to go back home and putting it off would not make the task any easier. She also knew she couldn't do it without Justice present.

Everyone, including Tre slept in that Saturday morning. As she and Justice sat at the breakfast table she said, "Justice, I think it's time. You go back to work next week. We can't live here with mom and dad forever. I'm eventually going to have to face the house. I know it will take a while before I'm comfortable being there by myself..."

"Sweetheart that's not going to be a problem," Justice interjected.

"What do you mean Justice?" she asked.

"I sold the house," Justice replied. "I didn't talk with you about it because I wasn't going to take no for an answer. You may want to conquer that hurdle, but I don't want you to. Or Tre either for that matter. We don't know what going back there will do to him, and I had to take that into consideration as well. I stood there in the kitchen and watched Tre as he stood in the only spot in the room that was not covered in his mother's blood. He has done well. We all have at the counseling sessions with pastor, Talinda and Bernard. But sweetheart conquering the house is not something I want you to do. It will never be the same and I will not put my family through the torment of trying. The day I purchased the gun and went through that ordeal is the same day I decided to go ahead with the sale of the house, fully furnished."

"Justice—" she started to say.

"Don't worry, our personal things are in storage," he replied. "Sweetheart it wasn't on the market a week, and I had a buyer. I closed last week. But there is something that I want you to see today. There is a house right here in mom and dad's subdivision for sale. It's an older home, but I've always marveled at the beautiful architecture of it on the outside every time I drove by."

Nevette was almost speechless and relieved. She was talking a big game, but she knew inside the thought of being alone in their house plagued her. Even so, she was prepared to muscle through it, because she knew eventually they had to go home. She was also terrified of what it would do to Tre to be there as well.

"Thank you Justice. I really didn't want us to go back. But honey, we can't afford a house in this neighborhood," she replied.

"Yes we can. We already have the money in the bank from the sale of our home sweetheart. So we really only need to match the $265,000 we made from the sale of our home, with a mortgage loan. It's twice as much house. Go get dressed. I have been waiting for us to be able to see it. We'll be back before anyone gets up," Justice said as he rose from the table to place the dishes in the sink.

Nevette was excited and quickly went to get dressed. They drove about five streets over, and there it was. A beautiful corner lot with a 7500 square-foot home. She gasped at the sight of it.

He got out of the car and walked around to open her door. As she got out of the car she said, "Justice there is no way this home is going to sell for a mere $500,000 or less for us to be able to afford it. Its $600,000 to $800,000 easily. I know you're a partner with you dad and bring home quite a bit. However, you forget dear, mom is a doctor and that accounts for why they can afford to live in this neighborhood," Nevette stated in a tone that said there is no way this is going to work.

"Okay maybe. So let's just go have fun window shopping, "Justice teased.

Inside, the elderly couple watched them stand in the driveway conversing. They knew this was the couple. They could feel it in their spirits. They smiled and looked at each other.

Lately, Justice had taken chances to touch her stomach unannounced. Nevette was surprised that she reacted less and less which each passing day to his spontaneous touches. The prayer warriors at Grace were in overdrive praying for the Goodfellow family. They walked up to the front door, and Justice rang the bell. Nevette took a deep breath and expelled it like a kid who was just told it was open game at a candy store by their parents. Justice smiled and enjoyed her excitement.

"Hello may we help you?" Mrs. Santino asked.

"Yes ma'am. We noticed your For Sale sign in the yard. We were wondering if we could bother you to look around. If we need to have an appointment with a realtor, we will understand. We do not want to intrude on your privacy," Justice replied.

"Oh no, by all means, do come in," she replied. She looked over her shoulder and called her husband. My name is Leona Santino, and this is my husband David."

"Nice to meet you. "I'm Derrick Goodfellow II, and this is my wife Nevette," Justice said.

"Oh when are you due?" she asked Nevette as she beckoned for them to have a seat in the living room.

"I have just over seven more weeks," Nevette replied.

"How marvelous. Is this your first child?" she asked.

"Leona, so many questions," her husband teased.

"Oh no sir it's no problem," Nevette replied. "Actually it's our third pregnancy."

"Wonderful, do you have two boys, girls or one of each already?" she asked to keep the conversation going.

Justice smiled and replied," We have a boy who just turned eight. Our daughter was ten months old when she died. And the little one on the way is a girl also." He was surprised at how easy he could speak of Callisha.

"Mama that's enough questions," Mr. Santino said to his wife Leona.

"Oh it's alright," Nevette replied.

"Can I get you both some iced tea? It's hot out today," Leona asked.

"That would be wonderful. Can I help you with it?" Nevette replied.

"Sure, I would love the company," she replied.

Nevette followed Leona off to the kitchen. Derrick was surprised at her openness with the couple.

Nevette gasped at the majesty of the kitchen. "Your kitchen is heavenly," she said.

"Thank you," Leona replied.

They had more chit-chat about the house as they poured the tea and returned to the living room. The men were already engaged in conversation.

After Leona and Nevette served the men she asked, "So are you looking to upsize for the coming addition to the family?"

Justice looked at Nevette before responding. He wanted to get a read on what, if any, about their personal life he should mention about their house hunting desires.

She nodded and said, "It's okay sweetheart. Go ahead."

Justice smiled and gave them the short version of the events of their lives over the last year and a half. Leona and David listened carefully. Leona fought to keep from crying as Justice told their testimony.

When he finished David looked at Leona and said, "Well mama, is there any doubt?"

"Definitely not papa," she replied.

He looked at Justice and Nevette, who both had bewildered looks on their faces. Nevette wondered in anticipation, what God was about to do.

"Well, come. Let us show you the rest of the house," Leona said as she stood.

As they gave them the grand tour and told the stories of each room and the furniture pieces, Nevette kept commenting on how beautifully their home was decorated.

They finally ended up in back in the grand style, living room. Leona smiled as she gingerly gave her husband a pat on the shoulder.

Justice nervously said, "Well, I guess this is the part where we ask what you are asking for your home."

Leona smiled and looked at her husband. He returned the smile and cleared his throat, "Well son, Leona and I have been looking for just the right couple to sell our home to. God told us we would know the couple that was to buy it when we met them. He also told us the price we were to sell it to them for. Leona and I never had any children of our own. We bought this house so we could be a blessing for guest speakers at our church and for those in need of a place to stay briefly at difficult times in their lives. It has been a safe haven to many over the twenty years that we have been here. We decided that was time to retire and recently purchased a small condominium outside Atlanta. We no longer need this much house, and the stairs are getting to be a bit much for us. We recently had a new roof, plumbing, ventilation and everything the house was in need of repairing done, to get ready to put the house on the market. We have had several people come to look at it, but none of them could afford the asking price."

Nevette smiled. But inside her heart was breaking. She was already in love with the house and admired everything about it.

Leona added, "The moment we first saw you two in the driveway talking, we knew that you would be the couple that would get the house. And after hearing your testimony, we knew for sure that you were the ones." She smiled and rubbed Nevette on the shoulder.

Justice and Nevette were silent. They weren't exactly sure what they should say. They were sure the house was way out of their price range, and couldn't imagine having enough after so many couples had been denied.

Before Justice could speak David declared, "Thus sayeth the Lord, *I HAVE GIVEN YOU DOUBLE FOR YOUR TROUBLE!"*

Tears welled up in both Justice and Nevette's eyes. They remained silent.

David continued, "For less than double the price. Now I don't know what your last home was valued at, but God said he would tell us the couple that He wanted to bless with this house. He has set the price at $500,000.00, fully furnished. Everything in this house was staged and is to be left here for the buyers. We have already moved everything we need along with all our personal things into our condominium. The furniture pieces we took, we replaced with new things so every room would be furnished. As a matter of fact, we don't even live here anymore. We've only come over from time to time the last seven weeks waiting for the couple God wanted us to bless to come. We had previously been here only to show the house by appointment only with the realtor before that.

"But Sir, this house and all the furnishing has to be valued well over $700,000.00," Justice intervened.

Nevette was speechless. All she could do was cry as she leaned into Justices' arms. She felt weak at the knees at the blessing that God had just bestowed upon them.

"I understand that. Rest assured Mr. Goodfellow. The price we paid for it is well below the amount we are selling it for. We were blessed when we received it so therefore we have to be a blessing when we sell it. Now, do we have a deal," David said as he stuck out his hand.

Derrick could only nod and shake on the deal. He held Nevette, and they cried and thanked God. They were overwhelmed at His blessing. The Santino's were overjoyed and tears rolled down Leona's face as they all praised God.

They set up a time to meet at the realtors to close the deal. The Santino's had already started paperwork and ordered the appraisal for the sale. They were just waiting for Justice and Nevette to show up, so there wasn't much left to do.

They went home and shared the news with Tre and Derricks parents. They were just as stunned as Justice and Nevette were and gave God thanks.

A few weeks later Justice and Nevette closed on their new home. They called and had all of their personnel items that were in storage delivered into their new home.

There were four bedrooms up stairs and two more in the basement. The master suite was to die for. The home had three living room spaces and was full of bells and whistles with beautiful crown molding throughout. A laundry room on the upper level, as well as one in the basement for the bedrooms located down there. An eat-in kitchen and a separate formal dining area. They had two offices, one on the main floor and one in the basement, a game room, six bathrooms, a sun room and state of the art theater room. All updated stainless steel appliances. There was a hot tub and swimming pool in the back yard. All the yard care items were in the three-car garage, to include a like-new riding lawn mower. And the landscaping was immaculate.

~Chapter Eighteen~

Talinda was absolutely miserable as she neared the end of her ninth month of pregnancy. Her due date came and went and there was no sign that she was anywhere close to going into labor. She concluded that the due date was off from the beginning and wasn't at all worried. Dr. Harrell informed her that she would only allow her to go two weeks past her due date, as long as everything checked out at each appointment. She wanted to see Talinda every three days after her due date. Bernard's parents were there for the delivery as well as Talinda's and everyone played the waiting game. Teresa and Helen were back and forth on the phone every time they thought Talinda was close. Helen said she would meet them at the hospital when the time came. In the meantime, Bernard, Valetta and Teresa attempted to keep Talinda as comfortable as possible.

*****

Nevette and Justice settled into the new house, and she was now a little over thirty-five weeks pregnant. They were excited about planning for their house warming party the coming weekend. They thought of putting it off until Talinda had her baby. But doing so would have put Nevette close to having Zoé. So they decided to go forth with it as planned. Talinda and Bernard, however, did plan on attending along with Raymond and the twins. They inquired about bringing their parents along with Helen and Roger as well. Nevette was delighted. The more the merrier she told Talinda.

The Warner Robbins crew were also invited to include: Jaison, Tasha and their daughter Alicia; Terry, Stacy and their son TJ: and Michael and Gloria Thomas and their four boys. Of course, Pastor Tills and his wife Beatrice along with the entire teen youth group was on the guest list. Veronica and her husband Jeff, Nevette's and Derricks parents and siblings obviously; and of course, her best friend Lindsay, Trevor and their son Trevor, Jr.

Derrick entered the bedroom after he prayed with Tre and put him to bed. Nevette was still mulling over the list, making sure that everything was set for the house warming party the next evening. She knew the next day would be very busy and was relieved Lindsay, Shaundra and Yogi, would come over to assist her in getting everything ready.

"Alright Mrs. Goodfellow, you need to get some rest," Justice said as he gently took the notebook out of her hand and placed it on the dresser. "You've gone over that list at least twenty times today alone."

"I know. I just want everything to be perfect," Nevette replied.

"It will be. I'm looking forward to having all of our friends and family over as well," Justice said as he went into the bathroom to brush his teeth.

Nevette followed him to do the same. She was amazed at how comfortable she was with Justice and other people. She was actually looking forward to it. It had only been a little over three months since her attack. However, she felt perfectly fine with Derrick. But he knew she would most likely place herself in the vicinity of the women most of the time during the house warming dinner party. She had done okay at church the month before when she returned. People where careful not to crowd her. The house warming would be her first real test of close contact with a lot of people in one area. She welcomed the challenge. She was determined that this incident would not cripple her life or her marriage.

She looked at Justice in the mirror and smiled. He returned the smile, and she melted. She was surprised at her reaction to his smile. She waited for the moment that she would again desire her husband sexually. Although she had the feeling before today, she was particularly anxious in the bathroom with him. Not the bad kind of anxious. She knew what she felt was 'wedding night' anxious. As she looked at him, she knew that tonight would be their first night making love since it happened.

Her thoughts went to God and how awesome he was. He did a quick work in her indeed. Partly, because she confronted her fear and forced herself to lay down beside her husband every night. As well as be alone with him as much as possible. She actually felt more nervous when Justice wasn't at her side. She kept herself busy and anywhere but alone when he first went back to work. She spent most of her time with Talinda and Lindsay. But for the last two weeks, she intentionally stayed home alone during the day. She knew if she was going to be fully functional she would have to conquer the beast of solitude. However, she still had not returned to the store by herself. But that was mostly at Justice's request. He was extremely overprotective of her. The news of the rape had pregnant women on alert all over the city and surrounding areas. Most husbands required their pregnant wives to shop in groups or with them.

But tonight, her passion hit a peek and no amount of fear was going to stand in the way of her making love to her husband. She dabbed a little of his favorite perfume behind her ears before she headed out of the bathroom. Justice left the bathroom and was already in the bed when she entered the bedroom.

He saw her coming and said, "You are so beautiful."

"Why thank you kind sir. You are rather handsome yourself," she replied.

She pulled the covers back on her side and climbed into bed. He immediately smelled her perfume but made no reaction to it. She snuggled up next to him and sighed.

He placed his arm around her and gently pulled her into his chest. He was relieved that he no longer had to treat her with such kid gloves, or be mindful of every touch or movement in her direction.

She looked up at him and kissed him lightly on the lips. He wasn't sure if he should respond so he just allowed her to kiss him.

"Derrick Justice Goodfellow II, if you don't kiss me back," she declared.

He smiled and said, "I wasn't sure what to do. Where is this going Nevette? Because baby, if you think that you need to—"

"Shhhhh. Just kiss me Justice," she replied and kissed him again. This time he returned the kiss but was still somewhat hesitant. Nevette could feel his body tense up at her touch as she sensually maneuvered her hands over his chest and abdomen.

"Okay this is different. Tonight you have wedding night jitters," Nevette teased.

He chuckled, "Nevette baby. You know I'm a man who can keep it together sexually. You don't have to push or force yourself into something you're not ready for."

"Who says I'm not ready Justice?" Nevette replied. "Look sweetheart, I am not going to allow that man to control my life, my family or my marriage. I'm not going to crawl into a shell or under a rock and hide from life, or from you. I'm not forcing myself to do this. I want to make love to you. I was waiting for that warm tingly feeling I get when you smile at me to return. And tonight in the bathroom when we were brushing our teeth, it happened. So you just get ready Mr. Goodfellow because you're officially on the clock, now get to work."

He smiled and shook his head. Then with a look of concern he said, "Naythia what if something goes wrong? What if I put Zoé under stress? "

"Nothing is going to go wrong, and you're not going to put any stress on Zoé whatsoever. You were making love to me before everything happened," Nevette replied.

Derrick sighed, "I know baby but that was then, and this is now. And—"

Nevette cut him off with a kiss, and then she climbed on top of him. She straddled him and began to caress his chest.

She looked down at him and giggled as she said, "I guess I'm going to have to take it from you."

"Nevette—" he replied.

"Shhhhh—make love to me Justice," she said as she pulled her gown over her head.

"Baby at any time if this gets to be too much for you. Just stop okay Nevette?" he stated in question form. "You're going to have to lead on this sweetheart."

"Mmmmm your wish is my command," she teased.

"Come on baby. I'm serious. I'm nervous about this," Justice replied.

"Relax Justice. If I even remotely start to feel like I can't handle it. I'll say something," she replied.

The room was soon filled with an aroma of soft sweet love. Justice quickly relaxed and enjoyed his wife. Although it wasn't their usual powerful love making session, Justice was overwhelmed with the power that emitted off Nevette and flowed down unto him and penetrated his soul. It couldn't have lasted more than ten to fifteen minutes before she began to feel anxious and overwhelmed. But to Justice and Nevette, it may as well have been all night. They lay peacefully in each other's arms the rest of the night.

*****

Lindsay arrived first, and they got started while they waited for Shaundra and Yogi to get there. They spent most of the day helping Nevette get everything ready. Finally, the guests were starting to arrive. Even though Talinda had been having small contractions most of the day, she and her crew were the first to arrive. She introduced hers, Brandon's and Bernard parents to everyone again. She wasn't sure if there had ever been any formal introductions with them and the Goodfellows. As the rest of the guests arrived Helen, Roger, Teresa, Reginald, Valetta and Victor mingled as though they had known everyone their entire lives. Valetta and Shaundra, the two female doctors, hit it off from the start and were already inseparable.

Justice was out on the deck attending to the meat on the grill. Nevette was excited and greeted everyone with a hug. Most everyone was a little hesitant at first, but soon realized that she was okay with their contact. However, she still insured that she positioned herself close to the women most of the night when she wasn't up under Justice. All in all, she handled the situation very well thus far.

The teens were on their usual job and had all the kids in the backyard playing ball, and everyone was having a blast. Reginald held little Reggie as he talked with some of the teen boys.

Justice had gotten onto Nevette for working so hard that day, and finally with the help of Tasha and Stacy. They made her and Talinda both have a seat.

The ladies all gathered around in the hearth room. Some were sitting on the floor. Some on chairs chit-chatting about the men in their lives.

Valetta said to Shaundra, as they stood on the other side of the room at the refreshment table, "Now I know Talinda has been contracting off and on all day. However, as I watch Nevette, it seems like every twenty minutes or so, she is shifts slightly in her seat. She's wringing her hands and rubbing her stomach like she may be in pain."

"Okay so it's not just the pediatrician me," Shaundra replied. "I noticed the pattern to it. She is always accusing me of being overprotective with her."

"Well, it's not like you don't have a reason to be Shaundra. We'll just watch her for now," Valetta replied.

"Thanks. Let's synchronize our watches, so we can keep up with both of them." Shaundra said.

Stacy looked at Tasha as though getting the okay before she spoke. She looked at Nevette and said, "If this is too awkward and personal, you don't have to comment. However, Nevette, I have to say I'm just marveling at how well you are doing. It was a brutal act, and a lot of women would never be where you are right now. Like I said, you don't have to respond. I just have to give you kudos for facing fears and moving forward with life. What a powerful testimony you have. I believe God will use you and Derrick in a mighty way."

There was a two-second pause that seemed like eternity before Nevette spoke. "You know Stacy, the day it happened, I was terrified of everything and everybody. Well, everyone who was male of course. Justice was so beside himself with guilt and anger that I had to push my fear aside and minister to him. We talked a lot, and at first I would jump whenever he made any sudden movements. Whether they were in my direction or just in general. I saw how that hurt him. I would have nightmares and scream and hit him in my sleep. He would hold me until I would wake up and calm down, and then I would cry myself back to sleep in his arms. After a while, it changed from not wanting him to touch me to not wanting him out of my sight. He was my husband, my protector and where he went, I went. I forced myself not to crawl into a shell. With the help of my mother-in-law, Pastor, First Lady Tills, Talinda and Lindsay; I dealt with and still am, dealing with it."

"Wow," Stacy replied.

"I was amazed at how quickly the stab wounds started to heal. At first, it down right hurt to be touched. Now only a few of them are still a little sensitive. You know. I was determined that not another thing would take over my life or my marriage. I feel like the incident with Callisha prepared me. I think had they been in reverse, there is no way I would ever have allowed Derrick to touch me again intimately. And we definitely wouldn't have made it through Callisha after that," Nevette stated.

She shifted in her seat after she made that statement. Valetta and Shaundra looked at each other. This got Helen's attention, and she looked at Valetta who gave her a knowing look. Valetta stated she was going to get something to drink and asked if anyone wanted anything. Shaundra said she would go with her, and Helen follow behind them.

After they were at the table on the other side of the room Helen asked, "Okay what gives? I've been watching you two. I know Talinda is having contractions, but I saw you two just now with Nevette."

"Well, we noticed that about every twenty minutes she shifts in her seat," Shaundra replied.

"I saw that. I knew she wasn't extremely close to her due date, so I chalked it up to being tired and irritable toward nearing the last month," Helen replied.

Teresa noticed that they congregated a little long and came over to join them. "Okay what's the mother's jam session in this corner all about?"

"Our pregnant daughters what else," Shaundra replied. "It appears that Talinda may not be the only one we have to watch tonight. Nevette looks a little ready herself."

Back on the other side of the room Talinda finally had a contraction that got her and Tasha's attention.

"You okay girl," Tasha asked.

"Yeah. I don't think Dr. Harrell will have to induce me on Monday after all. I don't think I will make it through the weekend," Talinda replied.

The ladies went on in casual conversation about life, church and their families.

Meanwhile, the men were engaged in their own discussion downstairs. Derrick had just finished telling everyone about the day Nevette was attacked and raped.

Jaison said, "Derrick. I don't know what I would have done if I were to walk in my house the way you just described everything. I would have probably flipped out."

"If I wouldn't have had Tre with me, I probably would have," Derrick replied. "As a lawyer, I used to always wonder how people could just lose control and kill someone. I always thought, yeah right. You just couldn't control yourself. But now I see how it's possible. A circumstance or event can change everything. I was secretly angry with God. I couldn't believe he allowed my wife to get raped. I'm thankful to all the people who ministered to me. Mostly, my wife, who ministered to me the most in the midst of her own fear. She faced it and allowed me to touch her, when I knew she wanted to jump out of her skin. It's been a crazy few months. The last few years have been like open season on the Goodfellows or something."

"Tell me about it," Teddy added.

Roger asked, "So how is the case going? Do the police have any clues at all?"

Derrick sighed and said, "They have a ton of clues Mr. Travis. But they don't lead to anything. I haven't told Nevette yet, but it's considered a cold case already. They suspect he has probably gone back into hiding. This guy comes out of hiding, does his dirt and then disappears again. The only way they are going to get him will be to catch him in the act. The last five women he raped before Nevette were about three years ago, and then he disappeared until now. They said he usually attacks a few women back to back before disappearing. But because the news report gave the impression that Nevette may not have survived, they think that out of fear, he fled. Which is a good thing I guess. I mean no other pregnant women right now will fall victim to him. But bad also, because it means in a few years, he will probably surface to do it to someone else again. He doesn't have any priors. At least, not any that we know of, meaning he's not in the system. So the district attorney has already prepared us that this is most likely going to go unsolved. I'm thinking it's just as well. I'm being honest because the jury is still out on my actions, if I'm ever forced to sit in the same court room with this guy. I can't promise he won't take his last breath on earth that day."

Teddy said, "Well, you're going to have to beat me to him Derrick, because there's a line."

Jason added, "Yeah, a long line."

"Now gentlemen revenge belongs to God. Even though our flesh wants to react, we have to allow God to prevail in every situation in our lives. We can't trust God with the good, and take care of the bad in our own way," Pastor Tills interjected.

"Couldn't have said it better myself," Talinda's father replied.

"Yes sir and I understand that. I would definitely rather have closure on it. But Nevette and I are recovering, and my family is safe. I spent an extra ten thousand dollars on a state-of-the-art security system. We have a peace about it, and I guess that all that matters," Derrick replied.

They continue talking, but the conversation switched over to sports.

Back upstairs the moms rejoined the group, and the ladies were still talking and laughing.

Talinda smiled and said, "I am so in awe of God. Only an incredible God can take a tragedy and turn it into a ministry. There is not one lady sitting here tonight who hasn't gone through something, and yet we are all still standing."

"Tell me about it," Gloria added. "I never thought I would even be married right now, much less as happy as I am. God sent Stacy and Tasha right when I needed them. With you guys and your husband's help, Michael and I are so solid in our marriage now. I was ready for divorce court, then Talinda's testimony in the airport the day the guys returned from Afghanistan got me to thinking. More about God than Michael, but thinking all the same."

"What a mighty God we serve," Lindsay declared. I remember when I was fifteen and raped by the pastor. Then forced into an abortion to cover his sin. There was no one to minister to me. I suppressed it and it changed my life, and not for the good. I started sleeping with any and everything I could get my hands on. I decided I would control who had me. I wrecked a lot of relationships. I was convinced that all guys wanted was sex. That none of them really knew how to love anyway. But I watched Derrick love Nevette, and knew my thinking was off. Then along came Trevor. God used him to undo what another man abused. So when Nevette was raped my heart ached for her. I talked to her often because I was determined that she would move through this quickly and not get stuck. Stuck hurts. It's confusing, lonely and over whelming."

"I didn't know what to think or say to her," Yogi replied. "I mostly just stayed away. I would ask mom how she was doing, but I purposely stayed away from the house. I was like DJ. I had to let God deal with my anger. I knew all I would be was fuel for Derrick, and he was doing badly all by himself from what mom said."

"I understood Yogi," Nevette replied. "Trust me I did. I realized that sometimes we just say mindless things to people who have been through something that we cannot relate to. I think ministering to Derrick helped me. The more I ministered to his anger, the more I wanted him. I knew I was going to be okay. Last night, we actually made love for the first time."

"Oh my God Nevette! How did you do?" Lindsay asked.

"Ohhhh, so that's why DJ got that big ol' smile on his face today!" Yogi exclaimed as she laughed out.

"Yogi!" Nevette laughed. She answered Lindsay's question, "Girl. I had to almost force him to do it. He was so nervous. Mom, Yogi—Lindsay, y'all know why I got a kick out of that. Anyway, all I could handle was about ten minutes. But it didn't matter because at about three minutes Justice was *"explosion city"*. I teased him saying, "three minutes Justice—really?". Usually whenever he would say come on baby, give me five minutes. I would say, Justice you know you don't do nothing fast, he'll say five minutes and an hour later, we're still in bed going at it. But not last night, so y'all know I had fun with that. He was like, baby don't judge me, you know I'm a man who can control myself, but I'm so excited to be making love to you."

Tasha laughed out as she said, "Girl please. After a man has been without for five days much less a few months, five minutes is usually all he needs to play catch up!"

The room erupted in laughter.

Nevette said, "I can't believe I'm sitting here talking about making love to Derrick in front of his mother."

"Girl please, whatever. I'm married to his daddy!" Shaundra exclaimed.

"Ooooh momma!" Yogi said surprised her mother would make that comment in this open forum.

Teresa exclaimed, "I don't know what makes the younger generation think we "old people" don't have sex. What do they think, we spoke them into existence? Last time I checked, you still have to get busy to have a baby. And when the baby years stop, there's more freedom and it's just plain fun then, *ooookay!*"

Everyone burst out laughing as the mothers high fived each other.

Nevette laughed out and then yelled, "OH MY GOD! MOM MY WATER JUST BROKE! IT'S NOT TIME YET. MOM—SOMEBODY GO GET JUSTICE. HE IS GOING TO FREAK OUT!"

"Okay let's get you up and to the car sweetheart. Yogi go get Derrick," Shaundra said as she rushed over to Nevette.

Talinda said, "I'm going to go to the bathroom before we leave." When she stood her water broke, and the room went into pandemonium.

"OH MY GOD!" Yogi yelled as she flew down the stairs.

The men heard the commotion, and all thought it was Talinda. Bernard was about to fly by Yogi when she yelled, "DJ! Nevette's water just broke! And then when Talinda stood to go to the bathroom, hers broke too!"

"WHAT!" Derrick and Bernard both yelled at the same time.

Derrick was across the room up the stairs in about ten steps with Bernard hot on his trail. The other men were right behind him.

"Nevette! Baby are you okay?" Derrick asked in a panic. He turned toward his mother and said, "Mom. She's not even nine months yet!"

Trevor quickly assessed the women and said, "Calm down Derrick. Let's just get these two ladies to the hospital. When we get loaded up and on the way, I'll call the hospital to inform them of the situation. In the meantime, let's get them in the cars, so we can go."

Everyone was running around frantically. Nevette called out to Lindsay that she needed her coach with her in the labor room. They were trying to figure out who would stay and who would go.

"Michael and I will stay here with the teens and the children. So that way all of you can go," Gloria said as she took TJ from Lindsay and made sure she knew where the diaper bag and milk supply for him was. TJ was right at four months old.

Trevor said that he would stay there with the baby but Shaundra yelled, "You can't Trevor! Even though I will deliver Nevette's baby, I will still need an OB doctor on hand, in case there are any complications. Dr. Harrell can't be at two places at once. She is both Talinda's and Nevette's doctor.

"That's right Trevor," Lindsay exclaimed.

"He will be fine," Gloria said. "I've done this four times."

Trevor and Lindsay both smiled, and the adults prepared to leave. The hospital was only twenty minutes barring traffic from the Goodfellows neighborhood.

"Mom she's not quite nine months yet!" Derrick exclaimed again.

"Son, she will be fine. Her water broke, so obviously Zoé is ready to enter this world," Shaundra replied.

"Yes son, now calm down," Teddy Sr., said as he helped Derrick assist Nevette into the car.

Derrick breathed in and out a few times to calm his nerves. Nevette touched his face and smiled.

Teresa was about to blow a gasket from excitement, and Bernard was about pick Talinda up to carry her to the car. She was moving too slow for his adrenaline rush.

She protested, "Bernard, sweetheart. I can walk."

Everyone was soon loaded up and speeding down the highway with hazard lights on. Trevor called the hospital, so they could notify

Dr. Harrell that two of her patients were on the way to labor and delivery. That their water had broken, and he was en route with them to assist.

They arrived at the ER entrance about fifteen minutes later. Derrick and Bernard both jumped out of their cars. Terry and Jaison had parking detail as they quickly got the expecting mothers into the hospital.

Labor and delivery nurses were waiting for them at the ER entrance and took Nevette and Talinda straight in with husbands and grandparents in tow.

Dr. Harrell arrived about ten minutes after Nevette, and Talinda were in their rooms and hooked up to the monitors. She went to assess Talinda first because she knew that Shaundra and Trevor were with Nevette.

Trevor had Shaundra scrub and check Nevette under the circumstances. She surprisingly was already five centimeters dilated. Her contractions were tolerable, and she was comfortable. He had ordered the ultra sound machine because she was premature, to ensure all was well with baby Goodfellow.

"Well, looks like we're having a baby today Mrs. Travis," Yolanda Harrell said as she entered the room.

"Yes it does," Talinda replied.

When she walked in, Helen looked at Valetta and Teresa and said, "Well, the doctor is here now, and the room is going to get a bit crowded, so I will go to the waiting room. Teresa this is going to be so awesome."

She tried to hide her true feelings of being in the waiting room instead of the delivery room. This wasn't Brandon's baby and Talinda wasn't her biological daughter, so she felt she couldn't claim the right to be there for the birth of Bernard and Talinda's baby.

"Mom why are you leaving?" Talinda asked Helen.

"This isn't Brandon's baby. I just assumed—," she replied.

Teresa spoke up and said, "Well you assumed wrong Helen. Besides, neither the twins nor Raymond are Bernard's. But I feel I am just as much their grandmother as you and Valetta are. Brandon was my baby, and Bernard is yours. So Helen, we will have none of that. We are not going to start separating ourselves now. Who the biological parents of the Travis children are has never mattered. Now you will stay right here. We have all been in this and committed from the beginning, and we will not stop now. We are all grandparents, and we will all be in here when this baby is born."

"Yes Aunt Helen. We won't have it any other way. And neither would Brandon. He left me to take care of his family. All of his family. Anything that comes out of Talinda, is still a part of him. That's means it's still a part of you. I made a vow over Brandon's body at his viewing that I would take care of *"our"* mother. So you stand fast grandma, you will be here for the delivery of your grandchild," Bernard exclaimed.

Helen was in tears. All she could do was nod and walk back up beside Talinda. Valetta rubbed her shoulder and then pulled her in for a hug.

Teresa turned to Bernard and said, "Okay, so you guys never did tell us what you were naming the baby."

Bernard said, "Well, I think we settled on Natalie Amanda Travis for a girl, but we were at odds on the name for a boy—"

"No we are not at odds, Bernard. He is going to be a junior," Talinda stated.

"Talinda we've been over this. We can't have two boys named BJ for short. We have a junior already sweetheart. And anyway, Raymond is actually my first son, if you want to be technical," Bernard replied.

Teresa said, "Son him being your junior will work. You're Bernard Alexander Travis. So just call him AJ that way Brandon Jr., will be fine as BJ."

"Teresa that's an excellent idea! AJ it is," Helen agreed.

Talinda and Valetta both replied "yes" at the same time.

"I guess I'm out numbered. If it's a boy, then Bernard Alexander Travis Jr., it is. But I am still hoping for my little Natalie," Bernard replied with a smile.

"Okay so it's settled," Talinda replied as a contraction mounted.

They started to get stronger, and she moaned, closed her eyes and breathed through it. Valetta caressed her hand, and Bernard kissed her lightly on the cheek as he told her how much he loved her.

*****

Out in the waiting room everyone was in anticipation of hearing any news. They were concerned for Nevette and Derrick considering she was only just under nine months pregnant with Zoé. Some paced the floor and others sat, but all were in prayer mode. Everything happened so fast, they didn't have the chance to pray as a group before Talinda and Nevette were wheeled into their labor rooms.

Dr. Harrell talked with Trevor in the hallway before she entered the room to check on Nevette. He told her he ordered the ultra sound machine just to be sure. He told her he would return in a few minutes. He wanted to go give everyone an update on Nevette. She thanked him and entered Nevette's room.

"Okay Mr. and Mrs. Goodfellow, let's have a look at Miss Zoé," she said as she sat down in the chair beside the machine.

The nurse had already hooked Nevette up, and everything was ready to go. Justice took in a deep breath and let it out as Dr. Harrell turned the machine on and placed the wand on Nevette's stomach. He had only seen the first ultra sound via cell phone. The night of the rape flooded his mind, and he took a couple more deep breaths to steady himself. Nevette took note of his actions.

"There she is," Dr. Harrell stated. "Nice strong heart beat and everything appears to be fine. I don't see anything that gives me pause."

"Great," Nevette replied in relief.

"Okay dad, here's your baby girl," she said as she turned the monitor so Derrick could see it.

"Oh my goodness DJ. Look at her!" Shaundra exclaimed. She stood with her hand over her mouth. But the grin she sported could be easily seen through the cracks of her fingers.

"Yeah. I'm going to video this real quick. Just leave it right there Dr. okay," Derrick asked.

Lindsay also took a fifteen second video and sent it to everyone in the waiting room.

"Okay, if your have enough video, I'm going to turn this off. We will continue to monitor you. I have the neonatal on stand by for a preemie even though she looks pretty big. I took some measurements, and I'll look closer at them here in a few minutes. Well, since you're here Dr. Goodfellow, I'm going to go back over and check on Mrs. Travis," Dr. Harrell said.

"How is she doing?" Nevette asked.

"She is doing fine. Not quite as far along as you. But moving steadily," she replied.

Derrick had not spoken again since taking the video, and Nevette could tell he was struggling emotionally. She asked Shaundra and Lindsay to leave the delivery room for a minute, after she looked up and saw that Justice was about to lose it.

"Come here baby," she said after they left the room.

He leaned down in her bosom and cried out to God promising to protect Nevette, Tre, and the baby.

"Sweetheart you already are a good father, husband and protector," Nevette said.

"We both know the jury is still out on that Nevette. I couldn't protect you, Zoé or Callisha," he replied.

"Justice baby, those were three very impossible situations that you had no control over," she said as she showered him with kisses and told him how much she loved him.

"OH GOD JUSTICE!" she yelled as a whopper of a contraction hit her.

He instantly forgot about his anguish and despair and went into coach mode instructing her to breathe as he kissed her on the forehead.

Shaundra and Lindsay had been standing at the nurse's desk watching Nevette's contractions on the monitor. They saw how hard her last contraction had been, and headed back down to her room.

About thirty minutes later, her contractions started to come one right after the other. Trevor also headed back to the room. He'd also been at the nurse's station. He wanted to give them privacy until it was close to the delivery time after the ultrasound proved that baby Zoé was doing okay. He was making sure to take care of Nevette's emotional comfort during this time.

"I don't know what hurts worse, the contractions or the stab wounds at the top of my stomach. They're still tender and being stretched to the maximum with each contraction. It feels like they are going to burst open at any minute!" Nevette yelled as another contraction mounted.

"I love you so much Naythia," Justice whispered in her ear. He began to pray in her ear that God would ease the pain of the wounds.

Shaundra stood at the base of the bed and said, "Okay little momma. Let's check to see where you are. You've had some strong ones, and they are on top of each other already."

Shaundra checked Nevette's cervix and gasped. "Trevor check her! There is no way that she is at ten centimeters so quickly!"

Trevor donned latex gloves and carefully checked Nevette. Justice occupied her thoughts as he did. Trevor smiled, "Oh but she is. Come on back down here grandma. Let's get ready to push Nevette!"

A huge smile graced Derrick's face, and he kissed Nevette.

Trevor called the nurses station to find Dr. Harrell and tell her they were getting ready to push. She was in the room with Talinda, who was also getting extremely close to ten centimeters as well. By the time she reached them, they had Nevette into position, and she was set for the first push. He wasn't sure if he should be in the room when Nevette was fully exposed to deliver. Trevor was about to walk out of the room when Lindsay stopped him. She was on one side of Nevette and Derrick the other as they had been with both Tre and Callisha.

Shaundra had already begun to cry as she sat at the foot of the bed prepared to deliver Zoé with Dr. Harrell just over her left shoulder. "Okay Nevette, with the next contraction you know what to do!"

"OH GOD THIS HURTS SO BAD JUSTICE! OH GOD PLEASE I CAN'T PUSH. IF I PUSH I'M GOING TO BURST OPEN EVERY SCAR I HAVE ON MY STOMACH. JUSTICE I CAN'T!" she exclaimed.

"No, no, no, no, no, no baby! Look at me," Justice rambled out quickly. "Come baby trust God. He is not going to allow you to burst open. They are scars baby. Most of them are healed, and they're not deep. Come on sweetheart, trust God. Zoé is in the canal already. You're ten centimeters. It's too late to do anything else. Come on baby, you can't let the next contraction go by. She's in the canal. You have to push. COME ON NAYTHIA—YOU FOUGHT FOR HER LIFE. NOW YOU BRING IT FORTH!"

She cried and shook her head. She could barely get sound to come out of her mouth the pain was so unbearable, "Okay—okay baby."

"I love you—I love you!" he exclaimed through tears as he kissed her all over her face.

Lindsay was in tears. Trevor stood behind her to support her as she supported Nevette. Dr. Harrell stood just behind Shaundra just in case, considering how emotional she and everyone else was. She kept looking at her pager because she knew when she left the Travis' room that Talinda was extremely close.

The contraction mounted. Nevette let out a yell as pushed, "ZOOOOOOOOEEEEEEE!"

"I HAVE THE HEAD! STOP PUSHING NEVETTE THE CORD IS WRAPPED!" Shaundra yelled.

She suctioned her nose and mouth and cut the cord that was wrapped around her neck.

"I CAN'T HELP IT! I CAN'T STOP PUSHING! SHE'S COMING—SHE'S COMING!" Nevette yelled.

"MOM!" Derrick exclaimed.

"Trevor and Yolanda were both ready to spring into action.

"It's okay. I cut the cord off. Go ahead and push!" Shaundra replied.

Nevette pushed one more time and out came Zoé. She didn't make a sound.

"Do you have her?" Nevette asked.

"I have her—I have her!" Shaundra exclaimed through tears.

"I don't hear her. WHAT'S WRONG MOM?" Nevette yelled.

"Nothing is wrong dear. She's fine. A little smaller than Tre or Callisha, but she's fine," Shaundra replied through tears as she took her over to the table for be assessed, cleaned and measured.

As soon as Shaundra stood with the baby, Yolanda sat down to deliver the after birth and stitch Nevette up. She knew she was on a time crunch and needed to get back to Talinda.

Derrick didn't leave Nevette's side. Zoé weighed in at 5 pounds and 13 ounces, and was 18 inches long. When they gave her the first immunization shot, she let out a healthy cry.

"Oh God do you hear her Naythia? Do you hear Zoé?" Derrick exclaimed.

"Life—," Nevette whispered as tears rolled down her face.

"Yeah baby—life—abundant life," Derrick whispered as he leaned his face into hers and closed his eyes. He felt the peace of God that passes understanding.

Dr. Harrell ensured everything was under control. Trevor told her he would make sure the baby got down to the ward in a few minutes after mom and dad held her, and she left to head back down the hall to Talinda's room. When she passed by the waiting room, she stopped in long enough to tell everyone about Zoé's delivery. They were all ecstatic and praised God for a healthy delivery.

"Okay mommy, here's your baby girl," the nurse said as she brought Zoé over to the bed.

"Oh God Justice, she's so small compared to Tre and Callisha," Nevette replied as she looked down into her baby girls face. "I've been waiting a long time to see you Zoé."

Derrick was overwhelmed as Nevette handed her to him. He held her, and tears flowed down his face. He moved the blanket slightly to get a better look at her, and she grabbed his finger.

FLASH!—Lindsay always seemed to capture the perfect picture between Derrick and the Goodfellow babies.

"Hey daddy's little princess—hey—I love you," he paused to ease the lump in his throat down before he attempted to speak again, "I love you."

"Okay Nevette and Justice, we really need to get her down to the nursery. I know she is pretty big, but she is still a preemie," Trevor said.

"Yes, okay," Nevette said as she wiped her tears.

Derrick went over and placed her in the incubator to be transported to the nursery. Nevette nodded okay to him because she knew he wanted to accompany Zoé to the nursery. Lindsay stayed in the room with Nevette. Shaundra followed them out and went toward the waiting room to give everyone the rest of the details on the delivery, and to ensure Nevette's brothers and father that she was doing fine.

Tasha called Gloria and told them one down and one to go, that the Goodfellow baby had been born. Upon hearing the news Raymond called his father to ask how Talinda was doing. He told her she was really close, and he would call him back soon.

Teresa was about to go crazy with excitement. She began to move around the room like a mad woman.

Dr. Harrell walked back in the room. She washed her hands as she said, "Okay Mrs. Travis I noticed your monitor and contractions as I passed the nurses station. You have been pretty busy the last twenty minutes I have been gone for the delivery of the Goodfellow baby."

"Ohhhh, so she had Zoé!" Talinda exclaimed.

"Yes she did, 5 pounds and 13 ounces," she replied.

"Oh my, that's a nice size for thirty-five weeks," Valetta relied.

"Yes. That means she was probably fully developed. But I'm sure the stress of the rape had a little something to with her going in five weeks early," Dr. Harrell stated. "Okay, let's get you checked and see where we are."

"She's been having contractions like crazy! Long and hard ones!" Teresa exclaimed.

"Yes we had to stop Teresa from coming to get you," Helen teased.

"I'm just so excited," Teresa replied.

"We know exactly how you feel, Teresa," Valetta replied.

"Oh my, speaking of coming after me. We don't have a moment to spare. We are fully dilated. Let's get ready to have a baby, Talinda," Dr. Harrell said as she prepared to get Talinda into position.

The nurses assisted her, and Talinda was soon ready to push.

Bernard looked at her and kissed her, "I love you. Thank you again for doing this just for me." He chuckled, "I love you so much baby."

"I love you—" she started to say but was cut off by an enormous contraction. "JEEEESSUUUUSSSS!!!"

"Go ahead Talinda, you can push," Yolanda declared.

Teresa was in the position that Helen was when the twins were delivered. She had a bird's eye view and was in awe as the head crested.

"Oh my look at all that hair!" she yelled.

Helen laughed for joy at Teresa's excitement. This was an event she knew she would never forget. Childbirth was such an awesome miracle from God.

It took Talinda five more exhausting pushes to get baby Travis out. He came out in full volume screaming at the top of his lungs. She and Bernard waited for Dr. Harrell to state the baby's sex.

"It's a boy!" Yolanda declared.

"YES!" Talinda yelled.

Teresa, Helen and Valetta hugged and cried and began taking pictures of every step they took to prepare little AJ to see his parents. Bernard kissed Talinda and waited anxiously to see his baby boy. Talinda opted to allow Bernard to hold him first.

He weighed in at eight pounds, fifteen ounces and twenty-one inches long.

"Wow, he's a big boy!" Helen exclaimed.

They handed AJ to Bernard. He stood beside Talinda as he held him. Tears rolled down his face.

"Hello Bernard Alexander Travis Jr., welcome to this side of creation," Bernard said softly as he looked down into his baby boy's face for the first time. He gave him to Talinda, who immediately started to nurse him. He latched on with no problem, and the mother-son bond began. Helen went out to tell everyone that Bernard Alexander Travis Jr., had entered the world.

When she told them how big AJ was Terry joked, "Dang, that's' not a baby, that's a toddler."

Everyone laughed, rejoiced and thanked God for two successful and healthy deliveries. They called back to the Goodfellow house to inform everyone that Talinda had a boy. The teens congratulated Raymond as though he were the father. He called to speak with his parents to tell them how much he loved them and couldn't wait to see little AJ.

Soon everyone was in the nursery visiting babies and 'oohs' and 'ahhh's' filled the room. After a while, they left moms and dads alone with their babies and went back to the Goodfellows to relieve the babysitters and head to their respective homes.

Talinda called down to Nevette's room to see how she was doing.

"Hey girl how are you feeling?" Talinda asked.

"Better. It was pretty rough for a minute. I didn't know if I would be able to do it. Every cut and scar I had, burned with intense pain. Truly, I had to fight to deliver that life," Nevette replied.

"Wow, God is faithful," Talinda declared.

"Yes He is. I got the pictures of little—I should say, big AJ." Nevette teased.

"Yes girl. I didn't think I would ever push him out. The twins were about Zoé's size they were no problem. I had to put in some work with him," Talinda replied.

"Is Bernard there with you now?" Nevette asked.

"No. he's down in the nursery with the baby," she replied. "What about Derrick?"

"In the nursery with Zoé, where else? He's there while they give her a thorough check and determine if she has to go to the neonatal side," Nevette replied. "I hope to be able to go see her pretty soon."

"Yes, and I pray they will bring AJ to the room soon. Well, we had better rest while we can, because we both know the real work starts pretty soon," Talinda said as she smiled at the thought. She loved being a mother.

"You don't have to tell me twice. I'm exhausted. I'll talk to you soon. We'll have a lot of play dates in the near future girl," Nevette replied.

"Sure thing. Bye girl," Talinda said,

"Bye," Nevette replied and hung up.

*****

Derrick and Bernard stood at the nursery window looking at their baby boy and girl. You could tell that Derrick was finally relieved that Zoé was here and a stressful time that could have been deadly, was now filled with life.

"I heard it got pretty rough in there for Nevette and Zoé?" Bernard asked.

"Yes, she was in a lot of pain. More from the stab wounds. They made the contractions worse," he replied. "But we prayed and trusted God and made it through. For a minute, we weren't sure if she was born alive or dead because she didn't make a sound. Then when they gave her a shot, she let out a cry I'll never forget. It was music to my ears."

"I bet it was," Bernard replied. "I wasn't sure Talinda was going to be able to push this little guy out."

"Little! He's huge lying in the basinet next to Zoé's," Derrick laughed.

"Yeah I heard one of the guys teased that we had a toddler, not a baby," Bernard said.

Bernard shook his head as though deep in thought as he looked down at AJ and then Zoé, "Born on the same day, almost exactly an hour apart. Wouldn't it be amazing if our two kids ended up married to each other?"

Derrick smiled, "Well. I couldn't choose a better husband for her. I know the type of upbringing he'll have."

"Exactly!" Bernard laughed out. "Who knows Derrick? Only Time will tell."

"Yeah, to be continued—in about twenty-two years from now," Derrick teased.

They laughed and watched as the nurses came to attend to the babies. Zoé would spend a few days in the neonatal unit just to ensure all was well.

Soon they both left the hospital with their new bundles of joy, and the Travis' and Goodfellow's homes were again filled with the sounds of love, laughter—and LIFE!

~The End~

Discussion Questions:

1. Has reading this book changed your mindset of how the Christian should view and deal with tragedies?
2. Which character intrigued you the most in this edition of the series? Why?
3. Do you feel that the artist has properly shown the tragedies, situations and triumphs of the Christian world and battles Christians deal with in their flesh on a daily basis? Why or why not?
4. Has reading the series given you effective ammunition to minister to youth in your local church about sensitive issues in their lives?
5. What did the series speak to you about the most? Why?
6. What has the book opened your eyes to the most, on a spiritual level?

About the Author:

Minister Cynthia Middlebrooks Harris is a native of Atlanta, GA. She and her husband of 27 years, Minister Kim Harris, are the co-founders of T.O.S.O.T. (The Other Side of Through) Ministries, LLC. She has dedicated years in her local church writing plays for the Christmas and Easter programs. Her longtime friend and founder of Still Useable Ministries, Pastor Susan Marshall, solicited her to write a stage play for an upcoming women's conference. From that stage play, the series "The Other Side of Through" was birthed. Many of the instances in her works are inspired by challenges, situations and tragedies that have occurred in her own life. She implements the power and process of how God brought her through when the pieces of her own life, began to unravel and fall apart. She is passionate about writing and understands this is her mandate from God. She aspires to reach and minister to the hurt, confused and lost with her gift of imagination and knowledge of the Word of God, through romance and drama. She was born to write, for such a time as this.

~ Ministry is always.....Required! ~

Other works by Author Cynthia Middlebrooks Harris:

"The Other Side of Through: All Things Work Together..." Book one: The series begins with the introduction into the lives of Talinda and Nevette. One whose life is temporarily turned upside down while the other is in total bliss...for now!

"I Promise" Book Two: The saga continues, and Brandon speaks from the grave with a shout. The once total bliss of the Goodfellow marriage is threatened. Raymond is hit with another blow, and Lindsay's secret is exposed.

"The Valley of the Shadow of Death" Book three: Everything goes wrong for Justice as the journey continues. Justice and Nevette must walk the path that no parent ever desires to travel. Talinda's life is threatened to be changed forever. As new characters develop, adultery hits the scene and yet again is grace is put on trial.

"Legitimate Issues": Dysan Jamison and Laytoria James are about to enter the ugly, but real world of many prejudices. As they battle through discrimination from the worse source. A barrage of legitimate obstacles pop up like land mines, as they fight to decide if they are a compatible match.

Available at:
http://www.tosotministries.org; CreateSpace.com; Amazon.com and Barnes and Noble.com.

12201014R00154

Made in the USA
San Bernardino, CA
11 June 2014